W9-DHJ-797

# SOME KIND OF HERO

## A NOVEL

### James Kirkwood

A SIGNET BOOK

**NEW AMERICAN LIBRARY**

TIMES MIRROR

*For Lee Goodman*
*in fond memory of the nightclub years*

---

*with special thanks to*
*former P.O.W. Arthur John Cormier*

# Part One

Part One

# 1

The problem is this: when you commit a crime, pull off a big one—especially if it's not and never has been your line of work—there is one fierce compulsion to tell about it. It itches to get out, pulls and tugs, like the sensation when you stand on a high place and feel the urge to jump. You know you probably won't, still there's a nattering little voice inside that keeps insisting: Jump!

So—this thing I've done wants out. It's a matter of spilling it or coming apart at the seams. Splat! I don't mean showing up on national television and announcing it to the world; I don't even mean throwing a small bash and entertaining the gang with the fascinating details; and it's never entered my mind to go tearing into the nearest police station and confess. No. What I mean is, there should be one person you can lay it all out to.

Such as your wife, if she also happens to be your friend. Or your girl friend if she, too, happens to coincide with the friend part. Best of all would be your *best* friend, if you happen to have one.

Here I sit, alone atop my bundle, about to fall off, close to skidding straight out of my skin. With a dizzy combination: excitement, attacks of communicative nerviosity—I read that someplace—yes, nerves, despite my success, manic bouts of elation and confusion, and, at the risk of being maudlin—lonely. A big batch of the latter. The combination is an unruly twister.

What really made me start putting this down—I've taken to chattering to myself. While shaving this morning, I suddenly shouted at the person in the mirror, "You did it, Eddie! You actually did it!" At the same time my hand gave a sharp involuntary swipe, nicking my nose and drawing blood. I tried to keep a sense of humor about it as I blotted my nostril with toilet paper. "Yeah, you did it, you actually tried to cut your nose off. Three cheers! Want to try for an ear?" Then: "No, stop it, stop talking to yourself. Cool it, Eddie, cool it."

Therefore—splat! If you see what I mean . . .

# 2

I've fought and lost the battle about when and how to put down that, on top of everything else, I'm a P.O.W. No way to avoid it, no slipping it in later on, first things first.

I'm not as angry now at being one as I am bored with it. Most people are undoubtedly bored with P.O.W.'s, too. Maybe not bored but certainly turned off, either by conscience, in some cases, or the same embarrassed pity that makes you turn away from a spastic person industriously jerking his way down the street. Or turned off in plain disgust at the whole stinking Southeast Asia mess. Understandable. I'm not crabbing, only acknowledging it.

So I'll say, in partial relief, the entire report will not be about my time as a prisoner. Sighs all around. A portion, yes; and I'll make every effort to keep it to that.

Would you believe a lot of the time spent stashed away could possibly be classified as good times? Yes, in a cockeyed way, the good times. Not all, of course, but some. It wasn't that the cuisine or entertainment was the best at the Bel Air Country Club, the name of our particular camp. But the companionship, at times, was unbeatable. And the hopes! And plans. Never was time so filled with hopes and dreams, daydreams, nightdreams, all sorts of dreams, half-assed and otherwise. Because that's the stuff of which we had the raw materials.

And we were not hard up for the time to spin them out.

Also, you could see the enemy daily, get a fix on him. The enemy was on target. Now the enemy is—all around, like a plate of spilled soup in the sky.

Last one who says he isn't confused gets his tonsils ripped out. And *then* tossed in the pool.

Some pertinent details. Captured in February 1968 during the Tet Offensive outside Hue. At the time a corporal in communications.

I was having trouble with my walkie-talkie along the side of a large hill I didn't know whether we were still trying to take or hold or get the hell out of. I slipped down into a gully to see if I could do a quick repair job. Two riflemen in my platoon were in another gully maybe fifteen-twenty yards away from me, over a small mound and down a bit. All hell had broken loose and it was a problem trying to figure out where the firing was coming from, whose it was, and where it was going.

Was I scared? Oh, yes, I was scared. My unit had split up in the general mass confusion of the attack and I was trying to get the walkie-talkie working so I could find out where everyone was and whether we were supposed to hold steady, strung out as we were, or retreat and regroup.

I'd had to piss for about two hours but I'd been so busy running and dodging and keeping myself together that I'd put it out of my mind. Now, kneeling in the gully and impatient with my shaky hands as I worked on the radio, I felt the strong urge to go again. I stayed on my knees—wasn't about to stand up and become a target—but swiveled around to the side so I wouldn't wet my equipment, unzipped, and let go. The relief was tremendous and so was the stream. I was aiming as far away as possible so it wouldn't run back and wet my knees.

It happened quickly. I just happened to look up, still peeing—I didn't hear scuffling or footsteps or anything because of the gunfire all around—and there were two Charlies (V.C.'s) standing at the top of the gully and then there was a third. They all held rifles aimed at me. And there I was with my limp dribbling dick in my hand. Great!

Only one of them grinned at the sight. One of the other two shouted something and motioned with his rifle for me to stand up. I was in no position to argue. I stood up, still peeing. Hands over my head was the next order pantomimed to me. I obeyed and the stretching motion caused my cock, still peeing away like crazy, to snap back inside my pants of its own accord. At this, they all grinned and laughed. Now you see it, now you don't.

I heard gunfire very close, heard Ernie Bagetta's voice in the next gully down the hill shout "Jesus—Morty!" Morty being the other guy in the gully with him. More gunfire and Bagetta cried out, "You turds!" Then there was silence.

The three Charlies were looking down and to their right toward the other gully. I wondered why they didn't have their rifles aimed in that direction. They were not laughing when they turned back to me. I'd stopped peeing finally, and glanced down to see the wet stain along my pants leg.

More pantomime as two of them jumped into the gully with me; quickly got my rifle, the walkie-talkie, and the rest of my gear and turned me around. One of them took a piece of rope and tied my hands together around the wrists. Tight and uncomfortable. Now they jabbered to each other and to me, poking me in the back and prodding me out of the gully.

Starting down the hill, I wondered if Ernie Bagetta and Morty Wilks would pop up out of their gully and start shooting. I got nervous as we neared it, because I realized my three captors had been looking in their direction when Bagetta shouted, "You turds!"

Seven, eight more steps and I could see down into the gully. Both lay on their backs. Morty had been shot point-blank in the face: his face was shattered. His legs were spread apart at a crazy angle like he'd fallen from a tree. Bagetta, a few feet away from him, was still bleeding through his shirt. His legs were together, like he'd been laid out. He was dead, too.

I stopped at the sight of them. Such a short time. And where were the Congs who shot them? Gone already, no sign of them. I couldn't believe it. Bagetta called everyone "You turd!" when he was mad at them. Had he called his killers, as he'd been shot, "You turds!"? Jesus, what an understatement.

A poke in the back. I turned around. One of the V.C. shouted something at me, then the other two nodded toward Morty and Bagetta and grinned. One of them spat out a few chopped-off words and laughed. I looked back down. A huge black fly had landed squarely on Bagetta's nose.

"Very funny!" I muttered. The one who wasn't laughing spoke; the inflection was a question. "Very fucking funny!" I said.

If I was scared before, I was scared shitless now. Two buddies lying there dead, shot and left in a matter of minutes. Another poke in the back. I was sure I was going to be shot, too, as we walked down around the side of the hill. I kept hoping we wouldn't run into the trigger-happy clowns who'd shot *them*.

I wasn't walking fast enough—another shove in the back. I fell forward on my face. I lay there, nose in the dirt, thinking: Oh, God, I'm never going to see my baby, I won't even know if it's a boy or a girl. (I'd learned in October that my wife, Lisa, was pregnant.) I simply lay there in the dirt waiting to be shot in the back, thinking: I'm twenty-three years old and I'm never going to see my baby. Finito.

Then a kick in the side, a shouted order or two, and I scrambled to my feet.

I have never, to this day, understood why some of us were shot and some of us were taken prisoner and when I do think about it, I get a case of the shudders.

# 3

A little over two months later I arrived at the P.O.W. camp known as the Hanoi Hilton. Outside of the last five hours in a van, I had been marched all the way, over into Laos, then up north and back over to Hanoi. There were stopovers, days at a time; the food was incredibly bad; the treatment was sometimes worse than the food, and sometimes not all that bad, depending upon the mood, the weather, the terrain—whatever.

My feet were a mess by the time I got to the Hilton, running sores all over them. I also had a miserable cold. I was given medical treatment, my clothes and what possessions had not already been stripped from me were now taken, including my wedding band. I was issued two pairs of rough cotton shorts; a pair of sandals, the straps made of inner-tubing; two pairs of cotton socks; two pairs of black pajamas; two cotton T-shirts and a toothbrush.

A North Vietnamese officer, a lieutenant, interrogated me: age, serial number, unit, home address—all the basic information. I attended a lecture, along with about twenty other prisoners, most of them officers, during which we were told of our high crimes against the people of Vietnam. We were criminals of the worst order, not war criminals, because it was not a declared war. Just plain criminals and would be treated as such, no Geneva Conventions applied to us.

Still . . .

There was a certain basic joy at—simply being alive. And out of the fighting, which had been fierce. I've never had a hero complex; if I had, this war of all wars wouldn't trigger it. There was also fascination being prisoner in North Vietnam. It was exotic at first. And there was curiosity. What was going to happen next?

Among the P.O.W.'s I got to talk to at the Hilton there was little fear we'd be killed. It was apparent we would be used as hostages for bargaining and for political reasons.

Five days later I was taken in a truck and transferred to a smaller camp for enlisted men only, which came to be known as the Bel Air Country Club. Sitting in the back of the truck, which was covered with canvas, I heard traffic sounds and I was curious to see if we were going through Hanoi itself. Seven other prisoners and three guards were sitting there. The flap in the back of the truck was down, we couldn't see out, but the canvas along the sides was tied down loosely, so I bent over on my bench and lifted it up a few inches to have a look.

A guard jumped at me and smashed his rifle butt against my right hand. He mashed my thumb, mashed it good.

I howled with pain, calling him every name in the books. The other P.O.W.'s shouted for me to quiet down, for fear we'd catch more slamming around. My thumbnail was hanging loose and I was gushing blood, but I managed to control myself. This thumbnail I grew to replace it is still gnarled and discolored as I look at it now. I call it my atomic thumbnail.

The Bel Air Country Club was on the northwest outskirts of Hanoi, what would be the suburbs. It had once been the private estate of a rich man and his family. The following page shows a sketch of it.

Other camps were called Little Vegas, Heartbreak Hotel, The Zoo and Dogpatch. There was a slight pun in the naming of the Bel Air. To the east, across the railroad tracks that ran by one side of the camp, was an enormous dump where all sorts of refuse was set afire and left burning for days at a time. The smell, when the wind blew toward us, was incredible—thus the Bel Air Country Club.

The main house, brick covered in stucco with vines growing up around the sides and front and cut away from the doors and windows, was three-storied, the top floor being sloped dormer rooms. Downstairs was a large main room that had been the living room, a general outside office adjoining it, then the Camp Commander's office, a large kitchen, a pantry and a dining room. Bedrooms were upstairs, but in the almost five years I spent there I never actually saw the upstairs.

The building I was quartered in had six double rooms on either side of a small corridor. The rooms were fourteen feet long, twelve feet wide, with fifteen-foot ceilings. One clear lightbulb was screwed into a socket in the center of the ceiling. A loudspeaker sat on a ledge up in a corner to the left of the door, which was wood with metal bolts and a small peephole. There was one small window, about two by two, with no glass, only metal bars and wooden shutters inside. The floor was concrete, and two wooden platforms, supported by bricks, were the beds; two or three inches of loose straw was the only mattress. Two coarse blankets made up the bedding, along with a piece of much-needed mosquito netting. I was issued an earthen mug and a spoon that had been stamped out of tin. A cake of soap, like yellow laundry soap, and two rough brown towels were also given me.

No heat or running water. For going to the john there was one large slop can with a board you could lay on top to

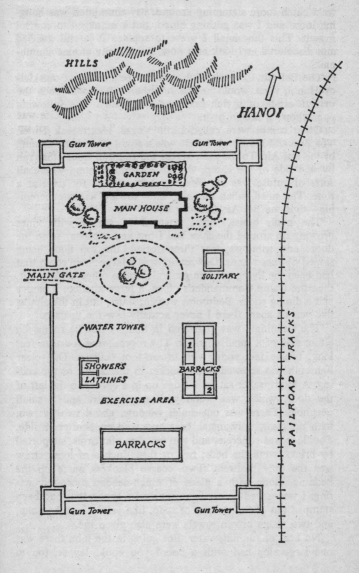

cover it. Toilet paper came in separate sheets about the quality of fine-grade sandpaper, very rough on the ass.

I was alone in the room I've marked "1" for almost five months. For a while my feet were still giving me trouble, and once a day a paramedic who spoke no English came and painted them with a violet-colored solution that stung but eventually healed them. My right thumb was cleaned up and bandaged. It throbbed for days. And nights.

The description of a general day won't take long. Life was simple, life was basic. A gong went off at 5:00 A.M. I got up and made my bed—not much making, just straighten the blankets out. An earthenware pitcher of water was brought to the room and with that I brushed my teeth and washed up. The water was always ice-cold.

Around six or six-thirty the loudspeaker went on for a half hour or so. News in English, "The Voice of Vietnam," mostly bad news about the war we were losing, the terrible casualties we were suffering. Sometimes there'd be a little Vietnamese or Chinese music after the news.

Between nine and ten we got our first meal. Meals were always brought to the room. There'd be a bowl of soup—sometimes cabbage soup, sometimes squash soup, or something we called "green" soup, made up of almost any vegetables boiled in water, and my unfavorite, pumpkin soup. Pumpkin soup was served for two months straight at one point and I came to hate it with a passion. We would get a large hunk of French bread; often there was lukewarm tea. That took care of that meal.

Some prisoners were taken out for their exercise and their showers after that. I was in the afternoon shift. From noon to about a quarter of two was quiet hour. As opposed to what, I wondered. We were supposed to lie down and nap. This was impossible after sleeping from approximately nine in the evening until five in the morning. But the Vietnamese are into siestas, even in winter.

Sometime after two I was taken out to the yard by myself, where I first emptied my slop can in a large trench used for sewer purposes and then was allowed to sit or stand or exercise for twenty or thirty minutes. This included time for a shower, which you could take every day in summer and twice a week in winter. We also washed our clothes when we washed ourselves.

I was disappointed that I was not allowed to exercise with any other prisoner, talk to any other prisoner, or even see one. Isolation was number one on the list of priorities. Isolation kept us vulnerable for purposes of interrogation and indoctrination.

At first, in April, my shutters were always supposed to be kept closed, but I used to peek out to see what I could. Not much—a guard or two walking by, sometimes another prisoner being escorted on the way to his exercise period or the showers. Later on, when the weather got hot and humid, we were allowed to open our shutters.

After the exercise period I was given three Vietnamese cigarettes. Dien Biens, they were called—short and strong, something like the oldtime Camel cigarettes.

Around four in the afternoon we got our second meal. This also featured a soup of sorts, more French bread, perhaps some bean curd, which I liked; sometimes a bowl of rice with a little pig fat in it, and if you were lucky maybe there'd be a little stringy bit of meat hanging onto it.

At five o'clock the lightbulb was turned on and that was it. It was left on all night long and turned off the next morning.

The worst of it? Loneliness, the no-contact with anyone, the not knowing what was going on. The no one to talk to. Hunger came next. I've always had a huge appetite, especially in the morning when I wake up. I wake up hungry. The wait from five until nine-thirty or so for anything to put in my stomach was a killer. Often I would save some of my bread from the afternoon meal so I would have a little taste of something in the morning; just as often I'd wake up in the middle of the night, starving, and eat it then. The cold and the heat were next. Not that it got down below forty—it didn't, not often—but it was damp and rainy and the chill ate right into my bones. Although the straw was itchy I couldn't afford to use one blanket to cushion it. I needed both in the winter to keep myself anywhere near warm. Of course, in the hot weather I slept on top of both of them.

But loneliness was the worst. It left my mind too much to itself. The mind is a tricky clown to deal with. Stubborn. Tell it not to think of certain things—sex, baked spareribs, snuggling warm and safe in bed with Lisa until noon on Sundays—and it won't do anything but flash them on in mile-high letters.

After a while I actually looked forward to the days when I'd be brought over to the main building to be interrogated or fed propaganda, what they called "indoctrination." At least I was involved in an activity and got to see a new face or two. I should add that as a corporal I was not hassled as much as an officer would be; it was taken for granted I didn't know that much about our military operations, which was true. The real squeeze was put on officers for information; they were also pressured much harder than enlisted men to sign statements against the United States, especially the pilots who'd been shot down.

Outside of these days, there were only two people I saw, except when I managed to look through the shutters. One was the Turnkey, who came and opened and closed the doors and brought the morning water and the meal. He spoke no English. The other was what we called the English Speaker. He spoke a very broken English and was there in case we needed something or got sick or in some sort of trouble. He took me out for my exercise period, and also brought the afternoon meal. He went off duty about five in the afternoon; then there was only the Turnkey and occasional patrolling guards who you rarely saw and were forbidden to speak to, unless there was an emergency.

One problem: my first English Speaker didn't want to speak to me. I'd try to strike up conversations with him in the yard during exercise periods, but he'd give me the shortest possible answer. Or shake his head, meaning no, he'd better not talk—and point to one of the guard towers or gesture toward the main building, indicating any lengthy conversation was verboten. Difficult to connect with him; also, he did not have an ounce of humor in his entire make-up—or, if he did, he was brilliant at concealing it. At first, we were also not allowed to know the names of any of our captors.

Looking out of my shutters, I often saw sets of two prisoners being taken for their exercise periods. This indicated some of the rooms in my building were shared by two P.O.W.'s. Over a period of months I finally learned that seven out of the twelve rooms were double-occupied, three were singles and two were empty. One of the empty rooms was next to me; the room to my left was another single.

In that room was another corporal, Calvin Sprague. Naturally I wanted to make contact with him, so I could have some sort of communication. The walls were thick enough so that if you wanted to talk, you would almost have to shout. If you shouted you faced getting caught, and that led to solitary.

In my second month there, about a dozen of us were taken over for a group indoctrination session. I was marched over with Sprague, a tall, thin, big-eared guy who seemed nice enough if a bit cowed and jittery. I'd seen him now and then in the yard through my shutters. I started to talk to him on the walk over to the main house, but one of the guards slammed me in the shoulder and shut me up.

After the indoctrination talk, as we stood and got ready to be marched back, another P.O.W. slipped me a note. It turned out to be several pieces of toilet paper with the tap code on it. I'd known there was a tap code, but I didn't know what it was. I was overjoyed. I felt like a rich man.

The code went like this:

| A | B | C | D | E |
|------|------|------|------|------|
| ·· | · ·· | · ··· | · ···· | · ····· |
| F | G | H | I | J |
| ·· · | ·· ·· | ·· ··· | ·· ···· | ·· ····· |
| L | M | N | O | P |
| ··· · | ··· ·· | ··· ··· | ··· ···· | ····· ··· |
| Q | R | S | T | U |
| ···· · | ···· ·· | ···· ··· | ···· ···· | ····· ···· |
| V | W | X | Y | Z |
| ····· · | ····· ·· | ····· ··· | ····· ···· | ····· ····· |

The letter K was missing, in order to make the code even with five rows of five letters each. If a K was needed, we used C.

I could hardly wait to use it. About an hour after we got back to our rooms, I started tapping to Sprague, asking him how long he'd been there, etc.

I got no answer for a long time. I kept tapping away, different questions, then I'd wait for a reply. Nothing.

Finally I heard a thumping on the wall. I stood very still and listened. I had the two sheets of toilet paper in my hand and referred to them as he tapped out SOLITARY. I waited, that was all that came. I tapped for him to go on. He tapped

back SOLITARY again. I tapped back WHAT ABOUT IT?
He tapped back SOLITARY a third time. This went on until
he eventually tapped out STOP DANGER.

We were not tapping loudly, so I continued until he
thumped again, then tapped out NO MORE.

Christ, my luck. I found out later he'd been caught tapping
and put in solitary for six weeks. He'd only got out about the
time I arrived and was terrified of being caught again. That
ended my tapping days for the time being.

I began brooding more and more about not having a roommate. I wanted company badly. The need wouldn't have been
felt so strongly if only there'd been something to do—books
to read, writing material, a deck of cards even. I'd have sold
my soul for a dictionary. That became a thing with me, the
desire to have a dictionary. If I'd had one I'd have read it
straight through from the beginning, then I'd have begun
memorizing all the words. When you're forced to waste time,
you feel miserable about the time you wasted on your own,
lying on the beach or sitting in a stupor watching ridiculous
television shows. I vowed never to lie on a beach again—if I
ever got the chance to. The endless drag-ass hours stretched
out on my bed started to get to me.

Wondering: Does Lisa know I'm a prisoner or does she
think I'm dead? Does my mother know—does anyone—does
the army even know? Was my baby a boy or a girl? I'd asked
if I could write a letter. The answer was no.

The first six months were by far the roughest. Looking
back, they seem almost equal in time to the next two or three
years.

# 4

If anything got me through this time alone without breaking in two, it was Lisa. And, to an extent, the idea of our baby. Really only Lisa. You can't love someone you don't know, you can only love the idea of him/her. Lisa was the ledge I clung to.

I was deeply in love with her, with everything about her.

If asked what really sent me into a spin, I would say medium-to-tall small-waisted girls with ample breasts, thin shapely legs, long dark hair, and green eyes. That would approximate my composite drawing of heaven.

After I'd finished my basic training and been assigned to an army depot in the Bay area, I spent most of my free time in San Francisco. I'd been to Fisherman's Wharf one Saturday afternoon and was taking the cable car back toward Market Street about five o'clock when I spotted my composite riding a cable car in the opposite direction toward the wharf.

The cars slowed down and stopped briefly side by side, only inches apart, at a cross street while the conductors exchanged a few words. She was reading a paperback, sitting about four people to my right, across from me. I stared at her, willing her to look back. Nothing, until her car started with a lurch; that caused her to look up briefly. God in heaven, green eyes, too. She glanced over, saw me staring straight at her, looked at me for a brief moment, but didn't change her expression or smile. I smiled. Still no smile. She looked back down at her paperback as the car pulled away. As my car started in the opposite direction up the hill toward the Fairmont Hotel, I leaned forward watching her go down the hill. Why doesn't she look? Come on, come on! When we were about three quarters of a block apart, she did glance back. I quickly waved. Come on, wave! She didn't wave but she did break into a smile. Then her car went swinging around a curve and out of sight.

The second my car slowed, even slightly, I was off it, galloping down Powell Street, trying to keep my footing and not take a nose dive. I couldn't possibly catch up with her car but I tried nevertheless. Finally I gave up; all I could do was hurry the rest of the way, eight or ten blocks, to the end of the line and hope I would find her down around the wharf somewhere.

I tore around the small restaurants and shrimp stands and import-export shops like a madman. I must have looked like a hunting dog who'd lost his master. I ducked into a few restaurants but I automatically skipped the bars, telling myself a girl, one that spectacular, wouldn't be going into a bar alone. Alone! How did I know she was alone? The cable car was crowded, but she'd caught my eye so, I hadn't noticed who she was sitting next to. Then, again, if she'd been *with* someone, a date, she probably wouldn't have been reading a paperback. I was confusing myself more and more, and by the time I'd scouted around for almost an hour I was getting depressed. The sight of bleak, abandoned Alcatraz sitting out there in the harbor didn't help.

Still, I couldn't get over the girl on the cable car, although I'd given up hope of finding her. I wandered around the area, allowing myself a decent period of mourning. Until I spotted her standing on the boardwalk leaning against a railing overlooking the small fishing boats tied to the docks in front of DiMaggio's restaurant.

She leaned with her elbows, calmly looking out over the fishing fleet, her dark brown hair shining, her lovely profile etched out for all to see. Surprise and joy at finding her overcame any stage fright I might have had. I walked up next to her, took my place at the railing and coughed up a rather explosive "Hello!"

I startled her. She took a little step back from the railing as she turned to face me. Then she smiled, "Oh, you again!"

Her words contained great humor: *"Oh, you again!"* I loved it, laughed instantly, and leveled with her: "I followed you."

She laughed. "You did? What for?"

"I fell in love with you."

Now a wise look in those green eyes. "Oh, brother . . ." she said, in a down-flat voice.

"I did, no use lying."

"Really fell in love, huh?" she asked.

"Yes."

"Not kidding me?"

"No."

Her next line killed me. "Enough to *marry* me?"

I didn't even blink. "Of course," I said.

"Oh, no." She shook her head. "Not so fast."

"Then you're not ruling it out—completely?"

"Oh, no," she said facetiously, "I wouldn't do that."

"Good. Why don't we have dinner and discuss it further?"

She pulled back and gave me a solid looking-over. I could tell she was seriously appraising the situation, deciding whether to go on with the charade or end it. Quickly I added, "I mean, we don't want to do anything rash, do we?"

"No . . ." she said, still looking at me, the charade having left her voice.

A crucial moment, I knew. I could feel my heart banging away. I was so attracted to her I could barely stand still at the idea I might blow it. "Listen," I said, purely out of nerves, having not rounded up the right words, having no idea what they might be. "Listen . . ." I repeated.

"I'm listening," she said.

The flat tone put me smack behind the eight ball. "Look," I badly stalled, "I mean—"

"You mean what?" she asked, not hostile, but as if she simply wanted to know.

"I mean," I told her, completely unzipping myself, "I'm so nervous you won't have dinner with me that I can't think of any right words, I can't go on being cute, or kidding, or—I just would love to spend a few hours with you." Still, she looked at me. "I would, I really would."

She smiled briefly, a small smile. "All right." Before I could reply, she added, "Let's walk a while."

"Okay."

We walked along the dock by the boats. Suddenly she stopped and looked at me. "Oh, my God," she said. "I forgot, how old are you?"

"Twenty-one."

"You are? You wouldn't lie to me, seriously?"

"No, I'm twenty-one, almost twenty-two. I know I look younger—"

"Way younger."

"I know, but I'm twenty-one. I'll be—"

"I don't lie either," she said. "I'm twenty-three, almost twenty-four."

Her face struck me again. "You are so beautiful," I told her.

"Thank you. You're very good looking yourself."

"Thank you."

We walked for a long time without talking. But once we started we never stopped. We had dinner at a restaurant on the wharf, and we got along so well it was scary. Lisa Woodruff, from Sacramento, a graphic artist for an ad agency in San Francisco. She was funny, with a very special under-the-surface humor, and independent, and still she never lost her built-in warmth. She was also candid about herself; she'd lived with a man for almost a year but he'd been edging into the drug scene, beyond pot, into L.S.D. and other, heavier stuff, and she had recently broken off with him, although she said she still loved him.

That I did not like to hear; she saw it in my face, laughed and said, "That doesn't mean I can't love anyone else."

She had moved out of his place and now shared an apartment with a girl who worked as a reporter for the San Francisco *Chronicle*. We lingered over coffee forever; she would tell me a part of her life, I would drop a part of mine. I was in civilian clothes, and there was one part I dropped that did not go over well at all. She was not pleased to hear I was in the army. *I* was not happy to be in the service by that time either. But I was stuck; I was in and that was that, but only for two years, and a quarter of that time was up.

Long walk after dinner. Cable-car ride. A few drinks in a few bars. All the time talking and connecting with each other more and more. To find a girl as beautiful as Lisa with such a delightful sense of humor, and of herself, was exciting. I could feel the excitement in my stomach, the tiny shakes, like you're coming down with the flu.

Around midnight, sitting at a table in a bar named The Frump, it was she who suddenly said, "Should we go to bed tonight, or do you think that's"—she broke off, smiled and shrugged—"or not?"

"Yes, I'd like to, if you would," I said, trying to keep the tiny shakes from mushrooming up into my throat and strangling me.

Another one of her considering looks, then, "Yes, I would."

It was an exceptionally warm August night for San Francisco. "What if we drive down the coast?" she asked.

"I don't have a car."

Lisa said she could get her roommate's, adding, "I'd like to make love with you outside."

"Outside where?" I asked. "In a field?"

"No, at the beach."

I absolutely shouted, "Oh, God, yes—how great, at the beach, we'll get a blanket!"

This had exploded from me. The two couples at the next table could not help overhearing. The meaning was obvious. They laughed, and we laughed, blushed, got the check, and left as one joker called out, "Watch out for sharks."

Lying on my bed, how I replayed that first evening! Constant reruns, summer, winter, spring, and fall. We drove to Half Moon Bay down the coast from San Francisco. I had not been apprehensive until we'd found a sheltered spot by a deserted Coast Guard lighthouse, put down two blankets and started to undress. Then, because I was feeling such love, I could not help hoping I'd be an exceptional lover for her. As I stepped out of my pants, she put a hand on my shoulder. "I hope you're not nervous," she said, without waiting for a reply, "because I find you very attractive; I've been looking forward all night to the feel of your body next to mine."

Well . . .

Seven times we made love that Saturday night and Sunday. Four of them outside, including once in the ocean and three in a motel room we took. She was not only beautiful and warm and funny and touching but she was just about the best sexual partner I'd ever had. She could not touch me without arousing me. If I seem to concentrate on the sexual aspect, endless months cooped up in that cell made me dredge up those specific memories constantly.

I didn't have to dredge them up; they came up and sat on

the head of my cock like demons, thumbing their horny noses at me.

By the time we said good-bye late Sunday night I was hooked, helpless and punched-up happy.

Our courtship was intense. As indicated earlier, I've never been known for gratuitous bravery. Although I'd been in communications I had still availed myself of every opportunity to forestall going overseas. Now that I had Lisa I redoubled my efforts, and through a series of moves—ingratiating, chicanerous, and using every contact I possibly could—I was able to get myself transferred to duty at the base, doing clerical work.

This gave me almost every weekend off, except perhaps one in four or five. I stayed with Lisa and her roommate, Sammy Moorehouse. Sammy was pretty in an offbeat way, not beautiful like Lisa but energetic, bright and terribly ambitious. I liked Sammy; we got along fine.

It had never occurred to me that I would want to be married until I was at least in my thirties, if then. Suddenly I found myself proposing to Lisa every weekend. Without even thinking about it. I suppose marriage is when there is no other alternative, when you can't see anything else but being glued to someone for eternity.

I knew she loved me but she would not agree to marriage, not with me in the service. "You're tied to the army; wait until you're free before you tie yourself down again," she'd say. There was a look in her eyes, though, that indicated there was some other reason. I finally nudged it out of her: she cringed at the idea of being a war widow, of sweating it out if I ever got sent overseas. Besides loathing the war, she actually felt if we got married, that might put a jinx to work on us.

We talked it over and over; I would not let up. I thought I was secure in my clerical job, thought unless there was a big shakeup at the base I might never be sent overseas. After a while, Lisa thought so, too.

Almost seven months to the day we met, I convinced Lisa to marry me. We were married on the seventeenth of March, 1967. If I attempted to describe my happiness, our happiness, it would probably make you ill—that's how sweet our time together was.

In July the shakeup came. I was taken out of clerical work,

put back in communications and assigned to a company scheduled for Vietnam.

Lisa tried to be brave about it, but the foundations inside were shaky. She became extremely irritable and edgy. When I attempted to humor her, she would barely respond. It was as if her humor, which she had in abundance, had been put in the freezer compartment.

Our last two days together, a week before I was shipped out, I spent consoling her, assuring her I had no intention of getting killed. She, who had such everyday strength and independence, who was so much her own woman, was suddenly a little girl.

I was touched by her love and caring. I held onto it. I clung to my memories of Lisa. She was my lifeline to remaining sane. You come through difficult tests—for yourself, I know, but you also make a special effort if someone else is included.

Those first strange isolated months comprised the Big Adjustment to life as a prisoner.

Trains going by the camp would always depress me. The mournful low muffled whistle reminded me of travel and distance. And distance from everything I knew and loved was the problem.

The lack of any discernible personality in my captors was not only depressing, it was scary. They were dehumanized. I could imagine North Vietnamese being prisoners of Americans, and the treatment they would receive from our guards might at least differ according to the wide swing of personality in the individual, even if it should take the form of anger or disgust or bullying on a personal level. But these guards were so detached. If they treated us well one day, badly the next, you knew it was the result of orders, nothing inherent in the men themselves.

Although I didn't wish being captured on anyone else, I couldn't help thinking if the Viet Cong kept taking prisoners, even half as many as they claimed on "The Voice of Vietnam," I would eventually have to get a roommate.

The first year was the rockiest, by far. And when I did get a roommate, it was even worse, in a way.

# 5

On the twenty-seventh of August, 1968, at about three-thirty in the afternoon, the Turnkey opened my door and in walked Sergeant Jerry Harker.

Joy. Christ, I bounded up off my bed; it's a wonder I didn't somersault. He looked like a nice guy, but then a rattlesnake would have been welcome: sure, yeah, hey what groovy skin; ah-ah, no biting now and I'll give you some of my pig fat.

Jerry Harker had been captured during Tet, too, and had been at the Hanoi Hilton in a general barracks with eleven others until this day. He was regular army, thirty-four, married, three kids, husky build, five-ten, coarse brown hair, like a horse's mane it was so coarse, and smallish hazel eyes set a little too close together over a prominent nose.

The first three, four months were great, the honeymoon period. You tell each other everything there is to tell, you wonder everything there is to wonder, you share your thoughts, you try to cheer the other fellow up on bad days, you cooperate.

After the honeymoon, you start getting on each other's nerves. So happened we shared a hundred basic differences. Jerry was square, square about the war, too. The U.S.A. had no failings; we were right all the way down the line, except for our refusal to use atomic weapons. He thought we were actually fighting to keep the Communist Hordes from moving into Trenton, New Jersey, where he was from. I told him I thought people were moving *out* of Trenton, New Jersey; I didn't think even the Communist Hordes would care to move in. Mistake.

He was that strange animal, a square philosopher. Sample: "Pisher (He named me that on account of the way I was

captured; even I thought it was funny—for a few months)—
Pisher, you know how you gotta look at life? You gotta take
the good with the bad. So we got the bad right now. We'll get
the good when we get out of here. Wait'll you get home, kid,
you're going to find out you're some kind of hero. Some kind
of hero! You wait, you're gonna see parades and meet
presidents and—we are each one of us going to be some kind
of Lindbergh. So just remember, take the good with the bad."

That kind of aimless chatter can get on your nerves. I re-
strained myself, at first, from telling him he sounded like
some kind of asshole.

He had a nasty habit of talking pidgin talk to the English
Speaker. He would say things like "Me no likee cat food" or
"Me wanna make shave-shave" or "Velly nicey, velly nicey."

The English Speaker didn't like it and I didn't like it. It
was chicken shit. When I asked him to please stop it, he said,
"Oh, Christ, they don't know any better; they're nothing but
a bunch of moronic goons."

We had some particularly rough times over the U.S. bombing raids on North Vietnam. He'd watch out of the shutters,
cheering them on: "That's right, bomb the shit out of their
Oriental asses, bomb the shit out of those fucking moron
goons."

To which I would counter that if they really kept on bombing and bombing and bombing, the North Vietnamese might
start knocking off prisoners in retaliation.

"No, we're gonna win this war any day now, any day. Not
long before we're gonna be some kind of hero. Christ, the
United States of America and this pissy little half-assed
Mickey Mouse country. Pisher, you got a bad attitude."

"Okay, think of all the years the United Almighty States of
America has been fighting this pissy little half-assed Mickey
Mouse country and you don't see any victory, do you? Some
kind of hero, my ass! You're their prisoner, that's what you
are. Look around, where do you think we are, roughing it at
some Y.M.C.A. summer camp?"

"I'm gonna report your Communist ass when we get out of
here."

"Oh, go report your petrified brain!"

Jerry and I exchanged a few punches, hit the floor and
wrestled around. The Turnkey came, then the English

Speaker with a warning that if we fought again, one of us would be put in solitary.

By these examples I don't mean to present a blanket denouncement of Jerry Harker. He had many good qualities: he could not be bullied by the guards, nor would he stand by while I was bullied; he was not a down-head—he kept his morale up and would try to cheer me on bad days; he was a loyal friend and a good soldier; although he, too, was not allowed to write, he received two packages from home while we were cellmates and he insisted upon sharing the goodies fifty-fifty.

It was the little things, little idiosyncrasies that rubbed against the grain. To show how petty it got, we actually demolished our relationship over Marilyn Monroe in January of 1969. Marilyn Monroe, dead and buried, and the two of us prisoners of war, fighting over *her!* We were talking late one night about movies we'd liked and I happened to mention I'd like to see *Some Like It Hot* again.

"*Some Like It Hot?*" he asked, "what was that about?" I reminded him. "Oh, yeah, that fag movie." We had a few words over that when I corrected him that it wasn't a fag movie.

"What do you mean, it wasn't a fag movie? The two of them dressed up as fags, didn't they?"

"Jesus, Jerry, you don't know what you're talking about. In the first place, if you'd use your head, they didn't dress up as fags, they dressed up as girls."

"Same thing."

"Wrong, it's not the same thing."

It went on like that until he suddenly dropped that he wouldn't want to see it because it was a fag movie, and besides, Marilyn Monroe was nothing but a cheap whore, had always been a cheap whore and—I cut in and said the poor girl was dead and to leave her alone.

"Sure, she's dead, probably screwed herself to death."

Now, oddly enough, I'd never been that wild for Marilyn Monroe; I could take her or leave her, but suddenly it became terribly important to stick up for her. The more I'd defend her, tell him to stop talking like that, the more he'd dump it on her. "She's the kind of chippy would screw a police dog!"

"Stop it, she's dead."

"Christ, she'd screw her own brother or her father—yeah, she'd screw her old man!"

"Jerry, quit it, come on!"

"She'd screw the Pope if she could get her hands on him, she'd screw little kids if—"

Then I was up and over and on top of him, pinning him down and, of all things, trying to make him take it back. Shows how punchy you can get; it was like the fever.

He sort of half-defended himself but he was enjoying getting my goat and he started laughing, too, and going on: "She screwed other women, too. She was also a lesbo, Pisher, everyone knows that. Why she'd screw—"

By that time I was choking him, and the fight was on for fair. I was suddenly out to kill him. Because it was late, around ten in the evening, it took a while for the Turnkey to hear us and come around. Trying to stop us, he got roughed up a bit. He summoned the officer in charge from the main house and that evening I was put in solitary.

Solitary was not fun. Jesus, what an original, brilliant sentence! You mean *solitary wasn't fun?*

The two solitary cement bunkers were back to back, off in the yard by themselves. They were about six feet high, no more than three feet by four feet in area. You couldn't lie down in them. You had to sit with your knees doubled up most of the time. I had one blanket, that was it. No light, no nothing in there but a slop can. There was a small grated peephole at the top, mostly for looking in rather than for looking out. The floor was—just dirt, damp and filthy. The concrete walls didn't help in damp weather, either.

Bread and water was it for the most part, with perhaps a little soup and some greens, a little rice, a couple of times a week. The hunger for the first week was killing; then the stomach shrinks when it's not getting anything and you don't feel it so much, unless you don't watch yourself and start fantasizing about food.

The best thing to do was put yourself into a state of numbness. At least numbness to the present, what was going on, where you were. Mostly I relived my entire life, went over it from my very first memories. When I'd done that I would change the scenario; I would imagine how it would have been if I'd made certain decisions, or my mother had made them, and how these decisions at crucial times would have changed things. Then I'd go on from there, charting my life along another course.

There were, of course, days when I was afraid I was losing my mind. There were other days when I hoped I *was* losing it.

In early March I got a bad fever—I'd lost almost twenty-five pounds and I was sick. That resulted in my being let out, but instead of being put back in my old room with Jerry I was put in the room I have marked "2" on the sketch. I was alone again. It didn't matter, I was so sick. I got medication twice a day and I was given a third blanket, which came in handy when I got the chills. It took me three weeks to get back on my feet.

In May I got a letter, my first, not from Lisa but from my mother. She had moved to New York from California. She said she was on the wagon for as long as I was in the service. She felt responsible for the fix I was in and would never forgive herself (more about this later), but the biggest news was that she had met Lisa before she left California and she had seen my daughter—Lauri!

Daughter! I'd always wanted a son, but just the news that my baby had been born, was alive and well and living in California, was enough for me. This news did one other thing. After all, Lisa was a terribly attractive girl. And not only to me; I was always aware of the glances she attracted. The idea that she was not just alone, wandering around on her own, that she had someone to direct her love to as well as someone to love her back, that there was a living link between us, made me relax about Lisa and not worry about her being so lonely.

My mother didn't tell me too much about my daughter, except to say she looked exactly like me. I could tell from her letter she presumed I had tons of information I didn't have because obviously both Lisa and my mother had been writing to me regularly and had also sent packages. She hoped I would be able to answer her letters soon. She had phoned Lisa before writing me this time and Lisa had told her she still hadn't heard from me.

At least they believed I was alive. I can't explain how important that was. If people thought you were dead, it was almost as if you were. The idea they knew I was alive and were thinking of me day after day—this would keep me alive.

The last three sentences in the letter had been censored, so thoroughly blacked out there was no hope of deciphering them. Maddening as it was, still I'd had a letter. Immediately I asked if I could write. No, not at this time.

## 6

Nineteen seventy was a dull year. Most of it was spent alone in my corner room, two small windows. There was a change of guards, a new Turnkey and a new English Speaker. The new English Speaker, whose name, I learned, was Ti (pronounced Tie), was one step up from the first in personality, although his English was worse.

The major events of 1970 can be put down on the head of a pin. The biggest was a letter from my wife in March. She and Lauri had been staying with her mother in Sacramento, but she was thinking of moving back to San Francisco and looking for a new job. She loved me, missed me, and lived for the day I'd return. Lauri was a beautiful baby, who looked like me, had my coloring and my blue eyes. Lisa hoped very much I would be allowed to write her; she hoped I'd received the packages she'd sent. (I had not received them.) Again I asked for permission to write. No, not this time.

In April an arrival took place in my cell. I had a visitor. There was a large crack between the outside wall and the concrete floor, perhaps two inches at its widest, narrowing down to less than an inch and running half the width of the room.

One afternoon during a heavy rainstorm, a mouse scurried in, shook itself off, stood up on its hind legs, looked around, sniffed over to the corner and just sat down. I was sitting on my bed at the time. I kept very still, so's not to scare him off.

After a while he seemed to huddle up there in the corner and go to sleep. I carefully swung my legs up on the bed, swiveled around so my head was nearest him and observed him. Brown, with a ratty coat, he had one ear torn off, patches of fur missing, and a wisp of a little spiny tail.

Soon he appeared to be sound asleep. I had saved a piece of bread from the morning meal for myself. I got it out from under my blanket, tore off a few small soft pieces so the crust wouldn't make a noise and frighten him, and tossed them over between him and where the crack was widest. He didn't move. I must have lain there an hour waiting for him to wake up.

When he did, he shook himself off again, sat up, looked around, and then sniffed about the floor. Suddenly he looked up and spotted me, still lying on the bed, my head right by the edge. Immediately he sat up again. I didn't move a muscle. He twitched his whiskers; then, when I remained completely still, he turned and started toward the crack.

Oh, God, how I begged him not to go.

He found the bits of bread, squeaked a little and fell to them, devouring them right on the spot. He'd pick them up in his claws, like a cartoon mouse, and nibble at them. When he was finished he began a tour of the floor to see if he could find more.

I waited until he'd gone under the other bed, across from me; then I tore off a few more bits and tossed them near the crack, away from him, careful not to frighten him.

He heard them hit, poked his head out from under the bed, froze for a few seconds, then scurried over to retrieve them. I got to feeling more secure, and this time, when he'd finished, I threw some more in his direction, but one piece landed too close and bounced over, almost hitting him. He scooted out the crack.

I lay there for another hour or so waiting for him to come back and claim the rest. As time went on and he didn't return I went into a fierce depression, berating myself for throwing too close and scaring him.

Now, it all sounds ridiculous, a grown man grieving for a mouse, not a snowy white little pink-nosed lab mouse but a ratty motheaten one-eared North Vietnamese varmint, an enemy mouse at that. But you cannot imagine the importance of contact with any living thing.

I actually think I'd have made a major confession for the entire United States if I'd been promised a dog or a cat: "Yes, it's true, the military-industrial complex has plans to work up from North Vietnam, take over China and eventually Russia and then the whole bloody world, call it the *United Countries of America*—now give me the goddam cat!"

Before I turned in that night I littered the floor near the outside wall with crumbs so there'd be no mistaking the place for a bare cupboard in case he chanced by during the night. I awakened several times and checked the bait. Still there, no mouse.

Next morning about six-thirty I was sitting on the slop can—I would balance a slipper on each side of the can and sit on it, providing a cushion from the sharp edge—and in came the mouse, cautiously at first, whiskers twitching.

He could not miss the breakfast put out for him. I sat on the can, not moving even my bowels for fear of frightening him, while he went from crumb to crumb. Finished with them, he went on an investigatory trip around that part of the room to see if there was more. There wasn't, and soon he wandered over to the corner and went to sleep again.

When I was finished I almost didn't wipe myself for fear of disturbing him. But then I started to laugh. How stupid—life has to go on, mouse or no mouse.

Still, I tended to myself gently and then carefully made my way back to my bunk, where I lay down and watched him sleep.

He dozed until the Turnkey came with the morning meal. The door opening, the general racket, awakened him and he scooted out. Before I ate, I tore up crumbs and set a line of them along the crack. About eleven o'clock he reappeared, ate and then made a thorough search of the room, even standing up on his hind legs to get a better look at the stretched-out giant staring at him from the bed.

I blinked at him, he blinked at me. No sweat. And went on exploring the place. He would often pause, stand up, sniff, and make a little pawing gesture with his claws, almost like a boxer, before getting back down on all fours. It was a feisty little gesture, as if to challenge anyone who might be lying in

wait. As I watched him on his inspection rounds I thought I'd
never seen a mouse do that. It also occurred to me I'd spent
relatively little time documenting the life, times and physical
attitudes of mice.

Soon he worked his way back to the side of my bed, stood
up once more, twitched his whiskers and made the little
pawing gesture before getting back down to a crouch; even
his crouch, I noticed, was a defiant one, feet splayed out,
head jutting forward.

"Wanna fight, do you?" I said. Right then his name came
to me. "Okay— Spike! Yes, Spike!" I could imagine him in a
little fighter's cap. A very little one. "Christ, you've even got
cauliflower ear."

He soon went out the crack again. Immediately I put out
more crumbs. Spike knew a good thing and took up residence
in my cell on a regular basis. For the next few weeks I never
went to sleep or left the room for exercise period or a shower
without placing food out for him.

Eventually Spike spent the greater part of every day with
me. But no evenings. He had better fish to fry. He was a
night mouse; every evening around five or six he'd leave and
I wouldn't see him until about five in the morning, when he'd
come in, eat his breakfast, and nap for a spell.

After a while I could move around with ease without disturbing him or seeming to be a threat. His favorite spot was
the lefthand corner of the room. Eventually I collected some
bits of straw from outside and a few little pebbles and made
a little separate place for him, which I would have to dis-
mantle when we had inspection. I'd just scatter the stuff under my bed, thin it out, and then rebuild for him after.

It was a good relationship. I'm embarrassed to say how
fond of him I became. And if you'd heard me talking to him
you'd have thought I'd gone bananas.

Especially when he'd show up in the morning. "Well,
Spike, where the hell have you been, you little bastard? Out
all night, every night, you must be all fucked out." Then:
"Tell me, Spike, do you get a lot of ass? I bet you do, I'll bet
that little ass of yours hammers away all night long—wham,
bam, squeak, squeak! Listen, if you've got a lady-friend bring
her around sometime for breakfast. Go ahead, there's
enough, and I swear to God I won't touch her. Unless she's
one helluva cute little mouse." And on and on. Silly dumb

chatter, but at least I could pretend to be having a conversation.

There was other conversation, too, with Wally Briggs and Eugene Gronowicz, who shared the room next to me. They knew the tap code and we spent many hours tapping away back and forth. It was tedious but it was worth it.

Then I found myself doing push-ups over a large nail out in the yard during exercise period in July. I sneaked it back to my room, and a few days later, when I emptied my slop can, I dropped a rock in the bottom and managed to get it back to the room undetected.

Slowly and as quietly as possible I began gouging a hole in the wall between our rooms, underneath the wood bed platform that stood next to the wall. Within two weeks I had a small hole chiseled away, perhaps half an inch around. I'd lie under the platform and we could talk back and forth: Wally Briggs, Eugene Gronowicz and me. Not much in the way of lengthy or comfortable communications, but it was something, it was contact. It also reminded me of when I was a kid—the secrecy, the danger if we were caught.

I got caught about six weeks later. We had inspection of our rooms twice a week, and for that period of time I managed to keep the nail and the rock hidden in the straw that was my mattress without either being found. I probably should have ditched them after I made the hole, but with so little in the way of possessions they mattered, so I kept them. Actually I was sort of fond of them. It was also a form of token defiance, having a nail and a rock.

When the Assistant Camp Commander found them on the inspection tour, he and the Turnkey immediately searched the room thoroughly. It didn't take them long to discover the hole. It was my hole, and in order to save Eugene and Wally I made a full confession.

Back in solitary, but only for three weeks, which surprised me. I thought it would be longer. My main worry was Spike; without three squares a day I thought he might pack up and move out. I had other thoughts during those three weeks; I was hoping when I got out I might be moved and put in with someone, even Sergeant Jerry Harker, who I became much more attached to the longer I was separated from him.

But I was put back in my room alone. Spike was not there, but he'd been around sometime because I searched for mouse droppings and there were a few scattered about, especially over in his corner. As soon as I got my first meal I tore up bits of bread and set them out. One day, two days passed and no Spike. Anger and resentment against my captors began building up for putting me in solitary and lousing up my routine with Spike. Strange how one could live with the big disappointments: no mail, no packages, no word of the outside world, no sex. These items you got by without going bananas, but a little change in the routine—not being allowed out for exercise period or the disappearance of a goddam mouse—could get under your skin and drive you into a severe depression.

When he didn't show up on the third day I went into a funk. Even so, I kicked aside the old crumbs, which were stale by now, and set out fresh ones. The fourth morning, by God, in came Spike. He sniffed at the crumbs, then began breakfast. "Christ, Spike, welcome home, where the hell have you been?" At the sound of my voice, he turned, scurried over near the bed, stood up, looked at me, and made his little pawing gesture. I interpreted this, of course, as a sign of extreme delight at seeing me back.

He soon went back to eating and, after a brief inspection tour of the cell, made his way to his corner and went to sleep. I was happy to a ridiculous degree that day.

I had been weakened by my three weeks in solitary but I was not really sick, just in bad shape. It was about this time I began concentrating heavily on push-ups. I became a push-up nut, eventually working my way up to one hundred.

In November of 1970, around Thanksgiving, we were taken one evening to the main house, where we were shown movies of the Russian Air Show. There were about twenty-five of us. I spotted Jerry Harker immediately and went over to sit next to him. Odd, so odd; like we were long-lost friends. We began chattering away, but a guard quickly came over and told us no talking. We were sitting on a bench, and when the lights switched off for the film Jerry put his hand on my knee and kept it there for five minutes or so. It was nothing more than a little quiet communication. After a while he gave me a squeeze and a few pats and took it away. When the movie ended, the lights were quickly put on and we were ordered to stand and start moving out. Jerry quickly whispered, as we marched off, "I take it back about Marilyn Monroe."

# 7

There was 1970, until the very end. On the nineteenth of December around seven in the evening the door to my room opened and the English Speaker and Turnkey helped in a badly bruised and messed-up guy who was, despite his beat-up condition, mad as a bobcat. His right arm was in a sling, he had various bandages on him. I don't ever recall seeing such wild eyes on anyone; they burned red they were so angry. He muttered and swore as they put his earthenware bowl, spoon, towel, blankets and things down on the bed across from mine.

I had stood up when they came in. But he no more than glanced at me. When they left, bolting the door behind them, he started pacing back and forth and before half a minute had passed he'd given the slop can a hefty kick and sent it flying. There were no solids, thank God, but there was some urine in it.

"Jesus," I said, "that's the slop can."

"No shit!" he said, through a badly swollen jaw.

Oh, Christ, I thought, here we go again.

He kept limping back and forth, although in his condition this was obviously extremely painful for him. I went to my bed and sat down. I sat there watching him, trying to decide which approach to take.

After a while, he flashed his eyes my way. "Well, what the fuck are you looking at?"

I almost said, "Nothing," but thought, what the hell, it was plain I was looking at him, so I said, "You."

He hobbled over and stood glaring down at me. "What are you, some kind of smart-ass?"

I ducked back on my bed against the wall. Immediately angry at myself for cringing, I only sputtered, "Yes—no—oh, shit, I don't care."

"I do, I fucking care, mind your own fucking business!"

His attitude got to me. "Jesus, what's eating you?"

"What's eating me, what the fuck do you think's eating me for Jesus Christ fucking sake?" It hurt him to shout but that didn't stop him. He stood over me and shouted louder. "What do you think's eating me? Huh, tell me! *What the holy fuck do you think it could possibly be!*"

Now, he was bigger than me, older and stronger and mad as hell and the whole situation made me nervous. When I'm nervous I sometimes get punchy and try to dodge my way out. "I don't know," I told him, "you just found out you got the clap!"

He swung a backhand to the side of my head with his good hand, the left one. I saw it coming and ducked but he still stung my ear and the side of my head. I only yelped and took it, staying right there on the bed.

Many reasons: I didn't want solitary for Christmas, that's when we got special treatment and a great meal, a meal I looked forward to all year. I didn't want to fight with him anyhow because it would have been a nasty one with him all beat up, one arm in a sling and out-of-his-mind angry as he was. I also thought I'd pull in cool and make him feel sorry about it. I only sat there and put a hand up to where he'd hit me.

He did not feel sorry. He stood there, glaring down at me. "Fuck around with me and you'll get more. You got that straight?"

I couldn't help thinking: what a nervy fucker, all bandaged and messed up and *threatening me!* I didn't answer; I stared him in the eyes; he stared back.

"Keep to your fucking self, I'll keep to mine. You got that?"

I still didn't answer him, just kept staring, trying to let him know with my silent glare how much I was hating him.

"Okay," he said, "okay." He resumed his pacing for a while, then finally he lay down. After a while I went to sleep, but I don't think he slept all night.

At one point I woke up, dripping with sweat, something nagging at my mind. I couldn't pinpoint it until I looked over at him, lying on his good side, three-quarters turned away from me. As I watched him he moved slightly. I heard him mutter something, and he readjusted his arm, the one in the sling. Then it hit me, and I was on my feet standing next to his bed.

"Okay, listen," I said. The suddenness of my move and the sound of my voice startled him, but only slightly. He glanced up over his shoulder at me, then turned his head facing away again. I went on: "I got what you said and it's fine by me, you won't hear another word from me except one thing I got to tell you. There's a mouse comes in here every morning, he's a pet, he's my mouse and—" At that a derisive snort came from him. "I don't give a fuck what you think, I've been here since 1968—after you've been here that long, you'll start playing with cockroaches. Now this mouse lives here during the day, he doesn't bother anything, stays over in the corner. You do anything to that mouse, hurt him or even scare him and I swear to God I'll kill you!" I was almost screaming, my voice was way out of control and I was breathing like I'd just run the mile. "I mean it, cool it with the mouse. Okay, that's all I got to say. You got my point?"

Silence. But I wouldn't leave it at that. I wanted official acknowledgment. "Did you hear me?"

Without moving, his reply was issued in the form of a rather substantial fart.

"Terrific! A class act all the way. Hope you didn't get any in your shoes!"

I went back to bed. Once there I had to press my face down into the blankets. Actually it was wildly funny, after my histrionics. It was a great putdown and I got a sudden case of the giggles, which probably were part nervous-tension from my scene and standing up to him. I almost smothered myself to keep from laughing. I would not let him think I thought anything he did was funny, not for anything in the world.

I went back to sleep, fairly sure he'd leave Spike alone. But not entirely certain. I kept waking up during the night, anticipating Spike's return. I'd always look over at the New One. He finally arranged himself on his back, laying there with his eyes wide open. Once, when I woke up about four in the morning, he was standing facing the shutters at the window. Not trying to look out, just standing there facing the wooden shutters.

Spike came in around six the next morning. He was not happy to have two people in the cell. Especially with the New One in such a restless mood. He ate, sniffed around, went to his corner for a while and then left. When the New One noticed him, Spike earned a snort of contempt, nothing more.

We did not speak a word to each other for the next day, or the next, or the next. Not one word. For those three days his anger stood at fever pitch. It was fascinating to see how he could remain so mad. It showed in everything he did. He ate angry, two or three times spitting out his soup in disgust and shoving it away. He shit angry, it flew out of him. When he finally went off to sleep the second night, he even slept angry, tossing and jerking around on his bed, then waking and cursing to himself because he hurt where he was bruised.

Though there was a definite strain being in a small room with someone furious as he was and who wouldn't talk to you, it had its points. First off, there weren't many projects to get involved in. Even though this was a negative project, it was still a full-time one—cooped up in a small cell and not speaking to someone. That takes working at. There was also suspense involved, wondering how long it would go on, ringing up a victory of sorts at the end of each day. And there was the plain novelty of having a stranger in the room, someone you didn't know, didn't know his background, didn't even know his name.

Now and then I'd observe him, sitting on the end of his bed in his black pajamas, looking toward the shutters. Even sitting still, he filled the room with his anger.

I made as much of a game out of it as I could, trying to imagine what his first name would be. He was about six feet tall, had a lithe build, not overly muscular but strong and hard in its leanness. Black hair, bold, straight black eyebrows, brown eyes that I avoided looking at, but they were lively, that was for sure, and a light olive complexion. Even with a badly swollen jaw and cuts and bruises on his face, he was good-looking, in a snarky way, what my mother would call "a smooth devil." Straight-nose, thin-cheeked. I'd have put his age at thirty-two or three. I thought maybe his name would be Burt, or Vic, or Clint. Something sharp. Maybe Robert, or Roberto. He could have been Italian, maybe even Spanish, some Mediterranean background: he certainly had the temperament to go with the Latins.

The fourth day, December 23, he was taken over to the main building for medical treatment. When he returned, just before the afternoon meal, his bandages had been changed and his right arm was in a smaller sling. Still no talking. I was beginning to dig it, maybe we'd set a world record, together in this dump of a room for one year and not a word.

December 24, his anger had cooled a bit, he lay on his bed most of the day with his eyes shut. Christmas Eve, we got rice and tinned fish (Russian), bean curd, Chinese cabbage, cookies, tea, a whole pack of Dien Bien cigarettes, and he got a third blanket. I already had my third one.

During the meal the loudspeakers were turned on and for a while they played French music; I remember Edith Piaf sang "La Vie en Rose." There was some Chinese or North Vietnamese music, too.

I started feeling sorry for myself along about this time. A train went by, blowing its mournful whistle. I saw Lisa trimming a tree, Lisa in bed Christmas morning. My second Christmas stashed away in cold storage. And now for a Christmas present I finally got a nut roommate, who instead of a handshake gave me a clop in the head. I glanced over at him, actively hating him now. He was an intruder. Suddenly I wanted him out of there, I wanted to be alone again.

The whistle sounded way off in the distance now. I couldn't stop thinking about Lisa and our daughter, wondered what they were doing right now at this moment. I got hit in the stomach with the intense ache of missing her, so much so I stopped eating.

If I'd have been alone I probably would have had a brief Christmas cry for myself.

When they played "Silent Night, Holy Night" I really wanted to let go. But with him over there, struggling to eat with his left hand and becoming more and more impatient, I wouldn't have cried if they'd told me my whole family had been wiped out by an earthquake.

I concentrated on him again. Better to feel angry than sorry for myself. He did the trick, I was able to get back to my meal.

Christmas morning the gong didn't go off until seven o'clock. We'd both been awake for a while, though. About ten minutes later the loudspeakers went on, a North Vietnamese girl's voice wished us all a Merry Christmas and then Bing Crosby's recording of "I'm Dreaming of a White Christmas" came on.

I was sitting on my bed, smoking. He was still lying down.

Suddenly he sprang up from his bed, grabbed his sandals and started throwing them, with his left hand, at the speaker up on its ledge in the corner of the room. And swearing. Every combination you ever heard and a few you haven't. He grabbed *my* sandals and threw them, he threw his spoon, his soap, and finally he picked up his mug and threw it. He hit the speaker head on, knocked it down and the sound cut off—wham, like that.

I was still sitting on my bed. The sudden silence, the slice-off of Bing Crosby's voice was wildly funny, although I wouldn't allow myself to laugh. Certainly not in the face of his rage.

He sat down on his bed hard. Bam. Just sat there for a while breathing hard and staring down at the floor. I suddenly thought to look for Spike, who'd come in, eaten and gone to sleep. Spike had taken a powder.

I looked over at him, still staring down at the floor. Then he looked up at me. He shook his head, his lips curled into a smile and we both started laughing. We laughed and laughed, laughed ourselves sick. I had to lie down on my side and turn away from him; it was beginning to hurt. He had the same problem, only because of his bruises it hurt him more.

Eventually we laughed ourselves out. I turned over to look at him; he was lying on his back, panting, out of breath. When he glanced over and saw me looking at him, he swung up to a sitting position and said, "Merry Fucking Christmas!"

"Merry Fucking Christmas!" I replied.

# 8

Sergeant Vin Poirier, twenty-eight—younger than I thought
—was of French Canadian parents, now living in Dorset,
Vermont. He'd been shot down on a search-and-rescue heli-
copter mission about thirty miles from Hanoi. It was to have
been his last one before returning to the States. He had thirty
days' leave coming and he and his girl friend, Ginger, were
to be married. That explained his outsized rage at being captured.

He had parachuted from the copter and even with an
injured right arm, a few cracked ribs and other bruises, he remained uncaptured for six days, by hiding out in an old silo
for four of those days without food or water. He said at
times his searchers came so close to him he could have
reached out and touched them. He was forced to leave the
silo the fourth night to hunt for food and water.

On the sixth evening, after grubbing around for odds and
ends to put in his stomach, he went to sleep in a pile of straw
in a large barn on a farm. He woke up when people, older
men, and women, young to old, began arriving with lanterns.
He lay there very quietly, after burrowing down in the straw
farther over in his corner. Soon there were fifteen or twenty
people. When the group was called to order and from the
tone of the conversation, he realized it was some sort of civilian militia meeting.

One woman had brought her two young children along;
one of them, a little girl, crawled over and eventually sat on
him. When he moved slightly she got the giggles and the jig
was up. As Vin said, "And a little fucking child shall lead
them."

That Christmas Day we had our great feast. Even though

it was Christmas it was still brought to our rooms: roast chicken, dumplings, vegetables, a real salad, bread, tea, canned fruit, a bag of hard candy, cake—the works. It's difficult to describe how much this meal meant. I'd begun salivating weeks before whenever I thought about it.

Because of Vin's bum right arm, I had to cut his chicken up for him. There was an intimacy about this act that cinched our friendship.

Although Vin took a long time to get over his anger at being taken prisoner, that evening I was happier than I'd been in a long time. My belly was full and I had a roommate I suspected I was going to connect with.

Vin and boredom didn't go together. He was full of life; even when he was lying down, a field of energy generated from him. There was a hum in the air around him. His karma would be a humming thing.

Right away I clued into his humor. Thank God he had it. I'd rather be locked up with a disturbed person that had a sense of humor than a dolt without one.

He admitted he'd taken an instant dislike to me the night he arrived. Then, when he swatted me and I didn't retaliate, that cinched it, he figured I was a washout. "But," he said, "I got a kick out of your sermon about the fucking mouse. You meant it, too, didn't you?"

"You're goddam right I did."

He laughed. "Yeah, I got a kick out of that."

"Yeah," I told him, "I got a kick out of your reply, too."

"It just slipped out," he said.

We both laughed.

He had some pet phrases I got a kick out of. For instance, having sex, any sexual act, he called "performing the Dread Deed!" Everything down, bad or dull with Vin he referred to as the Pits. The camp was the Pits, the food was the Pits, the bed was the Pits. Going to the john squatting over a slop can with someone in the same room was the Pits. Despite his original fart, as soon as we became friendly, this took him a while to get used to. I liked that about him. At first I offered to stand facing the shutters and hum.

"No," he said.

"Why not?"

"Your singing would constipate me even more."

He was high on nicknames. Our room was the Henry Ca-

bot Lodge Suite, later changed to the Henry Kissinger Suite.
When I told him how I was captured, he got a huge kick out
of it. "That's too much," he said. "You're too much." I gave
him permission to call me Pisher if he wanted. He shook his
head, thought a minute and said he'd just call me T. M.

"T. M.?" I asked.

"Yes—Too Much."

From then on I was T. M. Or Eddie, my name.

Because of his temper, which he had in spades, I came to
call him El Exigente or D. O.—the Demanding One.

Vin had certain blind spots. He'd had two years of college
but mostly he was self-educated. He was a heavy reader and
it drove him crazy that we were given no reading material. It
made no sense to him at all. He requested an interview with
the Camp Commander and oddly enough he got it. When he
came back to the room he was shaking, his light olive
complexion was a reddish purple. "Jesus Fucking Christ (he
could work fucking into almost any sentence), what harm
would it do to at least let us read a book or a magazine? Our
fucking minds are going to rot."

I was able to help him in those early weeks with his attitude. Vin's temper was what you didn't need as a P.O.W.
You paid for a temper and paid heavily. With almost three
years behind me at camp, I explained that you had to take it
easy, very easy, day by day. I equated it with being an alcoholic. This I knew from my mother when she had, now and
then, gone to A.A.

You had to take one day at a time, not think about time in
large spans. Concentrate on getting through each day with as
few hassles as possible. This meant not looking forward too
much to when you might be getting out. It meant not
pressing down hard on thoughts that bothered you, not wor-
rying the why, how, rightness or wrongness of us being in Vietnam in the first place.

To my mind, we never should have become engaged in the
Vietnam mess. But I couldn't let myself think too much
about this. I'd been there, I'd been captured, and that was the
situation. To dwell on the obscenity of our entire involvement
would have been dangerous territory for the mind to wander
in. It would have been magnifying a bummer.

I'd learned by this time to tranquilize myself when I found
I was getting wound up over—name it—the cold, the heat,

the bad food, bad treatment, no sex, the discouraging news
we were constantly fed over the loudspeakers in the morning
about the war and our losses.

Of course, you couldn't avoid having rotten days, no matter how much you tried to control yourself or your thoughts.
They had to come. And they did. Black days. When I was
having a bad day I even got so I could tranquilize myself
along on that: okay, I'm having a pisser, I'm depressed, I'm
lonely, I miss Lisa, miss the feel and warmth of sex with her,
of going to sleep after wrapped up in each other. Or whatever else was specifically bugging me.

Have your bad day, but have it underwater, keep it
numbly bad. Don't fight it, that could only make it worse.
Don't activate the bomb. Tomorrow it won't be so bad, some
little thing will happen that will give you a kick in the morale.

Gradually I began conning Vin out of his temper. At first
he wouldn't look at me when I'd talk seriously to him, he'd
glance away. After a while, he began focusing on me, he'd
nod his head, sometimes smile. Later on he explained he
thought I was about nineteen or twenty. He could hardly believe it when I told him I was twenty-six. And he didn't like
taking advice from a kid.

My regret, but I've always looked much younger than my
age. I told Vin what my mother used to say: "He may have
the face of a babe, but he's got the soul of an old man."
When she saw I got a kick out of that, she'd add, "Not a wise
old man, just an old man."

Vin's and my relationship, the quality and intensity of it,
bears directly on what happened later, so I will explain it. As
best I can.

# 9

To say we hit it off is an understatement. The way I looked
at it, God, or whoever, had dropped a reward on me for having gotten through two rocky years without falling apart.

Although we were totally different in many ways—background, me, city-raised, him, mostly country; family, me, the
only child of a split marriage, him, parents still married plus
two brothers and a sister—we shared certain parallels in our
lives that were eerie.

We had each gone into the service, instead of avoiding it,
out of a combination of disappointment and anger with a
dash of spite thrown in. Neither of us thought we would
necessarily ever marry; there was no need for it in this day
and age. Neither could avoid it, though, because both had
fallen in love to the nth degree where you no longer weigh
the pros and cons of marriage—you simply do it. Although,
of course, Vin's marriage was in cold storage for as long as
he was prisoner.

As if these parallels weren't enough, Vin and his father
and older brother had been in the construction business,
house builders and carpenters. They were doing well, making
a go of it, building houses on contract for architects, and
soon they'd built two or three of their own on spec.

His father had always had a problem with gambling—
compulsive—but for a few years he was on the straight and
narrow. Then his mother underwent a mastectomy; although
she came out of it well, this triggered something with his father, who went on a prolonged binge, drinking and gambling
and pissing away most of the money they'd accumulated until
their business went down the drain. Vin went into the service,

anything to get away from a family situation that was no longer possible to deal with.

Because I had never lived in a home of my own, I mean one that either my mother owned or, say, a stepfather, when I was about eighteen I suddenly got hooked on real estate. Perhaps living in California, where most people seem to own their own homes, got to me. We'd always lived either in rented houses or apartments. The idea of owning my own place became a goal. This spread to being in real estate in general, developing it, dealing in it, eventually having houses built and selling them. (Not doing the actual building like Vin, more in the management end.)

I don't mean suburban split-level ranch homes or any other crap housing. I mean special homes for special people who know and care about the basic feel of a house, about texture and materials and privacy and, also, ecology. No crowding. So I'd started taking courses at U.C.L.A. that would help me toward this end: business management, real estate, and the like.

It was my plan to get my real estate license and build up a nest egg so I could start buying a piece of land here and there and gradually expand my operation. I suppose I had in mind to become a benevolent minor tycoon-landlord. Dreams of youth and all that.

I was on course, headed in that direction, when I was drafted. I gave in to the draft because of the situation with my mother. Now, to get to her, because our relationship also bears directly upon what happened later.

My mother, Bebe Keller (pronounced Bee-bee), was a costume designer, mostly for films—a good one, too, when she was paying attention. She walked off with an Academy Award when I was seven and was nominated several times. My father, Leonard Keller, left her when I was five. I barely remember when we were a family; he remarried and went to live in Maine with his second wife and their children. I spent an uncomfortable hour with him in New York when I was eleven. He kept telling me how much he wished we could spend more time together; he also kept looking at his watch.

The year before I was drafted my mother was heavy into the bottle, having a long, drawn-out breakdown of sorts, precipitated by the bust-up of a two-year love affair. Soon she was unable to work.

When my mother was deep into these rocky periods, I was the one who took care of her. Even when I was little. I loved her—loved her talent, looks, warmth and humor. But I loathed her drinking. It was the single most frustrating downer in my life and had been since I could remember. When she was out of control I was sickened, saddened, embarrassed, disgusted and angry. And confused about why she could not or would not take steps to help herself. Looking back on it, I was also naive in my supposition that since she loved me—and she did—why wouldn't she attempt to pull herself together, if not for herself, for me? (I know, *they* say you either do it for yourself or you don't do it. Still . . .)

By the time I was in college I was just plain weary of taking care of her, of begging and reasoning and coaxing her away from the bottle. The last six months I'd had to leave school and take a job doing accounting and paperwork for a real estate agency in Santa Monica. I took it because we needed the money; at least I was getting practical experience in the field I was interested in.

We were living in a small rented house, a depressing little gray two-bedroom stucco cottage on Fountain Avenue in Hollywood. I know some people think living in Hollywood is tacky, period. But this was really the tacky side of it. It was at that time I first read *Day of the Locust* and I had a feeling we'd moved right into the book.

Bebe was not eating, pale, skinny, and her usually pretty oval face was taking on a blotchy red angry look. I would not bring liquor to her but she would get it if she had to crawl down to Highland Avenue on her hands and knees in a nightgown during a parade.

Bebe also had two slightly more controlled alcoholic women friends who were forever driving around in a stoned daze with their bottles of vodka in paper bags nestled up against their thighs like pet cats, driving around keeping each other drinking company. How either Nan or Dotty managed the freeways without major disasters none of us ever understood.

Funny, but it was a small incident that finally snapped it with me and Bebe, a week before I received my draft notice. I'd met a girl, Joanne, at a party; she was married but about to leave her husband. We liked each other and decided to go to bed. We couldn't go to her place and she didn't like the idea of a motel, which I suggested. My mother was usually passed out by ten, so I brought Joanne home.

The TV in the living room had gone on the blink and for several days my mother had been watching the small one in my bedroom. When Joanne and I came home, the only light on was one in my mother's bedroom. She was asleep in her bed with the door open. I shut off her light and closed the door, then made us a drink in the kitchen.

When we eventually went to my bedroom, because it was our first time together—modesty and all—I didn't turn the light on but left the door slightly ajar, allowing just enough light from the hall to filter in so we could undress and get into bed without breaking our necks.

I undressed and went to the bathroom to brush my teeth. When I walked back to the bedroom Joanne was naked. "Okay, everyone in the pool," she said, making a playful lunge onto the bed. Immediately she moaned, "Oh—Ohhh—Oh, my God—Eddie!"

"What?"

"Turn on the light—oh!" She scrambled up off the bed.

I turned it on. My mother had thrown up on my bed and just left it there.

The fuck, as they say, was off.

That Joanne and I didn't go to bed that night was not the point. It was the sloth, the not caring or even being aware on my mother's part.

When my draft notice arrived, my mother was panicked. She even sobered up enough to plan some string-pulling. She knew a general, she knew a political bigwig in Los Angeles—she would fix it.

I would have none of this. I wanted to get away; I'd finally had a bellyful. I'd been through years of her drinking. Oddly enough I took it better when I was younger. When you're young you don't have much else of importance to do except go outside and play or watch TV. Also, at first, when I was ten or fourteen, taking care of her had given me a sense of being an adult. Now I was grown up and had my own life to tend to.

Bebe was only forty-nine at that time and I could look into the crystal ball and imagine another twenty-five years of messy, depressing on-again off-again bouts with the bottle. Something had to break it. Perhaps if I went into the service she might pull herself together. With no one to take care of her, except occasional friends, she'd more or less have to.

Bebe went into a rage when she realized I was serious about going into the army. The scenes and drinking got worse. I was a traitor (to her, not my country) and what was I running off to get myself killed for, and on and on.

It got so bad I had to move out two weeks before I was to be inducted. But not before her friend, Nan, moved in, having been kicked out by her husband. The two of them sitting around in a stupor—vodka and grapefruit juice for breakfast, Bloody Marys for lunch, slipping in the serious vodka martinis about midafternoon.

Except for one time, just before I went overseas, I did not see my mother again. Naturally, since becoming a prisoner I had developed a hefty conscience about leaving her; I also worried about how she was getting along.

There was consolation in talking this over with Vin. He understood my problem and I understood his. We used to kid about his father and my mother getting married. What a pair, jokers wild! Her drinking, him gambling.

On the war itself Vin and I were in agreement. We'd both seen enough of the incredible damage, the laying waste of an entire country and its people. No war, certainly not an undeclared war with a people who had instigated no hostility toward our own country and, for the more practical-minded, a war we could not really hope to win, was worth this.

The destruction, corruption, confusion, the day-by-day live-in fear of the people of South Vietnam were testament to the reckless waste of men, money, time and energy.

How fantastic if the President could tighten his guts and admit to the world that the Almighty Great and Powerful United States of America had actually made a blunder.

What this would have done for our national conscience, for our morality and for our limping drop-assed prestige in the eyes of world opinion! King Kong withdraws.

I forget when I first heard of Nixon's bolstering, self-serving phrase "Peace with honor."

Horse shit! There is no honor to a fragmented peace a decade late in coming. There is only shame. To say nothing of the fact that what will happen in Vietnam eventually, *is* happening now that we're out, would have happened had we never been there. It's only a matter of time.

Excuse the soapbox. Vin and I talked about this, but as I explained earlier, we couldn't dwell on it in any great detail or it would have been demoralizing in an already demoralizing situation.

For the first few weeks Vin and I exchanged not only our feelings about the war but the pertinent details of our lives up to the time we were captured. Basically a country-reared boy, he still had a sharp sense of humor, slightly bitter and ironic, but funny.

At first Vin fostered plans about a possible escape. I kept explaining it wasn't like you were escaping from a prison in the States. Even if we managed to get away from camp, and the chances were not likely, where the hell would we go?

We couldn't check into a sleazy little hotel in downtown Hanoi and lay low till the heat was off and we could head south. We looked like what we were—a couple of Americans. Two American P.O.W.'s who couldn't speak the language, running around in sandals and black pajamas trying to look inconspicuous. I told Vin if we could get eye-jobs, we might have a chance; otherwise—to forget it please.

# 10

Vin's sense of game playing was a welcome, and sometimes dangerous, addition to time as a P.O.W. About five weeks after he arrived we got a change of personnel—a new Camp Commander, a new Turnkey and a new English Speaker—although some of the guards remained the same.

The previous Camp Commander had been a relatively mild sort; you rarely saw him except on inspection days. Most of the officers one came in contact with, especially the interrogation officers, spoke French and preferred to speak it if you could. Vin spoke French Canadian and for those five weeks he would speak it to the Camp Commander on inspection days.

The new Camp Commander was a different sort altogether. When he first took over, he called all of the prisoners to a meeting outside in the yard in front of the main house and made a speech, in almost perfect English.

He was short, not more than five three or four, and plump with a shaved head. He had a round pleasant-looking face when he walked out of the main house to address us.

"Hey, look," I whispered to Vin, "we've got a little Buddha."

He looked us over before speaking; there seemed to be a smile on his face. The minute he began, though, his features firmed up like cement. He gave us his name, Captain Nguyen Tan Tai; this was unusual because they rarely gave their names right off the bat. He came on like gangbusters, telling us we would all get along fine as long as everyone stayed in line, obeyed orders and refrained from causing trouble. Troublemakers would soon learn to change their ways unless they wanted to spend time in solitary.

The more he spoke, the more I got to thinking if Erich von Stroheim had been North Vietnamese, that would have been Captain Nguyen Tan Tai.

He appeared to have a chip on his shoulder and underground camp scuttlebutt soon verified he'd had problems with his former commanding officer, a colonel, and this assignment to a relatively minor P.O.W. camp with only enlisted men was a demotion of sorts.

When he seemed to be finished speaking his face relaxed back into a semi-pleasant expression. One of the P.O.W.'s standing a few rows in front of Vin and me raised his hand and at the same time started to speak.

The Camp Commander's face froze and he shouted, "No! That is what I mean, you have not been given permission to speak!" He allowed for a long pause, as he looked us over; then he glanced back to the man. "You wish to have that permission?" he asked.

"Yes," the man said.

The Captain nodded. "Speak."

"Jesus," I murmured to Vin.

"I have lice and—" the man began, but this got a laugh from most of the other P.O.W.'s before he could go on.

"Quiet! Quiet!" the Camp Commander shouted. It did not take us long to calm down. Then: "Americans think lice is a funny thing?" No reply. In a brief time he'd got across the idea he was not to be fooled with. He turned his attention back to the man, who went on to say he had lice and would like to have treatment for them. The Captain did not reply, only nodded and spoke in Vietnamese to his assistant, who wrote something down on a pad. When he was finished he looked up and asked if anyone else had any questions.

On those rare occasions when all the prisoners got together, there was a manic something in the air at just being in a group. Meetings, assemblies were stretched out as much as possible, for the sake of prolonging a novelty and our time together. But now no one said a word. It was clear no one wanted to get off on the wrong foot with Captain Nguyen Tan Tai.

Back in our room, Vin said, "When they stack them in short compact packages like that, they can be mean as cat shit."

The first time the Captain came to our room on inspection day, toward the end of that week, Vin began speaking French to him. Vin had only gotten a few words out when he was stopped cold.

"You will speak English."

"I thought you might prefer French," Vin said.

"I have just told you," he said, instantly angry, "you will speak English." A thought occurred to the Captain. "You do not think my English correct?"

"No, it's very good."

"Then we have no problem."

"Let's hope not," Vin sighed, with an off hand attitude acknowledging that he couldn't win with him, no matter what.

"What tone is that?" the Captain asked, quick to pick him up.

Vin only muttered, "Christ, I don't know, I don't know."

Furious, the Captain snapped, "You will not speak French and you will not swear. Are you correct on this?"

I could tell Vin was about to say "If you say so," but the Captain marched right up to him and repeated "Are you correct on this point?" in a way that indicated he didn't want one more ounce of anything from Vin but strict obedience—

no insinuation, no tone, no nothing but what he got, which was "Yes, I understand."

"Fine, that is good."

When we were alone Vin said, "I knew all that talk about Hitler living in South America was a dodge to throw us off the track. But how did he get so much shorter?"

"Maybe he wore lifts in his boots."

"That's it, he wore lifts and had a face-job and we got him."

That day we named the Captain "Mine Fury" after *Mein Führer*. Later on we also worked up a few other names for him. "Mr. Correct" because "correct" was a favorite over-worked word of his. We also called him "Mr. Chips," that stemming from the chips on his shoulder.

Vin's theory was that he didn't speak French. Mine was that he did but he was proud of his English and wanted to use it. "Why not? He does speak it better than anyone else I've come across."

"I still don't think he knows French."

Next inspection day, as Mine Fury was leaving the room, Vin turned to me and said something in French.

Mine Fury wheeled around, face red, eyes narrowed—more than usually—and said, "I have told you not to speak French to me. Is that not correct?"

Vin played it with total innocence. "Sir, I was talking to my roommate. We often speak French together, just to keep in practice." (Which was a lie, I don't speak French.)

"From here on, you will speak only English in my presence!"

"You don't speak French?" Vin went on. "I thought all—"

"You do not worry. You speak only English in my presence. Correct?"

"Correct."

When he left, Vin said, "I knew he didn't, I knew it."

"Why, what did you say to me?" I asked.

Vin laughed. "I said, 'Well, at least he didn't find the dirty pictures and the dynamite.' "

"Jesus, Vin—what a chance to take!"

"No, I was pretty sure. He's the type if he spoke it, you'd know it. He'd run through his whole repertoire just to let you know how bifuckinglingual he was."

"Still, Vin, don't try to get his goat, it's not worth it."

"Okay, okay," Vin said, but he was chuckling. I could tell he got a kick out of Mine Fury. And it worried me.

The new English Speaker, Kwan, was the best yet as far as general intelligence. Although his English was very broken, he was bright and he wanted to learn. After he got to know us, now and then he'd bring pictures of objects to our room, cut from magazines or newspapers, and ask us the English words. I remember a tractor, a bridge, a building crane, and once a picture of a mouse. As soon as he showed us the mouse both Vin and I said "Spike!" But we blew it by laughing, so we told him the real word. In return for this information Kwan would often slip us extra cigarettes.

The new Turnkey assigned to our building was very young, not more than eighteen, with unblinking eyes that seemed glued open and unusually high-arched eyebrows that gave him a look as if he'd just been goosed. His nickname, of course, was "Goosey."

He did not speak one word of English but he was friendly. When he brought our water in the morning, Vin would speak to him in a calm gentle voice that belied his words: "You know what?" he'd say, "I would like very much to defecate in the umbrella of your grandmother, then I would like to cut off your grandfather's withered testicles, bronze them and make a pair of earrings for Pat Nixon." In an inquiring way Vin would ask, "Would that be all right with you?" Goosey would smile and nod or shrug. Vin would continue in his gentle voice, "No, come to think of it, I shouldn't talk like that, I like you, you've been okay with us. What I'd *really* like to do, as a peace gesture, I'd like to cut off Nixon's withered balls, bronze *them,* and present you with a pair of souvenir earrings for your grandmother? Friends, okay?" He'd offer his hand and Goosey would smile and shake it.

Vin had all sorts of variations on this theme. If my delight in them seems childish—after three years as a P.O.W. you'd be surprised at the things you start getting a kick out of.

In the middle of May 1971, the English Speaker came one afternoon about three o'clock to take Vin to the main building. What was up? Vin wanted to know. Kwan didn't know, or wouldn't tell. As he left the room, I said, "Vin, whatever it is, take it easy. Keep cool. Remember, solitary is *really* the Pits."

"They probably want to know the secret of my famous

New Year's fish-house punch. Don't worry, I'll keep it cool."

The afternoon meal came, time went on, by six o'clock when Vin wasn't back I got worried. He'd been taken over for interrogations quite a few times right after he arrived, but nothing lately. Seven, eight, nine o'clock. This was unusual. The idea of losing Vin as my roommate shook me up. I started pacing, I started swearing, until I noticed I was sopping wet with sweat. Jesus, I told myself, talk about cooling it. Cool it, you're a grown man, you've been prisoner over three years now, what the hell is this? I simmered down, but not really.

By eleven o'clock I was paced out, but I sat there on my bed, almost at attention, like I was waiting for the phone to ring. Finally I heard footsteps outside in the corridor, then the jingle of keys. Up off the bed as I heard the bolt slip and the door open. Two guards I hadn't seen before carried Vin in.

He was conscious, but just barely. He'd been beaten so badly tears came to my eyes. I saw blood; it took every bit of will power not to jump the guards. Whether they were the ones who dished out the punishment or not made no matter, the strong impulse to jump them was there.

Trembling, I took his hand as they put him down on the bed. Praying, I was praying to Christ they'd get out fast. They did.

Vin opened his eyes in response to my squeezing his hand. "Pits," he mumbled. "The Pits . . ."

His face was a mess—nose, lips, eyes—cuts and huge welts all over. They'd also given him the rope treatment and his right arm was killing him. I used our towels, soaked them in cold water and sat up with him all night. He was out of it until the middle of the next morning.

I wanted to kill.

Vin had gotten into trouble with Mine Fury, who'd held a letter up, saying it was for Vin and he would give it to him if he would agree to make some tapes denouncing the United States bombing of civilians and nonmilitary targets.

Fury would not tell Vin who the letter was from, only that he'd be given it after the tapes had been made. The tease went along for over an hour. Until Vin lost his temper and made a lunge for the letter. The beating was on.

Vin was in bad shape for a couple of weeks with severe

pains in his kidney and liver, and his right arm and shoulder were out of whack again. He was tough about it, though. He knew the mistake had been his, realized he had nothing to gain by losing his cool. But this did not stop his hatred of Mine Fury. He could not stop plotting a way to get back at him for what had been dirty pool.

I told Vin to try to forget it. There was really no way to gain the upper hand, the percentages were stacked against us.

Still, I could tell in his mind he would not stop gambling with some form of revenge. After that, every time inspection day came around I'd get knots in my stomach for fear Vin would do or say something that would get under the Captain's skin.

# 11

As we got to know each other better, I kept waiting for the honeymoon period to end, kept waiting for us to start frazzling each other's nerves. This did not happen to any great degree. The more I knew Vin the more I liked him; I trusted him like I'd trusted no other friend.

Oh, there were little things that drove me up the wall. Vin had hay fever. In the spring and summer he would wake up in the morning and sneeze sometimes twenty times in a row. He had one of the loudest sneezes on record. It was more of a shout than a sneeze; it could have shattered glass. I knew he couldn't help sneezing but I did think he could turn the volume down. One morning, after a half hour of solid blasting, I finally said, "Jesus Christ, Vin!"

"What? What?" He was up off his bed. "What do you want me to do? You think I like it? Huh, do you?" Another sneeze.

"No, but can't you cool it a little?"

"What does that mean—cool it a little?"

"I mean, do you have to let them go that big, can't you sort of shut your mouth and muffle them?"

"No, I can't. It hurts if I do. Jesus, cover your goddam sensitive ears!"

Then from me: "How the hell did you get in the army with such hay fever anyhow!"

"How the fuck do I know! Go ask the Defense Department."

Another sneeze and he lay back down on his bed. We didn't speak for an hour or so. I wished I hadn't said anything because of all the mornings he woke up sneezing. It made for some itchy beginnings to the day.

His hotheadedness also got on my nerves. For a while, after the letter-tape episode, Vin pulled in on inspection days, he would not speak unless spoken to. But the longer time went on, the more I could sense his restlessness whenever Mine Fury came around. I knew it was coming to the point where Vin would let go.

In the spring and summer we had pumpkin soup until it came out of our noses. P.P.S. we called it—Putrid Pumpkin Soup. I didn't like it any better than Vin. One day, a day that Mine Fury was in an unusually good mood, he asked us if everything was going all right.

"Okay," Vin said, "except for the pumpkin soup!"

"The pumpkin soup?"

"Yes, we're getting it every day, it's sick-making," Vin said.

Despite Mine Fury's having asked us, he did not care for routine complaints. So go figure. "Ah, you do not find the pumpkin soup pleasing?" He said it facetiously; turning to his aide, he added, "Make note of such, Sergeant Poirier does not find the pumpkin soup pleasing!"

I did not like the look on Vin's face. As Mine Fury was going out the door, it happened. Vin suddenly shouted, "No, I don't find it pleasing and make a note of *this*. When I get out of here, I'm going to come back as a civilian and shove a pumpkin up your ass!"

Christ, my heart stopped. That was enough, with Mine Fury, to get you solitary.

The Captain wheeled around, gave him one long murderous stare and left.

Before I could even say anything Vin shouted at me,

"Well, he asked us, didn't he? What the fuck did he ask us for?"

"But, Vin—what a dumb-ass thing to say!"

"No lectures, I don't want any lectures from you. I said it, it's on me."

"On you, my ass! I've already got a bad record, twice in solitary, and stupid crap like that only makes him come down hard on this room."

"I told you, no lectures."

"Sure, keep running off at the mouth, you keep on like that, maybe that's why we don't get any mail or packages."

"That's right, blame me for the whole fucking situation."

"I'm not blaming you, I'm talking to you about it. I'm just asking you to cool it."

"Cool it, cool it!" he shouted. "Everything is cool it, cool this, cool that. I'm fucking sick of your cooling everything!"

"Go cool your ass!"

Another sulk. That afternoon we were not served our meal. The explanation came through Kwan. Since pumpkin soup was again featured on the menu, Mine Fury had taken Vin's complaint to heart and spared us. Pumpkin soup was not the only thing we were spared. We also didn't get our French bread, our bean curd or rice, and our pig fat with a little bit of meat. Or our tea.

I was pissed off. "Great! El Exigente didn't like the quality of the food so I don't get to eat. You satisfied?"

No reply. We didn't talk for the rest of the night. In the morning Vin offered his hand and said, "Merry Fucking Christmas."

"Merry Fucking Christmas," I replied and it was over. That turned out to be our peace phrase.

These minor annoyances had to happen, no way for them not to creep in. But on the whole, we got along fine.

This being the case, eventually we started making long-range plans.

# 12

Even though we were kept as isolated as possible, rumors were bound to sweep through camp from time to time. Most of these had to do with peace talks. Or peace itself.

We tried not to latch onto them with high hopes, but it was hard to resist. The tap code would swing into high gear, like in those old movies—the jungle drums were sounding—and this would cause periods of elation when our hearts beat faster and our brains whirred at the prospect that, after all, the war couldn't last for-fucking-ever (as Vin said). Could it? No, it couldn't, it had to end sometime. Everything has an end. Perhaps this was the time.

In the morning the loudspeakers constantly fed us any news of peace demonstrations at home, peace marches, peaceniks, word of opposition to the war by members of Congress or other political figures, by the wives of P.O.W.'s, by almost anyone of importance, even movie stars like Jane Fonda.

Two ways to look at this. Jerry Harker, for instance, had flown off the handle, saying if all the un-American Americans kept opposing the President and the war, the fighting would go on forever, we could never win. "A country divided cannot win a war," he would say.

I looked at the other side, so did Vin. (Perhaps because we wanted to, it gave us hope.) If the opposition to the war kept up, if more and more Americans joined in, Nixon would have to end it, he'd be forced to. As Vin said, "When it comes down to the line, Nixon would grind Pat and his two little vanilla princesses through a sieve to keep his job."

It was always in our minds that the war would be ended, not won. Unless some trigger-happy clown decided to use "limited atomic arms." Limited to what? To blowing up only a few countries instead of the entire world. Great!

A rumor spread around camp in September of 1971 that the opposition to the war had grown so strong in Congress it looked as if Nixon and Kissinger would have to make a deal and get us the hell out. Of course, we had no reason to believe it, because of the way news and propaganda was fed us. We also had no reason *not* to believe it.

It was around this time that Vin and I started talking seriously about what we would do when we got out. Because Vin was a carpenter/builder and I was interested in real estate and houses, it was my suggestion that perhaps we could go into business, form a partnership—first buy a piece of land, then put up a house on spec, take the money from that, buy more land, eventually expand and have a going business we both cared about.

Vin went for it right off. I suggested California; Vin took to this, too. He'd never been there except for a few days on his way to Vietnam and those were spent mostly at an army base. He was still bitter about his father; getting away from Vermont suited him fine.

I told him there was still beautiful undeveloped land up the coast from Malibu and down the coast from San Francisco and filled him in on the richness of the Santa Clara and San Joaquin valleys. Forget it between Los Angeles and San Diego. If we got a start in California and it eventually became too crowded, too difficult to find the right land, we might move up into Oregon and Washington.

We grew more and more excited over our plan. Being single, Vin would have had his pay put away for him. Lisa would have gotten all mine, but her one letter said she was going back to work, so she should have saved some money. We were also positive we'd be getting so much per day or week for the time we'd been prisoners. I was into my fourth year already. There would also be bonuses for P.O.W.'s. So we were sure of a nest egg between us. There would probably also be G.I. loans in the event we wanted to move faster.

We talked more and more about our plan—building on it, elaborating, jumping ahead ten years to view our own small empire from our own small Cessna plane. It was good. It was a foundation to hang onto, a destination. We would not come out of the war as displaced persons; we knew where we were headed. It was not only good, it was cheering. I remember the fall of 1971 as a happy time, full of hope and plans. Vin and I grew closer, more thoughtful of each other than ever. We played more games, thought up more ways to fill the time and keep ourselves entertained.

The little red pills we were given for diarrhea, when squashed and dampened with a little water, made good ink. The head of a toothpaste tube had lead in it and could also be used as a pencil. Vin drew sketches of types of houses on toilet paper. We also found a jagged piece of brick out in the yard and Vin sketched with this on the concrete floor. More talk, more plans.

Vin began giving me French lessons, Canadian French, which has a much harsher sound than Parisian French. I'd had three years of Spanish in high school and I'd also had some Mexican friends in Los Angeles. I liked Spanish and was good at it; although I didn't speak it half was well as Vin spoke French, we taught each other what we knew.

We would also play the dictionary game. Pick a letter of the alphabet and then alternate, trying to think of every possible word beginning with that letter. Amazing, the words you can come up with.

We'd have Movie Night. One of us would pick a movie we'd seen and then tell it as exactly as he could, scene by scene. Many times we'd get stuck and have to fake it through to the end but that was often more fun than if we remembered.

We would go back and try to dredge up the earliest possible memories from when we were children. One's memory would jostle the other's and he would come up with something previously unthought of. After Vin had reconstructed the first time he remembered his father ever hitting him, I came up with an incident that happened with my mother.

Bebe had beautiful long chestnut hair, gorgeous hair. One day when I was just a little kid she had it cut off short and bobbed. I was shocked that afternoon when I saw her. She could tell I didn't like it from the look on my face and I verified that for her. In the evening after she'd gotten all dressed up to go out she was doing some last-minute primping at her dressing table and I was just hanging around, when she turned to me—she was in a good mood—and asked how I thought she looked. Did she look pretty?

I missed her long hair, she looked like a stranger to me. "No," I told her, "you used to look pretty but now you look like a duck!"

She gave me a quick slap in the face. I cried and then she cried, hugged me and apologized. I'd forgotten all about that. All kinds of memories for both of us came to the surface.

We made lists of things and people that bugged us, things that seemed so unimportant now that we were P.O.W.'s. Vin couldn't stand to see a woman with curlers in her hair. I could not stand watching Dean Martin on television; here's a guy making millions a year and winging his shows. I wanted to see him put forth a little effort—at least not let me see him reading the cue cards. Vin disliked Dr. Joyce Brothers. He was forever arranging for her to be gang-fucked. "Then let her psychoanalyze *that!*" I wouldn't buy a used car from Billy Graham. Vin could not stand the smell of oilcloth, it made him sick to his stomach. I couldn't possibly get a piece of tongue down my throat without gagging. And so forth.

Of course I would have given a month's pay, at this point, to watch one Dean Martin show, and Vin said, "If Joyce Brothers showed up for a half-hour visit, I'd cuddle her like a kitten!"

So it went that fall. Peace did not come, but that did not stop our planning. The food was getting a little better. Twice a week or so we were getting tinned meat or tinned fish, both Russian. I was in good physical shape, all things considering, and I was up to a hundred and fifty push-ups. Vin "cooled it" on inspection days.

On Thanksgiving 1971 we were taken to the main house and shown an excellent documentary on China.

More rumors of peace around Christmas.

Now, although I had not intended to, I would be cheating if I did not document the closest and strangest part of our relationship. During those days I thought that when the time came to look back on it, I would be ashamed to speak of sex. Now that the time has come, I find I'm not.

# 13

The lack of normal sex was not a minor matter. I recently read an interview with one P.O.W. in which he said, "Sex was a problem the first few months, but then, when you're completely deprived of it, after a while you just put it out of your mind. It's like a taste for sweets."

Beautiful for him. Bullshit for me.

I had always needed, at least preferred, sex several times a week. I was healthy, twenty-seven, and when I woke up in the morning with an aching hard-on, I could not pretend it wasn't there. Difficult to ignore, there it was wagging in front of me.

No pretty smooth-skinned tiny-waisted Vietnamese girls were brought in for our pleasure Saturday nights. Outside of wet dreams, masturbation was the obvious solution for release.

There'd been no problem mixing that with my fantasies when I was alone. Whack away, even refine the art to its ultimate. There had not been much of a problem either with Jerry Harker in the room. It was done when he was asleep. And vice versa, I imagine. We never discussed it.

Now, with Vin there, it was trickier. First off, I'd been there nearly three years by that time. Secondly, there was a good deal of animal in Vin. Some people strike you as sexual, others don't. Some men and some women, you cannot imagine them having sex, can't imagine them anywhere near a sexual situation. Some have the scent all over them.

Naturally Vin and I talked about sex. No way not to. We talked of everything: parents, girl friends, friends, ambitions, fears, death. And sex. In the first few weeks as we were getting to know each other, we touched on the lack of it.

"What do you do for sex around here?" Vin asked.

I shrugged, made a fist and the appropriate gesture.

Vin laughed. "Old Freddie Fist," he said. "I always thought jerking off was the Pits, but, yeah—I guess that's it."

As we told each other more and more about our lives, we exchanged sexual histories from the very first time to the present—Vin, at sixteen with a whore in Montreal, me at fifteen with Rhonda, a friend of my mother's who had offered to stay the weekend and look after me while my mother went to Palm Springs. Rhonda looked after me, all right, she looked after me three times that weekend. For the next eight months, before she moved back east, two or three times a month I'd ride my bike over to her house, where she'd make my favorite, chocolate pudding with walnuts, and then she'd look after me.

We filled each other in from those early times up to my relationship with Lisa and Vin's with Ginger. Including fascinating side trips like the time Vin caught his younger brother, age thirteen, screwing a calf held in place by his brother's ten-year-old friend.

"Oh, shit!" his brother, Buddy, said when he saw Vin walk around the corner of the barn.

"Right!" Vin replied, "and that's exactly what you're going to get if you don't watch out!"

Besides Movie Night, we started having Hot Date Night. In the beginning one of us would describe how he'd met a girl and made out. A little exaggeration was allowed, embellishments were welcome, but the incidents were basically factual. When we ran out of real-life experiences we decided we'd simply make them up. There would be entire scripts involving mood, place, time, infinitesimal descriptions of the girl and eventually of the Dread Deed itself.

"Okay okay," one of us would say if the preliminaries were dragging on too long. "Let's get to the Dread Deed."

One morning about six months after Vin arrived he slept late. He was still sleeping by the time Goosey brought our water. As he gradually came to, yawning and stretching, I asked, "What's the matter, big night on the town?"

"No," Vin said, "Freddie Fist dropped by early this morning—wore me out."

A week or so later, Vin asked if I'd ever had any homosexual experiences. "Not really," I said.

He laughed. "What does 'not really' mean?"

I told him I used to jerk off with Boots, a friend of mine in high school. When we were juniors, his mother, who was extremely wealthy, remarried' and Boots's new stepfather, two years younger than Boots's oldest brother, took us on a camping trip to Big Bear Lake.

He got drunk during dinner by the campfire and was still drinking rosé wine when Boots and I went to bed in our tent. I awakened to find Boots's stepfather going down on Boots. Boots looked over in the semidarkness, saw me, and shrugged. His stepfather, who was about thirty, good-looking, a drinker and swinger with an aversion to working, mumbled one thing that I got a kick out of. To explain, so it makes sense, I should tell you that Boots's mother was in her early sixties and one tough lady, the kind who really runs the whole shooting works. At one point, Boots's stepfather grabbed Boots's cock with his hand and muttered, "Jesus Christ, you've got a bigger cock than your mother's."

When he finished with Boots, he came over and performed the same act with me.

"Those were my only experiences. What about you?" I asked Vin.

"Hitchhiking once, along the Boston Post Road, a great big hulking truck driver, really a big monster of a guy, offered me five bucks if I'd let him blow me."

"Did you take it?"

"Sure," Vin said, adding with a grin and an exaggerated shrug, "I was broke."

"What did you think of it?" I asked him.

Long silence. Then Vin looked at me and grinned again. "I don't know," he said. "What about you and Boots's stepfather?"

I grinned back at him. "I don't know . . ."

"Um-hmn," Vin said.

A month or so after that conversation I woke up in the early hours of the morning and heard sounds coming from Vin's bed. I slowly turned over. Vin was facing the wall, turned away from me. His pajamas were off, he was naked, and he was masturbating.

He had a long lithe body, a graceful strong animal body, the kind of animal that could run and jump. The sight of him there on his side, the way his head rested on his curled-up left arm, his right hand working away, his buttocks tightened—it was sexy.

I started masturbating. After a while I stopped to slip my pajamas down. He heard me, stopped his own movements and turned his head around to look over. He saw me, saw my erection. I didn't want to abort what was happening, so I quickly put my hand on myself and began again, slowly, gently.

Vin watched a while, a serious expression on his face; then when I looked him in the eye, still masturbating, he smiled slightly, a small smile, turned over on his back and we both continued, watching ourselves and each other.

After three and a half years of nothing, except myself, it was terribly exciting. It was hot and horny—and all without even touching. Still, in a way, we were doing a spin-off of the Dread Deed together.

When we'd finished, after we watched each other shoot up into the air, we lay on our beds on our backs without looking at each other, without saying a word, for a very long time.

Finally Vin got up, got a towel and handed it to me. "Here." I wiped off my belly and legs and cock. He stood there during this and when I was finished he took the towel and cleaned himself off. This struck me, that he would use the same towel. There was kind of a—*no-fear* of intimacy to it.

When he lay back down, he said, "Have a good sleep."

"You, too."

That was all we said.

A couple of hours later, when the gong went off and we woke up, Vin said, "Hey, did you hear the news?"

"No, what?"

"Freddie Fist dropped by, brought along his twin brother."

"Oh, that, yeah . . ."

That was all that was said. Period. I can't honestly say I didn't wonder if this would continue. Or if there might be some variations.

# 14

Certainly we became more intimately aware of each other. Usually when we took our showers we'd talk, laugh and horse around in general. For one, the cold water made showering a peppy time.

After that one evening, now and then we'd take our showers without saying much. Before this, Vin would often kid me, swat me on the rump and make some comment like "The best ass on a captured enlisted man above the Red River!" Now he rarely kidded around like this.

One evening when we'd gotten into sex talk about different positions and what we both liked, Vin asked if I'd ever done it with Lisa dog-fashion. I said I had, with her kneeling on the edge of the bed and me standing. Vin joined in about his experiences with Ginger, how it was extremely snug and exciting and that the angle, the thrust under and up was so great. Then Vin asked, "Did you ever do it the other way?"

"What other way?"

"You know, go in the back door?"

"No," I said.

"Oh . . ."

"Did you?" I asked.

"Yes," he said, "a couple times, not with Ginger, with another girl who really dug it that way."

"Did you dig it that way?"

A pause, then, "Yes . . ." Followed by, "I didn't think I would, thought it might put me off. But when someone else is getting such a charge out of something, then I guess you automatically do."

We sat there for a while without either of us speaking and

when we did pick up the conversation it veered away from sex.

The next time I masturbated Vin was asleep. I was half-hoping he might wake up. He didn't; he was sleeping one of those sound sleeps. When I'd finished, I was half-glad he hadn't awakened.

In November, late one night, a high wailing sound woke us up. "Wheee-ah! Wheee-ah!" "Jesus, what in the—what's that?" Vin asked.

"I don't know."

We both got up, went to our shutters and opened them. It was almost a full moon, just minus a little slice of the full pie, scattered clouds scooting along under it. "Wheee-ah! Wheee-ah!"

The sound was thrown way back up high behind the bridge of a man's nose. It was coming three or four rooms down the hall from us, aimed out in the yard from a window like ours. Soon it turned into more of a scream, as if there were something crawling all over the person. Christawful. Then a lot of jabber. "I see you out there—I can see—what you do to me! I see y'all." There was a southern accent to it, or else hick-western.

"Wheee-ah, wheee-ah—y'all keep away now!" Then, "Hey, Rose-mare-ee! Rose-*mary!*" The first with three definite syllables, the next call with two and the last part pronounced "mary."

"Christ, someone's gone squirrelly!" Vin said.

We knew the voices of the other P.O.W.'s in our building; this high shrill scream didn't belong to any of them. "I'm gonna git you—git you boys. Wheee-ah, wheee-ah! Hey there, hey, you Rose-mare-ee! Rose-*mary!*"

Another prisoner shouted for quiet, goddammit, and pretty soon we heard guards come inside the building. The man took to screaming again—high wails, long sustained ones. Until the guards, shouting in Vietnamese, finally got him to stop. The last shout, short and sharp, seemed to be the result of a hit, a punch. Then he was quiet.

Right away I named this new P.O.W. Fay Wray. Vin didn't know who Fay Wray was, so I explained about *King Kong,* which he'd seen on TV, and how her specialty was screaming.

We soon found out Fay Wray's real name was Sergeant

Leonard Barnes, from Tennessee originally. He'd been a P.O.W. in South Vietnam, held in jungle camps for three years, and he was profoundly squirrelly. He never yelled much in the daytime, but sometimes at night he'd make your skin crawl. The bombing raids set him off something fierce.

We didn't catch sight of him for a few weeks but when we did, he turned out to be a tall, frighteningly skinny fellow with bushy hair and a very long curved nose. We would kid about him because you just had to, but we were both angry that he wasn't simply turned back to the U.S. forces where he could get help. Why keep a prisoner in his pitiful condition? Give him back.

Fay Wray would never talk to anyone, not a word; screaming was his only thing. He would scream some pretty far-out things, but whatever they were, Rose-mare-ee would always be worked in.

Some nights after he'd gone on for quite a while, Vin would say, "Where the hell is Rose-mare-ee, she's not going to make an appearance?" But she would, he never left her out. All it would take for him to stop would be for one of the guards to go in and hit him, that would end it. We used to wonder why, some nights, it took so long for anyone to tend to him.

Two days before Christmas 1971 I received my one and only package, sent by my mother from New York. It was all beat up and torn and looked like it had been dropped from an airplane but it contained: strawberry jam, chocolate fudge, a small fruitcake, a can of mixed nuts, pâté, a jar of caviar, sardines, a jar of antipasto, a large bottle of vitamin pills and a carton of Lark cigarettes, from which four packs were missing.

Naturally I shared it with Vin, although we agreed not to demolish it at once, what with our big Christmas feast coming up.

About two weeks before Christmas I'd found a pencil in the yard near the latrine area. I smuggled it back to my room, wrapped it in toilet paper with a bit of string I'd stashed away earlier and gave it to Vin as a Christmas present on Christmas Eve.

At first he laughed—so did I—because it was one pitiful, silly Christmas present, a used pencil wrapped in toilet paper. But I figured he'd like it to make sketches of houses with. After we stopped laughing, he just sat on his bed looking at it, shaking his head, and he was actually very touched, I could tell. Finally he said, "T.M.—that's really a great little present." He looked up at me. "I wish I had something for you."

"Forget it; later, when we get out of here, you have to put in overtime in the business."

"It's a deal."

Christmas dinner 1971 was even better than the two previous ones. I gorged myself, so did Vin.

New Year's Eve day we kidded about what a big night we were going to have. "You have to promise," Vin said, "that if you see me getting bombed out of my mind and making a fool out of myself, you'll stop me." Stuff like that. In the evening, between five and seven, we had two hours of good music. Chinese/Vietnamese (it was hard to tell the difference), French, Russian and some American. They were not especially up-to-date tunes. I especially remember Johnnie Ray's "Walking My Baby Back Home" and Tony Bennett's "I Left My Heart in San Francisco." The latter, naturally, got me right where I lived.

During the music we each had some caviar on French bread we'd saved from our meal, then we ate some fudge. Fudge and caviar, an unbeatable combination!

Even though it was New Year's Eve, the camp remained on the same basic schedule: early to bed, early to rise. We talked for a while after the music, and when we eventually got sleepy, Vin said, "Maybe next year we can really celebrate."

"Let's hope so."

"Well, T. M.—Happy Fucking New Year!"

"Happy Fucking New Year." After a while, just on impulse I said, "It hasn't been all that bad, has it?"

"No, not all that bad," Vin said.

"Good night, Vin."

"Good night, Eddie." Then Vin added, "Hey, maybe we'll wake up later and celebrate a little." It was now around ten.

"Yeah, maybe we will."

We did. I awakened a few hours later to see Vin standing up looking out of the shutters, listening to a passing freight train. I leaned up on my elbows. When Vin turned around to go back to his bed he saw I was awake. I noticed he had an erection.

"Hi . . ." I said.

"Hi . . ."

Nothing more was said. He took off his pajamas and lay down on his bunk. I got out from under the blankets and took mine off.

It happened just as it happened the first time, watching each other, each on our own bed.

From that Christmas on, maybe once every ten days, sometimes more and sometimes less, we would repeat the same ritual. We never talked about it, never planned it. It would just take place, usually in the middle of the night or early morning. Sometimes I would instigate it, more often Vin would. Whichever one had it in mind, he would get up out of bed, make some noise or movement, open and close the shutters, some little movement like that, and the other would awaken.

This went on from Christmas until July. In July there came a change, one that I half-expected and half-feared.

# 15

Off and on, all year, there had been the usual peace rumors, but now, in the summer of 1972, there was a momentum building, like peace just had to come.

Vin was keeping his cool but not without effort. He had been upset, when I got my package, that four packs of cigarettes had been taken. He was positive there'd been a letter enclosed or a note and wondered what else had been removed. I prevailed upon him not to pursue this line of thought. We had what we had and that was special enough.

As time went on, however, Vin became increasingly upset over the notion that Ginger and his family had most certainly been writing and sending him packages. He was convinced Mine Fury would never allow anything to get through to him.

I kept telling Vin I was positive the breakdown in communications from the States occurred at a higher level and a more distant one than at our camp, that it was not Mine Fury who decided who got what and when. I also reminded Vin perhaps he had not been listed as a P.O.W.; maybe Ginger and his family thought he was dead or missing in action. He had never really got a look at the letter he was supposed to receive if he agreed to make the tape.

This was by far the healthiest way to look at it. Even so, Vin worried the problem. He was still furious over the lack of reading material, except for the propaganda pamphlets we were fed. "Christ," he said, leafing through one, "I'd even welcome these if they weren't so allfucking-mightyboring."

The heat that summer got to us both. The mosquitoes were bad, too. We'd lie on our beds in puddles of sweat, unable to go to sleep for hours and then struggling through a hot restless on-again-off-again sleep once it came.

The bombing in July accelerated; sometimes it got terribly close to our camp. We would stand at the shutters, in the totally blacked-out camp, peeking out, listening to the explosions, watching the sky light up all around Hanoi, hearing the antiaircraft ack-ack back at our planes.

The night of July 27 all hell broke loose. We'd never heard such bombing. In between explosions Fay Wray was going at full pitch. Every so often he'd come out with something wildly funny. This night after an extremely loud explosion he shouted out, "Wheee-ah, you guys watch out for Mama's good china! Whoo!" That got a huge laugh from Vin and me, as someone else shouted out, "The *good China!* Man, the squirrel's goin' good tonight!"

It was impossible to sleep. We both stood at the shutters looking out. "Jesus," I whispered to Vin, "wouldn't it be the Pits to get knocked off in this shitty camp by one of our own bombs!"

"Yeah . . ." he answered, also in a whisper.

"I hope they know where the hell these camps are? Do you think they do?" I was still whispering.

"Sure they do, they've got to, they sure knew where Son Tay was," he whispered.

"Yeah, great . . ."

Bam, a bomb hit so close we could feel the ground shake.

"Je-*sus!*" I whispered.

Suddenly Vin slapped me on the shoulder. "What the fuck are we whispering for?" he laughed.

I laughed, too, a shaky laugh. "I don't know, I don't know."

"If we shouted, they could barely hear us in the next room," he said in a normal voice. "Not with all that going on out there!"

"I know."

We stood there for a long while, listening to the bombs hit, the antiaircraft, watching the flames light up the sky a mile or so away. We didn't speak for along time. Fay Wray had quieted down. Our shoulders were touching. I was shaking, I remember trying to control my shaking so Vin wouldn't feel it. But I knew he could.

Another bomb struck close by, the ground shook again. I tried to make a joke. "Hey, will you people stop dancing out there, we're trying to sleep!"

I laughed nervously; Vin didn't. I could feel his shoudlers trembling.

We kept standing there. We heard a plane coming in low, very low, seemed like it was coming right toward us, the roar of its engines was heavy and deafening. We froze, thinking it was going to crash into us. It roared on over—we couldn't see it, it was right overhead—close, very close, right over us, then by us, and there was a terrible explosion to the north. The entire building shook as the plane hit.

"Jesus Christ!" I said, turning to take a step away, to pace, just out of nerves, when Vin suddenly grabbed me by the shoulders, swung me around and slammed his mouth against mine. For a second, I wasn't sure what was happening. The gesture was so abrupt and ferocious. But he was attempting to kiss me.

With great force, his hands going to my head, one on each side, holding me like a vise, he did kiss me, kissed me hard. I tried to pull away. "Vin—Jesus—Vin—!"

But he was a wild man.

It was such a panicky moment all the way around—the camp guards outside shouting, then one, two, three explosions as the plane's remaining bombs blew sky-high.

He kept on. Our teeth bumped, grazed, bumped again. It hurt, my lip was cut, but he wouldn't let up. I kept trying to pull back. But then he had his arms around me, holding me in a bear-lock.

This made me struggle more. The surprise and suddenness of his attack had really frightened me. As a result of my struggle, we lost balance and fell to the floor. Not an easy fall, either. Because he would not let go of me, we crashed down together.

All I remember him saying, over the general noise and confusion outside and in the hot humid darkness inside, was "You bastard! You *bastard,* you!"

Although it was swearing, there was more to it than that, a hundred times more in those few words.

He was on top of me, then all over me, ripping my pajamas off, and I was suddenly excited and clawing at his pajamas to get them off. Like we'd both been napalmed and had to get our clothes off.

It was completely violent. The wildest experience I've ever had. It was mutual rape, out of control, terrifying *and* exciting, hot, steamy and unspoken except for what strange animal sounds we made as we thrashed around on the floor, doing, by groping instinct, almost everything two men can do to each other.

The bombing continued, sometimes at a distance, sometimes dangerously close, as we kept up our physical taking and forcing and giving-up and taking and wrestling until we had each come through two massive orgasms. And we lay on the floor awash in sweat and semen and blood, too.

We lay there in the dark, panting, trying to allow control to return, listening to the bombs, and every so often the guards or other soldiers shouting in the distance.

Finally, more to bring my breathing to a normal in-and-out and make some return to the world of sanity, I panted out, "Oh, Jesus, Jesus Holy Christ!"

"Yes," Vin gulped, almost choked, "Yes—Jesus Holy Christ!"

And that was all we said.

## 16

From July to mid-October, it happened three more times. With only slightly less violence. But not much less.

It was always pure animal although there was a mutual giving and taking, still it was entirely raw and unrefined. But there was passion in it, too, a hard, pounding jackhammer passion, mixed with anger and guilt and a certain tacit embarrassment that we were forced into having it off this way.

As we never planned it, we also never spoke directly of it. It was now truly—the Dread Deed. It happened out of the blue, like a sudden sharp thunderstorm. As it had started with Vin being the aggressor, it remained that way. Strangely enough, although the first rough move was his, once underway he was the more abandoned, the more wide-open, anything-goes giving than I was. I was not far behind, though.

Each time it was accompanied by other violence. Actually the energy and impetus sprang from an outside physical force. Twice it happened during raging storms, and once during another fierce bombing raid, the same night Fay Wray went completely bananas and was finally taken away screaming "I want my fucking mama! I want my fucking mama and my fucking daddy and my fucking brothers and sisters!"

He'd hardly ever sworn before. But this night it was different. He'd been screaming off and on for several hours. The guards had come, he'd been slammed around, but then he'd start in again. The sounds were different, too, not as high or shrill. Rosemary had appeared, but the screams and words were tearing harshly from his guts. Finally, when they were taking him away, we heard a wild shrieking laugh as he tapped his own slightly saner sense of humor: "Yes, and I want my fucking hamsters, too. You guys—no deal without my fucking hamsters!"

Those were the last words, then there was only gibberish as they hauled him off. We never heard from him again. Vin kept pumping Kwan for word of what had happened to him. Finally Kwan said he would tell us if we promised not to reveal the source. We promised. Kwan pantomined a shot to the head.

Vin and I couldn't believe they would shoot the poor bastard, that they wouldn't simply release him, or put him in a hospital where he could get badly needed treatment.

Vin took Leonard Barnes's death hard. (I can no longer refer to him as Fay Wray.) He brooded over the plain inhumanity of it. The next inspection day I got a nervous twitch when Vin asked Mine Fury, "What happened to Barnes?"

"Barnes?"

"Yes, you know, the guy who screamed?"

"Oh, yes, Barnes," Mine Fury said, averting his eyes and checking our room. "That is no concern of yours."

Vin started to speak. "Vin," I said, putting a hand on his arm.

Vin shook me off. "If you killed him, you'll pay for it."

Mine Fury wheeled around, started to say something, then abruptly cut his words off. His reaction had all but trapped him.

"You killed him, didn't you?" Vin said.

Mine Fury shook his head. "This is not true, this is ridiculous."

"What happened to him, then?" Vin asked.

Mr. Chips snapped, "No words from you!" Vin started in, but he repeated, "No more words. Silence. Nothing!"

The Captain left the room.

In October the peace rumors were documented by the North Vietnamese. The talks with Kissinger were close to agreement, we were told on "The Voice of Vietnam." You could feel it in the air. The food got better. Not only that, we were given a book of Chekhov short stories to read. Vin was delighted, he ate them up. There was even a basketball game outside in the exercise area among some of the P.O.W.'s. Vin and I were not allowed to participate, however. Vin was not pleased about this.

Toward the end of October a Canadian inspection team

came to our camp. It was the first inspection team we'd ever had. When Jane Fonda and Ramsey Clark had been over we'd heard about it but we hadn't seen hide nor hair of them. We were spruced up, given new pajamas, haircuts, and we were also given magazines. Vin and I got a *Sports Illustrated* and a *National Geographic*.

The team, or the part of it we saw, consisted of three men. They came to our room about eleven one morning, along with Mine Fury, an aide of his, and Kwan.

We stood at attention by our beds. One of the men asked how my health was. I told him it was good. He asked if there was anything special I wanted or needed. I told him I wanted very much to write a letter to my wife. He asked how many letters I'd written during the time I'd been there.

Vin cut in, saying neither of us had been allowed to write any letters, not one. The man seemed surprised. Mine Fury was not pleased, but he kept his face dialed to stoic. The man who'd been speaking asked Vin if the general treatment had been good. Vin looked at Mine Fury and I held my breath. "All right," Vin said. Thank God, I thought.

Just then one of the other men spoke something in French to the man who'd been questioning us. With that, Vin opened up in a whole string of French. Mine Fury immediately ordered Vin to speak English. But Vin was off and running and the danger signals went up when I heard the word "Barnes" mentioned in French and also *mort*. By this time I knew *mort* meant "death," although Vin was speaking so fast I could barely understand him.

Mine Fury's face was pure concrete as he called for a halt. The Canadian thought a moment, then turned to Mine Fury and said, "The report on Sergeant Barnes stated he died of natural causes, complicated by pneumonia, didn't it?"

"That is what happened," Mine Fury said.

Vin took off in agitated French again. Mine Fury shouted for him to stop. He then turned to the three men and reminded them that they were being "allowed" to visit the camp, that if they did not speak English he would have to bring an end to their visit. He held in his temper when he spoke to them—it was not easy, but he was firm and suggested that perhaps they would like to visit another building. He ushered them out of the room without looking at Vin or me.

When the bolt had slipped and we heard their footsteps go

on down the hall and the bolt to the outside door release, I said, "Oh, Vin! Vin, what's the good of that? The poor guy's dead, whatever happened, he's dead."

Instead of flying off the handle, Vin only said, "I know . . . I know . . ." He sat down on his bed.

The rest of the day I was so nervous about possible reprisals I couldn't even mention it to Vin. I didn't want to put my mouth on it. I told myself if peace was really near, perhaps Mr. Chips would let the incident pass. But I was scared. Vin lay on his bed reading *Sports Illustrated.* Every time we heard footsteps or the jangle of keys we both tensed, although we didn't put words to our feelings. I actually said a few silent prayers.

We took our exercise in the afternoon, were brought an extra-good meal at four, and were tucked in for the night at the usual five.

Later on, about nine, when we were in our beds, I said to Vin, "I've been scared shitless all afternoon."

Vin laughed. "Yeah, I was for a while, too."

"No more hassles with Mine Fury, Vin. It's not worth it, the news is too good. Easy does it, okay, Vin?"

"Okay."

"Promise?"

"Promise." After a while Vin said, "You know what's bugging me?"

"What?"

"I keep thinking if I hadn't opened my mouth, you might have been able to give them messages for Lisa and your mother, or gotten a promise to write a letter—"

"Forget it," I told him.

"No, I'm really an asshole. I'm sorry, T. M."

"Forget it."

Actually I hadn't even thought about that. I was so worried about Vin there was no room for anything else in my brain.

At five the next morning three guards came to take him away. We were both asleep when the sound of the door opening awakened us. As they stepped inside the room, I came to quickly. Vin was groggy, but when he focused on them, he blinked his eyes and looked over at me. "Shit," he said.

They hustled him out of bed, put chains on his wrists and irons on his feet. Vin took it calmly. He looked at me, smiled and shrugged when they were having trouble with one of the clamps.

As they headed him for the door, I said, "Vin, take it easy now, will you?"

"Only way to take it," he said. "You be a good boy, too, will you?" He looked over his shoulder. "No matter what happens, you keep your cool. Don't be a pickled asshole like me."

"I'll be okay."

He winked at me and they hustled him out.

# 17

That was October 23. I was miserable and badly shaken up for days. Outside of Vin, the news was good. Peace was definitely in the air. I learned from Kwan that Vin was in solitary. Nothing worse. To my mind, the best place for him; there's not much trouble to be gotten into in solitary. I just hoped he would keep up his strength, stay in good health, despite the damp rainy weather we were having.

Life at the Bel Air was on the upgrade, if not the smell when the wind was blowing the wrong way. I wished Vin could have enjoyed it. Food got even better, still not gourmet cooking but the improvement was noticeable and the portions larger. They were fattening us up in case peace actually came. Early in November I was allowed to play basketball one afternoon. Jerry Harker played, too. It was good to meet other P.O.W.'s and talk to them.

Not only were we getting into the holiday season, there were extra high spirits because of the peace negotiations. I was given another book to read, a collection of translated Russian short stories: Pushkin, Turgenev, etc.

Inspection day about two weeks after Vin was put in solitary, I decided to appeal to Mine Fury. When he and Kwan came into the room I told him how much I was enjoying the book of short stories. He smiled and said he was glad I appreciated the book; then he added, "I would believe it is only a matter of months, perhaps even weeks, before a treaty is signed."

"I hope so," I said. "If there will be peace soon, couldn't I write a letter to my wife?"

"That is not up to me," he said. "Not at this time."

I decided to try something that was up to him. "If, like you say, it's just a matter of time, couldn't you let Vin out?"

"Sergeant Poirier?" he asked.

"Yes."

Automatic frown. "He is trouble."

"Not really," I said, immediately kicking myself for such a weak rejoinder. *Not really!* "Wouldn't you think about it, though? We've got our Thanksgiving coming up and then—Christmas. It would be a great favor."

"Favor?" he said, smiling.

I had to smile, too. Favor, indeed, as if he owed me a favor. My concern over Vin had immobilized my brain. That and Mine Fury's quirks. You never knew what word or change of tone he might pick you up on, pick you up and turn you off. I didn't know how to act, what words of appeal to string together. "I know you don't owe me a favor, still—wouldn't you think about letting him out? I promise he won't cause any trouble."

"You promise?" Again he smiled.

Good God, I was acting like Mr. Goodbar, Mr. Goody-Good. I couldn't tell whether he was getting his kicks from that or if he took his delight from having me royally skewered. For an instant, I wanted to grab him and shout, "You really are one miserable son-of-a-bitch!" Instead I kept on: "I know you'll think about it, what with Christmas coming up soon—and peace."

He said something in Vietnamese to Kwan and laughed. Kwan answered him, without laughing. Then they left.

I was angry with myself for my inadequacy. On the other hand one had to tread lightly with Mr. Chips. There was no winning by doing or saying anything that would set him off.

The next day Mr. Chips returned to my room with an aide. He was in a pleasant mood and handed me a piece of paper.

It was a blanket denouncement of all our "high crimes" against the people of Vietnam. When I finished reading it, he told me if I would copy it out in my handwriting, sign it and also read it "into a recording machine" Vin would be let out of solitary.

I thought of Vin, of how he would react if I did this. I loathed the blackmail of it. Vin had refused. If I did it for Vin, it would almost be as if Vin had done it. (This, yes, despite my feelings about the war.)

When I looked at Mine Fury, he was smiling at me. It was a self-satisfied smile. "I'm sorry, I can't do it."

"You want your friend out?" I could tell he was surprised.

"Yes," I said, handing him back the paper. "But I can't do it."

"You *can* do it, you mean you will not do it."

"Whatever you say—no."

"So—" he said, folding up the paper. "So it is."

He signaled the Turnkey, who had stayed outside, to open the door. As he was leaving, I said, "I hope you have a Merry Christmas."

This stopped him. He turned around in the doorway. "What?" he asked.

I smiled and said, with as honest and straightforward a reading as I could summon, "I said I hope you have a very Merry Christmas."

He actually looked confused. I was filled with joy at his confusion. He said nothing but turned and walked out.

Several weeks passed; then on the eve of Thanksgiving, after our afternoon meal, at sundown, two guards I had seen around but did not know came to my room. They told me to stand and one of them put leather cuffs joined by a chain on my wrists, their version of handcuffs.

"What did I do?" I asked. No answer. "Where am I going?"

They gave me no information. They took me out and marched me across the yard toward the solitary back-to-back sheds. The tail-end of a fantastic winter sunset was disappearing. For some unknown reason I suddenly thought of New Mexico. They marched me right up on one of the sheds. I could hear Vin coughing before I got to the small grated peephole, the only ventilation there was. They shoved me up to it.

I looked in, squinting to see. The heavy smell of human

waste and mildew hit my nose before I could even see him. But there he was, sitting in the semidarkness on the ground, knees up, huddled, shivering, coughing and wheezing. Although it was dark in there, I could sense how awful he must look.

"Vin!" I said.

I scared him, his head jerked back.

One of the guards jammed a flashlight against the side of my cheek and shined it in. Vin put up a hand to shield his eyes. He had a heavy growth of beard; his nose was running; he hadn't bathed in weeks. He was a mess.

"Buddy?" he said. "Buddy!"

"No, *Eddie*," I said, but the guards grabbed me and shoved me away, marching me back toward my building.

I could hear him thumping around, trying to get up. I heard him calling out, "Buddy! Buddy—in here!"

My blood turned icy. Buddy was his younger brother. Without another thought I said to the guards, "Tell the Camp Commander I want to see him."

That evening I copied out the statement and signed it; the next morning, Thanksgiving, I read it into a tape machine.

They carried Vin back to our room at noon. He was very sick with a wracking cough and a fever. He was not, as I'd feared, out of his mind. He'd been temporarily delirious and had been thinking about his brother. He'd lost way too much weight and was terribly weak. I'd bargained for medical care and he was given pills and a shot.

He'd been on bread and water but still he couldn't enjoy the meal we were served. I tried to feed him a little bit at a time but he was so sick he had no interest in food. He only wanted to be able to lie down and to be warm. Although the weather was chilly and damp I gave him two of my blankets. He slept on and off for two days and nights.

I never told him what I'd done to secure his release. I didn't want him harboring any more hostility against Mine Fury. As he gradually got his strength back and we talked about it, he wondered why they'd brought me to see him.

"I asked if I could see you," I told him.

"Why?" he asked, "Wasn't there anything good on TV?"

"Because I was worried, dumb-ass!"

"And they let me out the next day?"

"It was Thanksgiving, they were obviously going to let you out anyhow, they probably wanted me to see what a mess you were, so we'd be good little boys from now on."

"Oh, Christ, I'm going to be the best little boy in the whole wide world. Don't worry about me. I wouldn't say 'shit' if I had a mouthful."

By Christmas Vin had regained most of his strength. There had been a long halt in the bombings while Kissinger was negotiating terms, then to our surprise the Christmas bombings of 1972 began around the eighteenth of December. They weren't kidding around either, great waves of B-52's lumbered in and dropped their Christmas presents on Hanoi.

We stood at the window looking out that first night as the bombs went off and the sky lit up in the distance. "No," I shouted out the window at the planes, "you guys got it wrong—it's *Christmas* coming up, not the Fourth of July!"

"Somebody fucked up in Paris," Vin said. "Jesus, this doesn't mean it's all off and we're in for another year of this shit, does it?"

"Maybe Nixon's finally on L.S.D. You don't suppose he's flipped out and pressed all those buttons? Maybe they're hitting Moscow right at this moment and Peking and Havana."

"I hope they slip a couple to Miami," Vin said. "I hate Miami."

"But seriously now," I said, "I wish they'd cool it. They keep this up and we won't get our Christmas dinner!"

The bombings kept up, though. I'd been hoping we might get mail or packages around the holidays but we didn't. Christmas Eve the bombing stopped. Christmas Day, despite the recent havoc, we were given a feast of a meal, more magazines, cigarettes, candy and several hours of music over the loudspeakers.

You just couldn't figure the North Vietnamese.

Or the United States either. December 26 the bombing started up again and went on until December 30. When they stopped this time, the word was out that terms for peace had been reached, it was just a matter of working out the details.

We got another surprise. On January 2 we were given entertainment. A live show, the equivalent of a U.S.O. troop, North Vietnamese-style, was put on for the P.O.W.'s out in the yard in front of the main building. There was a team of five acrobats—three men and two girls—a girl singer, a dance team and a magician.

A wood platform was set up only several feet off the ground as a stage. The P.O.W.'s all sat on the ground on mats that had been spread out. Mine Fury and about a dozen of the camp personnel sat on chairs to the right of us. I commented on Mine Fury. "He looks like death warmed over."

Vin said, "He's probably heartsick at the thought of losing us."

Vin and I were in the front row, only about four feet from the edge of the platform. With three musicians accompanying them, the acrobats opened the show. They were very good and the two girls were both pretty; one of them especially was petite and doll-like, the other was a bit more husky, but she had a pretty face, too. Toward the end of their tumbling act the three men formed a triangle; the two girls, atop their shoulders, made a pyramid. When they finished this, the two girls jumped down, did a series of cartwheels around the platform and ended up doing the splits right down in front of us.

As they landed in the splits, the unmistakable sound of a rather substantial fart could be heard despite the music. The two girls immediately shot each other surprised sidelong glances, no more than fleeting looks, as if to say "Did you do that?"

There was no sign of amusement on their faces, only a very slight disdain tinged with embarrassment as they glanced briefly at the first few rows to see if anyone had caught this extra added attraction.

With that, Vin and I turned to each other at the exact same moment and whispered, "Did you do that?"

We tried not to laugh, but the moment, the subtlety of their exchanged looks—together with the timing and translation of their glance all at the same instant—was too much for us. Also, as we later talked it over, there was something fortuitous about this happening, in light of Vin's first communication with me the day he arrived. Now it looked like we were at the end of our stay in North Vietnam and we accepted this last fart as a punctuation mark.

We howled with laughter as the team lined up for their applause. When they took their bows, by definitely *not* looking at us, we knew the two girls knew what we were laughing at. That made it all the worse.

We had a good solid laugh for ourselves, although we did our best to conceal it, and then we calmed down. We made it through the girl singer's act but she was followed by the dance team, a young boy and girl in their early twenties who looked to be brother and sister.

Their first number was a fragile little dance in which they both used their fans a lot. About halfway through, as they did a little gliding step side by side, they each flicked their fans and exchanged glances. Their looks mirrored the looks the girl acrobats had exchanged and Vin immediately whispered "Did you do that?" again.

Brutal. There we were once more, choking back our laughter. We were not all that successful and someone behind us said "Okay, calm it down!" and that made it worse.

I glanced back and to my right to see who'd spoken, and Mine Fury's attention had been caught by what was going on. His eye was on us. I whispered to Vin, "Cool it, Mr. Chips is onto us."

Vin glanced over, saw the look on his face and whispered, "Shit . . ."

To which, for some insane reason, I replied, "Who did? *You* did?"

Off again, hunched down, hands to our mouths, shaking with laughter. Another look toward Mine Fury told me we were soon going to be in serious trouble. "Vin—Jesus—stop it!"

We managed to get out of that spree all right, but not until they'd finished their second number, a short peasant dance based on harvest time. To the delight of the P.O.W.'s the third dance turned out to be their version of a jitterbug to the tune of "Boogie Woogie Bugle Boy of Company B." Great response from the audience to this, whistling and shouting. Toward the end, as the boy slid the girl forward between his legs, just as her face was under his crotch Vin made a very loud raspberry sound with his lips.

We were convulsed again, way out of control, punching each other, howling, rolling from side to side. Childish, I know, but—years stashed away, the holiday season, peace any day.

The magician came on next but we were laughing so hard

I barely remember what he was doing. All my concentration and resources were put to use trying to control myself. Now a few louder comments from fellows sitting behind us and the guy to my left was getting bugged, too.

Suddenly Mine Fury was standing at the end of the first row. When he saw me looking over, he quickly motioned for us to get up. I nudged Vin. "Curses," he muttered. We stumbled up, still unable to control ourselves completely, and walked over to the Captain. He said nothing, only motioned for two guards to escort us back to our room.

I could tell by the way he looked at us he thought our laughter was derisive, aimed at the quality of the entertainment, rather than at some specific item that set us off. There was hatred in his eyes.

Still, once Vin and I got back to our room, we lay on our beds howling off and on for about another half hour. We were caught by a binge that just had to be laughed out, that's all there was to it.

We would alternately make raspberry sounds or whisper "Did you do that?" "No, I didn't do that, did *you*?" "No, I thought Mr. Chips let one go!" And on and on. It made no sense but it was hysterically funny to us.

When we were finally all laughed out I said, "You don't think he'd put us in solitary for *laughing*, do you?"

We both agreed we didn't think there'd be any serious reprisals, not at this time, not with peace so close at hand.

# 18

That evening and the next day there was no word from Mine Fury, nor did we see him.

The following night Vin and I got back into our plans. During whatever leave we had before we were discharged, he and Ginger would be married and take their honeymoon in California. After a week or so, Lisa and I would join them. We'd drive around the state and Vin could see those parts of California I thought might be best for us to investigate. The four of us would be together. We were as optimistic as we'd ever been.

After we'd got into our beds, I said, "Hey, Vin, what if Lisa and Ginger hate each other?"

He thought a moment, shrugged and said, "Fuck 'em!" We burst into laughter. After a while Vin said, "What if Lisa takes one look at me and decides I'm the Pits?"

I thought for a second, shrugged and said, "Fuck her." Vin laughed and I added, "Suppose Ginger hates me on first sight?"

Vin rubbed his chin, then said, "She just might, she's a very perceptive girl."

We laughed again, said good night and went to sleep.

About one in the morning I awakened to sounds of vomiting. Vin was kneeling by the slop can giving it all up. I quickly got out of bed. He was a pale greenish color and shaking as he supported himself on his hands and knees.

"Can I help, Vin?"

He only waved me away. When he stopped vomiting, I helped him over to his bed, got a towel, wet it and wiped off his face. He was extremely hot and flushed. He'd been in such good spirits only a few hours earlier. "What happened?" I asked.

"I don't know, woke up—all cold and shaky. Just lay there shaking, then—wham, I knew it was all coming up."

I felt his forehead. "You're not cold now."

"I know, I'm burning up. Hot, it's not hot in here, is it?"

"No."

"Whew—feel better now I threw up. Go to sleep, T. M. I'll sleep now, too."

"You sure?"

"Yeah."

But he didn't. I went back to bed and slept for an hour or so. When I woke up I could actually hear his teeth chattering. I looked over and Vin was vibrating under his blankets; he could have been plugged into an electric socket the way he was shaking. Lying there, just staring at the ceiling.

"Vin?"

His head jerked over toward me. "Oh, Jesus, T. M.—I'm freezing, I am fucking freezing."

I went over to him. The cold sweats had him, he shook uncontrollably. "Wait a minute, Vin." I got him two of my blankets; although he protested, he was glad to have them. Even so, they didn't do that much good. He was alternately seized by large jerking spasms and series of small shudders. I sat on the bed with my hand on his shoulder.

The next time large quakes shook him, he said, "Hold me down, I'll fall off the fucking bed!"

I pressed down hard against his shoulder with the palm of my hand. "Yeah . . . good!" he said. "Good." In another second he was struggling to get out of the blankets.

"What?"

"Throw up!" he gagged.

I got him over to the slop can, where he threw up, gagged and choked, and threw up some more. I helped him back to bed. The next time I heard a guard walk by outside I opened the shutter and called to him. I finally got permission to empty the slop can, an unpleasant task but a necessary one.

A good thing I did; Vin was struck by violent diarrhea early that morning. He was embarrassed to be having these massive attacks in front of me, although I told him, "Listen, Vin, after all we've been through together, what's a little more shit between friends."

"I know," he said, "but this is *really* shitty!"

When Goosey came on duty I had a long pantomime with him about Vin's condition. The smell of the room and the look of Vin didn't need translation. A paramedic arrived about an hour after that with diarrhea pills and a few other tablets for Vin to take.

Vin and I thought he just had a twenty-four-hour virus. But it was worse than that. He didn't throw up any more but he began having severe stomach cramps along with his diarrhea. This kept up for two days. Seems like he was struggling to get up and over to the slop can every fifteen minutes or so, sometimes even more.

Before Kwan went off duty one afternoon I asked if he would please get the Camp Commander. He told me he'd gone on leave. I asked him to get whoever was in charge, to tell them Vin was sick and needed to be put into a hospital.

Kwan said he'd do his best. The paramedic came in the evening and gave him more pills.

That night his diarrhea kept up and again he had the
feeling he wanted to vomit, but there was nothing left to
come up except a greenish bile. I only slept for a half hour
now and then.

The next morning when I was emptying the slop cans I
learned from another P.O.W., Sayers, one that I'd played basketball with, that Mine Fury's mother and younger sister had
been injured in one of the last bombing raids. They'd both
been taken to a hospital and his mother had died the morning
after we'd had the show.

This was not good news, not at all.

When I walked back to the room I suddenly got
frightened, really frightened about Vin's health. All the
P.O.W.'s went through sieges of diarrhea but Vin looked
godawful; his olive complexion was a sickly off-white, looked
as if he'd been bleached.

He tried to keep up his sense of humor but he was so
weakened it was pitiful. "I'd put in another year if I could just
have a regular flushing toilet—with a regular fucking *seat* to
sit down on!"

I asked Kwan around noon if I couldn't see the temporary
Camp Commander. Vin's stomach cramps were causing him
the most trouble now; all afternoon, between trips to the slop
can, he lay on his bed moaning and groaning, and when he
could summon up the energy, he'd swear. "Jesus, where is
that slant-eyed bastard!"

His pajamas, both sets, were messy and that afternoon
when I took my shower I washed all of his things and
gave him a clean pair of mine to put on. When I got back
to the room, he said, "T. M., I didn't go all the time you
were out." Seconds later he said, "Oh, no—I had to put my
mouth on it, didn't I?" I quickly helped him up. He was so
weakened I had to support him while he squatted. The look
in his eyes told me of his acute embarrassment.

The medic came later and I told him Vin should be taken
out and given care. He didn't speak good English but he understood and indicated it wasn't up to him, it was up to the
Camp Commander. I told him I'd requested to see the Camp
Commander, the acting one, a couple of times but no one

ever came. He gave Vin a massive dose of some liquid to bind him up, like paragoric, more pills and left.

Ten minutes later Vin threw it all up. I raised hell, banging and pounding until I got a guard to get the medic back. This time Vin threw the stuff up immediately. He was so sick he refused to take any more, just lay on his bed panting and gasping and waving the medic away.

"Vin, you've got to try."

Suddenly his temper. "Jesus Christ, Eddie, I can't keep anything down, can't you see that—what's the fucking use!"

I motioned for the medic to stay. "Vin, look, the bombings are over, you heard the radio this morning, they're practically typing up the treaty now. You don't want to shit in your pants as soon as you step off the plane. Besides, you'll probably be on television."

He finally agreed to take more medicine and try to keep it down. He managed to swallow the liquid and this time he didn't lose it. He lay very still, regulated his breathing, and after going to the can several more times, he fell asleep for an hour or so.

I slept for a while, too. When I opened my eyes, Vin was still asleep. Thank God, I thought, he's over the worst of it.

When he awakened he looked over at me and said, "Oh, God, I slept—wow, how beautiful!" Then, as he squirmed around on the bed and felt under him, "Oh, Eddie, Eddie—I shit in the bed. Oh, *shit!*"

He got up and I helped him clean himself and change his pajama bottoms. He'd no sooner lay back down when he had another attack. Vin had positioned the can so that when he had to go, he faced the door, away from the bed. He was squatting over the can when the door opened and Mine Fury stepped in.

He looked terrible; his plump Buddha-look had turned haggard; his face was drawn and tight. He glanced at Vin with absolutely no expression, as if he hadn't walked in and caught a man shitting in a can.

"Excuse me," Vin said, "but I can't help it. Would you wait a minute?"

Mine Fury stepped back outside in the corridor without saying anything. When Vin was finished and back in bed, I went to the door and opened it wide. As the Captain came back in I almost said I was sorry about his mother but something told me not to. Instead, as he walked over and stood looking down at Vin, I told him how sick Vin had been, that he should be taken to a hospital and given care.

To my surprise, Vin only sighed and said, no, he thought the worst of it was over. Mr. Chips stared at him, then mumbled. "Diarrhea, it will go."

"But it's been days now and he——"

"It will go." With that, he left.

After he'd gone, I said, "He looks like he's been through the meat grinder."

"Yes," Vin said, "who said they're all that inscrutable? The poor bastard!"

Vin slept on and off that night and I actually thought he was getting better. The next morning the news on the loud-speaker was extremely good. Vin hadn't eaten in days and he managed to get down a little tea and bread. Fifteen minutes later he was throwing it up, followed by more stomach cramps and diarrhea attacks every fifteen minutes or so.

I requested the medic again but he didn't appear. Finally, while squatting over the can, Vin simply fell down, knocking the can over as he fell and spilling it all over that part of the room.

I went to him. He simply lay there on the floor. "Oh, Jesus, *Jesus,* Eddie! I can't. I can't——"

"Can't what?" I asked.

A burst of laughter. "——I don't know," he blurted out, and then he was crying and laughing at the same time. "Just can't . . . can't keep on shitting." His eyes spurted tears and they widened as he looked up and asked me very seriously, "Can I?" Suddenly he glanced around at the mess he was lying in, as if it came as a total surprise, and he screamed, "Help me! Eddie, help me out of here!"

"Yes, I will. Here, Vin." I helped him up and he broke away, staggering to the door and shouting, "Help me—let me out of this fucking pigpen!"

I grabbed him and led him toward the bed. "Come on, Vin—we'll get you cleaned up."

He clutched my arm. "A shower! Christ, Eddie, help me get a shower!"

"Later, Vin, after you——"

"No, I want a shower—a shower, goddamit!"

Wally Briggs, next door, shouted, "Jesus, take it easy in there."

Vin staggered to the wall. Pounding against it, he shouted, "A shower! I want a shower, you pricks!"

Someone down the hall yelled back, "Give him a shower!"

"Vin, listen, I'll get you cleaned up, you're too sick to go outside for a shower!"

"No—no!" he screamed, and with a steely strength he summoned from God knows where, he shoved me away. I went crashing back over my bed and hit the wall hard.

"Vin, stop it!"

He assumed a wrestler's stance, legs apart, hands clutched into fists held out from his sides. "You want more? You want more, you bastard—or do I get a shower!" He gasped, felt behind him and instantly the fight was gone as he said, in a pitiful voice, "Oh, Eddie—Eddie, I'm shitting again! Oh, Christ, Eddie—*help me!*"

"Yes, yeah . . ." I went to him, helped him let his pajama bottoms down. They dropped down around his ankles and he hobbled, like a little kid, over to an unused slop can.

"Eddie—Jesus, Eddie!" He'd used his strength up, he was so weak and shaky he could barely squat. I fixed his slippers on the edge of the slop can and guided him down, then I knelt in front of him and he put his arms around my chest for support.

There was a closeness at that moment—him shitting, hanging onto me for support—I'm a goner just remembering it.

# 19

For two more days and nights Vin was wracked with diarrhea and fierce stomach cramps. He was so weakened by this time he could no longer always get to the can. He would sim-

ply lie on his bed, let the watery stuff go and either moan or
whimper or call feebly for help and sometimes—when he
could muster a spurt of energy—still curse. He seemed to
have lost, in this siege, at least ten to fifteen pounds.

I spent most of the time cleaning him up, trying to make
him as comfortable as possible. After a while I was so used
to the mess and the constant smell—the smell of grapefruit
gone bad—I treated it like a nurse would, something to be
dealt with, not criticized or focused upon.

I devoted my energies trying to get someone, anyone, to
pay attention, to get him to a hospital. Mine Fury was una-
vailable, the paramedic couldn't do it on his own, without
orders, and Kwan, although he knew Vin was seriously ill
and kept bringing clean towels and blankets, pajamas, toilet
paper and extra slop cans—still he was terrified of his boss.
He let me know the Captain was in no mood to be pushed.

Finally, though, after I'd been sending messages to him in
vain, Mine Fury appeared on his regular inspection tour,
about eleven in the morning.

Vin was out of it, weak and almost delirious. Mine Fury
walked over to the bed and stood looking down at him.
Again there was no expression on his face, only that tight,
drawn look. I decided to let him have a good solid dose of
Vin before I voiced the appeal that jumped around in my
throat.

Vin opened his eyes, saw Mine Fury and, to my surprise,
smiled at him, a real smile. "Hey," he said, reaching for the
man's hand. "Hey—" He grabbed hold of Mine Fury's hand.
The Captain pulled his hand away, but remained standing
there, didn't back off. "Oh, hey!" Vin said, as if: Why'd you
do that? I wasn't going to hurt you. "Hey," he said again,
reaching out and tugging Mine Fury's pant leg. Fury looked
down for a second, but didn't pull away, just looked at the
hand tugging at his pants.

"Good old Mine Fury," Vin said, calling him by his
nickname for the first time, to his face. If the Captain got it,
he gave no indication. Vin gave the leg of his pants another
little tug. "You wouldn't just let me shit myself to death,
would you?"

Mine Fury kept staring at him.

"Huh, would you?" Vin asked, giving another little tug.

When the man didn't answer, Vin smiled again, let go of

his pants and said, "Yeah, I guess you would." Vin glanced over at me. "Yeah," he sighed, "I think he would."

Without saying a word, the Camp Commander turned and stepped toward the door. I was right after him. "Can I speak to you?"

He stopped. "Speak," he said.

"Could we step out there?" I indicated the hall.

He considered this request for a second, then walked out the door and I followed him. A guard, who'd been standing outside the door, put his arm up to stop me but Mine Fury spoke to him in Vietnamese and he let me step into the hall.

As I left the room, Vin said, "Hey, buddy, I think I'm going again." Then a weak little laugh and he muttered, "I can't even tell anymore when I'm shitting and when I'm not."

We moved down the hall a few steps and I lowered my voice. "I want to tell you," I began, "how sorry I was—about your mother and—"

Quickly he turned and began walking away. I reached out and took his arm. The guard grabbed me. "Please, let me finish, please!"

A few exchanged words of Vietnamese between them and Mine Fury said, "Finish . . ."

"I was sorry—so was Vin."

He shook his head, no, and blinked his eyes, warning me off the subject.

"All right, I just wanted you to know."

Once again he started to move away but I went on in a rush of words: "Please let him go to a hospital. You can see how sick he is, he'll die if he doesn't get care. You don't want him to die."

He stopped walking, turned and looked at me. "You don't, you don't really want him to die?" No expression at all on his face. This was terrifying to me. "If you'll just let him go to a hospital—or just—even a room over at the main house—with care, real care—and—"

It was like talking to a lake, a chilled lake, no reaction, not a ripple. Panic struck. "I'll do anything if you'll—I'll sign whatever you say, if you'll put him in a hospital—or record anything, whatever you want—I'll—"

Now just a glimmer of a smile crossed his face. It stopped me for an instant, but then I went on. "Please, I know you don't owe me any—but, please, for Christ's sake, he's my best friend. Please, can't you give him a little—"

We ended up simply looking at each other. I'd already overstated my case. I knew it; we both knew that. Now I just let my eyes say, Yes, I suppose you would just let him die, wouldn't you?

He spoke to the guard, who took my arm, and then Mine Fury walked down the hall and out of the building, as I shouted out, "Think about him, Jesus, please think about him!"

That night Vin ran a high fever and most of the time he was delirious. He would talk about his father and forgive him. "You're okay, Dad," he'd say, "a little off the handle now and then but—listen, who's to say—huh? You're okay." He'd talk to his girl, Ginger. "Okay, honey, you're right—get the skiis and we'll go. Whole weekend. You pick up the skiis . . ."

He would have lucid moments now and then. Once he called me over and said, "It's true, you know, Eddie. I am fucking shitting myself to death. What a way to go—I wonder—did anyone ever go that way before—just shitting his way out?" He thought a moment. "Sure, probably in India—masses of—like the plague."

Every so often he'd sigh and say, "Yeah, well—wow—oh, yeah!"

Finally, about two in the morning, he went off to sleep. I sat there looking at him. He looked so young now, looked just about twenty, the skin stretched so tightly over the bone structure of his face. So vulnerable. The toughness, the fight had gone out of him. He was no longer so pale, though; there was a bit of color in his face, an unhealthy sort of light beige color, waxy.

I walked to the window. Coming up, very low in the sky, was the mammoth reddish-orange globe of the moon. It looked enormous, so low and close I felt it might just come straight on ahead and wipe us out, scrape us off the earth.

Now I made a bargain. I had nothing to bargain with, but I made it anyhow, to God—or whoever—the man in the moon, the goddam angels, whoever was up there to listen.

I aimed it at the moon because the moon was there and it was so outsized big and eerie looking.

I began with a reminder of what a supreme fuck-up it would be to let Vin get through the rotten war and prison camp—right up to the point where the treaty was being worked out—and then just have him shit himself to death. I told Him/Them/Whoever made the rules and pulled the strings that if they'd all get together and let Vin get well and go home, I'd make sure I performed some gargantuan good deeds in the rest of my lifetime. Some mighty hefty good works.

But if they didn't cooperate they would have one miserable pisser to deal with.

Then I took the threat back. "Cancel the last," I said. "Just let him get well, that's all."

# 20

The next morning, when I woke up and looked over at him, Vin was breathing heavily and his color was unmistakably yellow. There was the awful smell of rotten eggs in the room.

I went over to him. I could tell when he looked at me—the whites of his eyes were yellow, too—that he was seeing me in a hazy way. He had messed himself, that I could tell, but when I said, "Come on, Vin, let's get you cleaned up" he only muttered, "Uh-uh, leave me alone . . ."

I knew he had some disease now, probably hepatitis. About that time the Turnkey came with our morning water. I grabbed hold of him, dragged him over to Vin, shook him and hollered that he had to do something, that it was probably catching and someone better do something quick.

Other guards came from down the end of the building. Two of them went over to look at Vin and I kept up a barrage at them. Vin mumbled, "Jesus, Eddie, cool it, will you . . . cool it."

They didn't speak English but they seemed to be impressed that he was seriously ill. They left with the Turnkey, but when no one else came within a half hour I couldn't wait any longer. I banged on the door and said I had to empty the slop cans.

The Turnkey opened the door and followed me out into the yard. A light drizzle sifted down. I suddenly dropped the two slop cans and made a dash for the main building.

Goosey yelled and ran after me. Two other guards up ahead and off to my right by the barbed wire tried to head me off but I slammed right into them, knocked one down, and kept on.

Just as I made it up the front steps, a guard and the paramedic came out the door. They grabbed hold of me but I was shouting like a madman: "There's a man dying, you bastards! He's dying—now get him to a hospital!"

I went on, shouting and yelling, and soon five of them were holding onto me, trying to drag me off the porch.

Mine Fury came out. He didn't seem all that surprised to see me. Only spoke to them and then said to me, as they all held me down, "What is it?"

"He's got something—jaundice or—I don't know, but he's turned all yellow. He's got to go to a hospital. You've got to help him now, you've got to!"

Mine Fury was joined on the porch by an aide. More Vietnamese exchanged. They started to half-carry, half-drag me back to the building. "Let go!" I shouted. "I'll walk, let go!"

Mine Fury spoke to them and one guard dropped away; the other three escorted me back, followed by the Captain and his aide.

Back in the room, the aide and Mine Fury took a good look at Vin and spoke back and forth to each other. I could tell they were sufficiently impressed to take action. Vin didn't open his eyes until they were all leaving the room. "What's all the—what's going on?"

"Nothing," I told him, "but you're going to get the hell out of here and get some care."

"Wanna bet?" he asked.

"I'll fucking bet you."

"Yeah ..." he said, then he was off again, sleeping, eyes closed, breathing very heavily.

They came with a stretcher in about fifteen minutes. He

was still sleeping. When they started to lift him off the bed he woke up. He made no effort to help or hinder the two men who carried him, just sagged in the middle like a rag doll.

When they'd put him on the stretcher, he mumbled, "Going for a ride . . ." He glanced over at me and said, "Comin' along?"

"No, not right now," I told him.

"Going home?" he asked.

"Soon—I hope to Christ! Soon."

As they carried him out the door, he raised himself slightly, lifted his head and said in a commanding voice, "Now you cool it, T. M.!"

"You, too," I said.

And he did. Vin cooled it the most you can. Three days later on January 22, 1973. The ultimate cool.

# Part Two

Part Two

# 21

It's difficult to describe the rest of my days there, not much point to it either. Except to say I was stunned, completely stunned by Vin's death. By the immense bad joke of it.

I never spoke to Mine Fury again, although it was he who came to my room four days after they took Vin out and told me he was dead. Looking back, I imagine he was sorry to tell me that. I think he seemed to be, I couldn't tell. I was out of it.

It wasn't that I wouldn't speak to him, although I admit I had no desire to; it was that I couldn't. I was frozen by Vin's death. I sat there and listened, that was all I could do. Of course, I blamed the Captain; if Vin had been taken to a hospital as soon as he became seriously ill, he would not have died. But I could not even put words to the blame. I could only stare at him. With blame, without, no matter.

After that first day I vaguely remember eating, showering, cleaning up the room, doing a wash. All done numbly by rote. I gave up exercising and push-ups, I had no heart for it. The evening of January 27 the loudspeakers came on with a broadcast: "The Voice of Vietnam" saying the peace treaty had been signed. Shouting broke out all up and down the rooms. Guards came to shut everyone up, but there was nothing they could do. Celebration went on until midnight.

That was the night I cried for Vin.

There was a basketball game the next day. I was told I could play but I stayed in my room. On the twenty-ninth of January the entire population of the camp, about thirty-two of us, were assembled in front of the main house. Mine Fury addressed us, saying we would all get a copy of the treaty within a few days, that we would probably be going home within a month, perhaps less, maybe a little more.

From this time on the food improved greatly; we were allowed to mingle in the yard at exercise periods; there was a Russian film shown. I didn't attend.

The high spirits of the rest of the prisoners I certainly understood. But they grated, like laughter at a funeral. I only wanted to keep my distance from them. And did, as much as I could manage.

The Captain came to my room the day after the Russian movie, saying he understood my feelings, that he could not force me to partake of any activities but he suggested it would be better if I did. I did not speak to him. He said it would be all right if I wanted to move over to the barracks where I would be with twelve other men. I shook my head— no. He said he could have me moved whether I wanted to or not. I just sat there.

During exercise period Jerry Harker, Wally Briggs and Eugene Gronowicz all talked to me. They had offered sympathy about Vin but now they strongly urged me to snap out of my funk. I knew they meant well, that they were right, but I was still frozen and numb. I was simply not able to whoop it up, even though I knew I was going home.

My remaining time there was—dead time. That's all I can name it.

I clung to Lisa, held on to the picture of our reunion. I thought about my daughter, too, but Lisa was the anchor to sanity.

About the middle of February I had a serious talk with myself. I knew I was taking Vin's death unhealthily. So I sat myself down for a general review, reminding myself I was lucky to come out of the war alive, not only alive but in one piece, no limbs missing. The idea of coming back an amputee chilled me. I'd come through five years of imprisonment, I was still young, relatively healthy, fairly bright, and I had a beautiful wife and a child to return to.

It did some good, I picked up my spirits somewhat. It was a heavy haul and, still, when I was not paying attention, I slipped back into a terrible heavy quiet. It was way down inside me, sat in my stomach like a cold stone.

The evening of February 18 we were given almost a Christmas dinner. Early the next morning we were issued shoes, trousers, shirt, belt, a sort of handbag carryall, a comb, new toothbrush, toothpaste, etc. At noon we were lined up in the yard, dressed in these rough-hewn civilian clothes. We all looked so strange, as if we'd been on some chain gang and had been spruced up for church.

After an hour or so two large buses came; we were loaded into them, driven through the outskirts of Hanoi and across the Red River to Gia Lam Airfield, where we waited another two hours until a 141 landed. We were loaded aboard and flown direct to Clark Field in the Philippines. Stupid, I know, but as the plane took off and I looked back down at the soil of North Vietnam, I felt I was abandoning Vin.

It was a noisy ride. There were nurses on board—the first American women we'd seen in years—a flight surgeon, medics, an information officer, photographers. I remember being handed a copy of *Playboy*, a candy bar and a glass of ginger ale. The high spirits of everyone on the plane only quieted me down. I kept seeing this freedom activity through Vin's eyes. The view made me passive.

When we landed at Clark, it was all lights, camera, action. We were, as Jerry Harker had promised, greeted like heroes. The Admiral of the Pacific, various generals, the works, lined up there to salute and shake our hands as we got off the plane and were photographed by the news services and television camera crews.

After the initial hubbub, we were escorted onto a hospital bus and taken to the top floor of the hospital at Clark Field. We were given our first steak dinner.

Each P.O.W. had an escort assigned to him, a man of his approximate rank and age, who would stay with him and act as a buffer-friend-coordinator to ease him back into life as we had known it. My escort was Sergeant Richard Beagles—I had been promoted to sergeant—a nice enough fellow who told me my name had only been transmitted to the Defense Department after we'd been picked up at Gia Lam. They were getting in touch with my wife and mother and undoubtedly I would be able to speak to them by telephone the next day or so.

We were to spend three days at Clark, taking our first physicals, getting our records brought up to date, being outfitted with new uniforms, haircuts, all of that.

That night, after our steak dinner with all the trimmings,

Sergeant Beagles sneaked a bottle of Scotch to four of us who had nearby rooms on the top floor. Not having had liquor in five years, it only took a couple of drinks to get me blasted. I have to say my spirits began to percolate. Freedom was catching. Thank God, I told myself; I was beginning to get with it.

Suddenly I had a large glow on and the little things, the comforts, hit me. A hot shower, a *hot* one, without laundry soap, fresh pajamas, then climbing, unsteadily, into a real bed with real sheets and an honest-to-God pillow. Indescribable luxury. I had a great heavy sleep.

Even my slight hangover the next morning was a luxury, added to by bacon and eggs, waffles, toast and jam, coffee with real cream. And a toilet seat you could sit on without fear of falling in. The morning was taken up by a general physical examination. There was no official debriefing at Clark, that was all to be done when we returned to the States. I was to be flown to Travis Air Force Base outside San Francisco and then quartered at Letterman Hospital right in the city for further physicals and debriefing before convalescent leave and eventual discharge.

After lunch Sergeant Beagles said to come with him to one of the lower floors. He took me into an office and introduced me to a chaplain who was obviously waiting to see me. Sergeant Beagles said he'd be back up on the top floor when I got through.

The chaplain, all grins and smiles and the kind of glasses that reflect light and don't let you see the person's eyes, launched into a eulogy about how most all the P.O.W.'s were in such relatively good health, considering what we'd been through, how fine we all looked, how "splendid" our attitudes were and what terrifically strong characters we possessed, how amazing the shocks and strains the human spirit can endure. The last was my clue.

"Something's wrong," I said. "Isn't there?"

"Now my boy—"

"Not my wife?"

"No, no, but there's an illness—"

"My daughter?"

"No, your mother—about five weeks ago she suffered a stroke."

"Oh—oh, God!"

"Not all that bad, but—"

"How bad?"

"She's paralyzed on her right side—"

"She's young, she's only in her fifties."

"And her speech is—well, she can't speak all that well."

"How well?"

"Not good, but—"

"Oh, God!" The years we'd put in together rushed forward and hit me. Hard. Together with walking out on her. My insanity, going into the service. Not seeing her. How she must be feeling, the helplessness. "Oh, Christ!" I remembered I was talking to a chaplain and shook my head. "I'm sorry."

"All right, it's all right."

"Where is she?"

"In a nursing home on Long Island."

"Nursing home . . ." Such a heavy phrase.

"Naturally she's been concerned about you, very concerned. Now that you're back, I'm sure this will help her recovery. I spoke to her doctor earlier. She would like very much to hear your voice, on the phone."

"But she can't talk back?"

"Not really. We're putting in a call in about fifteen minutes. Will you be—all right to talk to her?"

"Yes."

"I wanted you to have more time to—well, get used to it. But it's already late in the States. She's waiting to hear your voice. We can put the call through right here in my office, if you like."

"Sure."

We sat in silence for a while. To break it I said, "Sergeant Beagles said I'd be able to speak to my wife, too."

"Yes, you will. I understand they're still trying to get her current telephone number. A report only six weeks ago indicated"—shuffling through my file—"that she and your daughter were both fine."

"Good."

Another silence. Just as I was about to ask him, he answered my unspoken question. "When you speak with your mother, I would just—well, make it brief. Just so she knows you're back and in good health and that she'll be seeing you soon."

I hadn't particularly taken to him before but I liked him

now, for sensing I needed help. "Can you place the call now?"

"Yes, of course."

He went outside and spoke to his assistant while I attempted—all muddle-brained—to rehearse what I might possibly say that would be *right*. When he came back he asked, "Would you rather be alone when you talk to her? I'd be glad to stay if you'd—"

"No, I guess it would be better alone."

"Of course. Why don't I step outside, if you need me I'll be right in the outside office there."

"Thank you. I'm just feeling a little—I mean, it was a surprise, I had no idea."

"I know. Here, sit at my desk, you'll take the call on that phone there."

"Thank you." I moved to his chair and he left the room, shutting the door after him. I looked at a framed color photograph of him, his wife and their three children, two boys and a girl. All five wore glasses. The Glass family. As I was wondering why the kids, at least, hadn't taken them off for the camera, the phone buzzed. I picked it up.

"Hello . . ."

"Hello, Sergeant Eddie Keller?" A woman's voice, brisk and cheery.

"Yes."

There was a whooshing sound, followed by long-distance waves echoing back and forth. "—right here with another nurse, Edith, right here beside Bebe, our favorite patient. Aren't you, Bebe?"

"Is she all right?"

"Oh, my yes, she's coming along just fine, aren't you, Bebe?"

Already I detected the overprofessional nurse in the woman, as she went on, "She's so excited, knowing her boy's back, all safe and well. So excited, she's just been raising *hade*s all evening, haven't you, Bebe?"

Oh, God, I thought, if she doesn't stop saying "Aren't you, Bebe?" and "Haven't you, Bebe?" The nurse started to go on, but I interrupted. "Can I speak to her, please?"

"Of course." She lowered her voice, I could barely hear her what with the whooshing noise. "Now, Eddie, she can hear you perfectly well, nothing wrong with her hearing, it's just her speech." Her voice switched back to normal, which bordered on the cheerful-shrill. "Just having a little trouble with our speech, aren't we, Bebe?"

She'd finally done it, used the plural.

"All right, now, I'm going to hand her the phone, she can hold it just fine in her *left* hand." The nurse's voice drifted away as she said, "There we go, all set now."

I cleared my throat. "Hello, Mother!" I heard myself shout. Shouting to keep control, I suppose. "Mother, I'm back and I'm fine. I'm in the Philippines and I'm—I'm in good health. I'll be coming home and soon as I start my convalescent leave I'll be back to see you."

I paused and then I heard a sound like "Eeh!" It came again: "Eeh!"

The nurse took over. "Your name, Eddie, she's saying your name, aren't you, Bebe? Yes, all right, that was good, wasn't that good? I'm handing the phone back to your mother now. Here we go . . ."

"Mother, I just want you to know—" I suddenly had to stand up from the desk to keep myself together. I pressed my free hand down with all my might against the top of the desk for strength. "I just want you to know I'm really fine and I can't wait to see you—I love you very much! I do and—"

Terrible gagging, choking sounds, like a baby choking on its food, struck my ear. Then a high, gasping, wailing cry. If I ever winced in my life, I winced now, all the way down to my toes.

The nurse's voice again: "It's all right, Bebe, all right, dear." Then back to me. "Eddie, she's just so happy to hear you sounding so fine, just made her cry for joy." Her voice turned away as she snapped, "Edith, help Bebe—there, now." Back to me: "I think we've had enough for now, Eddie. She's just so happy, it's too much for her, is all it is."

"Yes—" I said. "Give her my love, tell her I'll see her soon."

"Yes, I will."

I hung up the phone—*just*—before letting it all out. Great terrible-sounding sobs, sounds I'd never heard from myself before, came heaving out of me. The door opened. The chaplain. I waved him back. "—Alone—please—just a—"

"Yes."

He ducked back out and shut the door.

# 22

Phrases occur to me now. Hit 'em again, harder, harder! Two down, one to go. Quantum jump. Or is it leap? Let's make a quantum jump/leap. Let's get to the goodies, don't you want to hear the goodies?

By the time two days later, about to board the plane for the final flight home and I had still not been able to speak to Lisa on the phone—the phrase "two down, one to go" had entered my mind. They, the army, had certainly tried to contact her; finally the information came back that the phone was disconnected. The strangeness of that unsettled me; not like Lisa to have a disconnected phone. But then a call was put through to Lisa's mother, Marie, in Sacramento. Besides the wedding, I'd spent one weekend there and seen her several times in San Francisco. Marie was large and ungainly, likeable but a bit nervous and fretful for such a large woman; hard to believe she'd mothered such a beautiful graceful daughter.

The call relieved my fears. My daughter, Lauri, was in fact staying with Marie. Lisa had gone on a vacation for two weeks, was due back the night before. She was starting a new job. Marie was certain she'd hear from her today, had not known the phone was disconnected, and was bubbling over with what a wonderful daughter I had. She put Lauri on the phone for one of those happy discombobulated conversations between adult and child who don't know each other.

"Hello,. Lauri, it's your daddy." I laughed, hearing myself say that. Daddy! I'd never thought of myself as Daddy. I was a father, but—Daddy!

"What . . . ?" came this tiny confused voice.

"It's your daddy—" I almost said "dummy" but switched

to "sweetheart." Just the sound of that little voice had me giddy.

"It's my daddy?" I heard her say to her grandmother; it was more question than statement.

"Yes!" I shouted. "And I'm getting on a plane in a couple of hours and flying straight to you and Mommy."

"How come?" she asked.

"Because"—I laughed at the non sequitur of it—"I'm back and I want to take a look at you. And hug and kiss you."

"You do?" She didn't sound overly pleased at the idea and this tickled me even more.

"Yes, I do. And I will. Will you give me some hugs and kisses back?" Sergeant Beagles was in the room with me; I looked at him and said, "Well, what are you gonna do?" He was grinning for me.

"Maybe ..." came the reply. A tease, not even five and a tease.

"I can't wait to see you."

"All right." Such a little person's voice.

"We'll have such good times, you and me and Mommy," I told her.

"Mommy's away."

"I know, but she'll be back."

"Yes, I know."

"Okay, darling, I'll see you soon. Good-bye now, put Grandma back on."

"Okay."

"No, wait," I quickly said, "say 'Daddy' for me."

"*What?*" she asked, like it was a totally crazy request.

"Say 'Daddy' and make a guy happy. Come on, say it!"

A giggle, then: "Daddy ..." Another giggle.

Marie came back on, saying I'd never realize how upset Lisa had been and what she'd been through all these years but now that I was back she knew everything would be all right. "And just wait until you see Lauri, cute as a button and twice as bright." She had the information about when I'd be at Letterman and would pass it on to Lisa. We said good-bye and hung up.

News of my mother's illness had, of course, been a great damper on my spirits, but this phone call boosted them again. When the 141 took off from Clark Field late that afternoon for the long flight home, I was lightheaded with the excitement of seeing my wife and daughter.

There were twenty P.O.W.'s and twenty escort/sponsors aboard. We were spruced up in our new uniforms, shaved and barbered. I'd drawn three hundred dollars cash out of which I'd bought presents at the PX for Lisa and Lauri: perfume, a jade necklace and a kimono for Lisa and a little silver bracelet and a Chinese doll for Lauri. I'd also bought a watch for myself—and two dozen candy bars. I'd embarked on a sweets binge since arriving at the Philippines. I'd had two banana splits and three hot fudge sundaes within three days, along with cake, pie, cookies and all sorts of candy. Although I was way under my normal weight, I could see a small bulge protruding from under my belt.

On the plane were eight navy men, ten air force and two army: myself and a lieutenant who was going to a base back east. The flight took some twenty hours, with refueling and a two-hour stopover at Hickham Field in Hawaii. Liquor was not officially served, but almost everyone on the plane had managed to bring a bottle along and the eyes of the crew and other accompanying personnel looked the other way when we nipped.

Something about being up in a plane that gives me a sense of vast, almost eerie perspective. As if I can look down and back and, at the same time, forward to events and people and fit them all together into a master jigsaw puzzle that somehow makes sense. With a slight high-on from my Scotch, it was a mellow flight, mixed with fantasizing, stretches of sleep and bouts of camaraderie.

Of course, I thought of Vin. If we had been able to share this homecoming, it would have been so perfect. The plane would hardly have been able to contain us; we'd have been dancing in the aisles. But that was not to be. He was gone and there was nothing to be done. As he had been a good friend to me, I had been a good friend to him. I could only cherish our friendship and hold it close; I would forever, I knew that.

Bebe was something I could do something about. I was a grown man now, I'd been through something few men experience. I would take care of her, make it up to her, help her recover.

The mellow end—the ups, the rainbows, music and the

joy—that was my wife and daughter. And my life, itself, a life I vowed to spend wisely. I would not waste it. Suddenly, money, which had always been a large item, the making of money, dropped away in importance. No longer at the top of the list. Now it was using my time, accomplishing work I enjoyed, achieving relative happiness for myself and my family. The quest for good times.

Yes, sitting there looking out the window at the sun glistening on the flat endless view of sea-green, I actually thought I had the whole course charted. What a simpleton I can be sometimes.

At Hickham Field there was a message saying Lisa would be waiting for me at Letterman Hospital. I'd slept a few hours before landing in Hawaii and the relaxation provided by this latest news allowed me to put in a couple more after we took off.

There was a poker game for another two hours; five of us played and I was the only enlisted man, coming up winners for a hundred and twenty-two dollars. And I'm not a good poker player. Yes, my luck was changing. Right on.

It wasn't planned, but we sighted the California coast and the city of San Francisco as the tail end of an incredible deep burnt-orange sunset refracted off it. The lights of San Francisco, of the Golden Gate Bridge, strung out so graceful and jewel-like, the massive carpet of lights that was the entire California Bay Area, brought cheers from us, followed by window crowding and neck craning. I got the impression, from the wild quality of lighting, that I'd been in black and white for the last five years and now the world had turned Technicolor again. Little wisps and small patches of fog drifting in over the city from the Pacific made it more unreal and exciting.

Although Travis Air Force Base is about forty miles north of San Francisco, they buzzed us in a wide arc coming right in over the Golden Gate Bridge and banking south for a gradual circling of the entire city. I knew the Presidio section we were coming in over and looked down to see Letterman Hospital just inland and to the right of the bridge. Lisa was probably there already.

Spirits in the plane were so high as we dipped along the perimeter of the city, swinging back around over the Oakland

Bay Bridge and heading north in a gradual descent, it's a wonder the plane didn't explode from the mass energy we gave off.

I spotted more than a few men wiping tears away.

Rarely have I felt such excitement. It grabbed me by the shoulders, shimmered down my back, spreading all over me, like I'd been plugged into an electric socket, as the plane glided down, leveled off, let down again and finally touched the runway. It got me in the kidneys, too; I felt a strong urge to pee.

# 23

We could see floodlights and television cameras and a crowd of people as we taxied toward a stop. As opposed to the shouting and chatter when we flew in over the city, now a sudden inhaled hush filled the plane. Not a sound except for the movement of bodies, the shuffle of feet as we gathered our gear and stood up. And I thought: I'm on the same terra firma as Lisa, barely an hour away from her.

We'd already been advised of our order of disembarking, according to rank and service. Air force off first because it was an air force base, army next and then navy, highest rank off first in each branch of the service, grading down. This made me number twelve off.

Sergeant Beagles stood next to me, holding the manilla envelope with my record and a duffle bag. The hush stretched on as the ramp was rolled up, the door was finally opened and we began to file out.

Then sudden bursts of applause and shouts of recognition from the wives, parents, children and friends of the air force men who'd come out to meet them. No army wives or parents or navy. Stupid, but the other two branches were whipping their men away to their own receptions. Incredible joke that, after years in prison, the returnees were first treated to interservice rivalry.

A long line of brass, including two generals, stood strung back from the bottom of the ramp. As we stepped off they saluted, hurriedly shook hands and voiced gung-ho greetings. Flashbulbs popped all around, not only from the civilian press but from dozens of service personnel recording this event.

The air force men soon dashed past this official activity into the throng of those awaiting them to the cries and shouts of joy, tears and sobs, laughter, sounds of male-back-thumping. Microphones were set up in front of TV cameras for brief interviews with the air force P.O.W.'s.

A voice shouted, "Sergeant Keller?"

Sergeant Beagles spun around and called to an army colonel, standing off to one side, "Colonel Dwyer?"

"Yes, hurry it up!"

"Come on, Eddie," Beagles said, taking my arm and pulling me after him.

The colonel saluted me. "Sergeant Keller?"

"Yes, sir." I returned his salute, then we shook hands. The colonel indicated an officer standing behind him. "Captain Fitzmorris—Sergeant Edward Keller." We had barely saluted and shaken hands when Colonel Dwyer, a big beefy man, laughed and said, "Okay, enough of this crap, let's get out of this chicken-shit air force rank-pulling horse-shit! Let 'em have their own press conference, we got one set up for you, boy! Come on, let's make tracks!"

We trotted some twenty yards to an army staff car and piled in, the colonel, the captain and me in the back, Sergeant Beagles up front with the driver. By the time we took off, a California state trooper car zoomed in front of us, lights twirling, and another army M.P. car closed in behind us. The state troopers barely slowed at the gate. Two guards in uniform ducked out of the gatehouse and ran toward the car, necks jutting forward, arms waving.

Colonel Dwyer yelled at our driver up front, "Slow down and I'll put a bullet through your head."

One of the guards running toward us shouted, "Hey, sir, you're supposed to—"

Colonel Dwyer shouted out the window, "You're supposed to go fuck yourself!"

We laughed as our three-car convoy sped off the base onto the highway. I couldn't help thinking how Vin would have gotten a kick at the quality of this hero's return.

"Didn't forget anything on the plane, did you?"

"No, sir." Then, already pegging the colonel's personality, I added, "Only one thing, I got so excited landing I forgot to pee."

Colonel Dwyer laughed and shouted up to his driver. "Step on it, Benny, this P.O.W. has to take a piss. And we're not stopping at any gas station. This is gonna be the fastest ride into any city you ever had." He flicked the side light on and gave me a good looking over. "Five years?"

"Yes, sir."

"Shit, need a little fattening up, but outside of that you don't even look like you've been out on a forced march. How'd you come through it like that? Probably mean as a snake in heat, huh, that what did it?"

I laughed. "Yes, sir."

"Cut the 'sir' shit."

"Yes, sss . . ."

We all laughed again. Christ in heaven, I was feeling good. Way up, *way up!* For most of the ride until we hit the bridge, we were nearing eighty. Colonel Dwyer was head of the medical team in charge of the returning West Coast army P.O.W.'s. He was, himself, a psychiatrist, although you wouldn't have guessed it from the way he talked. I liked him enormously. He had Captain Fitzmorris break out a bottle of Scotch and paper cups and we all had a drink.

He leveled with me. "You're a big deal for us. Regular army only has a small group of P.O.W.'s, so you're gonna get more attention than a public hanging. We only got four at the hospital now, don't expect more than another three or four, tops. Oh, and watch out for them, their backs are up about you already."

"How's that?"

"They've all had a look at your wife. You have one gorgeous girl there, waiting for you right now. She had eyeballs popping." I could not help puffing up over that as Colonel Dwyer filled me in on my arrival schedule. "There's a plaza out in front of the hospital. We got a mike set up, there'll be photographers and some TV people, all you gotta do tonight is—just say a few words, whatever you want, have your picture taken."

"With my wife?"

"No, no. She's waiting up on the tenth floor. We've found it's best not to take chances with a public first meeting. Better for you to have it alone, more relaxed, not so many pressures."

He told me I could hold my own press conference in three or four days, if I wished to; it would be set up in an auditorium on the base. Then he got sidetracked into giving the air force hell for the way they took over the publicity and glory of the returning P.O.W.'s. "No wonder we couldn't win the goddam war outright. We got too much bickering between us for that." He stopped and turned to me. "I hope I didn't offend you, Eddie, I mean I don't know your feelings about the war."

"Didn't offend me a bit."

"Yeah, good, I figured," he chuckled. "By the way, don't kid the war with Captain Provo, Major Torrance or Sergeant Finley. Christ, they've all been prisoner for over five years and you'd think they just stepped out of West Point. Okay with Sergeant Hinsler, but it's pure Stars and Stripes, apple pie and Mom with the rest of them. You're not staying in, are you?"

"Staying in where?"

Colonel Dwyer roared. "Yeah, that's my answer. Staying in where!" He slapped me on the knee.

"Oh, the service, no."

He laughed even louder that I went on to verbalize it. We had another drink, passed around some words and nonsense, Colonel Dwyer insisting I call him Walter.

Soon we were zooming by Sausalito and next the lights of the city blazed into view. Approaching the Golden Gate Bridge, the state troopers activated their siren and within minutes we were across the bridge, circling down into the Presidio and entering the military base and the grounds of Letterman Hospital.

"Look at that," Colonel Dwyer said, "they got every light of the whole ten stories lit up for you."

A crowd of perhaps seventy-five or a hundred hospital personnel, nurses, plus a lot of army and some civilians stood by the flagpole at the plaza in front of the main hospital entrance. Television lights went on as the car pulled up and stopped. I noticed people looking out of almost every window in the hospital—more nurses, patients and their visitors.

"Here we go," Colonel Dwyer said, opening the door and getting out with me behind him. There was applause from the crowd and cameras flashed. The colonel took me straight over to the microphone and introduced me, ending with, "He's not going to make a long speech, only say a few words, because he's got the most gorgeous wife you ever saw waiting for him right up there." He pointed to the top floor. "Eddie, there she is, third window from the right."

I looked up and there she was, waving. I blew her a kiss, turned and faced the microphones, turned back and blew her another kiss. That got applause. Before I could speak, a reporter called out, "How many years?"

"Almost five."

A woman reporter asked, "How does it feel—being back?"

I was so overwhelmed, suddenly at being there, with Lisa right upstairs, I only mugged "Ehh!" and shrugged. It got a huge shock laugh and I thought Colonel Dwyer would fall over he roared so loud. When everyone calmed down, I said, "No, honestly, I can't really put words to my feelings, it's all too much." I felt tears backing up my eyes; I didn't want to cry. I looked down, I was standing on cement. "I could kiss the ground, if it wasn't cement."

"Go ahead!" someone shouted.

"Yes!" someone else seconded.

Without another word, I got down on my knees, spread my hands out, bent over and planted a kiss on the plaza as more flashbulbs popped and another round of applause broke out. When I stood up, the woman reporter who'd called out the first question asked, "What's the first thing you're going to do when you get up there with your wife?"

"I don't know, but I'm so happy right now—I'll probably bite her!"

More laughter. I got the feeling I was coming on as a stand-up comic, so I pulled down and in. "I just want to say I appreciate all of you turning out here. I want to thank you for a great homecoming and—it's unbelievable to be standing here, to be back home after five years of thinking and dreaming about it. I could really just about cry but I'm not going to." I turned to the colonel. "Oh, and I want to thank Colonel Dwyer for one of the scariest rides I've ever had!"

We quickly shook hands, more flashbulbs. "Okay, everyone, that's it, here we go!" The colonel and our little group whisked me into the hospital, an elevator was being held for us, and up we went.

# 24

My stomach was upside-down by the time the elevator stopped and the doors opened.

Lisa stood about five yards away; she wore an outfit I loved, a knitted two-piece suit, dark blue, trimmed in kelly green. She'd bought the suit when we were married, but it looked brand-new. Behind her stood a gaggle of nurses, orderlies and a few other people, all grinning a welcome.

A nervous little smile flicked across her face. "Eddie . . ."

With that I was into her arms, hugging and kissing her. She burst into tears immediately and Colonel Dwyer herded us, me with my arms around her, past the main nurses' station into a large clean double hospital room across from it. As he shut the door he said, "Take your time, Eddie. Then I just want you to check in out here and meet your doctor, any time you're ready."

We were alone. Still great sobs came from Lisa. I held her close, patted her, caressed her, squeezed her. She was shaking all over. She felt thinner, more fragile than I remembered. "There, Lisa . . . I'm back, I'm back and I'm okay."

"I know, I know," she sobbed. "I'm sorry, Eddie, I—it's just—for so long—I never thought I'd see you again." She cried off and on for another couple of minutes, her body still trembling, so I simply held onto her, soothed her with a whole string of comforting phrases. Finally she stopped. "Ah, there—I'm sorry. I'll pull myself together, I'm sorry, Eddie."

"That's okay, it's an occasion, you're entitled."

She stepped back away from me, all red-faced, mascara running, eyes blinking. She dabbed at them, then looked at me as if for the first time. "Eddie, you look—"

"How?"

"You look wonderful, I can't believe it, I was expecting you to be all—I don't know what, but—"

"I'm skinny."

"But your face, you look just the same." She caught my grin at the mascara running down her cheeks. "Oh, I must be a mess."

"No, you're beautiful."

"No, I'm not." She got out her handkerchief, turned and faced a mirror over the bureau. "Oh, look at me!"

"I can't stop!"

"I need some cold water." She headed toward the bathroom.

"You mop up, I'll go out and check in officially, see what the routine is."

"All right."

"Hey, that was quick," Colonel Dwyer said.

"She's pulling herself together."

He introduced me to the doctor assigned me, Colonel Floyd Martin, several nurses, an intern and two P.O.W.'s, Captain Provo and Master Sergeant Finley. After a few moments, Colonel Dwyer, Colonel Martin and I walked down to the end of the hall and stepped into a comfortably furnished glass-walled corner lounge with a spectacular view of the Golden Gate Bridge. I noticed a small dining table at one end set up for two with shrimp cocktails already in place. Colonel Dwyer told me Lisa and I would be served dinner in fifteen minutes or so. I'd forgotten all about time; glancing at my watch, I saw it was a little after eight o'clock.

We sat down and Colonel Martin said from my preliminary physical at Clark I looked to be in good shape. Outside of anemia and some badly needed dental work, nothing else of importance had shown up. However, they would be running me through more extensive tests—X-rays, the works—during the next week or so. These physicals would take place in the mornings; afternoons would be spent in debriefing sessions with army intelligence, counseling, psychiatric examinations and career planning.

I asked how long it would be before I went on my convalescent leave. Colonel Dwyer said he thought somewhere between ten days and two weeks, unless there were any unforeseen complications. I mentioned my mother's stroke and said I wanted to see her as soon as possible. They both knew about her and offered sympathy. We went over a few other points and formalities and then Colonel Dwyer said, "Your wife seemed overjoyed to see you, to the point of tears. I gather there are no problems there."

"No, sir."

"Good, because it's been rough for a couple of the others." Despite Colonel Dwyer's language earlier at Travis and in the car, he was extremely sensitive when it got down to serious matters. "Eddie, I hope you won't mind my asking, but we'd have to make arrangements—would you and your wife like to sleep together tonight?"

"I'm pretty sure we would. In other words—yes."

He smiled. "With two of our P.O.W.'s and their wives it was too soon, too rushed, they preferred to wait a day or so. With two others it wasn't, that's why I ask."

"You said—arrangements?"

"Either a do-not-disturb sign on your hospital room or—Captain Provo and his wife took a room over at Thompson Hall, didn't they?"

"Yes," Colonel Martin said, turning to me and explaining. "Thompson Hall is for officers or transient personnel right here on the base. The rooms are very nice, although Sergeant Hinsler and his wife just had a do-not-disturb sign on their room right up here."

"And believe me," Colonel Dwyer said, "you won't be disturbed!" He caught my expression. "What is it?"

"I thought I'd be spending the night, I mean all night, with my wife at her apartment. She lives right here in the city."

Colonel Martin said none of the P.O.W.'s were allowed to leave the base the first night, not until they got underway with their extensive physicals, perhaps the second or third night.

"But I'd check back in any time you say, early in the morning, early as you want."

"What objection would you have to staying on the base?" Colonel Martin asked.

"There's just a certain lack of romance. I wouldn't want to go to bed with my wife right across from the nurses' station, even with a do-not-disturb sign on the door. Also, nice as the room is, they do have hospital beds."

Colonel Dwyer smiled, so did Colonel Martin, who said, "Then take a room at Thompson Hall, we can fix that up."

"They probably have single beds there, too, don't they?"

Colonel Dwyer laughed. "Come on, Floyd—what the hell!"

"No, I can't. Besides, none of the other P.O.W.'s were allowed off the base the first night, we'd get all kinds of flack."

"I'll stand the flack," Colonel Dwyer said.

"No, I can't authorize it, Walt."

I liked them both and I didn't want to cause trouble. I broke in, "All right, we'll go to Thompson Hall. I just took it for granted I'd be allowed out the first night home."

"Fine, I knew you'd understand," Colonel Martin said.

There was a knock on the door, a nurse stuck her head in. "Dinner's here."

An orderly wheeled in a food service cart. I was even a bit disappointed to be eating there. I'd had, oddly enough, a good Chinese restaurant in mind. Colonel Martin stood, we shook hands and he said he'd have my wife sent in, he'd make arrangements and see me in the morning. Colonel Dwyer called out after him, "Floyd, a drink at the officers' club?"

"Sure, make it about five minutes," came the reply as he left.

Colonel Dwyer winked at me. "I'll fix it up, you'll get out tonight."

"No, it's all right over at—"

"Bullshit, he may be your doctor, but I'm in charge of the whole damned Operation Homecoming." I started to protest but he cut in, "You were right, they do have single beds at Thompson Hall. A couple of martinis and I'll fix it up, don't worry. I'll get back to you."

With that, he left, nodding to Lisa, who passed him in the doorway.

# 25

Lisa smiled at me.

"There, now you look like my Lisa."

She shook her head. "Not quite, I look a lot older."

"No, you don't." Even saying that, I noticed dark circles under her eyes that were never there before. Then, again, it could have been the remains of the mascara smudge.

"Yes, I do, I can see, I have a mirror."

"You're thinner, though, aren't you? Just a little bit?"

"Yes, a little." She glanced out the northwest window at the bridge. "Umm, what a view!"

"Yes, it's sensational."

"It's good from your room, too."

"I love that knitted suit."

"That's why I wore it."

"How do you keep it looking so new?"

"I haven't worn it all that much and I just had it re-blocked."

We were being so formal with each other, the view, you're thinner, the knitted suit, but then the orderly was clattering around setting up the food. Although I was hungry, I'd have preferred not eating right away until we'd gotten relaxed with each other, but there it was all being laid out.

"You hungry, Lisa?"

"Medium-hungry, actually I didn't have lunch today."

"Good, we might as well sit down."

As I helped her into a chair, the orderly took a towel-wrapped bottle of champagne from the serving cart. "There's not supposed to be any liquor served up here, but Colonel Dwyer sent this with his compliments." He shook his head. "He's some character, Colonel Dwyer, he really keeps it livened up around here." He opened the champagne with a pop and filled two glasses. "There you go. By the way, welcome home!"

"Thank you."

"Well, you two have a good dinner now." Almost out the door he said, "Oh, you want the color TV on?"

"No, thanks, not during dinner."

"Okay, most of the others, can't get 'em away from the color TV."

When we were left alone, I picked up my drink and held it out toward Lisa. She met my glass and we clinked. "Here's to good times ahead," I said.

"Yes, good times." Still, it was a nervous little smile she gave me.

I noticed her hand was shaking slightly as she lifted her glass. After we sipped, I said, "It must have been very rough for you, too, wasn't it?"

"The first two years were—were terrible. I didn't think I'd—then you get resigned, I guess you get used to it."

"I'm back now."

"Yes." She sipped her champagne.

As we started on the shrimp cocktails I peeked under the covered dishes set on the side. "God, I'm being steaked to death, if they keep this up I'll turn into a steer."

"Do you still like Chinese food, even after being over there?"

"God, yes." I had to laugh. "We didn't exactly get what you'd call Chinese food, you know?"

"I guess not." We ate in silence for a while, until she said, "Oh, Mother told me you phoned and talked to Lauri. What did she say?"

"Not much. I took her by surprise with a sudden 'Hi, here's Daddy!' routine. She sounded adorable, a real little person."

"She is, wait'll you see her."

I told Lisa about my conversation with Colonel Dwyer and my doctor, about the do-not-disturb sign and Thompson Hall and the colonel's promise to get me released for the night. When I finished she said, "Eddie, if that's the way they work it, maybe that's what we should do."

It wasn't what I wanted to hear her say. "Lisa, I want to

get out of here, I want to go home with you and see Lauri. I even half-expected you to bring her here."

"She's still with Mother."

"Oh, I thought you'd be picking her up."

"No, she didn't say that, did she?"

"No, I just—"

"What *did* my mother say?"

"Not much, it was one of those quick jumbled-up long-distance calls—why?"

"Didn't she tell you Lauri was staying with her for a while? I'm starting this new job and it seemed easier."

"No, I thought it was just while you were on a vacation. You mean she's living with her?"

"Only for a while. It does save money that way, Eddie. Otherwise I'd have to have someone full time to look after her."

"Oh ..." I cleared our shrimp cocktails away, took the covers off our steaks and the vegetable dishes. "More champagne?"

"Yes, please."

I filled our glasses. We seemed ill at ease with each other. Something I hadn't anticipated at all. But then I thought— five years! Five years, that was a large gap to fill, actually a much longer time than we'd ever spent together. I got an idea to jolly things up. "Wait here, I'll be right back."

"What—where are you going?" There was almost panic in her voice.

"Just to get something, I'll be right back. Hey, don't worry, I'm not going back overseas again!"

I went to my room and fetched the presents I'd bought in the Philippines. I carried them back to the lounge and gave them to her. "Merry Christmas—let's see, which year? Let's make it Christmas 1971."

"Eddie, you shouldn't have, you're the one who's been away. I should have presents for you, but I didn't know until last night that—" She looked down at her plate. "I didn't even know if you were alive." Looking back up at me she said, "Eddie, not one letter from you in five whole years, not one!"

"I know, but I couldn't, they wouldn't let me." I wanted to keep it light. "Open them, go ahead, the one who's been away is the one who's supposed to bring presents. So I've had this fantastic all-expense-paid trip to the Far East and I've brought you back some souvenirs. Go ahead, open them."

She opened the box with the necklace first, held it up and, instead of smiling, frowned. "Eddie, it's beautiful, but it's real jade, it's—it must have been terribly expensive."

"Money's no problem, you like it?"

"Yes, it's beautiful. Put it on me."

I stood behind her, arranging the necklace and hooking the clasp. The fresh clean smell of her hair got to me. Instant desire to bed down, not so much for the sex of it, but to discover the essential feel of her, to establish direct contact. We seemed to be filtered through to each other, like there was a layer of something, gauze, between us, thin, but there nevertheless. I wanted to dispel it. When I'd finished adjusting the necklace, she reached back and took my hand, holding it alongside her neck and leaning her cheek against it. "Thank you. Eddie."

There, that was more like my Lisa. "Open the rest."

"Oh, Eddie, what a gorgeous robe—kimono! It's absolutely stunning."

It was a pretty one, all orange and gold with flecks of green. "Damned clever those Japanese. The other's just perfume, don't bother now, your food'll get cold."

"All right. And thank you, Eddie, they're lovely gifts."

"That's only the beginning, stick with me, I'll have you plastered in diamonds." I noticed her glass was almost empty again. "Hey, my baby's got a taste for champagne, I'll have to keep you in diamonds."

She leaned back in her chair, sighed and said expansively, "What the hell, we're celebrating. I'd like to get a little high. Right?" She flashed me one of her full dazzlers. For the first time she sounded like the old Lisa, open, direct and peppy.

My heart warmed to her. I filled our glasses again, emptying the bottle. "There, we killed that one off."

"Good," she said, cocking her head at me. "Eddie, I can't tell you how good you look. I'm proud of you." She lifted her glass in a toast. "I am."

We drank, there was a knock on the door and Sergeant Beagles stuck his head in. "Hey, come in." I realized he hadn't even met Lisa yet. I introduced them, explained about him being my sponsor, and they exchanged hello's.

"Eddie, I got good news. Colonel Dwyer said to tell you it's okay for you to go home tonight."

"Good news, that's the best news yet!"

"But he says please don't louse him up, he's gone out on a limb, so be back here to start your physical by nine o'clock."

"No problem, I'll be here. Scout's honor. Pull up a chair, sit down, have some cold soggy French fries."

He held up a hand. "Oh, no, after five years, are you kidding? See you in the morning." He said a quick good-bye to Lisa and was gone.

"Isn't that great, Maw says I get to go out—" I laughed. "I can even sleep over, now if only Dad'll lend me the car."

Lisa did not respond the way I thought she would. She looked distracted. As I was about to ask why, she said, "Eddie, if he's gone out on a limb, maybe we should stay here. I wouldn't mind, really."

"Lisa! No, you heard him, it's all right. Why would you—I want to get away from the army. I want to see our apartment. Hey, where is it? I don't even know where we live."

"Hyde Street, the twelve-hundred block."

"Good, we'll pick up another bottle of champagne and—do we have a fireplace?"

"No."

"The hell with it, we'll fake it."

"Eddie . . . ?"

"What?"

"The only thing, I've got a roommate, I share it."

"Oh . . . well, send her out to the movies. Don't you have two bedrooms?"

"No, just one, we share it. I'd have asked her to stay with friends but she came down with a miserable case of the flu, got the trots and all that."

"How come you share a place?"

"Rents are expensive here now, Eddie, not like when you left. The city's expensive, it's cheaper sharing."

"Yes, but you've been working and you've been getting all my pay regularly, haven't you?"

"Of course, but I've been sending money to my mother for Lauri and I've been out of work for about three months."

"I thought she'd just gone to stay with her?"

"No, she's been with her for a while now."

"Oh, well—" Suddenly we were acting like an old married

couple, dickering over the kitchen money. "Listen, I know what we'll do."

"What?"

"Let's go to the Fairmont or the Mark Hopkins and get a terrific room with a terrific view and live it up, for God's sake. What about it?"

Pleased, she broke into a smile. "Could we? Oh, yes, let's do that!"

"Good, it's done."

Then, out of the blue: "Eddie, those hotels are so expensive, though. Maybe we should—"

"Expensive! Lisa, we haven't seen each other in over five years, I don't care if it costs five hundred dollars for three hours. You never used to worry about money, now you keep talking about how much everything costs."

"Everything does!"

"All right, so it does. But, my God, that's not what I want to hear about, not just yet. Let's enjoy for a couple of days before we start making out budgets!" I'd raised my voice, I was close to shouting. Lisa looked down at her plate. "I'm sorry, I didn't mean to shout."

She stood up from the table, reached out and took my hand. "No, you're right, we'll go, and we'll make a night of it."

I stood up beside her. "Lisa?"

"Yes."

"Were you nervous, seeing me again?"

"Yes—weren't you?"

"No, not until I noticed you were." She smiled at me. "Let's not be nervous with each other. I love you."

She leaned forward; we embraced and kissed, our first real kiss.

The door opened and the orderly stepped in; we automatically unclinched.

"Oh, shit," he said.

Lisa and I laughed, so did he.

# 26

The suite at the Fairmont—no rooms available, only two suites left—was pure luxury, outrageously expensive, and to me, at the time, worth every cent. The view faced the harbor, overlooking Fisherman's Wharf, where we'd first met, looking out beyond to Alcatraz, Angel Island, the lights of Sausalito, extending over to include the Golden Gate Bridge.

We stood gazing out the sitting-room window, each holding a glass of champagne, stood there for a long while watching a solid comber of fog roll in from the ocean, like one of those giant waves you see in slow-motion surfing pictures of Hawaii. Coming in low, lower than eye level on the sixteenth floor of the hotel, soon it had wiped out all sight of the Golden Gate Bridge. It moved toward us, obliterating lights, hills, buildings—everything in its path. It was hypnotizing to watch.

I switched the glass to my left hand and put my arm around Lisa. She moved into me closer. In that instant such a feeling of well-being and warmth swept over me my thoughts perversely flashed to Vin. A sharp twinge of guilt that I was experiencing this, while he lay rotting away in foreign ground. I shuddered.

"What?" Lisa asked.

"Nothing," I said, squeezing her closer to me.

"Someone walk over your grave?"

"I guess." *Not my grave* . . . Stop it, I ordered myself, taking a quick gulp of champagne.

"Were you frightened over there?"

"No, not really frightened, a lot of other things, but not frightened. Well, yes, sometimes during the bombing raids. Yes, then."

"You're so grown up now. You seem so—just grown up."

I laughed. "I should hope."

"You were such a—almost a boy when we met. Your own boy, spunky and all that, but a boy."

We played a round of let's remember, stretching back to our meeting and early courtship, until the fog had advanced to within several hundred yards of our window; it seemed to have raised in its travels and was now even with us.

"My God, look at that," I said.

"Yes, it's going to hit us soon."

"To the fog." We clinked glasses and drank.

Lisa hiccuped and put a hand to her chest. "I must be feeling the champagne."

"Good." I put my arms around her once more and we stood very close, watching while the fog smashed into the window with great eerie quiet, then swirled in a downdraft until there was no view at all, no outside world, nothing but us in that suite in the Fairmont Hotel.

I turned to her, we put our glasses on the sill, and we kissed and kissed and kissed. I was achingly erect and there were such dear little sounds coming from Lisa as we pressed our bodies together. At that instant I felt so in control of her, of life in general—yet so out of control of my passion.

Split controls. She reached down and took hold of me, fondling me during a long series of kisses. More sounds, then a larger, longer moan of pleasure from her.

"Yes," I said, feeling the faint beginnings of dangerous pulsations and quickly pulling away from her, laughing. "Oh, careful, be careful!"

"Were you that . . . ?"

"Yes."

"Good."

"Yes, but let's make it last."

"Oh, yes," she said.

I spun away from her, galumphing clumsily away in a large circle to the center of the room. "Oh, God! Oh, God! Oh, *God*! I can't believe I'm here. *We're* here! Why don't you get into your kimono?"

"Yes, I will." She went into the bedroom, quickly came back to retrieve her glass and disappeared again.

I turned on the radio and found music on a good FM station. Refilling my glass, I thought how quickly it would happen the first time, no matter how long we prolonged the event, no matter the foreplay or lack of it or whatever controls I could muster, it would be quick.

For a moment I thought of going into the bedroom and unleashing the first—almost perfunctory—orgasm, having done with the pressure of it, to clear the way for the intensive act of true lovemaking. There was no problem satisfying myself, not after five years, but I so wanted to satisfy her. To thrill her, to—in a way—recapture her.

For whatever reason I decided not to. Perhaps it was the state of euphoria I was enveloped by. Yes, I was in a state of euphoria. I took a drink, faced the mushroom soup outside the window and told it, "I am not in a state of grace. I am in a state of high euphoria!"

"What, Eddie?" This, from the bedroom.

"Nothing, just talking to myself. I think I'm getting punchy."

When she came out of the bedroom she was barefoot and completely lovely in the kimono.

"God, I could eat you up. And I don't mean that as a figure of speech."

"Eddie!"—as if she were shocked.

*"Elissa!"* (Her formal name.)

She giggled and there was a slight weave to her walk as she moved across the room to fill her glass. I was getting a kick out of it. Her back was to me as she poured a full glass of champagne, then drank several long gulps as if it was water. She coughed, put a hand up to her mouth, wheeled around and faced me. "Eddie—let's go to bed *now*."

There was urgency in her voice, close to a panicky look in her green eyes. The change in attitude from her entrance into the room was so abrupt, she had me stumped.

"Please! Right now."

"All right," I said, then jokingly added, with an aw-shucks snap of my fingers, "if I *have* to!"

She didn't react, only walked toward me, stumbled, spilled a bit of her drink. I steadied her, took her hand to lead her into the bedroom. Two, three steps only and she pulled her hand away. I heard a little catch-cry in her throat as she burst into tears, turning away from me and stepping back into the sitting room.

"Lisa, what is it? Lisa . . . ?" I followed her, put a hand on

her shoulder. She jerked away from me. "Lisa, you're not—
not nervous about us going to bed, are you?"

Laugher mixed with her sobs. Then: "God, no! But
that's—that's the only thing I'm *not* nervous about!" Her
voice was strident now. She kept turning away from me as I
tried to come around in front of her, so I could catch her expression.

"Lisa, are you a little drunk, is that—"

"Drunk!" she shouted. Now she turned around to face me.
Her eyes were red and watery. She had me totally confused.
"I wish I was—yes, a little, but I couldn't get really drunk if
I swallowed a whole still! Drunk!" she repeated, then
laughed. "It's not for lack of trying. I had three before I got
to the hospital, they barely touched me."

She stood in front of the window, the off-white-gray mass
of fog forming a nimbus behind her, indirectly streaked
through by other lights in windows above and below us. I
knew there was trouble now. The moment I acknowledged it
I berated myself for being so thick. I might have known all
wasn't exactly right, but still I hadn't owned up to things
being—wrong. Euphoria was slipping away fast.

Lisa sighed and shook her head. I stared at her, waiting for
whatever it was she had for me. When she focused again on
me, she only did so for a moment; then, glancing down at the
glass in her hand, she said, "Why are you looking at me like
that?"

I couldn't reply because the sight of her—slumped there in
front of the window, holding her drink, barefoot in the
kimono—so struck me; she looked like some hotel guest
who'd been routed out of her room and down into the lobby
by fire. The stamp of distress was on her.

"Eddie . . . ?"

"I guess you have something to tell me." She didn't reply,
only kept staring down into her glass. "Don't you?" I asked.

"Yes."

"So . . . tell me." I wondered if she knew about my
mother's stroke; not that that had anything to do with her
news. I simply wondered if she knew. I gathered she didn't or
she would have said something earlier.

She glanced up at me finally. "Oh, Eddie, I wanted so
much for us to go to bed. I still do. But that would have been
cheating."

"How cheating?"

She gave a little toss of her head. "It just would."

"Why don't you sit down?" I laughed, not a real laugh, more of a snort. "I suppose I'm the one who should be sitting. It's the receiver of bad tidings who should be seated, isn't it?" I sat on the sofa. "There, all set."

"Don't be flip, Eddie, it's not a joke."

"No, I'm sure it isn't." She remained standing there. "Go ahead."

She took another drink, hunched her shoulders. "I wrote you about—things, but I gather you never got it. I wish you had."

Nerves brought on an attack of impatience. "Lisa, let's not talk about 'things'—tell me what you have to tell me."

Eyes averted, she told me. "I'm living with someone, not a woman, a man." She glanced at me for my reaction. I didn't say anything; she seemed to be awaiting a response. I had nothing to say, except to myself: two down, one to go. "Eddie, I had no idea when or even if you'd ever be coming home. No letters, no official word, no nothing. I had no idea if you were even alive, can't you understand that?"

"I haven't said I couldn't understand anything."

"Oh, Christ, I've never hated having to tell anyone anything as much as this. I feel dirty and cheap and mean and yet I—" She stopped for a moment. "Yet, in a way, I don't. I didn't start out to—I didn't look to have an affair, it just happened. Christmas, two years ago, and I was thinking about you, wondering if you were alive, if you were, where you were, how you were. I went to a Christmas party and Jay was there."

"Jay?"

"Jay, I told you about him, the man I lived with before we—"

"Oh, Jay, who was on drugs?"

"Yes, he still was, but he was trying to get off it, trying to pull himself together. Eddie, whether you believe me or not, I hadn't been to bed with anyone since you left. Oh, I'd gone out to dinner with a few fellows I'd met through work, gone to the opera once and the theater a few times. But that was all. That Christmas I was feeling low and blue and—"

"Oddly enough I was feeling a little low myself that Christ-

mas." She glanced down, I certainly had the faculty for making her look down. "Coincidence, that thousands of miles
apart we were both feeling the same, huh?"

The room was so silent. I was being petty but I couldn't
help myself. I vowed not to be. She moved to a chair, took a
drink and sat down. "Shall I go on?"

"Yes." But suddenly I had something to say. "You know,
Lisa, whether you believe it or not I never thought much
about you going to bed with other men, it never really
worried me. Which is strange, someone as attractive as you.
But in all my fantasies, that was never one of them. Isn't it
wild I didn't brood about that, but I didn't. Funny, how that
works. You love someone so much you can't imagine them
with anyone else. That's one-sided thinking. Now that I do
think about it, I couldn't much blame you. Five years is a
long time."

"You're not being sarcastic now, are you?"

"No."

*"Gracias."* She took a deep, inhaling breath. "We did go to
bed and although, of course, I thought about you, of what
you'd—but I didn't have too much of a conscience, maybe
because it wasn't someone new, it was a man I'd known before I ever met you. I don't suppose that's mitigating circumstances, but—we began seeing each other. I'd moved back
from Sacramento and I was sharing a place with a free-lance
artist, which worked out well because Joanne worked at the
apartment most of the time and I could often leave Lauri
with her during the day.

"Jay said if I'd stick with him, he'd straighten himself out,
get off all the stuff he'd gotten into. I can't say that's the only
reason. I didn't just decide to turn into Florence Nightingale.
I was lonely and as time went on and I never heard from you
or anything more about you, nothing, I got to thinking
that—maybe you were dead. And that if you were—"

"You were never notified I was dead, were you?"

"I was never notified of anything, except in March of 1968
that you were missing in action during the Tet Offensive,
later on one other communiqué that you might have been
taken prisoner at Hue, were maybe being held prisoner in the
jungle, only because you were missing and no one had found
your body! My God, what is that to go on?"

"But you wrote me, sent packages?"

"On the chance you were *somewhere*. But we never knew, your mother never knew either. We kept in touch up until a little over a year ago. Then, I suppose it just seemed hopeless to both of us and we simply stopped."

It was apparent she didn't know of Bebe's illness. For a split second I thought of dropping it on her, but actually I was feeling some sort of sorry for her.

"Jay pulled himself together. He was marvelous to Lauri, he adored her and she got used to him and—"

"—Adored him?"

"Yes. But I've always told her about you, she has your picture, our wedding picture, she's always heard about her father." She sipped from her glass, sighed and went on. "By this time Jay had a job working in a bookstore down on Geary Street and when Joanne moved to Seattle—her fiancé was stationed there—Jay moved in. I had a part-time Mexican woman to help out with Lauri and I'd been saving money, what with my job and your pay, and—and—" She was in tears again. "Oh, Christ," she sobbed, "if I've ever paid for my sins, I'm paying for them now. Oh, God, Eddie—I don't know . . ."

I only looked at her; I wanted to help but I felt incapable of going to her and physically comforting her. She put her glass down and sat there, sniffling, trying to regain control. "Come on," I said in as easy a voice as I could muster, "it can't be that bad."

"Oh, Eddie!"

I even managed a smile. "We must have gotten to the worst of it."

This brought an anguished little cry from her that indicated perhaps we hadn't. She bolted from the chair, mumbled "Handkerchief" and hurried into the bedroom.

I sat there in the midst of a stupefying mess I had in no way anticipated. How could I have been fool enough not to entertain the prospect that I might not come home to a heady kettle of pure unadulterated bliss surrounded by flowers and candy hearts! I managed to direct my anger away from Lisa toward myself. Because my life had stopped for five years I'd assumed hers had. I'd suspended her in limbo, put her in a pretty gold locket, snapped her shut and held her close to my idiotic romantic-assed heart, only to be released when I was released.

All I could offer myself in the way of consolation was: Welcome home, Schmuck!

# 27

When Lisa returned, she sat down, then immediately stood up and paced back and forth. The possible worst of it occurred to me. "Do you want—" I'd been about to ask if she wanted a divorce, if that was it, but she cut me off, going on in a rush of words to spill it out.

"The bookstore he worked in was established, it did very well. About a year and a half ago, Jay heard of a stationery store-card shop on Polk Street right near where we live. The woman was retiring, going out of business. Eddie, it seemed like such a good idea, Polk Street is jumping now, it's a sort of miniature Greenwich Village, restaurants, movies, coffee houses, all sorts of shops. I'd saved six thousand dollars, it was Jay's plan to carry books, records, posters, all sorts of novelties and gifts. He's very personable, it seemed like such a good investment. We took a lease on it and he worked like a dog to make a go of it, night and day. But—I don't know—it had a great look to it and—" She shook her head. "It never really made money; oh, we broke even now and then, but the rent was high and—for the last six months I quit my job and worked there with him, so we wouldn't have to pay extra help, but—"

"You lost it?"

"We went broke, we closed it two months ago. That's why the phone was disconnected, it was a messy time, we still had some creditors after us." Now it was my turn to look down at the floor. Lisa stood up and came to me. "Eddie, I swear to

God I'll pay you back, so will Jay, we will, we've talked about it. It was your money, but you see I thought it would be such a good investment. I thought I'd be *making* money and when you came back—"

"And if I *didn't* come back, did you talk about that, too?"

"Eddie—"

"You've made a point of saying you didn't think I would, so you must have discussed the possibility?" She backed away from me, stood there without saying anything, only shaking her head. It had gotten messier than I imagined it would. I had alternate periods of wanting to comfort her and wanting to slap her. Yet I knew she was leveling with me, at least she was doing that and it wasn't pleasurable for her.

Finally she spoke. "I just didn't know, I didn't know what to expect, I was just trying to get through what had happened with the store."

"What do you know now? What happens now?"

She turned and walked away, almost shouting, "I don't know, I don't know!"

"Terrific!" I got up from the sofa and headed for the champagne. "Let's drink to that!"

"Eddie, please don't be—"

"What—mad? I hope you weren't going to say that, don't be mad."

"No, I wasn't. I don't know what I was going to say, I don't know anything."

"Like I said, let's drink to that." I got her glass, filled it and held it out to her. "Go ahead, take it, we've got to drink to something and as far as I can figure out—that's about all there is to drink to." She took the glass, I picked mine up. "There," I toasted her, "to not knowing."

We drank; she spoke in a soft voice. "I don't blame you for being, for feeling—whatever you're feeling."

I walked over and looked out the window into the fog. Looking into the fog, that was certainly appropriate. Now the sadness of the situation crept over me, not my sadness, the sadness of us. Neither of us spoke for a long time. After a while I heard her moving over—soft padding on the Fairmont's expensive carpeting—behind me. I was hoping she wouldn't touch me, but she did, placed a hand very lightly on my shoulder, just let it rest there. Oddly enough, it felt good. I was not pleased with myself for letting it feel good.

She spoke a variation of a line from the first evening we met: "Do you think we should go to bed—or not?"

"I don't know . . ."

"I think we've gotten enough mileage from that one."

"What one?"

"*I don't know.*"

"Oh, yes . . . true."

We stood there for what seemed ages; I tried to unblur my mind and reach some sort of perspective. It wasn't easy. After a while I said, "Maybe we should have gone to bed first, now—going to bed, not going to bed, seems almost anticlimactic. Not to make a pun."

She took her hand away. "Don't think it wasn't in my mind, don't think I didn't want to. The minute I saw you step out of the elevator, looking so—like my Eddie. But then, after it was all over and we were lying there all exhausted and happy, the idea of nuzzling into you and saying 'By the way, I have something to tell you'—I couldn't imagine that."

Her voice sounded like the old Lisa, not constricted any more. There was even a trace of humor in what she said, as if the telling had unburdened her. It triggered something in me, not that I was loath to let her off the hook, but nothing was really solved, the ends were dangling. "What do you intend to do now that I'm back?"

"That's more or less up to you."

I wheeled around to face her. "Up to me? It's too late for it to be up to me now. It's done." *Oh, Eddie, let's finish with the talk, get to the obligatory question.* So I did: "Do you love him?" She closed her eyes and before she could answer I said, "I wouldn't think you'd live with a man you didn't love, it wouldn't make much sense."

"Yes, I love him. I love you, too. I loved him because you weren't here to love."

"Those are the breaks. What do the three of us do, this love-team, all set up housekeeping together, you and Jay Mondays, Wednesdays and Fridays, you and me—"

"We'll work it out, we'll—unless you want a divorce." When I didn't reply, she said, "I wouldn't blame you if you did. That's what I meant by—up to you."

Suddenly it all rushed forward and hit me. "Could I have another couple of hours to think about it? Christ—" I looked at my watch, it was twenty to twelve. "I've been back, not more than six hours and—oh, shit!"

"Yes," she said, "I know, shit and more shit!" she said it with strength, snapped me out of the beginning nasty pressing of tears, snapped me out of it further when she announced in a firm voice, "I'm going to bed. Why don't you"—her voice dropped down, softly matter-of-fact—"just simply fuck me!"

"Yes," I said, looking around at our grand suite and nodding my head. "We've hired the hall. Why don't I?"

Walking to the bedroom, she began undoing the buttons of the kimono. I followed her, yanking the shirt out of my pants and unbuckling my belt. She was in bed in a matter of seconds; it did not take me long to join her, dropping down beside her and throwing my arms around her.

I was surprised, happily surprised, that within moments of our bodies touching, I was ready. I'd anticipated, because of the state my head was in—not good!—somewhat of an effort at the warmup. Not at all. If there had been, it would have provided my lovemaking with obligatory tenderness. Now there was no thought of tenderness as I kissed her and ran my hand over her body.

It was my intention to simply and energetically—fuck her. To screw her and myself into a near-coma of exhaustion that might give us release from all the messy talk we'd been through, to give us the relaxation to clear the air. Also, looking back now, I suppose I wanted to punish her. I know lovemaking shouldn't be punishment. Still . . .

I found I hadn't forgotten, for a moment or a touch, her body or the ways in which she responded. As if it had barely been five days, let alone five years. I loved the sounds she made during our kisses, the smothered lostness of them. Before long I had spread her legs and swung on top of her, arching up and then guiding myself with my hand and thrusting down inside her, forcing down all the way with enormous pressure. A cry of pain—not unpleasing to my ears—as she pulled her mouth abruptly away from me.

"Eddie—wait!"

"No." I heard myself saying strange detached words that didn't sound like me: "Jesus, now you're going to get it!" And arched my buttocks up and away for more.

"Eddie, please—my God!" There was such fright, such terror in her voice, that I stopped.

"What?"

"Please, please go easy." Her hands came up, bracing against my chest to prevent me from coming back down into her again. "It's been more than two weeks, I—"

"Good!" I shouted down at her.

"Please, be very gentle at first, please!"

She'd never been overly gentle herself. "Why gentle? I don't feel gentle!"

"We have to, at first." The bedside lamp shone on her face, contorted into an awful wince. It was unattractive and I wanted to erase it by engaging it in passion; I started to press into her again.

Again she screamed. "No, Eddie—don't!" Then she repeated, "We have to go easy, at first."

"Why so easy? We were never all that easy."

She moved a hand up to my face, caressing me and at the same time pulling my head down alongside hers. She spoke softly into my ear. "Darling, I don't want to go easy, but—just at first. I had a—a little female operation two weeks ago and—"

She felt me tighten and start to pull away.

"Oh, everything's all right, but this is the first time since and—"

My mind leaped right to it. I didn't want to but I did. "A little female operation? Not an abortion, you didn't have an abortion?"

"No, no, just a little female disorder." I pulled out of her, withdrawing as gently as I could. She winced again. "No, don't do—" But it was done. She searched my face for my expression, searched too closely and too anxiously. I only stared down at her. "No, it wasn't a—no, Eddie, not what you're thinking."

I knew she was lying. The capper, this was the capper. Jesus, what had they done? Eddie's coming home, wheel out the strokes and abortions and bankruptcies! "Yes, it was, you had an abortion! Didn't you?" I raised my hand to slap her, not really slap her but to scare the truth out of her. "Didn't you?"

Flinching, she cried out, "Yes—yes, I did!"

I was up off the bed and away from her. "Oh, Jesus Christ, how beautiful! Oh, Christ Almighty, your timing is fan-fuck-ing-tastic superb!"

"Eddie, it was—we caught it early—it was only—oh, Eddie!" Starting to cry again.

I turned back to face her, stepping quickly toward the bed. "Don't cry, stop it! I swear to Christ if you cry—I'll kill you!"

I stopped her tears. She ducked back, pulled in with a deep inhaling breath and spat out her words: "Yes, I had an abortion because I didn't want to have a baby, not his, not anyone's baby. Is that so terrible? It happens to thousands—millions of women. It was an accident anyway."

I stood looking down at her, disarrayed, clutching the covers to her. "Accident? *You're* an accident!"

"Eddie!"

"You are, I came home to an accident!" I had to laugh. "*We're* an accident, yes, I'm one, too. Why shouldn't I be?"

"I'm sorry you think it's such a horror. It's not, what should I have done, bring an unwanted baby into this gorgeous world? It's bad enough to bring a wanted one into it."

"It may not be a horror, but I'll tell you one thing: it's one spectacular turn-off. Especially announced during flagrante not-so-delecto." I could only sigh and shake my head. "Timing, Lisa—timing!" I picked up my shorts from the floor and stepped into them, feeling her stickiness on me, already drying. "I suppose we had the—quintessential quickie, wouldn't you say?"

Barely audible: "We could still . . ."

"Lisa!"

"It was only—you were being so rough."

Abortion has always given me the shudders; it's not that I think it's wrong; it's just the awful physical, mental picture of it. "Sorry, I didn't know you'd just been scraped out."

"How nicely you put it."

"And how nicely you deliver news. You sure that's all? No other little goodies?" She remained silent. "Lauri doesn't have leukemia or anything like that?"

"Eddie, stop it!"

I thought for a moment. "Yes, you're right, Lisa, let's stop it." I glanced around; how stale this beautiful overdecorated cushy bedroom had become. The air was dead in it. "Yes, I think that's it for one night. I couldn't possibly think of an encore to top it."

I gathered up my pants and shirt, walked out of the bedroom and closed the door.

When Lisa was dressed she came out into the living room. If I looked at her with anything, it was with a sort of detached compassion. Even cold compassion, if there is such a thing. Like someone I'd heard about who'd been through rough times, but only someone I'd been told about, not anyone I'd actually experienced. My energy was shot, I didn't get up, just remained sitting in my chair.

"Are you staying?" she asked.

"For a while."

"I'm sorry—for everything, Eddie. You must *know* that."

"Me, too."

I could barely mouth those simple words; I was out of words and out of thoughts.

"What should we—"

"I don't know."

"Let me know . . ." Then: "You'll want to see Lauri?"

"I suppose."

Lisa put on her coat, picked up her purse.

"You can get home all right?" I asked.

"Yes."

She left.

# 28

I don't know how long I sat there, staring out into the fog, until there was a click and the door opened. The night maid, a plump pleasant middle-aged black woman, stuck her head in. "Just checking, can I turn the beds down now?"

"No, thanks."

"Everything all right?" That brought a grin to my face. "Anything I can get you?"

YES, A GUN! sprang to mind. "No, thanks," I repeated, covering my mouth with my hand.

She'd barely ducked back out and shut the door when I burst into hysterical laughter at the incredible cleverness, the devastating wit of YES, A GUN! Rocking back and forth in my chair, I finally had to stand, I was laughing so hard. When I could speak, I spoke to myself. "Oh, Eddie, you must be in some kind of trouble!"

Now that I was on my feet, I thought briefly of going out on the town, tying one on, beating up the natives, getting laid, breaking a few large plate-glass windows.

I didn't have it in me; I was bushed. Picking up the phone, I left a call for seven-thirty and went to bed. Oddly enough, I fell into a heavy sleep. Deep depression is Seconal to me, always has been. But I suffered from an early awakening, a little before six. My mind began maneuvering me through the nasty maze of sorting out I'd expected to muddle through at bedtime. No more sleeping, I knew that.

The fog was no longer so thick but it was still there, in drifts and pockets and long streaks. Again I sat in a chair in the sitting room, now watching the dawn creep over the city.

Lisa had closed the magic circle. Vin, Bebe and now Lisa had closed it, formed the ring. Circle—circus! I felt cold and hard, felt a little cold nugget hardening inside me. It could have been my soul, if we have souls.

I decided to walk to Letterman, quite a walk, maybe three-four miles. I had the time and I wanted to get the feel of the city again, of civilization. Last night had not been civilized.

After checking out of the hotel, I found myself right at the corner of Powell Street, with its cable-car mechanism clacking along underground, the exact place I'd first set eyes on Lisa. I walked down Powell, docking the remains of the foggy night that dripped off the eaves of the buildings. Following Powell most of the way, I cut over at the bottom of the hill, ending up at Fisherman's Wharf and searching out the railing where I'd finally caught up with her. I stood there, looking out over the small-scruffy fishing boats with their tangle of nets and ropes and odd gear.

Flashed on me that I was holding a brief memorial service

for my marriage. That didn't hit home with any great jolt; it occurred calmly. Coldly, too. It wasn't anything I consciously decided, more like a decision *handed* me.

I accepted it, walking along the wharf area, heading toward Letterman. Too painful and messy to sort out the paths we could take in attempting to straighten it out. Mostly messy. She was not the girl I'd married, not any more, except for her physical attractiveness. And for that I softly cursed her. I was probably not the man she married either.

Still, the dream of our marriage, the memory of it, had been so strong, so tangible for all these years—hard to believe in one short night it was ended. Perhaps the memory of Lisa was the best part, the essence of it. It served in getting me through five long years. It was to be praised, she was to be thanked for that.

If only we hadn't had a child. Complication. I could face the complication and deal with it. But not the child herself. Might be best not to see her. She had no memory of me, why kindle one up for her? She would stay with her mother, anyway; certainly Lisa would provide her with a father, whether it be—this Jay, or not.

Decisions. Thank God, I was able to make them, instead of stew-braining around in a muddle. Felt good about that.

Found myself wondering, against my will, what Jay looked like, was he good-looking, was he a good lover for Lisa?

Stop it. No matter.

All proving, as I walked down the hill leading to the Presidio area and those immaculately kept two-story Spanish townhouses on the flat facing the bay, that decisions are not quite that simple; they have tentacles, loose ends, but they can still be made to work. And stick.

Couldn't they?

Another decision: hollow as I was feeling, I would not give the army the opportunity to keep me from my convalescent leave; I would get through my physicals and mentals and debriefing in record time. I would be a model P.O.W. To the observer, at least. Even if I had to make a game of it. Yes, a game might be the way to get through it.

Bebe was my target. I wanted to get back to see her as soon as possible. I could even, in these last few years, understand her drinking more, not *like* it any better, but certainly understand it. Because life was infinitely more complicated than I'd ever suspected.

Christ in hell, wasn't it?

Still, as I checked in at the gate leading onto the grounds of the Presidio Army Base I was complimenting myself on the way I'd pulled myself together on this early morning walk, stacked all my problem-blocks in a tidy row and was dealing with them. Yes, I told myself, walking along the side of one of those low wooden barracks built during World War II, wasn't I being sensible and grown-up and mature.

Laughter and shouts and the next thing I knew I was slammed into hard by a scrawny little private in fatigues rounding the corner of the barracks. Running and looking back over his shoulder, he was being chased by a buddy, the two of them playing a game of grab-ass. I got knocked back hard, hitting the edge of the building; I managed not to fall down but the collision sent the private sprawling to the ground next to me. Before I even knew what was happening, I was after him, hauling him up by the chest of his fatigues and slamming him up against the side of the barracks. Slamming him hard and screaming every curse word and phrase I'd ever heard in his frightened face.

Total blind rage as I kept slamming him while his buddy, a more substantial guy, attempted to come to his rescue. The minute I felt hands touch me I wheeled, letting go of my first target and knocking the second one ass-over-teakettle to the ground. I caught myself with my foot swung back to kick him in the side when he cried out "Jesus—Jesus—no, don't—help!" The same terror I'd put in the first one's eyes was now in his as he doubled up his arms and drew up his legs to protect himself and lay there, cringing on the ground.

Silence now. None of us spoke but I could hear my breathing, my gulps for breath. I walked quickly away. I thought for a few steps I might fall down myself, my legs were shaking so. It was another five-minute walk to the main hospital, and even when I got there I had to wait outside several minutes until I could stop trembling and regulate my breathing to normal.

Great, Eddie, you're doing fine. Just fine!

When I saw Colonel Dwyer mid-morning I thanked him for going out on a limb and arranging my night out.

"I trust it was worth it," he grinned.

"Yes, it was."

"That's an absolute stunner you have there."

"Yes," I agreed, taking his cue. "She's a stunner."

I knew he'd find out sooner or later, knew everyone at the hospital would, but as far as I was concerned—later was better.

That morning I began my physicals. Over the next week I was put through every possible test. It was V.I.P. treatment all the way. The small group of us at Letterman were treated with kid gloves; if we were celebrities in the civilian world, we were even greater celebrities to the army and staff of the hospital. We were each one of their own; we'd come through for the home team; we'd shown we could pass through hell and come out the other side.

That first afternoon I had my introductory meeting with my psychiatrist, Major Seymour Friedman, a gentle bespectacled owl-faced man in his mid-forties. This first session was devoted to general background, getting to know each other.

It was after this, on my way to my first debriefing with army intelligence, that an envelope was delivered to me. Inside was a large photograph of Lisa and Lauri taken in the country. Lauri, a most enchanting grin on her face, sat on top of a tree stump; Lisa stood behind, smiling down at her, arms resting on her shoulders, hands interlocked in front of Lauri's chest. Lisa had signed the photograph: "We love you."

There was an accompanying note.

> "Dear Eddie,
>
> Of course, I didn't sleep. Didn't because of the hurt I dealt you. Still, in a way, I'm glad I told you everything. Any other way would have been—there couldn't have been any other way. The phone will be connected this afternoon or early morning. Please call me. As soon as Jay's temperature (103) drops, even a little, he will go to stay with friends and I will bring Lauri into town. I won't go into further apologies in this—you must know.
>
> Love,
> Lisa"

No denying the picture of the two of them messed up my thinking and shook the resolves made on my walk to the hospital that morning.

Three army intelligence officers—in civilian clothes, which surprised me—arrived at my room on the tenth floor at two-thirty with all sorts of maps and photographs for me to identify. That first afternoon I told them the story of my capture, the march up to North Vietnam, the Hanoi Hilton and my eventual arrival at Bel Air.

When they'd left, after three hours, the head nurse in charge of the tenth floor, a warm, wise, concerned black major, Delores Freeman, told me I was free to go home to my wife any time I cared.

I cared, but not to go home to my wife. I cared to go in search of physical gratification on a grand scale that would sate me so completely I would be relieved of the desires that kept me thinking of Lisa every single minute, except when I was actively telling myself not to. And even then . . .

In my new uniform, lime-cologned, freshly shaved, showered and scrubbed, I set out on the town about seven in the evening.

## 29

Top of the Mark for two drinks, but no more, my point was not to get drunk. Dinner at the Jade Empress, where I gorged myself on spareribs, Peking duck and lobster Cantonese.

Then, the search. Remembering Lisa had said Polk Street was jumping, I took a cab there and strolled about until I passed the window of a tavern called Smuggler's Cove, large circular oak bar, gaslights, hanging ferns, looked like a good lively crowd inside. A blowup from a magazine article touting the bar as "the new in-place for the swinging singles crowd" was plastered on a small window near the door.

That propelled me inside, where I found one of the few vacant stools at the bar. Tables, mostly filled with dinner patrons, were in a room to the rear. There were more than a few attractive girls scattered about; the men were in their late twenties, thirties and early forties. Everyone looked to be fairly well heeled, young to middle-aged professional people. Hardly a hippie, aging or otherwise, in the group.

I'd barely ordered my drink when a guy to my right said, in a slightly fuzzy voice, "Christ, man, with those ribbons and—all that shit plastered over you, you look like you won the last two wars singlehanded!"

I was in no mood for a put-down, also I didn't particularly like his looks. Leaning toward him, I said in a low-key voice, "And you look like an asshole."

Surprisingly, this got a laugh from him. "Yeah, well maybe I am. Even so, I haven't seen a haircut like that since— Christ, I don't know when." I was winding up to let him have another when he laughed, reached over and patted my arm, saying, "No, I remember—not since Jack Armstrong!" (Our haircuts in camp were brutal; the barber at Clark Field could only tidy it up and I had the nearest thing to a crew cut he could manage.)

I withdrew my arm. "Don't touch me, I'm radioactive."

Another laugh from the asshole as the bartender put my drink down, leaned forward and said, "Hey—hey, didn't I see you on the early news?" He didn't allow time for a reply. "Yeah, yeah, sure I did, you're a P.O.W.!" Before I could make a pact and quiet him, he'd banged on the bar and announced, "Hey, we got a live P.O.W. here, goddam if we don't!"

He pumped my hand, refused payment, and all hell broke loose as heads turned my way and the guy next to me boomed out, "No shit, are you a P.O.W.?"

The bartender answered for me. "Goddam right he is, didn't I tell you? I spotted him right off, seen him on the early news, just tonight—kissing the ground, weren't you? Sure you were."

There were called-out "welcome home's," glasses raised, and a few people heading over to greet me as the man to my right held out his hand. "Je-sus, I'm sorry, man. I'm an ass-

*Richard Pryor, as Eddie Keller, an American POW in Vietnam, with his pet mouse, "Spike."*

*Eddie and his friend Vin (Ray Sharkey), fellow prisoner at the "Bel Air Country Club."*

*Eddie and Vin exchange feelings about the war and their previous lives.*

*Their meals are interrupted by constant questioning from the Viet Cong.*

*Eddie's homecoming is not quite what he expected.*

*Eddie has an unhappy reunion with his wife Lisa (Lynne Moody).*

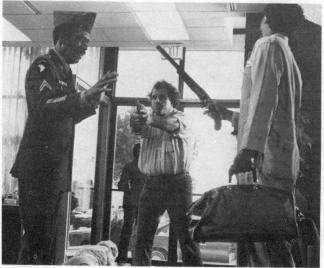

*Eddie tries to adjust to civilian life, but finds things getting complicated!*

*Eddie meets Toni (Margot Kidder).*

*Toni and Eddie get better acquainted.*

*Desperate, Eddie tries his hand at robbery.*

*Richard Pryor, star of SOME KIND OF HERO.*

hole when I drink. I apologize, will you forgive this asshole?"

"Sure," I said, extending my hand. At that, I didn't want him to get off scot-free and even though I'm not a tough guy and have never gone around looking for fights, I felt pretty secure with all the uproar going around and added, "Still, you ought to watch it, because in about two more minutes, I'd have kicked the shit out of you!"

"Je-sus, I bet you would, too. Here, shake on it."

We shook and by that time a small covey of men stood around, thumping my back, pumping my hand, asking questions. Only two girls came over and they were with two of the men. One offered her hand, saying, "You're lookin' good." The other leaned in after a while, pecked me on the cheek and said, "My brother was in Nam, two years."

We chatted a while, but her arm was linked with a tall fellow who'd already ordered another drink for me. It was getting a little thick and I was wishing the bartender hadn't been so eagle-eyed; I was also vowing never to wear my uniform out again, when I caught sight of a redheaded girl three-quarters of the way around the bar, sitting very quietly, sipping her drink and looking at me in a considered way.

When our eyes met, she acknowledged it only by the slightest change in expression, the tiniest flicker of a smile and a sort of inner nod, but nothing more, no come-on at all. Yet she kept looking at me. And as I went on talking to the group around me I could feel her eyes still on me. I checked now and then and I was right, she was looking.

It was a kick when the bartender, who had started the hub-bub, turned out to be the one to break it up, saying, "Okay, let him breathe, for Chrissake, come on, folks—back, back!"

The crowd eventually drifted away but by that time five drinks had been set down in front of me. I told the bartender that was more than enough and asked him not accept any more on my behalf. I checked the redheaded girl, still regarding me calmly. Just as the man to my right began moving in for further conversation, the stool next to her was vacated. I said a quick "Excuse me a moment," picked up two drinks and walked around the bar to sit next to her.

She didn't turn to me while I was settling down, only kept sitting there, facing front. For a few moments I thought: Oh-oh, bad move, she's not pleased to have me here. I began my usual rationalizing when things are not going my way.

Oh, well, I'd never particularly liked redheads, couldn't really remember any kind of alliance with one that had been rewarding.

Then a small sideways glance from her, followed by, "So, how's it feel to be a hero?"

There was only the slightest trace of a put-on in her voice, but it was enough to prompt my reply in a facetious whisper of enthusiasm: "Oh, Jesus Christ, it's just so exciting I can hardly keep from wetting myself!"

She laughed immediately, turned toward me and offering her glass in a toast. "Great! Hi, Fritzi Donavan here."

"Eddie Keller here."

We sipped our drinks and she laughed again. "You're funny . . ."

"That's what you think!" I replied in a flat, sinister voice.

Another laugh from her, then she looked me straight in the eye. "Oh, we're going to get along fine."

"I hope so," I told her, looking her right back.

We held the look and I knew we were a cinch. She had deep blue eyes and the kind of long red hair that is flax, not kinky, pale skin and no freckles that I could see, but the lighting was dark and she could have been wearing make-up, although if she was it was very white make-up. She was not gorgeous but she was pretty, with high cheekbones and a turned-up nose that, had it been acquiline and had her chin been more chiseled and not quite so short, would have pushed her over the top into gorgeousness.

"You don't look like a P.O.W.," she said.

"How do we look?"

"I don't know, but you don't look—well, beat-up enough. How long was it?"

"Five years."

"Five years, umm . . . no, you don't look it. How long have you been back?"

"Last night."

"Only last night?"

"Yes."

"Good lord." She gave me the same considering look I'd felt from across the bar earlier, then she smiled. "Shall we leave?"

"Sure, right now?"

"Yes, why not?"

It wasn't long before we were walking out the door, she ahead of me. The bartender called out, "Hey, Eddie, c'mere a minute."

Fritzi kept walking without even glancing behind as I said "Just a minute" and stepped over to the bar.

"Hey," he whispered, "how you fixed for money, okay?"

"Yeah, sure," I said, surprised.

"She's a hooker," he said, then seeing the expression on my face, added, "Oh, she's a great girl, but she's about the most expensive you could find, if you need money—"

"Oh, no, thanks anyway," I told him and started out, thinking: Oh, Christ, dammit to hell! I'd never been with a whore, never wanted to go with one, never imagined she *was* one and now faced getting out of it.

She stood on the sidewalk waiting for me. I was feeling annoyed with myself for being such an easy mark, for not having talked with her longer.

"Listen . . ."

She smiled and sighed. "Pat told you."

"Yes, and I—"

"Damn him. *I* wasn't even going to tell you."

"How could you—*not* have?"

"I just wouldn't have, that's how."

I felt awkward, was she telling me it was on the house for being a P.O.W.? Even if it was, I wanted no part of it. Not that I disapproved of hookers or whores, I didn't, it simply was not my thing. The professionalism turned me off, always had. Pride, too, no use hedging: adorable Eddie Keller *paying* for it! "Anyhow," I began, "I don't think we'd better—"

"What's the matter? If you're thinking about money, well, don't."

"No, it's not that."

"What is it? You were attracted to me, weren't you?"

"Yes." I gave her back the line she'd given me. "You don't look like a professional."

Smiling, she handed me *my* next line. "How do we look?"

I followed through, keeping to the script. "I don't know, but you don't look—beat-up enough."

"Touché."

We both laughed and she started to walk ahead. "No, wait," I said, "I really would rather not."

"Come have a drink with me, then."

"Okay, do you know of another place we could—"

"Yes, my place," she said, without looking at me and in such a tone I found it hard to contradict, although I was thinking of suggesting we stop at a bar instead when she added, "Let me tell you about myself."

"All right." I stepped up alongside her.

"I don't know what Pat said, not much, because you weren't there long enough, probably that I was expensive."

"Yes."

She nodded. "I am. For two reasons: I'm exceptionally good in bed and I like it. I put them backwards. I like it and that's *why* I'm good. So that's probably one reason, instead of two, huh? Anyhow, I like the boyish type, I really do. That's what attracted me to you when you first came in. I don't like the *dumb* boyish type, though. I like the bright boyish type and if you can find one with a sense of humor, all the better. You seem to have that." She looked at me and smiled. I was not smiling because she was being too analytical. I was still wanting out. Suddenly she laughed and said, "What would you have thought I did for a living?"

Her curiosity was so infectious that I laughed back at her. "I don't know, but not what you do."

"What?"

I thought of a few improbables and said, "Oh, probably a plumber or a brain surgeon."

She reached out and took my hand. "Oh, we're going to get along just fine." Abruptly she stopped walking and turned to me. "Do you want to bet we will? I know you don't think so, but my mind's made up. Do you want to bet?"

"Okay, I'll bet you a quarter."

"It's a bet."

We shook hands and suddenly the idea of me standing on a street corner sealing a bet for a quarter with a whore that I wouldn't go to bed with her for free—struck me. We continued walking as I thought: What's the big deal, so I'll have a drink with her, talk a while and probably win a quarter.

It hyped me into a good mood.

# 30

We sat in Fritzi Donovan's very attractive apartment having our drinks. Comfortable overstuffed furniture, good paintings and prints on the walls, several large green plants, a small fireplace, good music on the stereo.

She sat opposite me on a love seat. "Isn't it funny, now I suddenly feel shy with you. I suppose it's because I—well, I literally dragged you back here. I never do that, I don't go out to public places and get them. Besides, this was purely a night off, I had no idea of meeting anyone." She rubbed the edge of her drink with a finger, then looked up at me. "Tell me about being in prison camp, what was it like?"

This brought an involuntary "Ohh ..." from me, which I translated for her. "I'd rather talk about anything but that, if you don't mind." A look of disappointment. "I'll tell you about it some other time, okay? It's just too soon to get into it."

"Oh, sure."

"Is Fritzi your real name?"

"Yes, my father had a dog named Fritzi, had it since he was a kid, for eighteen years he had that dog. Fritzi died a month before I was born and my father named me Fritzi. Great name for a dog—" She laughed. "Not bad for a whore either."

"You don't really think of yourself as—a whore, do you?"

"Not really. I suppose I said that for shock value. Probably because I know you disapprove."

"I don't disapprove of it or you—it's just not for me."

"That's disapproval."

"No, it's not."

"Well, it's not *A*-pproval, let's put it that way."

"How did you happen to—"

"—Get in this line of work?"

"Yes."

She laughed. "Actually, to drive my father crazy. Isn't that funny?" I didn't laugh. "Well"—Fritzi sighed—"I guess you had to *be* there. He kicked me out of the house when I was seventeen because he was sure I'd been to bed with my boyfriend. The truth is, I hadn't. But you know those hard-hat crazy Irish Catholic types! My mother had died the year before and he just kicked me out, told me he wouldn't leave a penny of his hard-earned money to a whore, he'd leave it all to my sister. So I thought: Well, maybe I should take his cue. He's a building contractor right here in the city. It's been driving him crazy all these years. Crazy! I'm not unknown in San Francisco—among certain circles. One Father's Day I sent him a homemade card with a blowup photograph of me doing something rather bizarre to a black man. I thought he might have a stroke. No such luck, he's still around. Enough of that," she said. She looked over at me, stuck out her chin and there was pride in her voice. "Do you know how much I make a week?"

I had to smile. "No, what?"

"Not less than six hundred, sometimes a little more. And I don't work all that much."

"How much?"

"Three, four times a week, no more. I have a regular john who pays the rent and gives me two hundred a week. He lives in Los Angeles, with his wife, naturally, comes up here, oh, maybe twice a month. The other men I see are more or less regulars, too. I usually charge a hundred and fifty, sometimes only a hundred, sometimes two hundred."

She stood up and came over to refill my glass; as she took it she let out a little whoop. "My God, I'm chatty Fritzi tonight!" She went to the bar cart near the entrance to the kitchen and made us drinks. "Do you know how much that is a year—that's without taxes, too!" She laughed. "Well, it's a lot, I'll tell you. My God, why am I telling you all this? I'll tell you why, I'm trying to impress you. Imagine a P.O.W. who's been away five years, who gives every indication of being attracted to me, and then won't go to bed with me because he thinks I'm a common—"

"Ah-ah, I never said 'common,' or thought it. Especially not now."

She returned and handed me my drink. "Anyhow, that's probably why I'm telling you about my finances." She gasped and a hand flew up to her face. "Last night you got back—oh, but you went out last night, didn't you?"

"Yes, but I didn't have sex."

"You didn't?"

"No."

"You mean—five years and you haven't slept with a woman? In *five* years?"

"Right."

She crossed herself. "Holy Mother!" Then: "Is that the truth?"

"Yes." I grinned. She was bright and unselfconscious—and I just began to warm to her.

"You know," she said, "I wasn't going to tell you, I was going to play it straight. Oh, I wouldn't have brought you right home, I'd have suggested a couple of places, maybe a club, someplace with entertainment, made a night out of it—and then home. It would have been nice. Damn Pat, it's not like him. It would have been nice the real way."

Something about "the real way" touched me.

"Do you like the apartment?"

"Yes, it's very attractive."

"Want to see the rest?"

"Yes."

We got up, she came over and took my hand, leading me down the hall. Her touch was direct and warm. I was thinking seriously about losing the quarter. "This is my bedroom, down here, I mean the one I use most of the time."

She opened a door to the master bedroom. It was large and beautifully decorated, yet not overly so, in beige and browns with figured deep-orange drapes covering the windows at the far end. Again there were several good paintings on the wall, a large bookcase, and a small fireplace with a seating arrangement across from the bed. "You like it, it's nice, isn't it?"

"It's beautiful."

"I didn't do it, Clifford—Los Angeles—had it done by a decorator."

She went on, talking about how they'd found the apartment and although it was basically a man's apartment, she'd grown to like the masculine feel of it. As she spoke, I left her completely. My mind began to wonder what Lisa's apartment was like. I was overcome by a strong urge to see it. God, I thought, you can't cut someone off the way I'd imagined I could sever Lisa. You can't be totally in love with a woman for six years and then simply say no, stop, that's it. Memories of her were such a reality, perhaps they were more real than she was. I caught a quick glimpse of her as she appeared when I stepped out of the elevator at Letterman.

"—Would you?" Fritzi had asked me a question.

"What? I'm sorry."

"Would you like to see the other bedroom?" She'd let go of my hand, now she took it again. "Hey"—she was looking into my eyes—"you're crying."

"I am?" Then: "Oh, well—oh, shit!"

"Oh, baby!" Her arms were around me. "Oh, Eddie, what is it?"

"Nothing, nothing, I just—"

If it was nothing, it was a big nothing. I suddenly let it all go, not that I wanted to, there was simply no holding it back. She held me very close and I had a good cry, nothing hysterical, but a good solid cry nevertheless. She mouthed soothing little phrases, not asking me anymore why or how, just general comforting. When I felt I could control myself, I uttered little "Oh, Christ's" and "Shit's" and "Dammit's."

When I stopped, she asked, "All right now?"

"Yes." I turned my head away from her and wiped my eyes. She let go of me and walked away. In a minute she returned with a wet washcloth and started to wipe my face. "Here," I said, taking it and doing it myself, feeling foolish being wet-nursed.

"Isn't it awful, but when I see a man cry, I get—just terribly horny."

I coughed up a laugh. "A woman crying makes me feel the same way." It did, too, whenever Lisa had cried before I went overseas, I took her right to bed.

"I wish I could cry for you then," Fritzi said.

"You're doing all right the way you are."

"Am I?"

"Yes."

"Do you want to talk about it, tell me?" I shook my head no. "You sure?"

"Yes."

"Want to see the other bedroom? I bet you get a kick out of it. Yes, I bet that'll pick your spirits up."

"Sure."

She took my hand again and led me out into the hall, a few steps to the left, then opened another door on the far side of the hall and switched on a light.

"Oh, my God!" I managed a real laugh this time.

"Have to take your shoes off if you want to step in."

The room was small, only a little larger than the king-sized pink-sheeted water bed that sat in a wood frame on the floor. The entire room was mirrored, ceiling and four walls. A low sort of bookshelf-cabinet ran around two sides of the room, at water-bed level. Several lamps, ashtrays, cigarettes, a small television set rested on top of it, and a large tape machine was built down into one section. Glancing around, I caught sight of a black Afro-wig lying on top of a shelf next to a large hand vibrator; hanging on a hook affixed to one of the mirrored walls was a long leather riding crop with shredded bits of knotted thongs spraying out from the end, like a switch.

"This is the playroom, isn't it corny?"

"It may be corny but it's—really something, it's a whole production."

"Ain't seen nothin' yet," she said, snapping a wall switch which turned off a lamp and flicking another, setting a multifaceted revolving glass ball in the center of the ceiling to work bathing the mirrored walls and the water bed in a spray of rainbow-colored lights. "Now, isn't that the height of awful?" she asked.

"Yeah, but it's terrific."

She laughed. "Take your shoes off."

She took hers off, too, and we stepped into the room, which amounted to stepping up on the water bed. There was not an inch of floor space available. I stepped on it gingerly causing it to sway and ripple.

"You don't have to worry, it's solid."

"I haven't had much experience with water beds, they were just coming in when I got put away. Only ones I'd seen were in store windows."

"Oh, you never tried a water bed?"

"No."

"Oh . . ."

We stood there on the swaying water bed in our stocking feet and all at once—I'm sure we both sensed it—we were at the end of conversation. There was nothing more to be said. There we were, facing each other, with the overhead light swirling around, making its patterns not only on the mirrors surrounding us but on our faces. It had been funny in a far-out way a few moments earlier; it didn't seem funny at all now.

Fritzi leaned over and swung the door shut. Slam. The very next moment, I was terrified. Five years and dreams of hammer-ass Eddie driving it home were suddenly shattered. I was with a whore in a whorish room, if there ever was one, and I wasn't so sure at all what would happen. No more quarter bets from me.

# 31

Fritzi smiled, a shy smile, which made me feel slightly better. She walked across the bed to the tape machine—her movement upon it caused me to bounce up and down—and pressed some buttons, rolling the music. It was, to my surprise, Mozart.

She began unbuttoning her dress, a silky print material more greens than beige, which showed off her red hair. I took off my tie and shirt and started to get out of my pants, but the undulating water-bed movement made me lose my balance and I sat back down on it hard. This, in turn, caused Fritzi to topple over and hit the mattress. Fritzi giggled.

I slipped off my pants, socks and then my shorts. I was

facing away from her; I reached down, touching myself to see if I could detect a sign of life. I was completely soft.

Bravo, welcome home, big hero P.O.W.!

Five years without a woman, here she is, nada. As I sat there, dwelling on the perversity of the situation, I thought of Vin. Would he have laughed?

"Come here and hold me."

I swiveled around. Fritzi was lying on her side, naked now, the white of her slim graceful body a movie screen for the sweeping play of lights. I flopped over facing her and put my arms around her. Her skin felt as silky as her dress had. It was almost liquid skin.

She held me tightly to her, running her hands up and down my back and around my waist. After a while she spoke: "Oh, Lord, what a super young hard body, I can't tell you how good you feel. I don't want to put you off, but most of the men I—most of them don't have young hard bodies. As you can imagine. Young hard bodies don't have to pay, I guess." She kept tracing her fingers over me. "I hope talk like that doesn't put you off. It's just that—you feel so good, sooo good!"

She didn't put me off. Whether she was aware of what she was doing or not, I don't know, but I began to feel that delicious tingle, small wriggles growing into heavier surges as the blood filled me up. We kissed and I was hard and happy and the show was on the road.

In the middle of the first bout, the tape switched from Mozart to a sweeping Spanish type of music. I got a kick out of it and laughed.

"What?" she asked.

"The music."

"Yes, that, wait'll you hear what's coming."

No more talk, except her phrases of ecstasy, urging me on, and crooning praise, which I won't repeat because they would sound self-serving, and besides, she must have said them often. Still, I was in no mood and this was not time to disbelieve them. They excited me straight into orgasm. She joined me and for a few lunging plunging moments I thought we might even burst the water bed as our pelvic centers slapped against each other with sounds equaling the beat of the Spanish fandango.

We came to rest, me gently on top of her, but still hard inside her. We both uttered testimonials of our enjoyment. I added, "I'm sorry I couldn't make it last longer, but—"

"Baby, if it had lasted longer, I'd have been up on the ceiling."

"The next will be longer."

"I'll bet it will be."

We lay there for quite a while until she said, "You're still completely hard."

"I mean to stay that way."

"Good boy!"

After a while I started to move slowly, easily, and immediately her lovely sounds of response excited me more and more until we were once again back into a solid, wildly exciting encore. In the midst of it, the music abruptly changed to Wagner's love theme from *Tristan und Isolde*. I laughed again, so did Fritzi, saying, "Didn't I tell you?"

Laughter was no impediment, no danger at all. This second time was utterly fantastic, turning into the nearest thing to an athletic contest sex can be. We tumbled and rolled, covering every inch of that water bed, traveling and skidding and thumping and grinding, and when we came we screamed and shouted, drowning out not only Tristan and Isolde but the entire orchestra.

When we'd finished and were laying there, trying to get our breath, she reached up and touched her hair. "You know how I can always tell if it's an extra-special one?"

"No."

"I mean, outside of the *feeling itself*—my hair gets wet, feel it—" She took my hand and placed it up by her hairline; it was extremely damp. "See how wet it is?"

"Yes."

She laughed. "And it's not even summer, it's still winter. You win a kewpie doll."

As we lay there this time, now and then she'd reach over and touch my face, or run her hand up into my hair, scrubby as it was. After a while she said, "You know what? You're better than tuna fish!"

I laughed. *"Tuna fish?"*

"A passion of mine, hardly anything's better than tuna fish, but you are." She began to fondle me again and we engaged in gentle, easy foreplay. When I was aroused, she said, "Hey, would you like to smoke a joint?"

"Sure." I'd smoked now and then in L.A., but not much. I liked it when I had it, but I'd really forgotten about pot.

Fritzi lifted the top of the cabinet next to the tape machine, and soon we were taking alternate puffs and she'd put another tape on, now more contemporary music, rock and jazz, later getting into the psychedelic hair-raising stuff. "Don't worry, this is good grass but it's not gangbusters. I just want us to get a little high and dreamy. And then—" She giggled.

"Yes?"

"I'm going to show you what it's all about!"

I giggled, too. "What were we doing up till now, faking?"

"No, but I want to get freaky with you."

That evening, and into the early morning hours, was the best thing that could have happened to me. It was joyfully horny and therapy and total physical release and forgetting—all rolled into one.

If the marijuana was mild, you couldn't have proved it by me. Before long we were floating on that water bed. And it did get freaky. I'd never had poppers before, Fritzi introduced me to them. I'd never worn a cock-ring, Fritzi had the latest in equipment. She had the timing, the variety and the touch of a master technician. Whereas before, I'd been the aggressor, now she took over as ringmaster. I gladly followed, taking the tour as if we were going through a Disney World of sex.

The marijuana added a touch of unreality and there were times when I found myself staring into the mirrors, watching our activities as if I were a voyeur third-party.

The third orgasm was a long time coming. I don't remember how long exactly because I'd lost track of time, but it seemed like hours. She purposefully prolonged, stopping whatever delicious spin-off we were engaged in when I got close. There were rest periods; during one of them she left the amphitheater and returned with two bowls of ice cream topped with fudge sauce and almonds; the pot had made us crave sweets.

When we'd devoured the sundaes she said, "Now I'm going to taste your sweets, that's the way it's going to happen this time."

Oral sex had never been my favorite, only because it made

me feel inactive and I preferred an active role, enjoyed it. But now, in my dreamy state, I gave myself over to her completely—seeing it take place in those rainbow hues sweeping across the mirrors—and happily letting it happen. And when I finally came, because it was the third time, it was an aching explosion that began in my toes, paralyzed my legs and was two parts thrilling and one part exquisite hurt as it burst from me. I yowled like an alley cat.

"Oh, God," I said when I was able to speak. "I never— well, I never . . ." Then: "Can I ask you a favor?"

"Yes."

"Could we sleep a little while?"

We both laughed and she said, "Come on, we'll go into the bedroom, this place is a disaster area."

She helped me up and led me out of the room. When we got to the bedroom she said, "Why don't we take a shower first?"

"Oh, I can't, I'd drown."

"I'll hold you up."

"No, please, mercy, I have to lie down."

She put me in bed and the last thing I remember was crooning my thanks to her.

A conked-out sleep of pure exhaustion followed but it couldn't have been for more than a few hours. Fritzi awakened me with a cup of coffee. I could barely open my eyes, but it was eight o'clock and I had to be back by nine. "Now I'll take a shower."

Fritzi joined me in her large stall shower, soaping me up, and to my amazement there I was, hard again, even though I was half-asleep. "One more time?" she asked.

"Oh, no, I can't."

"Yes, you can. I like early-morning sleepy ones."

"So do I, but I don't think I can."

"Yes, you can."

And we began, right there in the shower, standing up, with the hot water pouring down on us, and we finished that way, too. It was our fourth time and I thought it would take hours but it didn't, it actually happened quickly. This one hurt, too, and not only the orgasm, my cock was raw in places from the night's activities and the soap stung. Again the hurt was the most pleasurable hurt one could imagine.

Afterwards I stood there hanging onto the built-in soap dish for support, my legs were so weak. Fritzi laughed. "You know what they call what we just did?"

"No, what?"

"A knee-trembler."

"They called it right." I suddenly laughed. "I've got more physicals this morning, I bet I flunk them all."

Fritzi helped dress me, like you would a little kid you were sending off to school. At the door, after she'd kissed me on the cheek, I said, "Fritzi, I'd really like it if you'd take some money."

She pushed the palm of her hand in my face, turning my head away. "Uh-uh." I started to speak. "Not another word. No. I enjoyed it as much as you did, believe me."

"You couldn't have."

"I did. You don't realize, they're all fifty or over. This was good for me."

I suddenly felt sorry for her. I kissed her again. "Could I call you and—"

"I don't think so." She saw the expression on my face. "I could get—a little hung up on you. I can't afford that, not now, it would get me all screwed up."

"I'll call anyhow, is the phone in your name?"

She didn't answer for a long beat. Then, as she gently shoved me out the door, "No . . ."

# 32

"Sergeant Keller? Eddie?"

I awoke to see Colonel Dwyer and Major Delores Freeman standing over me. I'd got back to the base a little before nine, lay down and tricked my body into thinking it was through for the day.

"Oh my, oh my." Major Freeman sighed. "I've seen old Red Eyes before, but you've really got 'em."

I grinned at them, my face was hot and puffy and I felt sweaty in my clothes. The sum total of the evening with Fritzi had flattened me. "I really don't think I can go through any physicals this morning, I'm whipped."

Major Freeman sighed. "Yes, I think he'd better take the morning off. No problem, I'll let them know." She left the room, shaking her head and chuckling.

"I don't get it, yesterday you were fine, but today—"

"Colonel, I'll level with you, there is a problem with my wife." His face went grave. "Oh, we'll work it out, but last night I went out on the town and, as they say, I fucked my brains out. I am one hundred percent bushed. I hate to louse up the routine, but—"

"Don't worry about that, we're not here to push you. Do you suppose you could pull yourself together for intelligence this afternoon?"

"Yes, if I get a few hours now."

"I'm sorry to hear there's trouble with your wife."

"Not serious," I lied. No energy for getting into that. "We'll work it out."

As Colonel Dwyer was walking out the door, he stopped and turned back to me with a grin: "How many times—or was it just one big wowzer?"

"No, four."

"Four? In one night?" I nodded. "Ah, youth—goddam youth!"

Lunch awakened me, brought on a tray by an orderly who had, from his happy conspiratorial attitude, been told the cause of my condition. I ate, then pulled myself together for an afternoon debriefing with the intelligence officers. The three-hour session drained me of whatever energy I'd gained from my nap.

Colonel Dwyer dropped by my hospital room about six that evening with a strong suggestion I spend the night at Letterman. No problem, I was happy to stay put. "You want to talk about your wife?"

"Not just now, I have to do some thinking."

"Sure. If you need anyone to talk to, besides Major Friedman, I'm here."

"Thank you."

"Have a good *quiet* evening," he said, laughing and adding, "And Eddie, try not to play with yourself!"

"I'll try."

Heavy rain had begun to fall in the late afternoon. Gusting winds slapped the wetness, snapping the gray sheets of it against the plate-glass windows. It was good to be inside.

The entire staff on the tenth floor seemed to be in on my exploits and when I went to the corner lounge to watch the news and have dinner with two other P.O.W.'s, Major Emanuel Torrance and Sergeant Thomas Hinsler, they too were aware. Manny Torrance nicknamed me "Old Faithful."

We had drinks smuggled in and there was a camaraderie that was comforting. It was a warm snug evening, like when you were a kid—the night you felt better after a long illness before going back to school the next day.

I basked, as much as I could, in the pure creature comforts of that night, knowing it was false comfort. Because I could not keep my mind from Lisa. I could keep it from dwelling on her, but I could not keep it from darting back to her. Was Jay's temperature down—yes, and *what did he look like, what was the essence of him?*—and was she there alone waiting for me to call?

I could not help thinking of my mother, sent up a quick prayer that her speech might return by the time I saw her. At least let us be able to talk.

Of course, now and then, thoughts of Vin stabbed me.

Sergeant Hinsler, Major Torrance and I played blackjack for a while before I turned in. Tom Hinsler could not stop talking about money, about what a good job his wife had done with his pay. She'd bought a house in Fresno, their home, that had been divided up into four apartments. It was more than carrying itself. They had no children and she held a full-time job with the phone company. She'd also bought two acres of land near the Friant Dam east of Fresno; just before he got back she sold one of the acres for more than she'd paid for the two and she was having a vacation cabin built on the remaining acre.

Talk like this made me think of what Lisa had done with my pay. I'd naturally given it thought before but that night after I went to bed I lay there, listening to the rain beating down, and I brooded about my financial condition.

A word about Letterman and the army. My fourteen-day stay there before going on convalescent leave was a good buffer between life as a prisoner of war and life as I'd known it before, civilian life. We were never rushed, never pushed, we were treated with dignity and aided with any problem they could possibly have anticipated. I liked the staff almost to a man and woman.

Having said this, I don't have the impulse to go into the routine in great detail. My escort, Sergeant Beagles, left after a week to return to his regular duty; I did hold a press conference at Schwartz Theater on the base; I found out that besides anemia I was host to some nasty little Vietnamese worms in my intestinal tract and was given shots and medication to knock them out; underwent extensive dental work administered by a dentist with the breath of a dead wolf, which, in a way, took my mind off the pain.

The treatment, care and attention could not have been better and, with one exception, were in no way responsible for what happened later.

Now for the exception. There was a bad afternoon with army intelligence when I identified a picture of Vin and told them of his death. By the time I'd finished I was depressed, the senselessness of it had swung back and hit me hard. About a half hour later the senior intelligence officer asked if I'd ever signed a statement denouncing the United States bombing of North Vietnam. He was looking over my file when he asked it; I could also tell by his tone that they somehow knew. Before I could answer he went on in a very understanding voice, saying many P.O.W.'s had been forced into signing statements, that every individual had his own threshold of pain and anguish, both physical and mental, and there was nothing necessarily to be ashamed of if I'd broken.

I admitted it. Immediately they all jumped in, asking how I'd been tortured, for how long, and exactly what means the camp personnel had used to coerce me. I told them the truth, that I had not been tortured, that I'd done it to get medical care for Vin. I felt badly that I had left this out in my account of his death, but I had. Although they seemed to understand, they came back to this area several times until the session was over. I had a strong impression they wanted me to say I'd been physically tortured. After they'd gone I was feeling very low. I'd wanted to ask if there would be any repercussions for what I'd done, but I refrained. I didn't want to seem anxious—or unmanly. I'd done it and that was it.

That evening a surprise picked my spirits up, a long-distance phone call from my father. Although we had not had contact since our luncheon in New York years before, it nevertheless came as a surprise that he'd not known I was a P.O.W. until he'd seen my name listed in *The New York Times*. He'd not been in touch with Bebe, had not known of her stroke, and although he seemed sorry to hear this news, he said nothing of contacting her, even when I told him she was at a nursing home on Long Island. No longer living in Maine, he'd pulled a reverse switch and was working as a stockbroker in New York, commuting to Nyack, where he, his wife and children had a house.

He was warm on the phone and sounded happily enthusiastic at the prospect of seeing me when I came back East, giving me both his home and work number. Although I rarely thought of my father, the phone call left me looking forward to seeing him. Perhaps, after all these years, we'd get to know each other and become friends, no matter how limited.

The next afternoon there was a fourth intelligence officer present for the debriefing. Things went along all right until the end of the session, when they led me back into the statement I'd signed. The new man took over, questioning me gently but still rather pointedly leading me into any other extenuating circumstances, any other torture, either physical or mental, I'd undergone to make me do such a thing. I explained over again why I'd done it. Still, he persisted. The only thing I could come up with was the twice I'd been put in solitary; that was akin to torture but nowhere near the time I signed the statement. After a while I lost control: "Jesus, what more do you want me to say? We knew the war was practically over, my best friend, probably the best friend I'd ever had was dying right in front of me, literally shitting himself to death and nobody would pay attention. I had to get help for him. All right, yes, to me, that was torture—seeing him die like that—for no good reason! Can't you understand that?"

Yes, yes, they could and did and apologized for making me go over it again. The session was ended.

Now to Lisa. As the hours and days separated me from

that first evening at the Fairmont, instead of softening the impact, the passage of time acted as a fixer—cement hardening—stamping the memory of the night, making it loom even more shabby, above all, dirtier. Why, I don't know, but the mess of it, congealed, became harder to clean up in my mind.

I was afraid of being seduced back into a hassling, punishing relationship (for both of us) by her attractiveness, her sexuality. I knew once we'd been to bed, I'd find myself in muddy territory and I didn't want to be led by my cock. I wanted to be led by some sort of logic that would determine whether it was best for both of us not to go through the hell of trying to patch up our relationship if it would only result in mutual unhappiness.

Unfortunately, Lisa phoned me at Letterman while I was getting cleaned up for dinner, only an hour or so after the four army intelligence officers had gone. I was not in the best of moods. There was a definite tone of rebuke in her voice when she first said, "Eddie . . . ?"

"Yes."

"I thought you were going to call?"

"I never said that, Lisa." I didn't mean to pick her up on semantics, but I hadn't said it.

"What does that mean? Oh, I see, we're going to play games, is that it?"

Struck me wrong, that accusation. "Games? You've played more than your share and now you say—"

"Eddie, let's not do this, just answer me—were you going to call?"

"Yes, of course, I was."

Silent air, then: "When, any time in the near future or should I just put myself on hold?"

"You're right, let's not do this." I was struck by our conversation not being at the right time, felt there was not much chance salvaging the tone of it. "Lisa, let's not get into a long nasty phone conversation, that's not the way to—"

"Fine with me." The voice turned coldly factual. "I do want to know one thing. Shall I bring Lauri in from Sacramento now or will it be a while before you get the urge to see her? I don't mean to pressure you but I've started my new job now and I don't want to bring her in without reason, I'd only have to get someone to look after her in the daytime."

"Lisa, can't you understand, I'm just trying to sort through the whole—"

"Poor darling, I know what you've been through, I hope you can pull yourself together!"

"I do, too."

"Yes, I hope you can manage." A pause, then the compulsory retort: "Did you ever think what I've been through, did that ever occur to you? Did you ever imagine it wasn't all just staying back in the good old U.S.A. and going to the movies and football games and kicking up my heels?"

"Yes, I have thought about it."

"Yes!" she echoed without much meaning, except anger.

"I'll call you," I said, weary to the soul.

"Grand!" She hung up.

It was not good.

## 33

Bought civilian clothes, no more walking around a certified hero. Asked Colonel Dwyer to get me the address and phone number of Ginger Collins, Vin's fiancée; I knew I should call her, see how she was taking his death, see if there was any way I could be of help. Sent an expensive arrangement of yellow chrysanthemums—her favorite—to my mother; also wrote her a letter, saying I'd be seeing her in a week or so. Went to see a hard-core porno film, *Deep Throat*, playing in a regular downtown theater, highly advertised. Content about the same, raunchy sex, but a new trend since my last movie-going days as far as better camerawork, color photography and especially the audience, no longer made up mainly of horny wolves-of-all-ages but now a good sampling of young folks on dates, married couples and a fair sprinkling of women alone or in pairs, even a few nicely dressed elderly ladies.

Times they are a-changin'!

There were moments, out in San Francisco, when the hustle, the crowds and activity, got to me, rattling me after years of quiet. There were times when I found it exciting, too. I became very much aware of severe ups and downs. One moment I'd be filled with celebration of my freedom, the next I'd feel rage against Lisa, a thumping ache over Bebe, and the indigo blues—yes, still—at Vin's death. The world is shit, I would think.

For the first few days after Lisa's call, I knew I should phone her back, but I couldn't bring myself to do it. My feelings were such a mix, they kept me immobilized. There were times when I wanted to be with her, to shake out the dirty laundry that had developed between us, but not on the phone. I bided my time.

During my psychiatric sessions with Major Friedman I now discussed Lisa and our problem. But I wanted to go easy on her, didn't want to strengthen any case against her by overtalking, until we'd had a chance to meet face-to-face.

Toward the weekend, on a Thursday afternoon, there was a message Lisa had called; Lauri was in town and if I wanted to see her, I could call. Still, I hesitated. Like a man with one foot in a tub of water and one foot out, I didn't know whether to let myself get wet or stay dry.

The next afternoon, Friday, I went out for drinks and dinner with Sergeant Hinsler and his wife, Emmy. They made a good couple; their affection for each other was catching. I could see the early married Eddie and Lisa in them and I was overcome by nostalgia for those days, felt downright homesick. We sat in a small Italian restaurant having a drink and I suddenly said, "I think I'll call my wife."

"Yes, ask her to join us," Emmy said.

"I will."

I'd told Tom there were a few problems but hadn't gone into details. Digging out the piece of paper with her number, I walked to the phone booth at the front of the restaurant and dialed.

After three or four rings, a man's voice answered. "Hello?"

Before I could stop myself I'd replied "Hello . . ." For an instant I was going to ask if I had the wrong number. But I'd dialed correctly, I knew it. The surprise of hearing his voice got to me. I held the receiver while he said "Hello?" again, then I hung up.

Sat there in the phone booth thinking: Was he still living there, why would she leave a message for me to call and let him answer the phone? Even if she was out, wouldn't she have told him not to pick it up? Wasn't Lisa home from work yet? I looked at my watch, six-twenty, maybe she was out shopping for dinner. If she'd hired someone to stay with Lauri, it wouldn't have been a man. Was he staying there with my daughter, taking care of her? Yes, he was out of work, having gone through my money, he had nothing else to do.

"Hey, Eddie, what's up?" It was Tom rapping on the phone booth window. I came out, told him she wasn't home. "You were just sitting there like you were waiting for your dinner to be served."

"Yeah," I laughed, "I thought I was back in solitary."

Timing. Cold water in the face, just when I was feeling warm.

Worse timing coming up. Does bad timing simply happen, or do we help it along, give it a little goose? I think this one I arranged for.

The next day, Saturday, I stayed at Letterman, although I didn't have to, I had a weekend pass until Monday morning. My thinking was that he (Jay) most certainly would have told Lisa I called, heard his voice and hung up. So I presumed she might call to say she was sorry I'd got him on the phone, the coast was clear, come see Lauri, let's meet, let's talk.

There was no call. Late in the afternoon I got dressed and went out. It was a warm March day. I thought of Fritzi, wished I had her phone number, considered just dropping by but thought, no, if any night would be a working night for her it would most likely be Saturday.

Besides, I'd stalled long enough with Lisa. I didn't want to talk on the phone, I wanted to see her, see Lauri, and if he were there, I'd take a look at him, too. All this went through my mind as I sat in a bar on Geary Street having one drink, then a second, slipping into a mellow mood. I went to the phone, thinking it might be best to call first. Busy. She was

home, Lauri would be there, too. The idea that my daughter
was only blocks away struck me.

I left the bar and decided to walk to the address I had on
Hyde Street. It occurred to me to phone again, but I was
feeling even mellower now that I was out on the street at twi-
light on such a clear beautiful day. I was feeling open to
whatever I might walk into. I felt excitement, too, when after
twelve blocks or so I came to the building, a typical beige-
gray five-story San Francisco dwelling with bay windows in a
row of similar buildings, inclining up the hill on Hyde Street.

Looking up from the sidewalk, I wondered which apartment was hers. In the foyer I saw the listing "Keller" next to
3-B. Strange, seeing my name on an apartment I didn't know.
Footsteps and the bark of a dog, a little girl approaching behind the thin curtains of the front door with a dog on a
leash. My heart jumped, was it my daughter? The door
opened. "Hi," she said, "going in?"

"Yes." I took the door.

"Come on, Commander." She trotted with the dog past me
down the steps and out onto the sidewalk.

No, it wasn't Lauri, this little girl was six or seven. I
walked up, two apartments to a floor, heard crying before I
got to the landing of the third, loud, wailing, unattractive to
the ear. The halls were bare, her crying came out underneath
the door and reverberated in the hallway.

Near the door of 3-B, I heard Lisa's voice, soothing, crooning to her: it was all right, nothing broken, no blood, only a
bump. I'd have rung the bell right then, but it would have
been a bad moment to make an appearance.

Then a man's voice approaching from what I guessed was
another room. "What's the matter—catastrophe strike?"

"Bumped her head on the hall table, a real knock."

"Hey, there," he said, "that doesn't sound like my big girl,
that's not my big grown-up girl."

Surprised that I could hear so well, I glanced down to see
a good inch of space between the sill and the bottom of the
door. I could see the shadows of their movement in the
changes of light streaking out from under the door, as their
comforting voices went on, working to stop the crying.

I sat down on the steps leading up to the next floor, only
two or three feet from the door of 3-B.

"Hey, there, look, Lauri. Look at this. I've rubbed it all away. I rubbed the hurt away, presto-chango, no more hurt."

The crying diminished, then Lisa said, "You may have rubbed it away but she's going to have an egg on her forehead."

Picking this up, he said, "An egg on her forehead? Did you hear that, Lauri? You're going to have an egg on your forehead! What *are* you, a little girl or a chicken?"

A giggle mixed with Lauri's tears.

"You're going to get in big trouble with a lot of chickens—marching around with an egg on your forehead." He imitated a chicken. "Puck, puck, puck pa-kaw! Puck, puck, puck pa-kaw!"

Now a burst of giggles, a few sniffles, coughs, more giggles. He went on with his chicken imitation, changed into a rooster crowing and soon she was laughing outright.

"You're silly!" Lauri said.

He broke off in mid-crow. "I'm silly! You've got an egg on your forehead—and *I'm* silly! You better straighten out your priorities, young lady."

"What's my pry—?"

"There you go, up we go!" I could tell by his voice he was swinging her up in the air.

"Time for bed," Lisa said.

"Yep, time to put the Mad Princess of Hyde Street away for the night. Fix me a drink, honey," he called out as he walked away with her.

"All right," Lisa replied. "I'll come kiss you good night when you're tucked in, Lauri."

The way he said "Honey" got to me. His voice was deep and pleasant, sounding as if it belonged to an attractive person. I sat there, numbed at having overheard this easy domestic scene, feeling as much an outsider as I'd ever felt. Quiet now, except for sounds from the kitchen, which must have been just to the right of the front door. I could hear a refrigerator open and close, ice-cubes being taken out, water running.

After a while I heard his footsteps returning. Lisa gave him a drink and he suggested "Let's go in and catch the end of the evening news." She wanted to stay in the kitchen and frost a cake. He stayed to keep her company. I could hear most of their conversation, except at times when an electric mixer and other kitchen noises obliterated their words. The longer I sat there, the more numbed I became. After a while, although I told myself to get up and leave—I couldn't get my legs going. Just sat there, pelted by snatches of conversation about an electric bill, a movie they wanted to see, about Lauri's shoes being resoled. "How much?" Lisa asked. "Four dollars," he said. "That's robbery!" "That's exactly what I told the guy." "What did he say?" Lisa asked. "Four dollars!" "Christ!"

He told her a joke, something about a drunk woman sitting in a cocktail lounge wearing a large picture hat; I didn't get the punchline because of kitchen noises but I could hear their laughter clearly enough.

Suddenly realized that what I was doing was waiting to hear some mention of me. Yes, then impatience turned to anger at the position I'd put myself in, at the scene they'd *presented* me with. Torn between crashing through the door and confronting them—SURPRISE!—and limping away, simply leaving in disgust. And the mix of these emotions so immobilized me, I only sat there frozen to the cold marble steps as their conversation went on, about a friend's dog dying, a job interview coming up for him, about everything else but "the situation."

Until the phone rang. That stopped them abruptly enough; total silence until the fourth ring, then I heard Lisa say, in a barely audible voice: "Oh, God . . ." A beat, and: "I'll take it in the bedroom."

Implicit to me was—*in case it's him.*

Her footsteps left the kitchen, fading away. I heard a door open and close.

With her gone it was so quiet, I even held my breath. The two of us sitting in silence, not more than ten feet from each other. Both wondering. Him, no doubt wondering if the call was from me. Me, wondering what the dialogue would be when she returned. Certain it would apply to me. Wanting to hear badly what their tone would be when they spoke of me; and just as badly—not wanting to hear.

Lisa didn't return for a long time. When I did hear the door open and close again and her footsteps approach, my heartbeat quickened.

*Go ahead, talk about the Returned One.*

"Was it . . . ?" he asked.

"No, it was Penny. She's giving a surprise birthday party for Herb next Sunday, wants us to come if we can."

"Oh."

There was a long silence. *Come on, come on, enough trivia, let's have the Big Guns!*

"I wonder . . ." Lisa said.

"What?"

"Nothing. Uh-uh," she cried out, "stay away from that frosting!"

The door opened on the floor above, sounds of a couple going out for the evening. I didn't want to get caught sitting there. I was sickened by this time anyhow. Not with them inside the door of 3-B, but sick of myself listening. Felt not only disappointed and frustrated but—grimy. I got up, quickly walking downstairs and out.

All I'd earned was "Oh, God . . ." when the phone rang and "Was it . . . ?" after. Their avoidance showed how they dreaded the subject. Mostly, they sounded so natural and at home with each other.

Saturday night. On the town? No. I didn't even have dinner. No appetite. I had three more drinks at a bar, the kind you have trouble getting down your throat and, once down, they sit hotly in your stomach. I took a cab back to Letterman and went to bed.

Isn't it strange how I couldn't go to sleep? In bed and out, up and down, staring out the window, pacing, thinking for a while of dressing and going out again. I wanted to talk to someone, a friend. Vin is who I thought of, naturally. Vin. I'd just got Ginger Collins' number and address that day, so, although it was almost midnight in Vermont, I put in a call to her.

Her voice was low and slightly husky, although she said she hadn't been asleep. At first she sounded confused, even guarded, but I quickly told her I'd roomed with Vin for two years, that I was with him when he got sick. She became very quiet then and I went on in a rush of words, not knowing how this call would affect her.

"Ginger, I'm calling on my own from San Francisco because Vin talked about you all the time. He loved you, but you know that. I thought you might want to hear from some-one who knew him. We were close friends, he was probably the best friend I ever had."

"Oh, God . . ." she said.

"You all right?"

"Yes, it's just hitting me now—how good it is to talk to someone who knew him. It's all been so—cold. An army chaplain came to see Vin's folks, but . . ."

"I'll be coming back east in a week or so, I'll be in New York. Would you like to see me, I mean would it help to have someone to talk to about Vin?"

"Oh, yes . . ." Then: "I'm sorry, give me your name again? The second Vin's name was mentioned my mind went . . ."

"Eddie, Edward Keller."

"Yes, I'd like to see you very much, I would. You know, Eddie—I still can't believe it, if anyone ever came back, I thought it would be Vin. Isn't it funny how I always felt that?"

"I know what you mean."

"We only heard—just two weeks ago. I still don't believe it, not really. I made up this story, he escaped and he's some-where, maybe he's—"

"No, don't do that."

"I know." There was a long silence. "I can't imagine him dead. I can't. He was so—I can't imagine him gone. I can't imagine no more Vin."

"I know, but he is gone." I said the words softly but I felt compelled to say them.

"Did you—*see* him, were you with him when he died?"

"Yes." I didn't hesitate a moment, lying about that. I knew she shouldn't hold on to any fantasies about him being alive somewhere.

"You did?" she asked again.

"Yes."

"Oh . . ."

I wanted to give her something good, but I didn't know what or how. So I simply said, "I loved him."

I heard her take a deep breath. "It's good to hear you say that."

We talked a while longer and I promised to call her when I got to New York. I'd either go up to Vermont or she'd come down to meet me. We said our good-byes and I hung up. I was glad I'd called her. It took my mind off my own worries and enabled me to go to sleep.

# 34

Monday morning I asked for an appointment to talk to legal counsel about a divorce. That evening I dropped Lisa a note saying I'd be going back East to see my mother at the end of the week, I thought it might be best if we considered divorce, that I would naturally contribute to Lauri's support, that I was sorry it worked out this way. I wished her happiness and ended saying I thought it might be best not to see Lauri at this time, not until I came back to San Francisco for my discharge, which would be in a few months.

Having wished her happiness, I had to acknowledge I'd said what I said with every intention of hurting her. And myself. I doubted it would hurt Lauri. She never knew me, how could she miss me? That would come later on as she grew up. Perhaps. Perhaps not. Depending upon Lisa and her life.

If I could have left San Francisco that afternoon, I would have. Gladly. I wanted out of there; the city, which I'd always liked, had turned sour for me. I began counting the time, grateful to be so occupied during the day at Letterman, trying to keep my off-duty hours crammed with activity.

Tuesday of that week brought the beginning of the Big Squeeze. I knew my life and times were not at their brightest but, to be honest, I thought perhaps the worst had already been dished out on the plate. There it sat, a certain amount of garbage, which needed to be sifted through or discarded or what couldn't be discarded—recycled.

Then a phone call came from a woman in New York, Monica Rohmer, who explained she was a good friend of my mother's and wanted to know if I'd had a call from a Hilda Munson, the proprietress of the nursing home where my mother was. I told her no, immediately asking if something had gone wrong with Bebe.

"No," she said, "Bebe's coming along fine, it's just a financial problem. Eddie, I hate to bother you with it, but I was sure the Munson dame would call you, even though I told her not to. She's a greedy bitch. I scraped up last month's and I've given them three hundred toward this month, but— oh, nursing homes are the most coldblooded—"

"How much is it a month?"

"Eight hundred."

"God!"

"And that's the cheapest we could find that wasn't an outhouse. Would you believe that?"

I told her I could probably get an advance on my pay and send the five hundred the next day, but she said no, as long as I was coming back within a week they could bloody well wait. There was a toughness, a directness in this woman's voice that I liked. No nonsense. Monica Rohmer told me how good it would be for Bebe to see me, how much she was looking forward to it, she also said she had a plan for getting her out of the nursing home, but she'd tell me about that when she saw me.

"Eddie, I realize you don't know me, but could I suggest one thing?"

"Sure."

"It might be good if I'm there the first time you see her. She's improving day by day, can walk a little now, but her speech is still, well, it's not good. I go out to see her about three times a week and we're onto each other, I can tell what she's trying to say most of the time. I think it would ease the pressure, for both of you. She'll want to ask you so many questions, talk about so much, and she won't be able to. I'm not a buttinsky, Eddie, and if you'd rather be alone, I'd understand."

"No, I'd appreciate your being there. To tell you the truth, I'm nervous about seeing her like that."

"Ah, don't be," she said. "You'll be surprised how good she looks. It's just the speech thing that's causing her trouble. It's damned frustrating for her, but Eddie, she's being so good about it all, you'll be proud of her."

She gave me her phone number and I told her I'd let her know when I'd be there. I liked her immensely, just from this phone conversation.

The money situation began nagging me badly that afternoon. I'd never anticipated that as a problem when I'd been a prisoner but now it was being brought home to me. P.O.W.'s would be receiving five dollars a day for each day we were prisoner, but that wouldn't be given to us for a while, not for two months or so. All of my pay for the entire five years was gone; I had no savings. I had my current pay and the pay I'd be getting for my convalescent leave, that was it. That afternoon I multiplied five times the number of days I'd been prisoner—1,825 days—which would mean I'd have $9,125 coming. Period. I could have used it now.

Thoughts of money only increased my anger with Lisa for what she'd done.

Because of Bebe's situation, the next morning I made inquiries about getting an advance on the five-dollar-per-day P.O.W. pay. The pay officer seemed downright nervous when I approached him about this, quickly referring me to Colonel Dwyer. I went to his office but found he was in San Diego at a P.O.W. center down there for a conference. His assistant, a young lieutenant, was also ill at ease when I mentioned getting an advance. He hedged and sputtered around until I finally asked, "Is there some problem?"

"No, not really . . ." When I kept looking at him, he added, "It has to do with the statement you signed—over there."

"I've already been over that in the debriefing sessions."

"I know, but now that several officers around the country have accused enlisted P.O.W.'s of conspiring to aid the enemy, the Pentagon has its ass in the air. They're kind of . . ."

"Kind of what?"

"Putting a hold on everything until the whole thing about signing statements has been checked out."

"But the intelligence officers—even they said lots of guys signed statements, or said things, at one time or another. Lots of them did."

"I know, but—for the time being, there's nothing I can do. When Colonel Dwyer gets back—"

"You mean because I signed a statement to save my best

friend's life—I'm not even going to get the fucking five
dollars a day coming to me?" I was starting to tremble.

"No, I'm sure you'll get it. It's just that—for the time
being, everything's kind of in limbo, until it all blows over.
You could probably get a loan on the outside for—"

"No, that's fine, I'll work it out."

I left, unable to believe the attitude I'd just encountered. It
threw me badly, put me in a black mood.

When Colonel Dwyer got back he arranged for me to get
my three months' convalescent pay in advance, which was
not all that much but it did help. About the lump sum I had
coming, he said no one was getting that yet and there was no
way at this time I could get an advance on it, although he
did his best to assure me I would not be done out of it by
having signed the statement. He was understanding and sym-
pathetic. Still, it hung over my head, unsettled me.

Thursday afternoon of that week, my last week there, I
dressed to go out in civilian clothes and when I got down to
the lobby, where the front desk and large waiting lounge
were—I saw Lisa and Lauri seated on a sofa facing the elevators. Stopped in my tracks. Lisa stood up, smiling, I
couldn't tell exactly how, not just a simple smile, something
behind it.

I hated her for surprising me, once again, with her beauty.
She was done up in her best, a simple dark blue silk dress;
she was even wearing short white gloves. She'd recently been
to a beauty parlor; her hair had that extra body and sheen
that comes from having attention paid it. Spiked heels gave
her a lithe filly stance, made her legs real winners. Thump,
thump, went the body's beat, against my wishes.

I walked toward her, unable to suppress a smile at the
presentation of her beauty.

"What's so funny?" she asked.

"Your ugliness," I grinned.

"Hah! Lauri, this is your father."

Lauri was standing by this time. She looked gorgeous, too,
in miniature. I saw myself in her immediately, she had my
nose, my chin, her mother's coloring, the same sable hair and
almost the same saucer eyes as her mother's, except Lauri's
were blue instead of green. She'd been dressed with care,

powder-blue little-girl dress, little black shiny shoes, white socks, she even wore little white gloves like her mother's, and a blue ribbon in her hair.

"How do you do?" she said, extending a tiny gloved hand.

An impulse to sweep her up in my arms—but just as quickly thought no, and took my lead from her. "How do you do," I said, shaking the tiny hand. "My, but you're pretty."

"Thank you," she said.

"I've been looking forward to meeting you."

"You have?"

"Yes."

"Mother said you didn't want to."

"Jesus!" Snapping my head around to Lisa, I wanted to slap her.

Wanted to slap her even more when she smiled, oh, so casually. "Well, you didn't, did you? One thing they don't do with kids anymore—is *lie* to them." She sighed, the second-hand scent of liquor carried on her breath. I suddenly realized, despite how pulled together she looked, she was slightly off-kilter. Not really drunk, but high enough so it was an effort to contain it.

"Well," I said, looking back down at this miniature person who had come from me, "you don't believe everything your mother says, do you?"

She smiled up at me and giggled. "No."

"Good." I got a bang out of her saying that. "I suppose you'll have to give me a kiss, but we can do that later on. Can't we?" I wanted to avoid the pushy adult dragging affection from a child.

"Yes."

I noticed a good-sized bump, slightly heightened in color just at the hairline on the left side. I almost commented on it but decided to wait. "Let's take a walk, shall we?"

"Yes," Lauri said.

As we walked out the door, Lisa said, "You look very spiffy in your civilian clothes, where'd you get them?"

It was such an inconsequential question I merely replied, "In a store."

Lisa giggled, "Oh . . ."

She was taking deep breaths, in and out; this came from trying to control (and conceal) the alcohol she'd consumed.

Although it was five in the afternoon, the day was still bright and glary, the huge sun was aiming directly at us as it dipped down over the Golden Gate Bridge. Lisa shielded her eyes against the harsh rays of it with a gloved hand, this action also having to do with her condition. No bright lights, please. She turned to veer away from the sun and we walked around to the side of the hospital, along a path cut through the thick springy grass.

"I brought Lauri because I'm taking her back to her grandmother's this weekend. She wanted to see you, whether you wanted—"

"Oh, stop it!" I said.

Lauri's head snapped up to regard my anger at her mother.

"Well, you didn't—want to." She was getting on a high horse, standing up very straight, taking a deep breath. "Whether you appreciate it or not, I still thought—"

"I'll tell you what I don't appreciate!"

"What?" she asked, tilting back away from me.

"I don't appreciate your drinking and then bringing Lauri out here!"

Although she didn't deny this charge, she looked hurt that I'd voiced it. "Eddie, you know what? I never realized how mean you could be. Maybe the years over there made you mean, did they?"

"No, Lisa, I think it was coming home to you that made me turn mean." Lauri was watching us closely. "Let's not get into this now, here, with . . ." I broke off. We were near a bench. "Why don't you sit here while Lauri and I take a little walk."

"All right."

"Come on, Lauri, take a walk with me."

She looked to Lisa for approval. "Go ahead, Lauri, he's your father, he's not going to bite you!" I didn't like Lisa taking it out on Lauri but I didn't want to be the cause of more friction.

"Come on." I took Lauri's hand and we walked away down the path, without talking for a time, while I decided to treat her as a person, not a child. "Lauri, how does it feel to have a daddy you don't really know?"

A look and a small squint. "It's—funny."

"Yes, for me, too, it's 'funny' having a daughter I don't really know."

"Is it?" she asked, seemingly surprised it worked both ways.

"Sure, it is." Then first things first. "You understand the reason I haven't gotten to know you was because I was away in a faraway country and—much as I wanted—I couldn't get back to see you. You understand that?"

"Yes."

"Do you miss not having a daddy?"

Pause. "Sometimes."

We came to a bench. "Let's sit a while." We settled down, I released her hand, swung around to face her, sitting there so dear, her legs dangling from the bench, her feet nowhere near reaching the ground. Thinking of the guilts dumped on children, also not knowing what words of caution Lisa had spoken to her about our situation, I wanted to dispel anything that might be fretting such a little conscience. "Do you think of Jay as your father? I mean, sometimes?"

A quick look up at me indicated the subject of Jay might well have been marked "verboten." I didn't want to put her on the spot; once again I took her hand. "I wouldn't be surprised or angry if you did. I don't know Jay but if he treats you nice, then I like him for that. He does treat you nice, doesn't he?" (I could tell from my eavesdropping scene he did.)

A guarded, small "Yes."

I squeezed her hand. "That's good, Lauri. I want everyone to treat you nicely. Anyone that does—I like. Anyone that doesn't—I don't like."

She smiled. "Me, too."

"Good. Only one other—serious thing I want to say, then we can talk about anything you want. Just because your mommy and I don't live together, doesn't mean we don't both love you very much. It also doesn't mean we don't like each other. Same thing when we were arguing just now, that doesn't mean we don't like each other very much. It just means—our grown-up lives, what we have to do, our work, have kept us from living together. Does that make any sense?"

She thought a second, then made a little grimace. "Not—I don't understand."

"I know." I made an exaggerated mugging face in return. "You know, sometimes *I don't understand either.*"

She giggled, I loved making her giggle. I'd been sounding serious, like a bad movie: "Just because . . . doesn't mean we don't love you . . . like each other," etc. "Hey, I'll tell you a secret, if you'll tell me one?"

A grin. "What?"

"I was nervous about meeting you. Were you nervous about meeting me?"

"Uhhuh. Why?"

"Why was I?"

"Yes."

"Because I wanted you to like me. Why were you?"

Her voice took on the singsong quality children fall into when they're being led. "Because I wanted you to like *me*."

"Did you really?"

She looked at me seriously, as if she'd really considered it now. "Yes."

"Good, that means we both care. And I think we do like each other. Of course, it's just a beginning, but I think we do." I didn't want to press her, demand an answer, so I went right on. "Oh, one other thing I want to tell you."

The way she said "What?" indicated she thought it was going to be a secret or a joke. I was sorry I didn't have one for her. "I won't be seeing you for a while again. I have to go back east, to New York, to see my mother, she's very sick."

"Your mother?"

"Yes, I haven't seen her for as long as I haven't seen you."

"Is she going to die?"

"No, no, she's just very sick, she'll get better but she misses me and I miss her."

"Oh."

"But I won't be gone for nearly as long as I was before. Just a month or two, then I'll be coming back here and we'll have some good times, won't we?"

"Yes. Will you come to live with us?"

A sticky question. Suddenly I wished she was twelve or fifteen so we could really talk. "I hope so. But if I can't, I'd at least see you often, take you places. What do you like best in the whole world?"

"My kitty."

"What's your kitty's name?"

"Squishy."

I laughed. "What a funny name for a kitty—Squishy? Why is it named Squishy?"

A little shrug. "Cause she almost got squished once."

"She did—how?"

"In a draw." (Sic—drawer.)

As I went on to the next question in line I was cursing for having to talk about Squishy, the cat, when I badly wanted to talk about us. "Why do you like her so much?"

"Because she sleeps with me."

"That's nice, to have a little kitty sleep with you all snug and warm, isn't it?"

Great joy. "Oh, yes! Do you have a kitty?"

I glanced down the path to see Lisa sitting on her bench; she was poking about in her purse, happened to glance toward us, saw me looking and went back to her purse. *No, and not even a pussy of my own, my dear. Oh, God, little angel, wait until you can see the view from where I am. I wish you could never see it, but you will.* "No, but I had one once."

"An orange one?"

"No, a black one."

"Squishy's orange."

*Oh, screw Squishy, hug me!*

"I'm going to school next—"

"Hey, would you do me a favor?" I asked.

"What?"

"Would you give me a hug?"

She smiled, a bit of tease in her drawn-out "Ye—ees."

"Good." I picked her up, sat her on my lap and turned her toward me. The small arms reached up and crawled around my neck. I hugged her and she hugged me back. I felt such a womping rush of affection for her in those moments, not only for her but through her for Lisa. All the love I'd been holding in Vietnam for all those years, that had been short-circuited inside me—wanted to come pouring out now. "Umm—what a good hug! The first of many, I'll want a lot of those when I get back!" I didn't want to be claustrophobically affectionate, so I didn't slam a strange wet mouth against her, only nuzzled her. "I guess we ought to get back to Mommy. Okay?"

"Okay."

Picking her up, I swung her to her feet, took her hand and

we headed back to Lisa. I felt easy with her, glad of our meeting, even such a brief one, probably best that the first one was brief, so she wouldn't get bored with me. Walking back she thanked me for the doll and the bracelet, which she had on and I hadn't noticed. She held up her small gloved hand and waggled her wrist to let me see it.

"What do you want me to bring you from New York?" (Why couldn't I resist buying further time and attention from her?)

"Oh—ah, I know—a puppy."

"A puppy? I don't know if I could bring you a puppy. Besides, what would Squishy do?"

"Play with it, Squishy wants a puppy."

"Did Squishy tell you that?"

Without a moment's hesitation. "Yes."

"Maybe later we could get a puppy."

Lauri sighed, one of those deep exaggerated little-girl sighs, as if they've just been through one helluva day. "I hope so."

Lisa stood as we approached, a gorgeous slightly drunk willow. Instead of asking how we got along, which I presumed she might, she brushed a hand across her forehead, saying in a chilly voice, "Hope you didn't mind us coming out here and—trapping you?"

I refused to pick her up on it. "No, I'm glad you did, I like my daughter very much."

"Not enough to make an effort, to call or come see her on your own."

No, she wasn't going to let me off the hook. Damn her for going on like that in front of Lauri. Much as I didn't want to indulge in game playing, she was forcing me. I dropped to my knees and brushed my fingers against the bump on Lauri's temple. "Hey, look who's got an egg on her forehead. Say—what are you, a little girl or a chicken? I'm going to swipe that egg and give it back to the chickens." I made a fake pass at it.

Lauri giggled. If she connected my dialogue with Jay's she gave no indication, only laughed. I avoided looking to catch Lisa's expression until I'd done my imitation of a chicken: "Puck-puck-puck pa-kaw, puck-puck-puck pa-kaw! What are you doing with that cute little egg anyhow?"

Another giggle. "I fell down."

"I bet you did." I looked up to see the confusion on Lisa's face. "You see, I did make an effort," I told her.

She started to speak, broke off, took Lauri by the shoulders and gently pushed her in front of us. "You walk on ahead, honey. Let Daddy and me talk a while."

Lauri ambled on, saw a squirrel over by a tree and ran toward it as Lisa said on the edge of a bitter laugh, "Daddy and me—hah!" Then: "What was all that about?"

"I'll tell you what it was all about. Saturday night I was feeling so—so ready to see you, to love you again—"

She laughed again. "*You were ready?* Oh, how great, we'd all been *wondering!*"

"Yes, I was, I phoned first, got a busy, then just came by on impulse, right after Lauri had fallen down and—"

"And you *listened?* Outside the door, you just listened?"

"Yes, I didn't intend to but—"

"Ah! How really—tacky!" She glanced toward Lauri, then wheeled around to face me: "Hear your name mentioned?"

"No, no, I didn't."

"Hear anything *juicy?*" Her anger was building. "My God, how long were you there?"

"I don't know."

"And you didn't hear anything good?"

"Yes," I said. This stopped her. "You both sounded 'good' together. He sounded 'good' with Lauri."

"Oh! Oh, my, aren't we being brave? So brave and *noble*, the returning hero!"

"No, you asked me and I told you."

"Next time you feel like snooping, let me know. I'll leave a beer out in the hall."

"I don't like beer."

"There, see how we forget!"

"Yes."

"Mommy! Mommy! The squirrel ran up the tree!" Lauri shouted.

"Well," Lisa said, in low tones ground through her teeth, inaudible to Lauri, "that's where squirrels live for Chrissake!"

Her response was part liquor, part anger at me and one part her old sass, a part I loved. I couldn't help laughing.

"What's so funny?" she asked, at the same time lifting a hand in a perfunctory wave at Lauri.

"The whole goddam—*us!*" I said. Lisa's ankle buckled, she

stumbled forward, a little catch step, and I caught her arm, steadying her. Such a small incident made her so vulnerable, I was filled with a sudden warmth for her as I held onto her arm. In a moment the essence of her came to me: the determined self-destruction of Kim Stanley in one of my favorite films, *The Goddess.* "Hey, let's have dinner," I said.

Another bitter laugh. "Do you want to have dinner or get a divorce?"

I kept my hand on her arm. "Dinner first," I said, in an attempt to keep my humor up.

"No, I can't, I have a—I can't."

"Oh."

She yanked her arm away from me. "Well, what do you—who do you think you are? I—you just expect me to sit around and wait for you to get the urge to ask me to *dinner?*"

"I only suggested it, I didn't expect anything."

"And aren't you cool! So cool about it all, that's the most infuriating—oh, I wonder how I ever loved you so much? So much! I wonder how I did!"

"Mother, the squirrel—" Lauri was coming back toward us.

"Oh, Lauri," she snapped, "can't you see we're talking!"

"Don't speak to her like that," I said, in a low warning voice.

"I'll speak to her any way I want, she's my daughter!"

"She's mine, too."

"Hah—some father you are!"

If Lauri hadn't been there, I'd have slapped her. "That's right, I actually deserted you, on purpose, didn't I? Got myself captured and put away for five years so I wouldn't have to stick around changing diapers and mixing baby formula!" I hated being sucked into this petty talk. "Oh, Lisa, come on, let's go someplace where we can relax and really talk."

"I told you, I can't."

"Can't you change your plans?"

"No, I can't."

"Can't or won't?"

"Both. Because, if you want to know, I think you're being a bastard!"

Lauri was standing next to her by then. She looked up,

squinted at me to see if I was, in fact, this word her mother called me.

"Okay, well—" I dropped down to my knees, gave Lauri another hug. "I love you, Lauri. Why don't you go inside and sit down a moment? Mommy and I'll be in in a minute or two."

We were only fifteen or so yards from the main entrance by now. Lauri looked to her mother. "Go on, I'll be right in," Lisa said.

We stood there waiting to speak until she'd gone in the front door. By now there was a spectacular sunset taking place over the Golden Gate Bridge to our left. "Look at that sunset," I said, hoping to mellow the tone of what we'd say to each other now.

Lisa gave it no more than a brief glance and a one-word review. "Shit!"

This triggered me. "Don't ever speak to me that way in front of her, don't ever call me a bastard in front of her— ever!" She turned to look at me, her eyes widening. "Yes, you heard me. Another thing, I may have come back mean, but I never realized how—how *coarse* you are." The snap of a laugh from her. "Yes, you are and you better watch it. Coarseness does not age well, it tends to toughen and leatherize, and pretty as you still are, the lines of your bitterness are beginning to show. You think I deserted you, don't you? You're acting like I did it on purpose, I can tell. On the other hand, I come back and you dump a bucket of shit—your word—all over me, you expect me to stand up, brush myself off and say 'Oh, well, great, okay!' You wouldn't even give me two weeks to think things through. By Christ, no, you just wanted a great big positive I-forgive-you and let's-get-on-with-it! And take it easy on the fucking—I've just had an abortion! What the hell is the matter with your thinking any-how?"

She looked at me for a long time before saying "I really am beginning to hate you."

"Hate on, baby. You make me sick, too!"

She started to dab at her eyes, now welling up with tears. "Ah-ah," I warned, raising a hand, "you can't come on with your snide nasty toughness and then pull a switch to crying when it doesn't go your way. That's not in the rules. Cry and I'll slap you—hard!"

"Bastard!" She screamed it out, turned and hurried ahead and on inside the hospital. I stood there, until she came out dragging Lauri by the hand, heading away from me. Lauri, looking confused, turned to me, glancing over her shoulder.

"Good-bye, dear, I'll see you soon!" I yelled.

"Your ass you will," Lisa shouted, without looking around.

"You want me to get you a taxi—*beloved?*" I called out, in some sort of mock-something.

*"No thank you and go to hell!"*

"Charming, you've turned into a real charmer!" I yelled, until I realized five or six people sitting across the plaza on benches waiting for the bus were glued to this little shouting match.

To get away from those amused pairs of eyes, I walked around to the side of the main building, where we'd been before, and sat down on a bench.

Sat there thinking: What a history of wrangling we've had since my return. No, not a history at all, this was only our *second* meeting. A phone call or two, a note or two—and only two face-to-faces. Seemed endless, this distortion of our original relationship. Light years ago. Cold and dead now.

She would never forgive me for my absence and the various unhappinesses it caused her. I would never forgive her for not living up to my dream of her.

I thought back to the days of dreaming and planning, the days with Vin at Bel Air, so fucking full of promise. How different from the anticipation it was, this coming back and waking up!

And, sitting there free as a bird, staring into the wild streaks of magenta over the Golden Gate, here in the home of the brave, land of the free, I realized I was looking back to those days as—yes, the good days.

Surprise—yes?

# Part Three

# 35

Saturday I was on the plane to New York. My hair had grown out to almost normal length; the worms in my intestines had been knocked out by antibiotics; I was putting on weight; my teeth were no longer in danger of falling out. After deducting the three hundred I'd drawn in the Philippines and another two hundred in San Francisco, I had exactly eight hundred and seventy dollars in my pocket, which was all I'd be receiving from the army for the next three months of my one-hundred-and-twenty-day convalescent leave.

Unsettling, knowing five hundred was owing immediately for my mother's upkeep. I'd phoned ahead saying I should be at the nursing home between four and five in the afternoon. I'd also phoned Monica Rohmer, who said she'd meet me there.

Colonel Dwyer had strongly advised counseling sessions for Lisa and me with Major Friedman. To avoid these, I said I would hold off a decision on divorce proceedings until I returned to Letterman for my discharge. I didn't feel like opening up our problems for discussion, not so soon after our last meeting. A cooling-off period was needed. Also, the closer the time grew to see my mother, the more her situation occupied my thoughts. I was not up to juggling two majors at once. I'd only drop one, or both, if I tried.

On the plane I felt certain freedom in escaping San Francisco, the scene of my own personal earthquake. But the trip was not relaxing; my mind kept flashing back to my desertion of Bebe and leaping forward to whatever condition I might find her in.

Although money was now a big problem, it was far easier to take a cab to Garden City, where the nursing home was, than attempt to find the nearest bus or train station to Kennedy Airport and make the necessary connections. I was getting anxious to see her and found a cabbie who gave me a flat rate of twenty-five dollars.

The Hilda Munson Nursing Home is an enormous old wood frame house three stories high with gables and turrets and a new addition jutting out in the back on the ground floor with another atop it on the second floor. A large veranda runs around one side and the front of the house, set well back on a tree-lined street in an old residential neighborhood.

A brisk end-of-March day and the late hour, it was a quarter to five, kept the veranda deserted. I carried my suitcase and a duffel bag up the walk and entered a large front parlor where several elderly people sat watching an old movie on television. It was warm and stuffy inside with a faint smell of rubbing alcohol and old flowers.

As I looked around for someone who worked there, a door clicked open off the hallway leading back from the staircase and a well-groomed woman in a smart navy blue dress with bluish hair stepped out, holding some manilla folders.

She glanced up, saw me and walked over, switching on what hit me right off as one of the most professional smiles I'd ever seen. Nothing at all behind it but a set of perfect teeth. "You must be Edward Keller—I'm Hilda Munson." We shook hands and she said, "So glad to meet you, Edward. Oh, Monica Rohmer called, she's running a little late, but she's on her way now, should be here by five-thirty. Why don't you step into my office? We can have a little chat before you go up to see your mother."

Hilda Munson led me in and sat me down across from her desk. She briefly acknowledged my P.O.W. status, commenting, still with that beaming smile, about "what absolute hell you must have been through!" But the little chat she wanted to have was all business. Within ten minutes, smiling all the way, she'd extracted the five hundred due for that month, plus seventy-three dollars in incidentals, and reminded me the next month would be due in little over a week. She did it all as gently as possible and when I'd paid in cash her smile even broadened and I thought she just might have a cheery bit of good news for me. Instead she said, "It's a shame one has to come home to face all the usual difficulties and problems of life!" I had a hunch if I'd hedged paying she'd have gladly signed an order sending me back to Vietnam. Still done with a smile, though. I also had a hunch I wouldn't want to catch her when that smile snapped shut for some reason or other.

After she'd given me directions to my mother's room on the second floor, I stopped to dig out some presents from my suitcase: perfume, a blue bed jacket, and a small gold locket I'd bought in San Francisco. Bebe liked gold. Walking up the stairs, I was as nervous as I'd ever been, praying that whatever happened—I wouldn't become too emotional.

At the top of the stairs, I met a nurse carting linens. "Eddie?" she asked. (I had worn my uniform.)

"Yes."

"I'm Mrs. Hershey. Well, your mother's been in a flurry, let me tell you. She looks good, you'll see. You must be nervous, don't be, she's fine. She's a love. C'mon, I'll take you in."

Liked her right off the bat, as I followed her down the hall. She knocked at room five, then opened the door. "Bebe—got a visitor, not a bad looker, either."

I stepped inside. There Bebe sat, dressed in a fancy rose-beige hostess gown, propped up against pillows in an easy chair to the side of her bed.

All I could tell from the first brief impression was that her face was still pretty. She took one long look at me, her eyes grew large, she held her arms out and then all I was aware of was her mouth—her mouth stretching wide, like a child's dark cave of a mouth when it's about to scream, not attractive to see because the stretch looks as if it must hurt. But there was not a sound, not until after I'd rushed to her, dropping the presents on the bed, and thrown my arms around her.

Then the sounds came, so much like a child's anguished shrieks, "Ahhh—ah—haah" almost on one tone level, long howls broken up after a while by choking.

Immediately Mrs. Hershey took over. "Okay, okay, Bebe—sure—there, that's all right." Then, to me: "Step outside, Eddie, the crying's bad, makes her choke, her gag reflexes aren't good. Out, come on, while we get pulled together."

I let go of her while Mrs. Hershey took over, massaging her throat with one hand and gently but firmly patting her back with the other. The sounds of her choking and gagging and crying followed me out into the hall. I hurried down the stairs across the foyer, opened the front door and trotted down to the sidewalk, fighting back tears and actually managing to by pacing up and down, muttering a whole string of "Oh, shit—Jesus Christ—fucking bastard—prick, son-of-a-bitch—my aching ass-almighty!" and other suitable combinations. On and on until a woman with a shopping cart rattled up behind me and, having caught this stream of charmers, gave me such a look of distaste as she passed by that it suddenly made me laugh and I was able to stop, pull myself together, go back inside and up to my mother's room.

I could hear Mrs. Hershey talking to her. "Honey, you wouldn't be alive if you didn't cry. But you've had it now. No more, promise? Good, if you do, I'll really give you something to cry about! Is that a deal? Good. You're lookin' good now, all pulled together. No, you are. Now don't blow it!"

I heard my mother's little bark of a laugh, "Ah-hah," and it made me feel better. Enough to knock on the door. "Okay to come in?"

"Just a minute," came the reply. Sounds of "There we go—here, I'll take that—yes, you look fine!" Then: "Come on in."

I opened the door. "Okay," Mrs. Hershey said, winking at me, "Let's give it another try, shall we?"

My mother shook her head and pointed to herself as if to say "Shame on me." She shook her head again and said, in a throaty voice, a perfectly understandable "Shit!"

I laughed, I was delighted. "Hey, I thought you couldn't talk."

Mrs. Hershey laughed, too. "Wouldn't you know, that's her one good word, has been for a month or so."

My mother laughed, choked a little, shook her head yes, said "Shit!" again, laughed some more, then went into a small choking fit.

"Uh-uh, that's enough, stop it," Mrs. Hershey said, patting her back. When Bebe calmed down, Mrs. Hershey said, "There, think it's safe for me to leave you two alone? Huh, Bebe?"

My mother shook her head yes. Before leaving, Mrs. Hershey said, "If she laughs or cries, she tends to choke because she can't quite control her throat reflexes yet, but it's getting better every day. And wait'll you see her walk."

When she'd gone, my mother pointed to the door and made a thumbs-up gesture. "You like her?" Bebe nodded yes. "So do I. But I'll bet you don't like Hilda Munson?" Bebe's face lit up that I'd discovered this so soon, then she made a frowning face, accompanying it by thumbs-down. "Me neither," I told her.

I went to the bed and picked up the presents; she immediately waved my arms back toward the bed and turned her head away.

"What?" I asked.

She shook her head no, then put a finger up to her eye. I caught on, she didn't want to cry again. She pointed to her watch, made a little waving-away gesture. "Okay, I see— later?" She nodded yes, then pointed to a chair, indicating for me to pull it up in front of her and sit. When I was settled in it, she looked at me, smiled, touched her face, meaning my face, and shook her head yes, meaning despite my years in captivity I looked good.

"You mean I'm still a stunner?" She made an exaggerated "no" sign. "Oh, you just mean I look okay?"

She nodded, then raised her hand as if to smack me. I knew we'd rely on whatever humor we could summon up to get through this first meeting. She raised her fists, shook them back and forth, as if to say how excited she was and there was so much to go over.

"Yes, it's been a long time, huh? Go ahead, ask me anything you want, I'll tell you."

Pointing to her mouth, she shrugged—how could she ask me if she couldn't speak? "Oh, yes, that's right. Shall I do some talking?" She shook her head yes. "Okay, well, I'm fine, in good health, I'm glad to see you and you know why I didn't cry when I saw you?" She nodded yes, then sat up straight, making a tough face, indicating "big strong man." "No," I said, "I didn't cry because you look so good. I was expecting to see something that looked like a head-on collision but you look very pretty, you do, and it made me happy to see you looking so good, *that's* why I didn't cry."

The gesture was: "Go on, get away with your blarney!"

"No, it's true."

"Ahh!" she said, thinking of something she wanted to ask,

then pantomiming cradling a baby. "My baby?" Big nod yes. "Oh, she's adorable, so pretty. She's fine, so is Lisa. They're both fine and send their love to you." No use getting into all that.

We went on talking, I say "we" because she was good at pantomiming, getting into the area of what she wanted me to discuss. At one point she pantomimed hitting, pulling out her fingernails. She wanted to know if they tortured me. "No, but they didn't go out of their way to give me back-rubs!" She grinned at this, motioned for me to lean forward and kissed me on the cheek. When she thought of something she wanted to talk about, she made fists with both hands and shook them back and forth as if she were holding maracas. "What?" I asked. She waved behind her, pantomiming "In the past," then she got all rigid, acting out having the stroke. "Yes," I said, "you had a stroke." She pantomimed "Half-right." Finally I got around to "When you had the stroke?" A big grin, she put a finger on her nose, like in charades, indicating I had it. She tried to speak; it came out guttural and tortured. "Ot—inken." Then she shook her head to the negative. "Again?" I asked. "Ot-inken!" she said, more affirmatively.

Oh, God, I thought, come on, get it. I couldn't. She saw the puzzlement on my face and said it again. She smiled, lifted her hands, as if to say "Now?" I shook my head no. "Ot-inken, ot-inken!" She pointed to herself, made a small negative shake of her head, then smiled with pride.

I could feel myself start to sweat, knowing this was important to her. "Ot-inken?" I repeated. She made a face, no, that wasn't it, of course it wasn't it. Then with impatience she said it again, bearing down hard, giving each syllable equal emphasis. "Ot—in—ken!"

Still I was puzzled. She made her hands into fists and shook them, saying the phrase over again three times and becoming increasingly impatient: "Ot-inken, ot-inken, ot-inken!" She quickly jabbed herself in the chest, meaning herself.

"Mother, I'm sorry, I'm just not thinking." She agreed with me. Having said the word "thinking" made me naturally think of "inken." "Thinking?" I asked. "Is it 'thinking'?"

She made a gesture as if to hit me, then quickly dug around at her side, in the chair, coming up with a large piece of cardboard with the letters of the alphabet printed on it.

She gestured for me to lean over and watch as she quickly pointed out with trembling fingers: NOT DRINKI—

"Oh, not *drinking!*" I said. YES, she nodded, jabbing herself in the chest again. "You weren't drinking when you had the stroke?"

Half-right, half a finger, she gave me.

"You hadn't been drinking *before* you had the stroke?"

Big yes.

Oh, Christ, how that got to me, that that was what she wanted so badly to tell me. "Ot-inken!" It hit me hard, I knew I couldn't deal with it. The ache behind my eyes was about to explode.

"Oh, Christ," I said, snapping my fingers and looking at my watch. "I forgot, I've got to make a quick phone call to Lisa, I promised I'd call as soon as I—be right back."

And I was out of the room and down the hall and bursting into tears, staggering way down at the end of the hall by a window and sobbing like a deranged person, telling myself what an asshole I was and then saying, oh, the hell with it.

# 36

Arms around me; I looked around to see Mrs. Hershey. "Oh, shit!" I said.

"Yes, yes, I know, I know. Here, come in here." Leading me into a large linen-supply closet, she closed the door after us. "Hope she didn't see you, did she?" I shook my head no, then just had one helluva good cry on her shoulder. She patted me, saying things like, "Good, get it all out, get rid of it, that's the way. Nothing wrong with crying, long as it's over someone else. But she's coming along fine, Eddie, she's going to pull out of this for sure. You'll see, I've been around, I know."

That began to snap me out of it. "You think?"

"Sure, should have seen her at first, all paralyzed on the right side, couldn't walk, she can walk now and move her arms, just her right hand is a little weak. Her speech will come back, too, might take a while but it will."

Pretty soon she'd worked me out of it by talking, by asking me questions. "What'd you tell her to get out of the room?"

"I had to make a phone call, a *quick* one."

"I'll bet," she laughed. "You okay now?"

"Yes, just a minute while my face gets back in shape."

"Stay here," she said, "I'll be right back."

I began pulling myself together and soon she returned with a wet washcloth and a paper cup with brandy. "There, give you a little pickup."

"Thanks." I downed it and went into a small coughing spell myself. Mrs. Hershey patted my back, saying, "Like mother, like son."

The second I opened Bebe's door I started talking, as if a line of fast chatter could camouflage my puffy face and red-rimmed eyes: "I'm sorry, couldn't get the connection, had to wait, but I finally got her, the goddam phone company! She sends his love, so does Lauri and—"

But my mother was shaking her head no, pantomiming with a finger to her eye, then rolling it down her cheek, pointing to me. She knew. I stopped chattering, looked at her and said "Yes."

Yes, she nodded, then she pantomimed "Done with it, all finished, that was good," and we settled down to another session of communicating.

If I'd been worried about Bebe's mind, I wasn't now. She was extremely alert. She'd always been good at charades and her pantomiming was excellent, although sometimes she was a little inside with clues, thinking because a particular association was clear to her, it should be to me. She would grow impatient when I didn't connect immediately with what she was trying to convey. She was able to give "Shit!" many readings; she could lay on joy, surprise, disgust or anger. I especially got a kick when she used it to mean "no kidding?" Like when I told her I'd had a press conference all my own and she said "Shit . . . ?" in a funny upward inflection as if saying "Really? . . . Say, that's something."

If we got stuck and several tries at acting it out didn't

work, she would quickly grab the piece of cardboard and begin spelling out key words, but, by that time, her finger would be shaking with impatience.

Her face, which had always been round, was thinner than usual, but this didn't make it any less pretty, it even accentuated the cheekbones, giving her better definition. Only her hair was disappointing, much shorter than before, the kind of close-cropped easy-to-manage cut sick people are sometimes given. The blue ribbon in her hair touched me greatly; her hair was so short it could barely support it.

She'd really been done up for my visit, dark red nail polish, eye make-up, which, because of her crying, had run and smudged, then been wiped away by Mrs. Hershey with the result that her eyes had dark raccoon areas around them. She was nicely perfumed but whoever had applied the make-up had gone a bit heavy on the rouge.

All in all, she looked very dear to me. Often I wanted to reach forward and hug her but I knew this would be dangerous.

There was so much she wanted to know: What was I going to do now? Where would I live? How long would I be back east? To most of these questions I made expansive general answers: "I don't know, I just want to relax for a while, enjoy, get my bearings." She would nod in agreement. To the question of how long would I be in New York, I replied, "Until you get bored with me." She gave me a wave of her hand and "Shit!" We both laughed.

After a while, she indicated she wanted to show me how she could walk. I helped her up, feeling the weakness in her as she held on to me. She was a bit unsteady and wobbly at first, but after she pointed to a cane and I'd got it for her, she walked better, using my arm for support on her bad side, the right one, and the cane on her left side.

Her right leg dragged as she pulled it after her, lifting it a ways ahead, then scuffing along until she gave it another little lift. She wanted to go out into the hall: there she hit a stride of sorts. When she forced herself to take larger, regular steps she was walking quite well, except for the limping right leg.

On our way back to Bebe's room, Monica Rohmer came trotting up the stairs toward us. My mother's face lit up, she said "Shit! Shit!" and jiggled my arm. It was obvious she didn't know Monica was coming.

They embraced and then Monica embraced me. Immediately I was taken by her outgoing warmth, by her breezy regular approach. If Eve Arden had been a brunette, shorter and a little more outdoorish, this would have been Monica. Above all, I could picture her taking a good healthy swat at a golf ball; I don't know why but that came to mind within a minute or so of our meeting. She seemed to be about my mother's age, early or mid-fifties.

Once we got back to the room and Bebe was settled into her chair, Monica turned out to be a fine go-between. She and my mother were completely connected and Monica was very up-to-date on current events with Bebe so there was hardly any time-lag involved in getting to the heart of a subject and Monica could invariably speak my mother's mind on almost any matter to her satisfaction.

After a while Monica said, "Oh, Eddie, come help me up with this plant I bought, will you?"

"Yes, sure."

As we left the room, she said to Bebe, "I'm gonna get a hernia yet on account of you."

When we got out into the hall and started down the stairs, Monica took my arm and gave it to me rapid-fire. "Gotta make this quick, she's sharp as a knife. I found an apartment on the upper West Side, old, rent-controlled, but spacious. Three ninety a month, have to give two months' rent, the first and the last. I live with a friend of mine, Alice, an old friend, a semi-invalid, in a tiny apartment in the Village. If I can swing this one, Bebe can move in with us and we'll take good care of her. I'm strapped for about another four hundred, if you could lend it to me, I'll take the place. Much better for Bebe than this and it'll be cheap by comparison. Could you make four hundred?"

"Yes, but it's not a loan, you've already paid for Bebe, I owe it to you." I said this without hesitation, although I didn't have it.

"Ah!" She waved away what she'd spent. "We'll work it out. But don't let Bebe know you're helping, she's dead set against taking money from you. Dead set. I've made up a cockamamy story about finances, which I won't bore you with now, no time, you'll get it when I tell Bebe. You just act dumb and go along, yes, it's a good idea and all that. Alice gets two fifty a month, I get unemployment and I think I might be getting a little running part on a soap so if you could manage a couple hundred a month for Bebe until she's able to work, we could swing it."

"I can manage."

"Good, it's a damned sight cheaper than this dump for eight hundred. Bebe likes Alice, too. Of course, Bebe and I are like sisters. Know where we met?"

"No."

"Alcoholics Anonymous, two and a half years ago, became thick as thieves. More about that later. There," she said, indicating a large potted plant, "just picked that up out here, near the station, so we'd have an excuse to get out, cost me twelve bucks for that lousy plant, but she's so quick, I didn't want her to catch on. Come on, right back, so she won't think anything's funny."

We hurried back up the stairs. After Bebe made a fuss over the plant and we both settled down in chairs, she made all sorts of signs, chiding Monica for buying it.

"Yes, well that's what you think," Monica said. "My ship's come in and I can buy a plant if I want."

My mother's eyes widened and she waved her hands for Monica to tell her.

"What do you think?" Monica shrugged, "that I *wouldn't?*" Bebe shook her fists impatiently, she wanted to hear. "All right, all right, take it easy. I have a surprise for both of you." Bebe looked to me, indicating "Why him, too?" "Because he's your son and he's probably interested to know where his mother's going to be living." Bebe's eyes widened even more. "Okay, remember the land outside of Phoenix I told you about, my brother and I own together?" Bebe nodded. "Well, the old bastard finally broke down and sold two acres, so I got a little windfall, not much but a little. I'm taking a new apartment at Eighty-seventh and West End and you're moving in with Alice and me."

My mother shook her head no.

" 'Yes' I said. You are, no nonsense. We need you for bridge, number one; number two, I can't wait to do Hilda Munson out of eight hundred a month." Bebe winced at the price. "Number three, I've been wanting to get out of that broom closet on Eleventh Street for two years now and this is my chance. Number four"—as Bebe started to pantomime about money—"I don't want to hear anything about expenses.

This apartment is rent-controlled, not much more than the mini-flat we're in now, with two large bedrooms, big living room, old-fashioned kitchen and a den and I want it. Costs—uh-uh!" she said, as Bebe went on protesting, "Listen to me. Costs a few cents more a meal to feed three than two, so all in all, it's a bargain. When you get back on your feet and can say more than 'Shit!' you can chip in on the rent, meantime—"

Bebe pointed to me and pantomimed "No money," shaking her head violently. "Don't worry, I wouldn't take a penny from a P.O.W. What the hell kind of an American do you think I am?"

Bebe gave her thumbs-down and they both laughed. Monica went on in quieter tones, now that she'd got the thrust of it out. "Listen, darling, you know how stuck Alice and I are on you. We'd really love it, also you and Alice would be good company for each other when I'm out pounding the pavement. It would be a favor and we won't take no for an answer. Hey"—she could see my mother's eyes tearing up— "and what about that bastard brother of mine finally letting go of two whole acres?"

My mother shook her head yes, but she'd no sooner done that when her mouth opened up, again the dark silent cave before the cries came out.

"Oh, no, Bebe, for Christ's sake, now don't do that!"

Bebe quickly shook her head in agreement but she couldn't stop herself. Soon long wailing sobs came from her and then the choking began. I headed toward the door. "I'll get the nurse."

"No," Monica said, "I know what to do, I've been through this about a thousand times."

"I'll leave the room while you . . ."

As I went out into the hall and shut the door, I heard Monica saying, "Honest to God, though, Bebe, the goddam crying's got to stop or we'll kick your ass out into the street."

In the midst of all the crying and choking came a burst of laughter, "Ah-hah!"

By the time I returned to the room, Bebe was quieted down. Monica turned to me as I came in and said, "It's all set, whether she likes it or not, probably doesn't, but what the hell can she do about it anyhow?" Bebe laughed, pointing to Monica and giving the thumbs-up gesture. Then Bebe laughed again, sputtered, said, "Ot-inken!" and gestured for me to explain it. I told Monica of our problem with "Ot-in-ken."

Monica picked it up and went on: "It's true, she hadn't had a drink in almost two years—" My mother waved a hand, gesturing back in time. "All right, over two years, was it?" Bebe nodded energetically. "Yes," Monica said, "I guess it was." My mother made a threatening gesture, meaning "Damned right it was." "Yes," Monica said to me, "she hadn't had one—but neither had I," she suddenly added, making the threatening gesture right back at Bebe. "What are you, the only saint? What about *me*? I never had so many Tabs in my life, I'm amazed I haven't turned into one gigantic bottle of Tab!"

My mother gestured approval of Monica, pointing to her and making a halo sign.

"Oh, I tell you, Bebe, I can't wait for our bridge games. Wait'll you see the den, it's perfect for bridge, it's got—"

Immediately my mother's eyes began tearing up and when Monica started to warn her off crying, Bebe only shook her head indicating "Don't worry, I'm not going to fall apart, let me feel a little something." She put a hand to her heart, making little fluttering, patting gestures, to indicate how happy she was over the apartment idea.

This got to both Monica and me and we quickly jumped to another subject. Several times before we left, my mother's eyes filled up whenever either one of us alluded to the new apartment. Monica was able to head off outright crying by treating it with dismay, if not outright disgust. After another hour or so, Bebe began yawning every few minutes. When Mrs. Hershey came in with medication, she caught one of the yawns. "Bebe, you better be getting into bed soon." My mother shook her head no, this was a big occasion, pointing to me, sitting up very straight and saluting. "Yes, I know," Mrs. Hershey said, "but you've had a busy long day with lots of excitement. You don't want to risk a setback, do you? You don't want anything to do with another stroke, do you?" Bebe shook her head in strong agreement. "Okay, then, fifteen minutes and that's it."

Bebe made a face and shrugged as Mrs. Hershey left the room. We talked some more, mainly I did, as Bebe would indicate questions and Monica would translate them for me.

Questions about my imprisonment, Lisa, Lauri, plans for the future—she wanted me to go back and finish college—and on and on.

After a half hour or so Mrs. Hershey stuck her head in. "Okay, folks, I gave you extra time, get ready to hit the road."

Bebe nodded and waved her out the door, saying, "Shit!" and yawning at the same time. We all laughed, then she picked up the cardboard with the letters printed on it and motioned for Monica to lean in and watch while she spelled. Monica spoke the words: "Leave quickly." She glanced at me, then patted Bebe's hand. "Yes, honey, we will. Don't worry."

I reached for the presents on the bed but again my mother warned me off them, pantomiming "Later" and quickly spelling out "Thank you."

I said I'd see her in a day or so, would phone and let her know exactly when. We all grew tense as time for leaving neared; there would be sudden little silences as we went on trying to keep the conversation light.

Finally it was Monica who said, "Okay, Eddie, up and out, I'll meet you downstairs."

I actually lunged forward from my chair, giving Bebe a quick embrace even though she turned her head away from me, already fighting back her emotions. I hurriedly left the room and I could hear Monica chiding her out of crying as I quickly trotted down the stairs.

The visit had been a good one, but it had taken its toll of energy. Although I was glad to see her in better condition than I'd imagined, still it got to me, way down deep, to see her so vulnerable, so basically helpless.

Waiting for Monica, I saw a phone booth in the downstairs hall and put a call through to my father. I gathered it was a maid who answered because she said, "Keller residence."

He was excited to hear my voice and when I told him I was in New York he immediately invited me to lunch Monday down at Wall Street. I was to meet him in front of the main entrance to the Stock Exchange at noon; he gave me instructions on how to get there and there was warmth in his voice when we said good-bye and he ended with "I'm really looking forward to seeing you, son!"

Son—after so many years. It sounded odd. Maybe not,

maybe he'd been saved for when I needed him. It was in my mind to borrow enough money from him to help Monica set up the apartment and get Bebe moved in. I would be getting my lump payment of five dollars for every day I was prisoner in several months so there would be no problem about paying him back.

I felt good about Bebe on the train ride back to the city and I liked Monica more and more. She filled me in on Bebe's life in New York before her stroke. She'd done costumes for several Off-Broadway shows, one Broadway play, and for two years had been with C.B.S., supervising wardrobe for several of their soap operas. They'd had a cutback about three months before her stroke and she was let go. Monica claimed if it hadn't been for Bebe she'd have gone back to drinking; Bebe had come to her rescue several crucial times when Monica had slipped back slightly and pulled her through. Monica was appreciative of this and said she'd never forget it.

At one point she suddenly turned to me and said, "Eddie, I want to tell you something. I know you've been through a lot so it probably won't make any difference, but I want you to know. Alice and I have both been married but for the last eight years we've been living together as—well, more than just friends."

She looked at me for my reaction. I only smiled and said, "I see."

"Good, then it doesn't make any difference. Of course, I keep forgetting you grew up in California around the business, so it's probably no shock." She laughed a wry little laugh. "Although nowadays that doesn't enter into our relationship. Alice's too sick for any shenanigans, also we're not getting any younger."

"What's the matter with Alice?"

"Oh, God," she sighed, "what isn't? She's got diabetes, arthritis, but the worst of it is emphysema. She can barely get from one room to the other without sitting down to catch her breath. She's a dear, though, you'll like her. Not a complaint, just goes on huffing and puffing, never hear a word. She's been a good friend to me." She sat there quietly for a while until she reached over and took my hand. "I'm sorry we're not rich," she said. "I hate to knock you up for money, I do.

And your mother would have a fit, an absolute fit. She feels responsible for what happened to you, she—"

"Ah! That's—" I started to shrug it off.

"No, she's told me how things were, she's very much aware of how it was for you. She loves you very much."

"I love her, too."

"I know you do."

Monica invited me down for supper to meet her friend, Alice Court. "That is, if you want to blow an evening with a couple of old bags."

I did. And liked Alice as much as Monica, although she couldn't have been more different: soft-spoken, gentle and terribly thin. Her constant struggle for breath was painful to watch. They did have one quality in common—warmth. And Alice seemed as fond of Bebe as Monica was.

Their apartment was small but extremely tasteful, simple and uncluttered. Alice had fixed a roast chicken, sweet potatoes and one of the best salads I'd ever tasted. A dry white wine was served, candles were lit. They might have been in narrow financial straits but they lived in a certain style that was clear from the large Turner (not an original) on the wall, their KLH and collection of records and books. Also the small television set was in the bedroom, not for company in the living room.

It was a lovely evening. Alice and Monica were excited about the new apartment and both were dedicated to nursing Bebe back to health. I realized I was lucky to have them. They apologized for not being able to put me up and Monica suggested an inexpensive hotel on Waverly Place only a few blocks from them. She phoned and arranged a room for a week for sixty-five dollars.

Before I left I promised Monica I'd give her the four hundred by Friday when she was planning to sign the lease.

The Breton Hotel was pleasant, unfancy but clean, and I had a single room with bath on the fourth floor in the rear. Still, when I climbed into bed I felt uneasy. Lying there thinking about my mother and the meeting with my father on Monday I realized I was feeling—what was I feeling? Not exactly depressed, I was feeling—disadvantaged.

I mumbled the word out loud. "Disadvantaged . . ." It was an odd word, one I never used or even thought of, but now suddenly I was feeling distinctly disadvantaged.

Alone in an inexpensive hotel in New York with two hundred and fifty-two dollars and sixty-five of that already pledged, having to come up with solid funds for Bebe. Even though I had security forthcoming for a loan, the pressure of *having* to borrow money from my father on our very first meeting after so many years—got to me.

Disadvantaged. Or as Vin would have said, "Disadfuck-ingvantaged." Clumsy, that.

# 37

Anxious was the word for me, standing in front of the Stock Exchange right off the corner of Broad and Wall streets Monday at noon. I didn't know what to expect, didn't even know if I'd recognize him on sight. It had been almost eighteen years and although he'd given me a snapshot of himself and his new wife at the time, I had, in one of those gestures of hurt youth and, also, out of loyalty to my mother, torn it up not an hour after we parted. As if he would know or even care, still I ripped off his head, also decapitating his wife, and then severed their bodies at the waist and once more at the knees, dropping the pieces down onto the subway tracks at Times Square for added measure. If mutilation didn't get them, the I.R.T. express would.

That was years ago. All gone, all forgotten. I was long past needing a father and exactly because of that I'd probably find myself with one. All right with me.

I had worn my uniform and I wasn't sure I liked myself for it, wasn't sure I wasn't using it as an added lever when the time came to borrow the money. But it *would* help him recognize me, standing there with the beginnings of the Wall Street lunch hour crowd spilling out into the lower Manhattan canyons. Then, too, I wanted to present myself, not just as his son, but as a grownup man, a soldier, too.

Bull, I wore it because I knew it would help get the money for Bebe.

"Eddie—oh, Eddie!"

I turned and there he was coming toward me—looking so almighty distinguished. I'd remembered him as a good-looking man, but he was downright distinguished, dressed in a smart light gray topcoat with his dark gray close-cropped hair and his steel gray eyes and a healthy tan, to top off his looks.

He grinned and threw his arms around me in one of those hearty embraces men give men in public. "My God, Eddie— all grown up! Say, if you don't look—what's the word we used to use? Natty!" He laughed. "You are one natty-looking soldier. Yes, sir."

"You're looking good, too," I told him.

"Marianne and I just got back from a long business week-end in the Bahamas. There's nothing like a tan to make an old bastard look pulled together." He paused, gazed at me for a long beat and said, "Son, it's good to see you."

"It's good to see you, too." I was sounding like Little Sir Echo but the warmth of his greeting, much as I liked it, had thrown me for a loss.

"Hey, would you like to take a spin through the exchange before lunch?"

"Sure."

"Come on." He led the way in past a guard who nodded, saying, "Mr. Keller."

"My son," he replied. "Five years in prison camp, North Vietnam, just back!"

"God bless you," the obviously Irish guard said as we breezed past.

"You don't look like you put in five years, not at all," he said, laughing. "Damned if you do." He reached around my shoulders while we were walking and gave me a squeeze. "Jesus, I'm proud of you, Eddie. I can't tell you!" He stopped walking and turned to face me. "Oh, now, isn't this some-thing? A father who's barely ever seen you, or even written, who didn't even know you were a P.O.W. until he read it in the *The New York Times after* your release—and suddenly I'm so proud of you. I guess that's what you call—a nerve!"

"I don't mind, better late than never."

He shook his head with pleasure at that, then said, "No, you must think I'm an old fart, sounding off like this."

"No, it's good to see you, I'm getting a kick out of it."

"You are—for real?"

"Yes."

"Good, come on."

The action on the floor of the exchange was dizzying. The yelling and waving, the clerks tearing around, the clusters of men bidding, the large moving neon tapes of stock quotations. The action was rabid. How did anyone ever keep track of what was going on? I thought of all the movies I'd seen with shots of the exchange, especially footage during the crash in '29.

My father (your what???) introduced me to several men during our tour, each time proudly as his son, each time giving my P.O.W. status. The third time he did this, the man he introduced me to said in good humor, "Your *son?*" Then: "No kidding, he's the spitting image!"

As we moved away from him we each sneaked a sidelong glance to see if it was true. We caught each other doing this, laughed and stopped. "Do we?" he asked.

"I don't know, what do you think?"

"Same beautiful straight nose and aristocratic chin. I guess so." He laughed. "Of course, I'm going gray."

"You're a little taller than I am."

"Only an inch or so."

"And your eyes are gray," I reminded him.

"They were blue like yours when I was a kid. Hey, what are you trying to do, talk your way out of it?"

"No," I said, smiling. "I guess there is a resemblance."

"Damned right there is!"

He explained the basic workings of the exchange and even took me into the smaller Bond Exchange, which was not nearly as hectic. I glanced up at a large oblong window overlooking from the second floor to see about twenty-five kids staring down at us, noses pressed to the glass. A school tour of some sort.

"That's the visitors' gallery, they've got one in the regular exchange, too, but that's not good enough for my son. I wanted you to get the feel of the action."

After we left, he stopped off at a large commercial bank a

block or so away to cash a check and I stood in line with him. Lunch hour and the bank was crowded. "Sorry," he said, "I should have done this before but I couldn't get away from the office." The line next to the one we stood in was for large commercial transactions and I was bug-eyed at the stacks of bills handed over by the teller. Some of the people on the receiving end, men and women, had guards with them, some didn't. I couldn't help a slight mental drool at the sight of all those white-banded stacks of green. My father caught the look in my eyes and said, "It's quite a place down here, isn't it? The money market of the world. I never thought I'd find anything like this exciting, but I do."

On our way to the restaurant, a walk of six or seven blocks, I asked how he'd happened to get into the stock market. He explained that his farm in Maine barely made a living, and a few years ago, with five children, three in high school and about ready to go to college, life had become more expensive. His wife's brother was partner in a firm; he suggested my father give it a try about four years ago when his wife's father died and left her the house in Nyack, about an hour's commuting from the city. He gave it a try and was what they call a customer's man. He liked the work, he said, although it was a tough business, getting tougher all the time, extremely competitive and not what you'd call relaxing. Weekends, however, he puttered around his house and garden in Nyack and it was a good change from city life.

He took me to the original Delmonico's, a restaurant founded way back when the only New York was down around Wall Street. After we were seated at a good table with waiter hovering, my father asked, "Drink?"

"Yes."

"Good." He turned to the waiter. "I'll have a Harvey Wallbanger. What about you?" he asked me.

But I was laughing. "A what?" I asked.

"Harvey Wallbanger."

"What's that?"

"Vodka and orange juice with a slight layer of Galliano. Very smooth, try one." I nodded and he ordered two.

I remember, right at that moment, feeling just about the best since I'd returned from North Vietnam. Here I was sitting in a fine restaurant, about to have a good lunch, and I simply felt filled with hope, felt my father and I were going to hit it off great guns. I laughed again.

"What?"

"Harvey Wallbanger, the name gives me a kick."

"You'll get a kick all right. They're subtle but they pack a hidden wallop."

The drinks came and a Harvey Wallbanger tasted smooth and good mixed with all the talk and questions we had for each other. He was hooked on hearing about my experiences in prison camp, insisted upon getting into that right off. His eyes were lively as I recounted the adventures and misadventures. He would lean in toward me and say, "Yes . . . ? Yeah, I see. . . . Uh-huh, go on. . . . What about . . . ?" and on and on. The idea of how we survived fascinated him.

When we were about to order, he caught my expression at the price list. Not only one of the oldest restaurants in New York City, it had to be one of the most expensive. "Don't even look at the right-hand side of the menu. Anything you want, this is an occasion."

I ordered baked oysters to start and trout amandine along with a spinach salad. My father ordered us another Harvey Wallbanger. As soon as the waiter left, he urged me to go on. When I got to the part about getting my one and only letter from Lisa I realized he didn't know I was married.

"My God," I told him, "you didn't know I'd made you a grandfather."

"A grandfather?"

I filled him in on Lisa and Lauri and, although he was interested, he did not listen with quite the same fervor as when I'd been talking about life at Bel Air. Later on he shook his head and said again, "A grandfather, what do you know? I'm already one by Marianne's daughter by her first husband, but now I'm a natural one. I had an idea it would be my oldest, Mathew, but—I mean," he added, correcting himself, "my *other* oldest. What's her name again, my granddaughter?"

"Lauri."

"Lauri, I'll have to send her something." He returned to the subject of his main interest: "And you only got one letter from your wife—in all those five years?"

"Yes, one from her and one from Mother." Natural time to bring her up. "Oh, I saw Bebe yesterday."

"You did?"

"Yes."

Pause. "How is she?"

"She can't speak well at all but outside of that she's coming along, a little limp in her right leg, but with the right care she'll pull out of it."

"Good." There was a pause, during which I hoped some of the warmth he showed me would spill over to Bebe. Instead he said, "What about writing letters, how many were you allowed to send out?"

"None."

"Not one?"

"No."

"But I thought, I mean the conventions of war would—" And he was back into war and life as a prisoner.

I went along with it, figuring to satisfy his curiosity and even, in a way, understanding it. Then, too, it was good to be able to entertain him. Afterwards I would get into family matters, perhaps even ask about him and Bebe and their early times together. Bebe never talked about him much, never really bad-mouthed him, except I was always led to believe he simply walked out. About all she would say was, "It was a mistake, we all make mistakes and I made a whopper. Beware the charm of the Irish. Oh, the Irish! The pride and vanity of that bunch keep them in constant trouble." Once, when she was drunk, she said, "Him? There was nothing wrong with Leonard Keller, it's just that he's one of the most selfish men ever put on this earth. Charm, oh, yes, when he wants to turn it on, but when he turns it off—watch out!" But she never portrayed him to me as a villain.

Smooth as the drinks tasted, by the time I'd finished the second one, I could feel it. In a good way. It made me relax, not be so uptight in anticipation of what I'd eventually be asking him. Besides, money was obviously not a problem, not with the way he looked, not with his entire attitude and this expensive restaurant.

When our first course arrived he ordered a third Harvey Wallbanger and a dry white wine to go with our main course. A few minutes later, as I was telling him about Vin and Mine Fury, the waiter and the maître d' returned in a flurry of apologies, saying they didn't have the specific wine he ordered. My father—might as well call him Leonard—wasn't all that upset at first but the maître d' went on explaining why they didn't have it and then held out the wine list. Leonard shoved it back at the man and snapped "No need for a big production, just bring a good dry white wine, a chilled one."

Still, the maitre d' held out the wine list. "If Monsieur would like to pick one—"

"Christ!" Leonard said, slapping the back of his hand against the wine list and knocking it back, "we're trying to talk, can't you just bring—"

"Yes, sir," the maitre d' said, as both he and the waiter backed off, trying to hide expressions of distaste.

"Go on, Eddie," my father said.

I have an aversion to people who are rude to waiters, but it was obvious his annoyance came not so much from whether or not he got the wine he ordered but from the interruption of my story, so I tried to discount it. Of course, I gave my father a more or less surface account of my relationship with Vin, but I did let him know we had a strong friendship and when I got to Vin's death, he reached over and put a hand on my arm. I could tell by the expression on his face he was touched, that he felt for me, and I warmed to him again.

"You know," he said, when I'd got to our liberation, "when I was a kid, well, not so much a *kid*, I had a strong— *thing* about the French Foreign Legion, always had fantasies about life in the legion, the life of a professional soldier, always on the go, one adventure after another, no ties, no responsibilities, no family, nothing but the life of a soldier. I probably romanticized it, but I never quite got over it. Matter of fact, when your mother ditched me, I thought about it."

"When she ditched you? I didn't know she ditched you? I thought you left—" I almost said "us" but changed it to "I thought you left her."

"That's what she told you?"

"I don't know if she told me, it's just the impression I got."

"Sure, she would have put it that way."

"No, she—"

"Don't tell *me*," he said, sharply. "I know her, I know what she'd do!" He quickly realized the tone he'd used and said, "Sorry, didn't mean to—but I haven't forgotten. May be years but I remember how it was."

"How was it?" I asked.

"What do you mean?" he asked, almost belligerently, as if I'd parroted his words sarcastically, which I hadn't done.

"I'd like to know," I said, openly and with interest.

"What do you want to know for?" he asked, as if there was some hidden reason.

"You mean, outside of the fact that you're my parents?" I'd said this lightly, trying to keep my tone one of casual good humor.

"Parents?"

"Yes, you're my parents, I'd like to know how it was."

"Ah, that's all so long ago, we don't have to get into that whole—mess. Some day I'll ..." He broke off, as if he were thinking about the past. For a second I thought he might even talk about it now.

His speech had turned slightly fuzzy; he was feeling the drinks. His features hadn't come unglued, but they'd slacked a bit. His eyes were not as clear and snappy, they were watery around the edges.

I felt slightly uncomfortable.

Suddenly he leaned forward with a new spurt of energy. "Did you ever think about going back there and getting even with—say, this Mine Fury? Hmn, what a name for him!"

"Not really, that would be pretty—"

"That would make quite a story, wouldn't it? About a P.O.W. who goes back, after—say a year or so, maybe he gets a job with a government agency and somehow gets back and then he seeks out one of his captors, kills him in revenge for the death of a buddy."

We talked about that for a while but I kept wanting to get back to our lives, what was going on now, what had gone on before.

When our main course was served he was edgy and abrupt with the waiter, although the service was excellent, the wine poured for him to taste, all the amenities. He seemed to be looking for something to find fault with and he did when he uncovered the rolls, felt one and said to the waiter, "These are cold, let's have some warm ones."

"Yes, sir," the waiter said, unfortunately adding, "I believe they were warm when they were first brought out."

They *had* been sitting there while we'd been drinking, but that didn't make any difference to Leonard Keller, nor the fact that the waiter was reaching to pick up the basket and was going to comply with his wishes. "I don't give a goddam when they *were* warm, they were warm when they were first baked, but that doesn't do us any good now." He slapped his napkin down on the top of the table as if he were initiating a duel. "Are you telling me—"

My stomach knotted. "I don't want any rolls, not with all this good food—"

"What?" He turned on me. "I don't care whether you want any—wait a minute, are you paying for this lunch?"

"No."

"Well, then—" Back to the waiter. "Are you bringing warm rolls or not?"

"Yes, sir. Right away." The waiter left.

Leonard looked at me, but not for my reaction to his outburst or to apologize, only to snort, "It's not like we're at McDonald's, for Chrissake, this is Delmonico's!"

I didn't want to linger in this area. I wanted to like him, had liked him up until these skirmishes with the maitre d' and the waiter. The bully in him was showing. He sipped at his wine. After he tasted it, he pressed his lips together. I hadn't noticed before but his lips were thin and gray and rubbery looking. I put a finger up to feel my lips to see if they felt like his looked, even though I knew I didn't have thin lips.

"What?" he asked, looking up at me.

"Nothing," I said, starting to eat.

Much as I hated to acknowledge it, he was turning me off. I wracked my brain for some way we could get back into comfortable conversation.

## 38

"Tell me about your kids?" I asked him.

"They're not such kids anymore, two are Marianne's by her first marriage, three are ours together. They're a great bunch, you'll meet them when you come out."

I was hoping he'd go into detail or perhaps even ask more about my wife and daughter, although I hadn't decided yet whether I'd tell him about our problems, or not, but instead he tapped his fingers on the table and said, "Five years, what a long time without regular food or—what about sex, well, I suppose you just did without, didn't you?"

"Yes."

He hunched his shoulders and leaned forward. "Say, did you ever try to escape?"

"At first Vin talked about it a lot, but it wasn't very practical."

"Why not?"

"Well, we were in North Vietnam, where could we go if we did get out?"

"Back down to South Vietnam, rejoin your unit."

I couldn't help thinking: Bullshit, but I said, "Yes, but we looked so different, it would have been impossible to get by."

"No, no," he said, energy up, as if he were planning it now. "You could travel by night, hide out in the daytime. I'd have tried it, yes, that would have been my point—escape!"

"Okay," I said, trying to kid our way out of it, "next time, *you* can escape."

He cocked his head. "You being smart?" he asked with a half-smirk, almost as if he hoped I'd say yes.

"No, I was only kidding."

"Oh," he said. "Oh, I see." He poured another glass of

wine for himself, then looked at my glass, which I hadn't touched. "What's the matter, you don't like the wine?"

"No, I'm still on my Wallbanger."

He'd finished his third but I was taking it easy; I was feeling the first two and didn't want to get drunk, didn't want to lose the control that comes with getting drunk. We didn't speak for a while. I glanced at my watch; ten minutes of two; wondered if he had to get back to work. The only sounds were those of us eating and the sounds of heavy breaths coming through his nostrils, the kind of breathing that comes when you're feeling the booze. I thought back to Lisa and our last encounter: everyone gets drunk at important meetings.

The silence was uncomfortable; I was trying hard to think of the best topic of conversation, one that would bring back the rapport we'd had at the beginning. I suddenly heard myself say, almost against my will, "I thought about you a lot during those five years."

He coughed slightly, a little piece of fish flew out of his mouth and landed on the tablecloth at the base of my water glass. He ignored it, saying, "You did, eh? What were you thinking?" He was pleased.

I was so surprised at what I'd said—I hadn't thought about him much at all—that I could barely respond. "I—you know, where you were, how you were doing."

"You did, did you?" He smiled, I noticed a bit of fish stuck between his teeth, wondered if they were his teeth or a very good set of false ones. They looked good, except for the fish.

"Yes." Hated myself for resorting to lies to be ingratiating.

He chuckled. "Thought of your father, did you? Jesus, I wish I'd have known, I'd have written you, son, I would have." A little wave of maudlin affection came over him. Seize it, I told myself, as he led into the opening more by patting my arm and adding "Too bad we never had a chance to—"

"Your rolls, sir." It was the waiter. Point-killer.

Leonard waved him off. "Too late, take them away."

The waiter was fed up with this treatment. His face tightened as he placed the basket on the table saying, "I'll leave them here in case—"

"I said take them away, we're almost finished with the goddam—" He stopped and flagged down the maitre d'.

"Say," he called out, stopping the man and drawing him over. "The service in this place stinks, what's the matter, this used to be one of the best restaurants in the city and I bring my son who's been a P.O.W. for five long years as a special treat and the service absolutely stinks!"

"What seems to be the trouble?" the maitre d' asked.

"The whole goddam thing *seems to be the trouble*," Leonard said, mimicking him. "that's what seems to be the trouble."

Now a whole little drama was played out—for nothing. The service had been quite good, the food was excellent, but something had galled him and when the maitre d' and the waiter attempted to find out what was the matter, beside the rolls, Leonard became angrier. "I'm just telling you it stinks and you're trying to put some sort of quiz to me. I'm a customer, a paying customer. I don't have to prove anything to you, I'm telling you it stinks."

His voice was raised now and we'd attracted the attention of more than a few tables. Scenes in restaurants are nerve-cringers; I loathe them, was wishing I could disappear. Three men were leaving and as they walked by, glancing at the commotion, one of them said, "Leonard? Give 'em hell, baby!"

"Frank, hey, Frank, come here, want you to meet my son."

And with that, the drama was over, Leonard waving it away and insisting Frank sit down with us. The man told his friends he'd see them, we shook hands and within a minute Frank had ordered us an after-lunch drink. As if we needed one. I bypassed it, but my father had a vodka-on-the-rocks. Immediately he set about giving Frank a rundown of my five years in prison camp. Congratulations all around. He also told him, "I've been a bastard of a father to the boy, but I'm changing all that now, you can bet your life, we're really going to get to know each other, aren't we Eddie?"

"Yes." Spirits picking up.

Leonard Keller's moods changed like cloud formations and once again the sun was shining through. His old enthusiasm was back and he said, "Tell Frank about your mouse, what's-his-name?"

"Spike." I told him a little about Spike and by that time my father had thought of another anecdote he wanted me to tell. This went on for a half hour or so, until Leonard had ordered a second vodka-on-the-rocks and I was hoping Frank would leave, because Leonard's speech was now more than fuzzy, it was getting downright thick. He was asking me to go on about Vin's death when Frank looked at his watch (it was almost three) and said he had to be uptown for a meeting. He quickly pumped my hand, slapped Leonard on the back and left.

"God, that's something you went through," my father said. "Can't get over it. Wait'll Marianne and the kids—I'll tell you who'll get a kick out of this, David, my sixteen-year-old, he'll eat it up."

The restaurant was nearly empty now; only a few other tables occupied. Time was running out. "I wonder if I could talk to you about something?"

"Sure, anything—of *course* you can talk to me about something." He snorted. "I'm your father, aren't I?"

"Yes." He'd given me an open lead-in. I quickly told him about Bebe, the nursing home, the two women who were willing to take care of her, the apartment and my need for a loan.

He'd sat there during this, bobbing his head. Instead of responding directly, he asked "You need *money?*" as if this were unthinkable. "After five years, you mean the government hasn't given you bonuses and all sorts of—"

I told him about the five dollars a day I'd be getting eventually, that there'd be no problem of paying him back out of that.

"What about all your back pay while you were in prison camp? That must have amounted to a whale of a lot?"

I explained it had gone to my wife and child for their support. He sat there, shaking his head. "So, well—how much did you want to borrow?"

I'd been going to ask for two thousand, there was four hundred for Monica, eight hundred would be due at the nursing home, although Monica had indicated they'd probably be moving in within two weeks, so another full month might not be necessary, and I needed some money, but his attitude made me change this. "Fifteen hundred would help a lot."

"Jesus . . ."

"I'll be getting over nine thousand when I get my lump sum, it's only that I need the money now or we'll lose the apartment."

"Yeah, I know, but—excuse me, be right back, gotta take a leak."

He stood up and weaved his way across the room. I'd been surprised at his attitude. Now I felt confused. Confused and also slightly dirty and angry with myself for even asking him. I also felt, in some wild way, I wasn't doing it right, I was letting Bebe down. Felt a clutch in my stomach when I thought of her getting all fixed up for me, sitting there with a ribbon in her short hair, playing gallant little games of charades. And "Ot-inken."

I took a sip of my wine, it tasted bitter. The earlier lift I'd gotten from the drinks had wilted; the letdown was on. I sipped the wine again, looked at the palms of my hands. They were moist. Christ, sitting there, rehearsing what else I could say that might appeal to him—how sickening!

When he returned, he glanced around at the bare restaurant, waiters and bus-boys clearing off the tables. "Getting late, I'll have to be going soon."

Trying to keep my spirits up, I smiled and leveled with him. "I'm sorry to have to ask you."

His reply jolted me. "I'm sorry, too. Hits me at a bad time. The market's been rough lately, but you probably know all about that. [I didn't.] And, Bebe, well you don't understand our whole past history."

I couldn't *not* say it. "But—she's had a stroke, she's helpless, she can barely walk."

"I can barely support my family, it's tough going, believe me."

"You know I'll pay you back."

"That's not the point, I'm having a squeeze of it now and—well, fifteen hundred dollars." I was thinking of dropping to a thousand when he said, "Christ, I don't know, son."

I suddenly wished he wouldn't call me "son." Anger for putting myself in this position, anger for him making me sweat it out surfaced. "Things are that bad, are they?" I asked in a level voice.

His head jerked up. "What kind of—listen, you think because I'm a stockholder, I'm rolling in money? Think again. You know what it's like to support a wife and five kids? You're damned right you don't. You know what it's like to have to keep up appearances, to run around—with this crowd?" He gestured an arm out over the room, caught sight

of a waiter and said, "Waiter, another vodka-on-the-rocks."
He spoke without looking at me. "You want anything?"

"No, thanks."

"And the check, bring the check." Then he did look at me,
shook his head, smiled and reached over, putting a hand on
my arm. "Oh, listen—you don't know, brokerage houses
closing all over the place, if it weren't a family thing I'd be
out on my ass. Still might be, they just use me for a lot of
bullshit stuff . . ." He seemed to want to salvage—what? Him,
us? "All right, I tell you what, you see what you can do; if
you get stuck, come back to me, I could probably let you
have a few hundred—"

The curtain was down. "No, I'll work it out."

"Yeah, well, I hope." He took his hand away. "Bebe,
Jesus—" He made a gesture with his hand and knocked over
his water glass. "Goddam it!" Sopping it up with his napkin,
he muttered, "Goddam water!" Then a snort: "Bebe, the idea
of money for—Bebe!"

I couldn't believe keeping bitterness alive for so long.
"Even after all these years?"

"Yes, after all these years!" he snapped. "You were just a
kid. Bebe, why she was hopping every belly in Hollywood
and I never even—"

"Don't say that!"

"Aw—" He even smiled. "Oh, Christ, come on, you're old
enough to—been through five years of prison camp, you
can—"

"She's my mother, I don't want to hear that kind of talk!"

"You want fifteen hundred dollars and you don't want to
*hear?* Who do you think you are, anyway?" He sat back in
his chair and he was one of the most objectionable men I'd
ever encountered. He had no ear for his jarring phrases or
offensive tone, or if he did, he didn't care. But he was not out
of curves; he could throw them all right, as he did now when
he suddenly said, "No, you're right, I shouldn't have said
that, that was—lousy, that's what it was." He sighed, looking
down at the table and saying, "Hmn, she was beautiful, Bebe
was, and sweet, our first year was—perfect. But, then,
well . . ."

And just as he handed me a shred of hope that perhaps
this meeting wouldn't end in total disaster, he looked up at

me, a smile curled his lips and he patted the flat of his hand on the table, shaking his head and saying, "Jesus, yes, of course. Of course, the only reason you looked me up—money for Bebe! What a dumb son-of-a-bitch I am!"

I could not believe him, could no longer deal with these jagged ups and downs. He'd finally shot the last bit of reserve I'd been holding in. "I think you've got that backwards. You called *me!*"

"What's that?" He looked confused.

I was no longer confused, I might have been shaking inside—the phrase "Hopping every belly in Hollywood" was sickening, even if he'd taken it back—but I was no longer confused. "You called me, in San Francisco, remember? And the only reason you did, after all these years, was because I was a P.O.W. You've got some strange crazy hangup about that!"

"Hangup?"

"Yes, hangup!"

The waiter arrived, putting his drink down and also depositing the check. We both had the decency to shut up until he'd left. I had gotten an American Express card in San Francisco. I took out my wallet, reached across the table and turned over the check. Lunch for two: eighty-six dollars.

"What do you think you're doing?"

"No, listen," I said, "if things are that rough—"

He snatched it out of my hand, crumpling it up. "Why you—" He coughed, wiped a hand across his mouth and then actually smiled at me. I wanted to hit him, to flatten those thin lips of his even more. "Hmn, I bet out of that uniform, you're a regular little snot-nose."

I stood up from the table. Way past leaving time. Now even my legs were shaking.

"Hunh," he said, staring up at me, and I could tell his vision was blurred. "I don't even—I don't even know who you are."

He gave me my exit line. "I'm not your son, there must have been a mistake."

I turned and walked away as I heard him mutter, "Little prick . . ."

## 39

The bright afternoon glare hit me when I stepped outside into the street. I put a hand up to shield my eyes. The sun accentuated the liquor I'd consumed, punched up the mood I was in, not one of anger as much as total disbelief. I couldn't believe the meeting with my father, experienced a moment of wanting to play it over, even turned around at the corner to stare back at the restaurant. No, it *was* over, he was in there, the way he was, whatever that was, however he'd arrived at what he was.

Turned around and began walking, next to blind in the sense I was unable to focus, walking in the general direction we'd come from. I remember bumping into a man, hard, almost knocking him down. When I came to a subway entrance I went down, taking the first train that came along. I didn't even look to see which subway it was, which way it was going; it made no difference.

Sitting in the subway car, my vision a blur, I rubbed my eyes, tried to focus them on—anything, a person across from me, the advertisements strung along above the seats opposite, but it was almost impossible. It was not from the drinks; I simply couldn't focus.

I concentrated, squinting my eyes and becoming aware of the massive graffiti splashed across the inside of the car, wherever there had been space: large swirling letters, names and numbers painted or sprayed on. The car was cartoon pop-art. I stood up abruptly. Rage made me stand. Away in prison camp five years while young punks and punkesses spent their time crapping up subway cars. I'd stood up as if there were someone I could challenge for this. But, of course, there wasn't, only a lot of people on their way from one place to another.

I sat down again, sat in a numb state, vaguely aware of stops, of people getting off and on. Someone got up next to me; a copy of the New York *Post* had been left on the seat. My vision had got all messy again. I picked the paper up, made myself focus on the headline, something about Watergate. Opening up the paper, I tried to make myself concentrate, read something, some smaller type to see if I could.

Although I don't remember the specific headline on Watergate, I recall clearly the specific column I made myself read, an interview with the historian Will Durant and his wife, Ariel. I can't remember the context of the line but it was a quote of his, saying he'd left a Roman Catholic seminary when he'd come across the ethics of Spinoza to the effect that "Desire is the essence of life."

That's all I got from the column and I had to force myself to absorb those few words; once absorbed, they took over with impact, slugging away at my brain. I repeated: "Desire is the essence of life." I translated that to simpler terms: I want. Then: I don't want to be wanting. I just want. I didn't want Vin or Lisa or Lauri, I didn't want my father. I wanted money. I didn't want to ask or beg or borrow. I didn't want to go through channels or agencies or paperwork. I wanted to take it.

About that time the train stopped again and I stood up to get off, surfacing at Fifty-ninth Street and Central Park South, by the Plaza Hotel. I started to go in the side entrance of the Plaza, got up the steps before I asked myself why I was going there. No reason. I came back down and walked to Fifth Avenue, crossed it and began walking downtown.

The windows of the toy store F.A.O. Schwarz caught my attention. I looked in at the stuffed animals, the incredible assortment of toys and games and—there was a display of chimpanzees aiming water pistols at each other. Beneath, resting on a bed of cotton, was a display of the water pistols. They looked like authentic weapons, black, lethal, compact, they looked like real guns. Without another thought I walked inside and inquired about them. Second floor. I went up, located the display counter and bought one. It cost four dollars and ninety-five cents; I had it put in a paper bag and left.

There was nothing to be done with me in uniform. I walked all the way down Fifth Avenue until I got below Fourteenth Street, cut over to Waverly and went to my hotel. There was a message that Monica had phoned; I returned her call. She'd been given tickets to a musical and wanted to know if I cared to go with her, or else I could have them if I knew of someone else I'd like to take. I thanked her, saying I'd already made plans.

"Oh, you know a few people back east then?"

"Yes." (I didn't really; oh, I had a few names and addresses of ex-Californians but I was in no mood to look anyone up.)

"I talked to your mother's doctor, he's very happy about the way she's progressing and thinks her speech will come back completely—slowly, but it will."

"Good. I'll get out to see her in a day or so. And, Monica, I'll have the money for you in a few days, don't worry."

"I'm not. I phoned the lady today and told her we were taking it, I've got a date to see her Friday."

We said good-bye and I hung up. I took the gun out of the paper bag and sat in the chair next to the television set. It was lighter in feel than it looked, but it looked as real in my hand as it had in the window. Made of molded hard rubber. I did not think it silly at all to be sitting there with a water pistol in my hand. It was a perfectly good replica of what I wanted—a gun.

I turned it over and over in my hand. It even had a hammer you could cock back.

I sat in the chair for a long time, until way after it got dark. By this time I had a slight headache. I suppose from all the drinks earlier. Maybe not, maybe I'd have had one anyhow, from all the thoughts tumbling through my head—jarring-mean flashes of Vin, of Lisa, that first night at the Fairmont, then the last time with Lauri at Letterman. Flashes of Bebe, sitting in her chair, reaching down at her side for the cardboard with the letters printed on it. And the most recent ones, of luncheon that day.

Unusual, but I had no appetite. There was no room in my stomach for food; I had a bellyful of hate.

After a long while I stood up, took off my uniform—just letting it drop onto the floor—and got into bed. At first I worried about waking up hungry in the middle of the night, turning and tossing, stewing about how I would ever pull off a holdup.

I needn't have. Severe numbing depression knocked me out for the count. I slept through until after nine the next morning.

# 40

Waking up the next day, I was not surprised to hear my stomach growling for food. I *was* surprised to find my resolve exactly as it had been the night before. If anything it was stronger, cold and hard and set; I was covered with prickly flesh as I showered, shaved and set about putting together an outfit that would be as nondescript as possible.

Brown shoes, gray slacks, a dark blue blazer, white shirt and the dullest of the four ties I'd bought. Best of all, covering this, a beige-tan raincoat I'd got in San Francisco, so plain it could have been a raincoat or light topcoat.

Once dressed, I looked in the mirror to see how easily I might be described. My eyes were blue, but how many blue eyes were there roaming around New York? It had been well over three weeks since my haircut and there was no trace of a crew-cut left. Brown hair, normal length, well not exactly normal according to 1973 standards, but almost. I wouldn't be easy to describe. My features were regular, there wasn't any one thing anyone could pin on me. No moles, no scars, no unusual identifying marks.

I opened the window of my room and stuck a hand out. Light clouds here and there but it was cool and very windy and one could easily wear a raincoat, which I needed not only because it was neutral but the large side pockets accommodated the gun.

Leaving the hotel about ten-thirty, I had no identification of any kind on me, no wallet, no papers, no nothing, except around twenty dollars. If I was caught I would give no information as to who I was. I would escape, somehow, before they found out.

After a large breakfast in a coffee shop on Fourteenth Street I started to go down into the subway station but now that I was setting out for real, I had more than prickly flesh; I had the shakes. Breakfast was not sitting well in my stomach. If I walked uptown I might exercise my nerves away by the time I got there; I went over to Fifth Avenue and headed north.

As far as the workings of my mind, I still can't pinpoint the reasons for specific decisions or actions at that time. I don't know what impelled me to go uptown. There are enough stores all over New York City available to be robbed, but it was in my mind to get uptown, to the heart of the shopping district.

There was no humor involved in setting off on this— what?—errand, mission, adventure? No, not adventure, it was a task. There was nothing of the prank in it. I never for a moment thought: Here I am loaded down with a squirt gun and, by Christ, I'm going to knock off a store! I don't even know how or why I decided to rob a store, instead of a person.

If I'd ever operated on impulse, I started off doing it this morning.

Somewhere in the Twenties on the west side of Fifth Avenue an Oriental import-export shop caught my attention. Expensive vases sat lined up in the window, Chinese figurines, prints, screens, several ornately carved teakwood cabinets and on the opposite side of the entrance door a display case of jewelry: ivory and jade and other precious stones.

No customers visible inside. The only person I could see was a small Oriental woman, Chinese, I supposed. She looked tiny and vulnerable as I watched her slide over a small metal stepladder and climb gingerly up on it to reach the top shelf of a display case.

My point was simple—to get the money. Not to be a hero,

not to pull a brave big-time robbery, not to overpower or terrorize. I only wanted to get four hundred dollars, or more, as easily and quickly as possible.

I opened the door and stepped inside the store. The woman, still on the ladder, glanced around and smiled. "I'll be right down."

"No hurry, I'm just looking around." My voice sounded strange, almost muffled.

But she was on her way. I quickly looked toward the front door to make sure no one else was about to come in, or was even looking in the window. No one. In that brief time I heard her speak Chinese. I turned to see two men carrying a large packing crate through a curtained doorway at the rear of the store. One was small and Chinese, the other was about my size and looked to be Italian. She was telling the Chinese man where to put the crate. They brought it to an open space, about ten yards from me, set it down and the Chinese man spoke in English to the other fellow, warning him there were vases inside and to be careful, as the two of them set to work opening the crate, one with a hammer and the other with a chisel.

"Can I help you?" The woman, smiling, walked toward me.

The three of them were too much to deal with; the noise of hammering and prying was jarring. I muttered "No, thanks," went to the door and left.

Disappointed but, on thinking it over, no reason to suppose the first store I picked had to be the right one. Such a strange mood I was in; I felt spiky, edgy, let anything act as a stimulus to drive me on. It was a breezy day; at one corner a gust of wind spiraling up from the gutter covered me with tiny particles of street dirt, dust and whatever else goes into making city grime. It stung my eyes, I could feel it coat my face and lodge in my hair. *What a lousy, filthy, stinking city; it deserves to be taken.*

A small park borders Fifth Avenue somewhere in the Twenties—I don't know its name—and a ragtailed assortment of bums sprawled on the benches along with a smattering of elderly folk squinting their wrinkled faces up at the cloud-scattered sun.

Poor fucks, I thought, you poor fucks! Get up off your

bony asses, go take what you need, don't just *sit* there. No, I'll do it for you.

In the Thirties, an army sergeant with a girl on his arm turned the corner and walked ahead of me up the avenue. The sight of the uniform brought me up short, reminding me I was still officially in the army. This was unsettling, an entanglement I'd much rather not have had.

*Don't let it bother you, you're not going to get caught.*

Still, as the uniform bobbed ahead of me I could not help previewing the headline: P.O.W. NABBED IN ROBBERY ATTEMPT. *Stop it, enough of that!* To get the army out of my mind I crossed to the east side of Fifth Avenue and hurried ahead.

Right before Thirty-fourth Street, across from the Empire State Building, I came to a small shop that sold tape recorders, cameras, watches and the like. One elderly man, stooped, with tufts of white hair, stood behind the counter showing a slide projector to a married couple with two young children.

He did not look as if he'd be much of a problem; in fact, I could envision the operation as quick and easy. Standing outside, rattled by the increasing wind, I decided to wait until his customers had made their purchase and left.

Before this could take place, three giggling teen-age girls stepped up to the display windows, two of them grossly overweight, all three looking as dirty as possible in patched, ill-fitting jeans and sloppy shirts or jackets, all with vast tangles of unkempt hair, like dead dusty ivy hanging from a building, the thin one a victim of acne as she even now chewed on a candy bar.

Jesus, I put in time (supposedly) to make the world safe for you mindless little fat-assed twats! The two of you ought to try solitary for six months, that would melt the blubber off your distended rumble seats. They paused before going in, one of the fat ones said, "Yeah, he did, and I told him—I said, 'Aw, go fuck yourself!' " They all laughed at this *bon mot.*

Enraged, I was enraged. "Cows!"

I'd thought it, not only thought it but said it. And loud.

"What?" the fat one who'd not spoken turned, they all turned, and asked, "What'd you say?"

"Cows!" I repeated, shouting it louder this time.

"Aw, go fuck yourself!"

I cut off their burst of laughter by taking a quick step forward, arm raised at them. "Watch your filthy fucking tongues!"

Two of them squealed, making for the door. The skinny one with pimples stayed facing me. She giggled and said, "Watch your *filthy fucking tongues!*"

"Come on, Janice!"

"Janice—watch out, he's nuts!"

They knew a nut when they saw one. Janice turned and followed them, laughing and repeating, "Watch your *filthy fucking tongues!*"

She saw the humor in it. I do now, looking back. Not then. I wanted to kill; if I'd had a grenade, I'd have lobbed it in the store after them. I stood there on the sidewalk cursing them. Inside, the fatties were telling the old man and the couple about the crazy person. I walked away muttering, "Future Mothers of America! Jesus, what a case for mass sterilization!"

Good to use my anger, it kept my adrenaline up. I let it build, go wild; whatever my eyes took in, I plastered with contempt. Fine, use it as fuel, put it in the tank, anything that will burn for you.

Kept on walking north until Fifth Avenue became too frantic, too many lunch-hour shoppers, the stores too large and unmanageable. I cut over to Madison, more likely stores there, small, expensive, exclusive. I cruised up and down for several blocks, crossing over from one side to the other. Madison seemed to be a good bet but, no doubt in order to stall, I decided to walk over to Park and Lexington and check them out.

And my anger slipped into frenzy the longer I hedged, eying this shop and that, almost zeroing in on a prosperous-looking florist's until I noticed the window plastered with every charge card imaginable: Diners, BankAmericard, American Express and others. There would probably be little cash on hand, probably most people charged flowers.

*Probably* I was frozen-assed terrified of pulling off a robbery!

I was scared, I had to admit it. The admission doubled my

feelings of anger and frenzy. Back to Madison, now in the mid-Fifties, where I forced myself to settle on a small, exclusive-looking men's shop staffed by two salesmen—one in his sixties, tall but thin and frail, convex and chestless, the other a cream puff of a man in his mid-fifties, and one elderly woman, grayhaired, sweater over her shoulders, glasses on a chain, who manned the cash register.

A pushover team, none of them could possibly have chased me for more than half a block. As I watched the store it was never crowded, but there was a steady patronage, one or two at a time, sometimes three. I would wait until it was empty of customers. After a half hour a middle-aged couple left, but just as I stepped off the curb to cross the street, two rich kids, boys, about sixteen or seventeen, stinking of prep school, entered the store.

They didn't look tough, they looked spoiled and effete, long-haired, lean and—they looked like two pedigreed Afghans—but they did look as if they could run. Yes, if they could do anything, they could sprint. They'd probably give chase to a robber, just for a lark. I'd wait them out.

Looked at my watch. Shocked, it was three-thirty. I'd been wandering around making up excuses for hours. Come on, you well-bred little turds, buy your little bikini underwear and get your little non-asses out of there. Within ten minutes they were on their way.

I took a deep breath. I knew this was the time.

It was also the time five or six people streamed out of a Hamburger Inn, four doors down from the men's shop, chattering and shouting, followed by drifts and spirals of smoke and two blacks in white aprons and chef's hats, and, within minutes, I could hear sirens way off in the distance and soon two police cars had pulled up, followed closely by three fire engines, and the entire block was a disaster area of police and firemen.

My first laugh of the day, I couldn't believe it. All set to go and the kitchen of a hamburger joint catches on fire. Go rob a store—*my ass!*

Terrific, are they trying to tell me something? At least I was laughing again. I hadn't cracked a smile all day. Walked north, heading uptown. Past Fifty-seventh Street the sidewalks were not nearly as crowded but still there were plenty of exclusive shops, antique stores, galleries, jewelry shops and smart women's stores. Kept on going uptown, into the Sixties. Even fewer people on the streets. And, looking west, I could see Central Park a block away. That would be a place to head for and disappear into instead of racing down the sidewalks, crisscrossing back and forth, making a getaway.

It hit me, the area was right. I could sniff it: exclusive, not overly busy, the refuge of the park nearby. Settle down and pick your spot. I moved slowly, considering shops on both sides of the street, weighing the pros and cons of each. Two fairly young healthy-looking male clerks. No. Too many credit cards in the window. No. Two elderly ladies, yes, but it was a card shop and lending library and, besides some elderberry wine, they wouldn't have diddily-zilch between them. No. A furrier shop—with a cop way back in the rear having a cup of coffee and laughing with the proprietor. No, keep moving.

All bummers—until I came upon a medium-sized ladies' dress and lingerie shop, very exclusive in appearance, no evidence of credit cards. Chez Madeleine was the name. The display windows were backed—no looking in from the street—they also ran in at an angle to the right from the sidewalk with the entrance at the end on the left, so you couldn't even see in the front door unless you walked in several yards.

I felt excitement, anticipation, as I inched my way back until I could see into the store through the front door. Very plush inside. I could see one lady, perhaps in her late forties, standing behind a display case of lingerie and gloves. Another saleslady was waiting on two women, same side of the store, toward the rear. Four ladies!

The act was suddenly so close at hand I started thinking of my opening line. Would I pretend, at first, to be buying something and then spring it on them? Or should I just walk in like I was going to sack Rome and stun them right out of their girdles?

Walked back out to the sidewalk. Doing the old hedge, natch. Four ladies! Not exactly a platoon of armed V.C.'s. Stepped to the corner. Oh, but I was loathing myself. To the point of the nasty sweats. And not from the weather. Feeling the weather now, the early spring chill. Wind still strong, heavy dark clouds had replaced the lighter scraggly ones and in the late afternoon the city was drenched in dusky sepia street tones that take hold before a rainstorm. The light was eerie. Electric lights were flicking on as the sky darkened even more and pedestrians moved faster to get to wherever they were going before the storm broke.

Glanced back at Chez Madeleine. *What in God's name did I want?* The perfect setup? A store *papered* in money on a deserted side-street, manned by an ancient arthritic lady in a wheelchair accompanied by a cat?

You poor chicken-hearted P.O.W. Oh, you are some kind of a piss-head hero!

The clouds let go as suddenly as if someone had dumped them upside-down. No thunder, no warning, just huge glob-drops of rain banging down onto the pavement. Pam, pam, pam! Pedestrians running, scrambling for shelter. I just stood there on the corner. Yes, you are now *truly all wet!*

Self-disgust rose up in my throat like a hot lump of vomit.

I used it, used more than that, running off a stunning series of charming vignettes and piling them on top of my soggy head, letting them drip down over me: Vin lying in his own mess; Lisa begging me to go easy; eavesdropping outside the door of 3-B; Bebe, her mouth open—only able to cry or say "Shit!" Poppa guzzling Harvey Wallbangers. "Little prick . . ." Was that my valedictory? Yes, Bebe said it for me, shit was the operative word for our life and times. What's a little more shit on top of such a winning score?

Winners never quit and quitters never win. Some whiz-brain coughed that up once. So—even if you botch it, you've got to do it now. You owe it to yourself, either way.

Turned, teeth chattering, feeling a little lightheaded now, and sloshed my way through the rain back to the entrance of Chez Madeleine. Took a deep (and shaky) breath, walked back between the display windows, and when I got to the door refused to look in for fear of stopping, just thrust out my hand, opened the door and stepped inside.

# 41

At the sound of the door opening and closing, all four ladies glanced over. Panic gripped me. The three toward the rear of the store went back to whatever business they were engaged in. The saleslady standing behind the glass case of lingerie and gloves running back along the store to my right smiled and nodded. She wore a simple black dress, one strand of pearls, smartly coiffed graying hair, no glasses. An attractive woman more likely in her fifties than forties, she was well made-up, wearing a shade of dark powder that almost looked like a tan. She smiled and said, "You're all wet."

You said the words, lady. I was wet with fear. Had no idea what to do first, hadn't budged a step, just stood there. "Yes," I said, the word sounding like it was strained through a blanket. Wanted to clear my throat but didn't.

"Can I help you?"

Another "Yes" and I walked toward her. The three other ladies were quite a ways from us and paying no attention. Soft music played on a radio in the rear. Hadn't noticed it before. The saleslady stood by a pass-through in the display cases running back along that side of the shop. Behind her and slightly to the side, the cash register was mounted on a wooden counter along with a file-box and a telephone.

"What is it you're looking for?" she asked, still the friendly warm smile.

Christ, *how do I put it?*—now approaching my side of the glass case—*what do I say?*

She'd said something else, I missed it. "What?" I asked.

"Are you looking for a gift?"

"Uh, yes . . ." I'd stepped up to the counter and was only a few feet from her. Wished she weren't smiling, wished she weren't so friendly and nice.

"What were you thinking of?" she asked.

Oh, Christ, *do it quick or you won't be able to. Say the words!* I suppose they came to me from the movies: "This is a stickup." I'd said it in such a low voice even *I* barely heard it.

"What?" she asked, an even bigger smile stretching her mouth.

I cleared my throat, now when my words came out they were strange to my ears but they were audible: "This is a stickup."

She heard me, but her smile remained as she cocked her head slightly, made a little "Uh ..." sound and then again asked, "*What?*" As I took a breath to give it to her once more, she added, "*What did you say?*"

"This is a stickup!"

Her smile froze for a moment, right where it was, then it even broadened and she almost laughed out her next words: "Why I—you don't mean that?"

"Yes, I do."

Still smiling, she leaned in toward me from her side of the glass-topped counter and I could smell the heavy scent of perfume as she reached out a hand to touch my shoulder. "Why," she said, kind of offhand chummy, "I have a *son* just about your age."

The confused me for a moment; I wasn't following her; what did *that* have to do with anything!

She gave my shoulder a little pat. "No!" I said, flinching back, "don't!"

"Don't?" she asked, confused.

"Don't touch me!" I'd said it in a loud voice.

She drew back away from me, her smile narrowed somewhat, but part of it remained. "You're not—"

"I mean it, this is a stickup!"

The smile snapped shut, her eyes—I forget the color but not the look—iced up. "No!" she said.

"Yes."

"Oh, no!" The sound of a warning was in her voice.

"Frances, what is it?" The saleswoman toward the rear of the store had spoken. I glanced back at the three ladies, all had quizzical expressions on her faces. "Frances?" the one repeated.

Frances kept her eyes on me, although she spoke back in a flat offhand voice. "Don't worry, nothing." She paused a moment, looking at me with cold hatred and not a sign of fear. "Now—you get out of here!"

I was so surprised at this order, issued like a general, that I only stood there. She repeated it, in an even stronger voice: "You heard me, go on, get out of here!" She even took a step toward the break in the counter, as if she were going to come after me.

I held an arm out, to ward her off. "Stay back there, open up that cash register!" I hadn't even thought of using the gun.

There was a short high little scream from the back; I glanced around and it was one of the lady customers, a hand up to her mouth. Her scream brought a surprise. Another saleslady, a third one, with another woman customer peeking behind her, stepped into view from a hallway in the rear and what I recognized to be several try-on booths. I'd had no idea anyone else was back there.

Now there were five ladies besides my opponent. It was good for me, rattled me even more. I spoke to the lady opposite me. "Open the register and give me the money!"

"No," she said, "not on your life." She took a little side step, putting herself directly in front of the cash register, blocking it off.

"Open it up!" I was shouting for the first time.

"No, get out of here!"

"Open it, goddam it, open it!"

She only shook her head, no, then smiled slightly and gave me a shock when she said, "Go on, get out of here, you're nothing but a little piece of shit!"

"Frances—don't!" This from one of the ladies.

"Oh, my God!" from another.

"You heard me," Frances said, smiling still. "*You get out of my store!*" Thrusting her shoulders back, she was now commander-in-chief. She telegraphed victory, that she would get me out of there if it was the last thing she ever did in her life.

I could feel my hand trembling as I reached into my pocket for the gun, trembling with fear more than anger because her strength—coming so quickly after the nice-saleslady person she'd been—had thrown me. Was it something about me, did she know I couldn't bring it off? What did my face look like? Did it show the uncertainty I felt?

"Go on, now, get out." This almost as if she were bored with my act. She even stepped toward the break in the counter again. "I've had enough of this, go on now, get—"

"I've had enough of you! *Goddam you!* Get away, get back there!" I took the gun out, she flinched, nothing more; several ladies in the back screamed. "Shut up!" I yelled. Another scream or two. "Shut up, back there!" Quiet. "Did you hear me?" I asked Frances.

"Yes," she said, in a low voice, but not moving.

"Get away from that register, get back there!" I waved the gun back toward the ladies.

"Frances, do as he says!"

"Oh, God!" from another.

She only looked at me, then at the gun. I stepped abruptly toward her. "Back there—or I'll kill you, I'll kill you!" My voice broke, that scared her, and she moved back toward the others slowly, but not more than six or seven steps. I stepped closer to the counter, then through the break separating the two long cases, behind it, turning to face her, pointing the gun at her.

I glanced behind me at the cash register. Realized I'd never operated one. All kinds of part-time jobs and the full-time one with the real estate agency but I had never worked a cash register. Turned back to her. "How do you open this thing!"

She smiled again, but didn't say a word.

"How?" I shouted, jabbing the gun at her.

"Frances, show him!" a saleslady said.

"No," she replied, staring at me.

"Open it, I'll kill you!"

"Go ahead"—in a fairly calm voice.

This enraged me. I backed up, until I was even with the register. I pressed several keys. Nothing. I looked back at her. She was actually smiling. Jesus, how I hated her at that moment! Hated her as if she were the demon lady of all time! If I'd had a real gun, I might even have shot her.

Turned back to the register and began pounding on the keys

with my free fist. Bang, bang, bang, until the welcome "ting," sound of the drawer clanging open.

"Don't you dare—get out of here!" Frances, shouting and stepping toward me, now tears of anger brimming her eyes. "You—you—"

"Stay there, not a move—*I swear to Christ I'll kill you!*" Shouted like I meant it. Greeted with screams from the other ladies and phrases imploring her to stop. She did. Stopped cold, fists clenched, making little chopping motions in the air as I turned, switched the gun to my left hand and with my right, shaking so I thought I'd tear my hand against the side of the register, reached in, grabbing the green stuff in bunches, unable to do it orderly because of the shakes, stuffing one handful in my pocket, then another and another, spilling some of the silver change out onto the floor in the process.

"No, no! It's not right—not right!" Frances screamed. "You're shit, you're shit!" She looked around at the other ladies and said in a helpless, imploring, almost questioning voice, "This city is shit!"

"Frances, stop it now, stop it, let him go!" A saleslady speaking strongly, authoritatively to *her*, because she, Frances, now seemed about to fly out of control.

I had all the money, wasn't about to bother with the change. My right-hand pocket was bulging with crumpled-up bills. I stepped to the breakthrough, backing my way out from behind the counter, switching the gun to my right hand and shouting, "Don't come after me. I'll kill anyone comes after me!"

All the ladies flinched, except for Frances, who seemed about to burst into tears of frustration. As I backed toward the door, she stepped forward again, indicating she *was* going to pursue me. "You won't get away with this! You're not going to do this to me!"

"Frances, stop it!"

"Back, get back there, get back you stupid cunt!" I shouted as I reached behind me for the door.

That did it, she stopped. I grabbed the handle, turned, opened the door and ran out. By the time I ran the length of the display windows and hit the sidewalk I could hear her screaming, "Help! Police! Robber! Help! Help!"

But I was running uptown in the rain, bumping into umbrella'd people, nearly blind with fear of being caught as I
raced to the corner, only aware of her voice following me
outside the store, shouting, "Help! Police! Robber! Help!
Help!"

Turned on the side street, running like a madman, not
many people on it, ran and ran, my heart banging away, still
scared shitless I'd hear a cop's gun explode, feel the thump of
a bullet in my back, not aware of who'd been on the sidewalk
or anything—but running as fast as I could. Didn't stop at
Fifth Avenue to see if the light was with or against me. Tore
out into the street, brakes screeched, aware of almost being
hit but not by what.

Dashed across and into the park—flat area with benches, a
walk or two, leading down a slope to my left and trees and
an underpass. Kept running, running, running. Passed a man
with a dog, almost tripped over the leash as the man jumped
away from the dog to get out of my path.

Kept running. Soon only the sound of my footsteps. It was
completely dark now. Still raining but not so hard. Ran under
the underpass, saw a sign "Children's Zoo," cut back over to
Fifth Avenue. Traffic was moving slowly south. Hailed a cab,
it slowed, I opened the door and got in.

"Where to?"

Couldn't think where, barely could gasp out "Downtown!"
I was panting so. He nodded. I was glad of the partition that
separated us, shielding the unglued condition of my mind and
body.

# 42

Wouldn't you think a grown man might start to feel a little
guilty—holding up a gaggle of terrified women? No. As my
breathing eased back to somewhere near regular, my spirits

rose and rose until I wanted to bang on the separation between me and the cabbie and yell, "Hey, I made it, I made it!"

All sorts of thoughts flicked through my brain. How much did I actually make off with? I hadn't seen the denomination of the bills, I'd been too rattled to take that in, was only aware of grabbing large fistfuls and jamming them home. Was there an outside chance I'd get caught? What about fingerprints? Did the F.B.I. have some master-genius computer that would whir away all night long and suddenly come to a screeching halt, bells clanging, lights flashing, announcing—yes, here they are, prints belonging to Edward Keller, army serial number so and so, born so and so, last known whereabouts such and such. Was that possible?

The cabbie interrupted my thoughts when he glanced back and asked, "Where to—downtown?"

"Ah—" No, don't have him take you directly to your hotel. There might be early reports of the holdup, he might remember you, might have noticed your condition, sopping wet, messed up, breathing hard, might recall the destination. "Fifth Avenue and Eighth Street." I'd get off there, double back and walk to the hotel.

I patted my bulging pockets, the money in one, my trusty squirt gun in the other. Caper successful. Thought of Vin. How he'd laugh.

When I got out of the cab I paid from the money I'd had with me at the start of the day. Didn't want to soil the spoils. Could hardly wait to get back to the hotel and add up the loot. Once in my room with the door locked behind me, I sat on the floor and straightened all the bills out neatly while I counted them. Six hundred and eighty-seven dollars. $687.00. Four hundred for Bebe and some left over.

Sitting there on the floor, grinning at my windfall, I realized, with surprise, that I had an erection. The potency of the currency! I felt horny and hot and loaded. This together with the happiness of a kid as I counted the money a second time.

I was not hungry; this was strange because I hadn't eaten since breakfast and my appetite was still making up for lost time in prison camp. I wanted sex. After cleaning up and changing my clothes, I went uptown thinking to try a few bars and connect with an attractive girl.

Instead I encountered a black hooker on the street near the Americana Hotel. She was an amazon, over six feet tall in her platform clodhoppers, plus an Afro hairdo that would put an English busby to shame, beautifully built, well-proportioned, but so tall and such a pair of shoulders on her—I felt she'd be too much for me to handle. I could imagine putting on a pair of nonskid deck shoes and climbing around on her, but as sexual partners, we seemed unfairly matched. I would need points.

She made the approach, after we'd engaged in eye-dancing, and it was her quaint opening lines as she stood on the sidewalk looking down at me that won me over. "You know what?" she crooned in a low voice, "Ermaleen would just love to feel your pretty pink dick in her hot black pussy."

I laughed. "That tickle your funny bone?" she asked.

"Yes, it kind of does."

"How much would you give Ermaleen to tickle your *other* bone?"

I'd only brought fifty dollars with me. I'd never paid a whore before, but the idea that the money was stolen somehow made it all right. Also, I was feeling raunchy and perverse. "Thirty-five dollars is it," I said, intimating that was all I had.

"Ermaleen usually gets at least fifty," she said, naming the contents of my pocket.

"Sorry, can't make it."

I turned to walk away but her hand on my shoulder stopped me. "All right, thirty-five, but only on account you're so cute!"

"So are you."

She howled with laughter, slapping the flat of her hand against my chest and almost knocking me out into the street. "Ermaleen—cute? I may be a whole lot of things but cute ain't one of 'em!"

I went with her to an apartment building on Eighth Avenue for a half hour of the most athletic sex ever. She was more of a decathalon champion than a sex-tress. She tossed and turned and bucked, flipped me over, twirled me around, sat on it, spun around herself—"Ermaleen's riding Big Red—Whoo!"—bounced me, jounced me up and down like a puppet and left me totally limp and done-in. I was physically exhausted, which was good because the robbery had me so hyped up I wouldn't have been able to sleep.

But I did, slept like I'd been out on a twenty-four-hour forced march. The next morning I had a hangover, not from liquor or sex but a hangover from the tension of what I'd done. Ups and downs fluctuating all day. The ups were obvious: I'd pulled it off, got the goods. The downs came from the fear I'd experienced. Kept going back to that, felt ashamed of myself. And the shame nagged me. I wanted to make it right. Strange moods hit me. I won't go into all of them because I want to take you on to the Big Caper with me. I'm revved up to it. But I'll give you the ones that made me decide to pursue my new Life of Crime one step further.

About noon I delivered the money to Monica for the apartment. Then I went to Lord and Taylor's and bought a gold quilted dressing gown for my mother and took the train out to the rest home.

Bebe'd had a slight temperature the day before; it was down now but she was tired and not up to the performance she gave on my first visit. She wanted to know what I'd been doing and I had to smile at the notion of telling her about my robbery, which I wasn't about to do. But the prospect of saying "Well, Maw, you won't believe it, but . . ." tickled me. She caught my smile and nodded, then spelled out, "Good time?" Oh, yes, I told her I'd had a good time, adding, "We'll have some good times as soon as you get out of here and into the apartment."

She got into the area of money, wanted to make sure I wasn't footing any of the financial burden. I assured her I wasn't, that Monica had insisted she was flush now and she knew Bebe would pay her back when she got over the stroke and back to work.

Mrs. Hershey wasn't on duty but another nurse came in while I was there and suggested that Bebe take a little walk up and down the halls. Bebe didn't want to, but the nurse said she should keep her muscles active, that the exercise of a short walk would be good for her, would tire her so she'd sleep better at night.

We finally got her up, and with a cane in one hand and holding onto my arm with the other she made a tour of the hall, slower than the time before. I also felt her weight more.

Finally she just stopped, putting a hand up to her chest, indicating she was bushed. I took her to her room, the nurse returned and put her back to bed. After she got all settled in against the pillows, she motioned with her hand: come on, tell me more, give me all the news. I chattered away, giving her bits and pieces, always trying to keep it light—until she closed her eyes and went off into a sound sleep.

I sat there, looking at her, feeling incredibly tender toward her. Sorting over memories of the good times we'd had together, not even touching the rough ones. Wondered if she was frightened that she might not recover from this stroke. Wondered if she actually would. Monica had made an appointment for me to talk to her doctor, that was to be in three days' time. Then I just sat and watched her sleep, letting my mind wander where it would.

Reconstructing my thoughts at the time: first and foremost, growing all during that day, the initial loathing of the fear and trembling that were so much a part of my operation at Chez Madeleine. Anger at the pettiness of it, the small-timeness.

Vin's death and Bebe's illness deserved—what?—revenge or payment on a much larger scale. Whether that makes good sense or not, that is what occurred to me. More based on Vin and Bebe than my own personal plight, although it was probably anger at Lisa and what she'd done with my money that turned whatever revenge I sought toward the financial. Who knows? My thinking was far from rational, it was definitely tilted.

There had to be security for Bebe, perhaps for a long while. I did not want her burdened by financial worries. She had enough to occupy her thoughts with recovery alone.

A flash of my father. A flash of Wall Street. Those banks. All that money changing hands. Big-Time Monopoly. It fell into place. I wanted a sizeable amount of money. I needed to buy time. Not only time for Bebe but time for me to straighten out what I knew was a very fucked-up life and would be for some time.

The more I sat and watched her, sleeping so peacefully, looking so vulnerable, the more I resolved to do it. And it would not be an operation so filled with panic and fright. I would see to that.

It might not be the healthiest motivation, that of *wanting to get even.* But I'll tell you one thing, it became my point that afternoon and I nurtured it, let it grow and fill me up until it was absolutely exhilarating. After a while, sitting in that room in the nursing home, I could barely hold still.

I wanted to wake Bebe up and say, "Don't you worry, darling, don't give it a thought, everything's going to be all right—with capital letters. ALL RIGHT!"

# 43

The next morning a deadening calm took hold—it was a pleasurable sensation—as I set out from the hotel, dressed as I had been two days before, no identification, nothing with me but around seventy-five dollars. Enough of squirt guns! Let's not press a good thing. I bought a secondhand .22 revolver at a hock shop on Second Avenue. I had decided not to buy bullets—I wasn't going to shoot anyone—but once down in the financial district I passed a large sporting goods store and for my own protection, I told myself, I bought a box of shells.

Strolling around the busy Wall Street area, it all hit me as a huge joke. I mean, it was so outrageous, what I was setting off to do, it had to be a joke! I also filled up with a sensation, as I cruised around, as if I were watching myself. Or that I was appearing in a movie, so I had to rein in, do nothing abrupt or jerky, just play it low-key and smooth. Or the film would snap. The strangest feeling, a feeling of lightness of body, of movement, as well as lightheadedness.

Advised myself to enjoy, not to block it, as I came to a large commercial bank several blocks from the Stock Exchange and drifted in. Instead of standing in the middle of the place like a sore throbbing thumb, I stationed myself at the end of the longest line, about seventh from the teller. I was less conspicuous and could watch people in the lines on both sides of me, also giving the impression I was there to conduct business, too.

Almost immediately my attention was attracted by a girl in the line to my left and about four people ahead of me. She had thick sandy-brown frizzy hair, clutched together at neck length by some sort of plastic clasp and frizzing out below that again. Although I couldn't see her face, I could see from my side-rear view she wore black-rimmed glasses. Dowdily dressed in a brownish-beige tweed skirt, a cream-colored blouse and a greenish-brown coat sweater, she was far from a stunner. What really attracted my attention was the black leather carrying case, like a briefcase only thicker, she held in her right hand.

As I watched her, she turned sideways slightly. She was, in fact, extremely unattractive, not much of a chin, freckles large enough to be taken for maroon blotches, and what kids in school used to call "liver lips." Her glasses were the thick bottle-bottomed kind. Her unattractiveness was enough to bring on a wince.

Wondered if she were depositing something from that substantial black case or whether she might be going to pick up something nice and green as she joggled up in line, soon next to approach the teller.

By the time she set the carrying case down on the marble ledge in front of the teller's window, I was three people behind her. The woman teller knew her, there were pleasantries exchanged while the girl, probably about twenty-eight or thirty, opened the case and, to my delight, was handed white-banded bundles of lush green money. Bundle after bundle she stashed down in her case. Now I moved up one in line and I could make out stacks of fifties and twenties and tens.

Close to the teller in *my* line, I made a little sound and gesture as if, oh, I'd forgotten something, stepped out of the line and walked over to a table containing deposit forms and the like, pretending to be figuring something out on one of them.

It wasn't until the girl with the black case concluded her business and turned to walk away that I noticed she had a defective foot, her left one. I don't know whether it was a club foot, but it was encased in a high black shoe, almost a boot, only with laces. Her other shoe was black, also, but it was cut lower. She walked with a limp but not a heavy lurching one, just a slight favoring of that left foot. I hadn't noticed this before, probably because her left foot had been farthest from me and I'd also been distracted by her looks and especially by that black case.

She left the bank, carrying the case in her right hand, and I followed as she turned right and made her way along the sidewalk. Despite her limp, she walked at a good pace. I kept about a quarter to half a block behind her. I was terribly excited. I knew she had a substantial sum of money and I knew she would be an easy mark. She certainly could not put up any sort of chase and unless she carried a gun, which I doubted, all I had to do was wait for an opportune time, snatch it from her and run like the wind. The street we were on was fairly crowded so I had no intention of making my move there.

She turned left on lower Broadway, crossed to the other side and walked in the direction of Trinity Church, which was about three blocks ahead of us. I was not familiar with the streets down there but when she made a right turn off Broadway after two blocks onto a narrow side street I noticed a sign, "Thames Street," on the corner.

About a quarter of a block behind her, I made the turn. The view was joyous. Although the sun was out, Thames Street was one long shadow, narrow, dark, almost an alley, and there was absolutely no one on the block between Broadway and whatever the next parallel street was.

I quickened my steps to catch up with her. Thoughts crammed my brain: Would she scream a lot? Would she in any way be personally responsible for the loss of the money? Would she lose her job? Was she bonded?

Became suddenly aware of my own footsteps clacking on the brick pavement as I closed on her. She must have, too. She stopped for an instant, as if to listen, then quickened her pace without looking back. But really quickened it. I almost broke into a trot; I wanted to get to her well before she reached the next cross street. When I was perhaps only ten yards from her and she was about twenty-five yards from the corner, she stopped abruptly, turned and looked directly at me.

She so surprised me that *I* stopped. Focusing on me through those bifocal glasses, she clutched the black leather carrying case up against her waist, slowly raising it so it was just below her breast line, like a quarterback would cradle a football close into him.

She didn't say a word, only stared at me, features motionless. It hit me: she knew exactly what I was up to. So patently clear it could have been printed on her forehead. She knew I knew. My intent was hanging in the air between us, filling the space.

And I thought: Oh, Jesus Christ, is it really fair to pick on someone that unfortunate! Doesn't she have enough troubles, simply getting through the day without jumping in front of a truck or turning on the gas oven?

Done, I'd done myself in.

She turned, and in the most pitiful attempt to run she broke into a sort of sideways lurching canter. Immediately she tripped, falling forward and emitting a little cry. In order to break her fall, she let go of the carrying case. It skidded ahead of her out onto the brick paved street. She didn't cry, only quickly turned her head to see what she entirely expected to come true—that I would run forward, snatch the case and make off with it.

She remained lying on her side, neck and head craned uncomfortably around, looking at me, immobile. Not saying anything or crying, just staring at me in that awful crouched position on the ground. Her skirt had hiked up by her thigh and I could glimpse an expanse of pink underwear, that nasty deep pink, like the cheap bloomers you see in dime stores.

I walked very deliberately up to her—now she flinched—past her, picked up the black leather case, turned and set it down next to her. "There," I said, and walked away.

The communication between us, when we'd been staring at each other, was so intimate that I was unable to touch her, to help her up in any way. She was probably just as glad I didn't.

Without looking back, I walked to Broadway and turned toward Trinity Church. I felt good and I felt depressed, not for my lack of success, depressed for her.

I did not feel ashamed for failing to pull it off. Or worried that this was a sign that I would not be able to score. I felt slightly shaken, but again, mainly for her. Wondered what her home life was like? Did she avoid mirrors? Could she possibly be married? Had she ever experienced the Dread Deed? With anyone? Ever?

Jesus must really love his children!

To get over her I entered the first bar I came to and, in deference to the memory of my late unlamented father, this being his territory, I had one Harvey Wallbanger. It was mellow, warmed me all over, gave me the proper lightheaded push to get on with it.

# 44

Vin became my silent partner. I started to use him almost as much as if he'd actually been there. I talked to him as I walked out of the bar. "Vin, it's not going to be like Friday. No big sweat, no shaky piss-in-my-pants deal, you'll see. And I swear to Sweet Jesus, I'm not going to wander around in a daze for hours making up excuses."

Came to a bank, a nice marble-columned big old bank that looked like it knew what it was there for. Yes. Walked in, marble floors, too, except for a red-carpeted area to the right where bank officers sat at rich-looking mahogany desks. Leather seats for customers waiting to talk to bank officers bordered that part of the bank, separating the V.I.P.'s from the deposit stands and the lines leading to the tellers. I sat down on one to see if I could spot a prospect.

I wasn't drunk by any means, but the Wallbanger had given me a pleasant lift, a slant at the way of looking at things. As I glanced around, getting my bearings, a man behind one of the mahogany desks called out, "Hey, Tank, what's a little runt like you doing without your mascot?"

Tank, a large florid-faced, big-boned, beer-bellied six footer in his early fifties with straight thinning black hair, wearing an ill-fitting silver-gray suit, a material with a metallic sheen, laughed and passed in front of me, approaching the man at the desk and saying, "Hey, listen—you know that little cashier, Ruthie, used to work here, so lah-dee-dah, hardly a 'Good morning' out of her?"

"Ruth Pulaski, used to work in savings?"

"Yeah, little Polish Ruthie, works over at the National Bank of Canada now. Well, get this"—his tone turned juicy now—"I bumped into her Friday afternoon over at Maury's bar, just got word her sister died of cancer, and she was in bad shape, slugging 'em down." He snickered. "I want to tell you, her nose wasn't up in the air Friday. 'Course, everyone was giving her the sympathy bit, me, too. Oh, I gave her sympathy, all right. Took her over to a friend's place up in the west Twenties, and I gave her the best medicine there is. I made her forget her sister, all right. Christ, I fucked her twelve ways from Thursday. You know what, Perry, I even made her blow me!"

"Ruth Pulaski?"

"Ruth Pulaski! I tell you, your sad gal is your horny gal. Oh, Christ, and didn't my wife want it Saturday morning? I could hardly get it up!"

There was a grossness about him, this guy, Tank, that knotted my stomach. They went on exchanging volleys of bravissimomachismo talk and I got to wondering about the bank officer's first remark: "What's a little runt like you doing without your mascot?"

Turning to look at them closer, I noticed Tank was carrying a large brown briefcase with a small combination lock on it. Did that crack mean—a guard, or what? They went on shooting the breeze, most all of the talk scroungy, until Tank looked at his watch and said he'd better be going or he'd get his ass in a sling. Some sling for that ass!

Instead of leaving, he went to get in line at the end teller's window. He seemed to know most of the people in the bank and leaned in to pass a few words with one of the bank guards. I got up and walked over to a table containing deposit slips near him. From his lowered voice and the leer on his face, I gathered he was telling the man the same charming story about his conquest of Ruth Pulaski. The bank guard grinned and patted him on the back when he'd finished.

Yes, I thought, congratulations are really due a guy who screws a girl whose sister's just died from cancer. I especially remembered the line "I made her blow me." Not "she blew me"—but *I made her*. Let's not leave anyone free choices.

When Tank stepped up to the teller, he kidded her, saying, "Everyone who got it over the weekend, raise their hands!" She blushed as he upped both of his and she said, "You're terrible."

"Yeah, I was so terrible last weekend I can hardly walk." A big leering laugh.

Umm, I thought, if at all possible, I'm going to give you something to laugh about.

Now the transaction began. He handed her several sheets of paper which he'd taken from his inside coat pocket. While she checked them over, he twirled the combination lock that allowed him to open the large brown briefcase. I was so hooked on getting him, so honed in to him, I fell into a moment of teeth-grinding meditation, begging that he be given something substantial to put in that case.

And he was, stacks of bills, stacks and stacks, all neatly banded, although I was not close enough to see the denominations, or if I was, I was so excited I wasn't able to focus clearly enough upon them for fear of being caught, as she slapped them into his beefy hands with the precision of a surgical nurse. It was obviously an operation they'd been through many times because he whipped them down into the briefcase with equal dexterity as if he were handling stacks of throwaway leaflets instead of cool green cash.

Standing by the table off to the side, I realized I had such a bead on him I hadn't even begun to feign an independent activity of my own to cover up being there. Even now that I was aware of simply standing there, I didn't. I was glued to the grossness of the man—and what he had for me.

After dropping the last few stacks into the case and snapping the lock shut, he leaned in, said something to the teller and reared back laughing as she blushed and said, "Tank, you're terrible, you ought to be put in jail!"

"Yeah," Tank chuckled, "with you as my cell-mate. Oh, baby, what a sentence that would be!" He made a little growling sound at her.

"Tank, you're just—oh, Tank!"

"See you Friday."

"Not if I see you first," she said, actually getting quite a jolt out of the line.

Tank turned, pleased as a ringmaster with himself, and, clutching the brown briefcase in his right hand, passed only a few yards from me.

Sent up a little prayer of thanks that I'd left the girl with the limp alone.

"So long, Seamus!" he snapped at a bank guard by the front door.

"See you, Tank."

Tank went out the door—with me close behind—and paused on the steps, glancing down and then hailing someone on the sidewalk. "Mickey—here," he said, starting down the steps toward the man.

Mickey was shorter than Tank, stocky and brick-like, though not big and beefy. Sandy-haired, about five-ten, he was rather nondescript looking. He also wore a suit, a brown one, but it was pressed.

As Tank joined him on the sidewalk, he said, "Just a minute." Tank walked to the curb, switched the briefcase to his left hand, bent over and, using two fingers of his right hand, squeezed the bridge of his nose and blew it, sending the contents shooting down into the street. Unattractive as it was, he was adept at it and the operation was a clean one, no loose ends left swinging in the breeze.

The pigness of him!

As he rejoined the other man, Mickey, I wondered what his wife could possibly be like. Did he have Little Tanks? If I could imagine him in any other situation it would be at a Fourth of July picnic, wearing an American Legion cap and winning the beer-drinking contest. Tankier than ever.

Falling in step behind them, I heard only the first part of their conversation. Mickey said, "Patsy came by while I was waiting for you, he said—"

"Yeah, Patsy," Tank replied, "I'm gonna fix that son-of-a-bitch's wagon, you better believe it."

Mickey glanced around as they continued walking. He seemed to include me in his look, no more than a glance, but I couldn't be sure. Just the same I let myself drop behind a few more yards and I was unable to hear their conversation as they went on talking.

Tank had become, in this short time, such a head-on target for me I hardly worried about his having a companion, felt the other man's presence no more than a minor complication. The idea of besting the bastard was thrilling.

Walking after them, I was also happily aware that I wasn't gripped by that old devil fear. Terrified, holding up a band of helpless women and now that I was on the trail of two substantial men and the stakes were much higher *and* the destination unknown—I was not in the position of picking my spot this time—there was still much more relaxation to this operation. I was taking to the hunt. I did wonder where they were headed and, of course, worried they might drop off the goodies before I had a chance to make my move. I couldn't quite see breaking into a trot, gaining on them, snatching the briefcase and whipping off down the street. Glanced at my watch. Twenty past twelve. The Wall Street lunch hour crowds were out.

When they turned a corner, with me following, I realized we were right across the street from the Stock Exchange. A fellow in kilts was playing a bagpipe at the corner of Broad and Wall streets. A large crowd stood around watching. The man had a blanket spread out with a basket for donations and a hand-printed cardboard sign: "Help Me Get Back to My Bonnie Scotland—Thank You."

Tank and Mickey stopped for a few moments to watch him play. I lagged behind, mingling with the crowd. After a while Mickey took out some change, threw it in the basket, and they walked on, moving away from the Stock Exchange, going south toward the Battery.

In the middle of the next block they suddenly turned left and entered an old, solid, gray stone office building about twenty stories high. I quickened my steps, almost ran, so as not to lose them, hurrying inside and over to the bank of elevators. Third from the end had the door open. I walked up to it and looked in. They were there, along with a woman and a younger girl. I stepped inside the car just as the door was closing.

Turning away from them, I looked at the buttons. Nine and sixteen were lit up. The woman and the girl were talking about needlepoint. Tank was ogling the girl, Mickey grinning at him. The two women got off at nine and I moved to the rear of the car while we rode up to sixteen. Neither Tank nor Mickey seemed to be paying attention to me; Tank said something about the girl having a great little ass, he'd never seen her before and wondered where she worked on the ninth floor.

I had no idea what was going to take place. I was simply following them as far as I could. Out of some sort of blind faith that it might work out. When the car stopped at the sixteenth floor and the door opened, they stepped out and I moved after them.

Right across from the elevator was a small glass-enclosed case with a listing of the offices on that floor. The most obvious dodge for me was to consult it as a stall but before I could even step over to it, Tank said, "I gotta take a crap, pick up the stuff for Reardon and Jones, we'll drop it off and grab some lunch."

"Okay," Mickey said.

They turned the corner by the bank of elevators and walked down a long hall. I followed. At a door marked with four names, ending in "Inc.," Mickey stopped and grabbed the handle. "Pick you up in a couple of minutes," Tank said and walked down the hall toward a door marked "Men" at the end.

Now my heart beat a wild little tattoo of joy at the call to arms. He was going to the men's room and he still carried the thick brown briefcase.

# 45

Walking toward the end of the hall, he took out a large ring of keys. *Oh, don't tell me you need a key to get in!* Just as I thought, well, there's nothing to stop you from going in along with him, obvious as that might be, he reached the door, put the key in the lock, then turned around and looked at me. Really looked at me with his puffy eyes.

I only allowed our eyes to meet for a moment, for fear of transmitting my intentions to him. Immediately I turned to an office on my left, the last one at the end of the hall, took hold of the handle, praying to Christ the door would open, twisted it—it did—and stepped inside.

There was a reception desk past a wooden half-wall, with a swinging wooden gate in it that allowed entrance to a main office, then a corridor with other offices off it. No one was visible but I could hear the laughter of women in one of the private offices down the corridor. After a moment or so I cleared my throat and said, "Hello?"

"Yes?" a woman's voice replied from inside an office down the hall and to my right.

"Ah . . ." was all I got out before she stepped outside, half a sandwich in her hand, and said, "Yes—can I help you?"

"I'm sorry," I said, pointing to the door, "I came way around from the other side. I didn't realize I needed a key to the men's room."

"Oh, sure," she said, walking forward to the reception desk.

"I'm sorry to bother you."

"That's all right." She opened the top drawer and took out a key attached to a wooden chip. Handing it to me, she said, "When you're through, just leave it on the desk here."

"Yes, I will." I thanked her as she walked back to the office where she was having her lunch.

Out in the hall, I turned left, put the key in the lock and opened the door. The smell that assaulted me was so putrid I just about stepped back outside, a smell that almost defied breathing.

Good old Tank. The sounds of blasting coming from the middle booth of three at the end of the spacious old-fashioned men's room indicated he was still at it.

On the floor inside the booth, right in front of his black shoes, now draped over by his pants and shorts—he'd simply let them drop to the floor, a class act all the way—sat the brown briefcase.

I acted at once, stepping quickly past the three urinals, two washbasins, the first booth, and reaching down to grab the end of the briefcase, knocking it on its side so I could slip it out under the foot or so of space between the bottom of the metal door and the shiny, tan granite floor.

"Mickey!" he shouted, "Jesus, come on, that's not funny!"

My mind worked clearly, none of Chez Madeleine's fuddle. And, oddly enough, now that the action had started—and I couldn't deny a certain amount of nerves—I was getting a kick out of the situation, that it was taking place in a toilet.

"Mickey!" he said again.

I didn't want to get caught waiting for the elevator or chased down the stairwell; the door to the john couldn't be locked from the inside. I had to incapacitate him somehow.

"Hey, Mickey—Jesus Christ, come on, I'm shitting."

Yes, as if anyone had to be told.

"Mickey . . . ?" For the first time his voice took on a tentative tone.

"No," I said, stepping back away from the booth with the briefcase in my left hand and reaching for the gun in my right pocket.

"No?" he asked, "not Mickey?"

"Not Mickey. Step out of your pants and shorts and kick them out from under the booth."

"Who is that? Who is that?" he demanded.

"Just get out of your—"

"Who the fuck—I'm taking a crap! Jesus, what a dumb trick to pull when a person's taking a crap!" He still apparently thought it might be a joke. I wanted to set him straight and

at once. I slid the briefcase back to the side of the main door
and then stepped forward to the booth, grabbed that door,
but it was latched from the inside. I dropped to my knees
and wagged the gun under the door, aiming directly at his
feet.

"Oh, Jesus—Jesus, don't shoot!" Tank said, his voice
coated with fear.

"Then step out of your pants and shorts, take off your shirt
and coat and throw 'em over here." I stood up.

"Okay, okay! Yes, okay, but don't shoot, I got a wife and
kids!"

The more's the pity. The big bad wolf was turning into a
chicken. I backed away from the booth as he stood up and
his head appeared above the top of the door. "Oh—you," he
said, recognizing me.

"Yes, me. Hurry it up, come on, get out of those clothes."

He only stared at me; the sight of me seemed to have
lessened his fear as he said, "Listen, you can't—"

I wanted no dialogue, no suggestions. I took an abrupt
stampstep toward the booth, aiming my gun at his head. That
did it, he let out a little cry and again pleaded, "Don't shoot!
Don't shoot!"—at the same time ducking his head down out
of sight so I couldn't see him.

"I won't, if you get out of those clothes—come on, snap it
up!"

"Yes, yes, okay!" I could tell he was fumbling to do just
that. For the hell of it, I gave the door to his booth a kick
with the flat of my foot. "I am, I am! Don't shoot, I am!"

He stepped out of his pants and shorts and kicked them
out from underneath the door. Reaching down to grab them I
couldn't help noticing his shorts were badly stained. Felt
sorry for his wife. I flung them back near the briefcase. "The
rest, come on, hurry it up!"

"I am, I am." The coat came over the top, then his shirt.
"My undershirt, too?" he asked.

"Yes."

The undershirt soon appeared. "You want my shoes and
socks?"

Obliging soul, this chicken-hearted bully. "No." The idea
of him running around stark naked, with that large beer belly
and big fat ass only in shoes and socks, was obscene enough.
While I gathered his clothes together in a large bunch to the

side of the door, thinking how lucky I was, really digging this fantastic stroke of luck, he asked, "What do you want me to do?"

"Sit down in there, relax and shut up!"

"Don't shoot, you won't shoot? I did everything you said."

I heard a key in the lock, ducked back against the wall to the side of the door as it opened up and swung back toward me, almost touching me.

"Jesus Christ, who died in here? Whew! Smells like a pack of dead sewer rats!"

It was Mickey, stepping in as the door slowly swung closed behind him. He carried an extra-large manilla envelope, both in dimension and thickness. It was bound around by several large rubber bands.

"Mickey—quick, your gun!" This from Tank.

"My gun?" Mickey asked.

"Yeah, that guy, isn't he there?"

"What guy?" Mickey asked, as he turned and saw me, but at the mention of his gun I already had mine aimed at him. Still, he made a fast reach for inside his coat.

"Don't!" I shouted, aiming to his left and firing a shot down at the wall next to him. A scream from Tank. The sharp explosion was amplified by the sound-box of this granite chamber as the bullet hit the wall, zinged off it and ricocheted wildly around the men's room.

"Oh, Jesus—Jesus—don't shoot—help!" Tank shouted.

I'd stopped Mickey cold. He'd dropped the large manilla envelope and his hands were frozen out to his sides.

"Up, put 'em up!" I heard my voice echo in the old-fashioned bathroom and I almost laughed. My dialogue was out of a crummy gangster movie. Mickey raised his hands, but not as high as I wanted them. "Higher—higher, all the way up!" I shouted.

He obliged, raising them high above his head and at the same time saying, "Jesus, what is this?"

"Don't fight him, do like he says, we'll get shot!" Tank again.

Now there was a silence. I figured he had a gun inside his coat or in his pocket or in a shoulder holster and I didn't know how to get it away from him. I also didn't like the look in his dull eyes; he was not as frightened as Tank, only confused at first and now sullenly angry.

"With your left hand unbutton your coat jacket, then put it back up."

He reached down, unbuttoning his coat jacket. "Open it up a little more." He spread his coat open and I could see a strap of leather and part of a gun holster near his left armpit. He kept his hand there, on the lapel of his coat. "Up, back up!" The hand remained there. "Up, goddam it!" I took an abrupt step toward him and he quickly raised his hand again.

"Be careful," Tank said from his booth. "He shot, you heard him shoot." Then: "Was that him—or did you shoot?" he asked. Struck me funny, the Mark Brothers stage a hold-up. "Who shot?" he asked, when neither of us replied.

"Shut up or I'll shoot again, that's who shot!" I said.

How did one man disarm another without getting clobbered! I guessed just by chutzpah. He could always grab me, or hatchet down with his hands as I reached for his gun, but I could always shoot him. Or I could make him toss his gun on the floor. No, don't give him a chance to get near it.

"Okay now, I'm going to press my gun up against your stomach and if you make one move I'm going to pull the trigger!"

Mickey only looked at me.

"Did you hear me?"

"I heard you," he said, but there was no fear in his voice. I wanted to put some there.

I shouted now, taking another abrupt step toward him. "I swear to Christ I'll shoot you if you make one move, you even cough and I'll shoot you, do you get me? *Do you?*"

"Yes, yeah, I get you," he said, flinching back at my outburst and pressing back against the wall.

*Take it, take the fucker's gun, Eddie. Shit, do it!*

Stepping up to him, I flicked his coat open with my left hand and stuck the muzzle of the revolver right into his stomach, making a little indentation. His body gave a little jerk but only from the pressure against his belly. I reached in, took hold of the butt of his gun, pulled it out and quickly stepped back away from him. As I did this, my foot kicked the large manilla envelope he'd dropped.

I glanced down at it. "What's in that?" I asked.

He looked at it, then up to me. It was a stall, I felt it, especially by the forced offhand tone he affected when he did speak: "What? Oh, that, just a lot of papers and shit. You got the money, *that's* the money!" he added, jabbing his head at the briefcase with the lock.

"Okay, now, get in that end booth, shut the door, get in there and take your clothes off."

"What?" he asked. "What the fuck—"

"Do it, do like he says, Mickey. I took mine off."

"Yeah, you're a big help," Mickey said, moving to the booth.

Suddenly the idea of them both being in adjoining booths rubbed me wrong. I didn't want them close to each other. "No, don't go in there, just step up against that end wall over there, back to me, and take off your clothes."

He walked to the wall at the end of the john, past the booths. "What do I have to take my clothes off for?" Mickey asked.

"So we can't chase him," Tank said. "Do like he says."

"Chase him? He's got the guns, who's gonna chase him?"

It was getting too chatty. "Shut up and strip."

"Okay, okay."

While he took off his coat, holster and shirt—no undershirt on Mickey—I retrieved the manilla envelope. It was large, slippery and ungainly to handle. I almost decided to leave it. What with two guns and the briefcase, I'd have my hands more than full.

"Now the pants, come on, hurry it up."

Mickey had little curly furrows of hair running up the sides of his back and clusters of it sitting on his shoulders. He stepped out of his pants and underneath he wore a loud, flowered pair of boxer shorts. He only stood there. "The shorts, too, take 'em off!"

"The shorts? Why the shorts?"

Suddenly I felt crazily, completely in control. It really seemed like I had them, there was no way for it to go wrong. The feeling made me a little punchy. "So we can all have a look at your ass!" I told him.

"What?" He turned his head around. "What are you—nuts!"

"Don't kid with him," Tank warned. "*He is nuts*, don't fool with him!"

"Take off the shorts and kick 'em back here!"

"Jesus." He slid down his shorts, stepping out of them and kicked them back. To my delight, there was a bumblebee tattooed on the right cheek of his ass. Just as I was about to comment, he snarled, "No cracks about the tattoo!"

Right. No cracks about anything. It was time to get out of there. I quickly gathered up all their clothes. I'd had the idea to take them with me, but together with the briefcase, the guns, and the manilla envelope it would be too much. A frosted window to the side of the washbasins was open an inch or so. I opened it wide, got the clothes and dropped them out in the dark narrow space between the building we were in and the next one.

On a hunch I decided to pick up the manilla envelope. As I did, Mickey turned his head around and said, "Aw, don't take that shit, it's just a lot of papers, records, it'll fuck me up good—come on, guy!"

"Turn around," I told him. "Now, listen, the two of you. I got a friend, Vin, out by the elevators. He's got a gun and he's going to be covering this door until I'm long gone. If you come out of here within five minutes—he'll shoot the shit out of you. You got that?"

"Yeah," said Mickey.

"Yeah, we will—no, I mean we won't," big brave Tank sputtered from his booth.

"Remember it then." I stuck Mickey's gun, which was much heavier than mine, in one of my pockets, backed toward the door, arms full, grappled with it, opened it and in a moment of improvisation shouted, "Vin, cool it, it's me!"

Out into the hallway, almost broke into a run, but stopped myself, walked quickly to the corner by the bank of elevators, turned and pressed the button. Set the manilla envelope down and, with the briefcase in my left hand and the gun in my right, peeked around the corner to see if the john door at the end of the hall might open.

Heard a clang, looked up to see the red bulb over the elevator light up. Scooped up the manilla envelope, the door slid open and I stepped into the car.

# 46

Relief was so intense, it swamped me, being in the elevator car, moving down, fast getting away, so intense I forgot I held the .22 clutched in one hand along with the manilla envelope. Forgot, until the other three people in the car drew my attention to the gun by their complete and respectful silence and their stares.

In fact, when I was guided to it by the wide eyes of a tiny, birdlike fifty-ish secretary, I uttered a little surprised "Oh ... !" as I fumbled with my bundles and finally managed to shove it in the other pocket, the one not containing Mickey's gun. By that time we were stopping at a lower floor to pick up two more passengers, two men.

Acute nerves made me break into a wide grin at the sight of *me*, as seen by them, when I first stepped into the car with the loot and the gun all jumbled together. If anyone had ever been caught by the human eye in the middle of a getaway, it was me.

Could not wipe the grin off my face. The two men, who had turned and stood in front of me facing the door, didn't notice but the secretary, an elderly man and a young messenger boy did. They broke into grins in return, happy and relieved, I'm sure, to know that whatever it was, it was sort of a joke, to be laughed at.

When we landed at the ground floor, the door opened and as soon as the men in front of me left the car, I was out, scooting along the narrow lobby and out into the street. Expecting, at any moment, those two bare-assed babes, Tank and Mickey, to come charging out after me with all the appropriate shouts and gestures. But I made it to the corner and into a cab, doing my best to induce deafness so as not to hear sounds of pursuit.

And then, sitting in the back of a cab heading uptown—I told him Eighth Street and Sixth Avenue—it dawned on me, dawned on me with the impact of creation, that I had

## DONE IT!

"Oh, Jesus—Vin!" I said. "I really did it!"

"You say something?" the cabbie asked, glancing back.

"No," I happily admitted, "I was just talking to myself."

"Umm," he shrugged, as if to say, yes, there's an epidemic going around.

Another grin was plastered on my face. The cab was one of those small nasty ones, with a barricade up between the driver and passenger and locks on the doors operated by the cabbie, so no one could get in or out without his cooperation. It was only fitting and proper that, sitting there with my loot on the seat beside me, I should have my own private armored car. It was completely right that I should be guarded like that.

In the darkest corner of my mind, of course, I fully expected to hear sirens and look back to see police cars in pursuit. But there was just the usual jumble of traffic. I glanced out, along lower Broadway, at the huge office buildings on either side, and realized this was the part one always saw in ticker-tape parades.

I held a little secret parade of my own as we moved slowly up the street, grinning and acknowledging the nonexistent paper fluttering down to hail me, because, I was feeling for the first time—Some Pretty Big Fucking Kind of Hero!

I was in joy-shock, overcome like a diabetic, dizzy with it. Wanted to shout, wanted to proclaim, make a speech. The first overpowering urge to tell someone. Anyone. The compulsion that finally mushroomed into forcing me to write this down.

Sat there awash in it. Until it occurred to me to look in the manilla envelope. But you know how you make up stupid superstitions: step-on-a-crack, break-your-mother's-back? I made up that if I opened the envelope in the cab there'd be a reverse surprise for me, nothing, nada of value. Although I knew I had a bundle of cash in the briefcase, I did want there to be something good in that manilla envelope. Wanted a double-header.

Before long I was being let off at Eighth Street. Walking east with my boodle I glanced down, taking notice of the small lock on the briefcase. When I came to a hardware store, I went in and bought a hacksaw. Hurried over to the hotel, feeling the sweat of anticipation eking out under my armpits, and up to my room, breathing heavily both from the physical hustling and mental exhilaration. And suspense.

Much as I wanted to count the cash, I couldn't wait to dive into the manilla envelope, as I dumped it all onto the bed. "Come on, Mickey-baby, don't fail me now in this hour of my need!"

Slipping the rubber bands off and ripping off the Scotch tape, I opened it up to find other small manilla envelopes, about ten-by-twelve size, inside. All had different names printed on them, some names of people, others had names of companies. I took one envelope and ripped it open.

Mickey didn't fail me. He presented me with a stack of lovely dull-green sheets—like the backside of regular bills—United States of America Treasury Notes 5 ⅞% due date 2-15-75. The value of each note was five thousand dollars. I quickly counted them, thumbing through with shaky fingers. There were twenty-three, bringing the total for that envelope to one hundred and fifteen thousand dollars.

From my business courses at U.C.L.A. I knew these were the equivalent of bearer bonds, they were negotiable. Anyone having possession of them could sell them, trade them, or borrow on them. Even though they had serial numbers and were originally registered someplace, still—they were highly negotiable.

Admitting to greed, I whipped through the other envelopes. Nine others contained stock certificates and corporate bonds. Disappointment, they were not negotiable. But the next envelope held another surprise. Six United States of America Treasury Notes, each one of these worth ten thousand dollars. That was another sixty thousand.

I was getting dizzy, overcome by this good fortune. I remember switching on the television set. There was a terrible compulsion to call out, make some sort of noise. Celebrate. To calm down, take the sting off this, I needed an outside activity. Too much to deal with in a quiet hotel room by myself. A soap opera flicked on. I paid it no mind, only needed the company of other people, no matter how removed or unreal.

Several more envelopes of non-negotiable stocks and bonds and finally one more containing two additional five-thousand-dollar Treasury Notes—another ten thousand dollars.

Total: one hundred and eighty-five thousand dollars' worth of negotiable securities.

Punchy, I turned to two women whining at each other over coffee in a kitchen on the soap opera and laughed: "You think *you've* got troubles!"

So excited I'd forgot about the briefcase. Ripped the hacksaw out of its paper bag and sawed through the lock. On top of it all, I had sixteen thousand five hundred dollars in cash. $16,500.

Jesus must really love this child! *After all.*

# 47

That afternoon, the rest of the evening, was a rough time. Rough holding myself in. I wanted to spend, give away, make an announcement. Kept telling myself not to do anything rash, nothing splashy that would draw attention.

Around six, when I thought I could no longer contain myself, I walked over to Monica Rohmer's—almost danced over—and gave her two thousand dollars to put toward buying furnishings and when she and Alice protested they had furniture in storage, enough to take care of the new apartment, I told them to put it toward another few months for Bebe's share of the rent. To cover my windfall I explained I'd gotten an advance against the nine thousand I had coming from the army for back P.O.W. pay.

That evening I went out on the town, Harvey Wallbangers

all around. I can hold my liquor fairly well, but I found myself getting drunk quickly. It was the excitement. At the bar at Michael's Pub, which I'd wandered into off Third Avenue, I connected with three very attractive girls and an older man. One of the girls was his secretary, it was her birthday, the other two were her roommates. After several drinks, the man invited me to join them for dinner. I'd have liked to but I was getting very high. Actually I felt if I stayed with them I might come apart and spill the beans. Thought: No, you're not fool enough to do that. I made an excuse to think things over, saying I had to make a phone call. Sat in the booth talking to myself. Cool it, Eddie, go easy. You've pulled it off, don't blow it now.

There was still work to be done. I'd already been forming a plan about how to possibly convert the Treasury notes to cash. It would be a tricky operation, a delicate one to bring off safely.

The excitement of my win had centered in my stomach; I was nowhere near ready to receive food, had no desire to eat. I'd go on drinking and who knew in what state I might end up—or with which girl? And I just might spring a leak.

Back at the bar I explained I couldn't get out of a previous engagement and left, taking a cab back to the hotel. Locking and bolting my door, I put myself in solitary. *You will not leave this room this night!* I laughed as I got out of my clothes, remembering Dr. Jekyll and how he tried to lock in the Mr. Hyde of himself.

I turned on the television set as I stumbled drunkenly into bed and to my woozy delight caught an interview on the ten o'clock local news with Tank and Mickey filmed in the hall outside the men's room.

Tank didn't have much to say, only stood there sullenly, while Mickey described "the perpetrator" as over six feet tall (I'm five-ten and a half), rugged, armed with two guns (Yes, one of them was his), accompanied by one or two more persons out in the hall, whom they had not seen but heard, one being a man named "Vin." My age was put at "twenty-one or twenty-two" and I was described as "extremely dangerous" with "crazed eyes," as they cut to a shot inside the men's room and Mickey pointing to a chip in the wall where the bullet had struck, saying I had fired at him but he'd ducked out of the way.

I don't know how you duck a bullet fired at close range but, by God, he'd done it. Of course, Mickey, who was a bonded guard-messenger, had to beef up the account to save face. Although the news commentator ended up saying the loss was covered by insurance, he added that new regulations about to go into effect in the financial district would prohibit stocks and bonds from being carted about the area and something about transactions being conducted on paper, "in the books."

If that was the case, I'd got in under the line. For once—timing was with me.

I was blessed with the heavy drugged sleep of a happy drunk man.


My plan to get cash for the securities involved going back to Wall Street, so I decided to wait a week until the matter had simmered down.

In the meantime I opened a bank account, only depositing six thousand in cash. Didn't want to attract undue attention. I sent off a check to Lisa for two thousand, along with a note, a mellow note, to my surprise, telling her to put the money toward taking care of Lauri. At the end I tacked on a P.S. saying, "Use it for anything you want. I'm sorry about us, I know you are, too. Be happy!"

I felt good.

Had a meeting with Bebe's doctor, who thought she would come out of the stroke, her walking was getting better every day, perhaps her speech might always be a little thick, especially when she was tired, but he was optimistic about her regaining it and over the outlook in general, saying she had a strong heart and good blood pressure.

I visited Bebe every other day. The first visit after I'd pulled off my caper I wanted to free her of any worries she might have about money. After we'd taken a walk and she was back sitting in the easy chair to the side of her bed, I pulled up a straight chair and took her hands in mine. She cocked her head and indicated "What?" Immediately tears formed in her eyes and as I patted her, saying I had something to tell her, she shook her head and pushed my hands away, picking up her spelling board and pointing out "Know you have to go—I'm O.K." She'd stopped the tears and waved a hand, indicating she was all right now, tell her.

"I'll tell you a couple of things." I was smiling; her eyes widened. "For one thing I'm not going back until my leave is up." Immediately she wanted to make clear she would not have me staying back east because of her, but I cut her off. "Now don't *you* be worried about this, because I'm not, but Lisa and I are separated." Look of surprise, dismay, then a series of questioning gestures. "I won't go into it now but I'll tell you later. No sweat, Maw, it just didn't work out, not after all those years being away." She motioned for me to explain. "No, not now, because I'm feeling happy today and—I'll tell you later on. Okay?"

She nodded, then pantomimed "Why happy?" I'd rehearsed the lie on the train coming out to see her. "I had a best friend in the service. Before I was captured I saved his life, out on patrol. He was an unmarried guy, you'd have liked him. Soon after that I got captured, that's the last I heard of him. Until a few days ago. He had put me down on his service life insurance as beneficiary. He was killed in action later on. I have come into twenty-five thousand dollars, Maw!" Bebe's large eyes widened even more. "Twenty-five thousand dollars," I repeated, taking her hands again. "So what I'm telling you is—there's no money problem. No panic about that at all. Have you got that?"

She shook her head to the negative, then pointed to me. "What?" I asked.

The muscles of her face tightened, the veins in her neck stood out, her mouth opened and she uttered a garbled "Or you!"

"Or me?"

Shaking her head, she pointed to me with one hand. "Or you," she repeated, quickly taking the board up and spelling "for." "Oh, *for* me?" She nodded, suddenly I realized she'd spoken, said something besides "Ot-inken" and "Shit!"

"Hey, you're talking!"

She grinned, then shrugged as if to say, sure, repeating "Or you!"

"No," I told her, "for me and for you, for whatever we need."

Shook her head no again. "No?" I asked, "what are you going to do for money—start hooking?"

She laughed, coughed, shook her head and then had a nice

little cry for herself, at the end of it picking up the board and spelling out, "I don't deserve you."

"No, but you're stuck with me!"

Oh, God, I was feeling good. So happy to be able to do this for her. So happy!

When I got back from the nursing home, I put in a call to Ginger Collins. The same low, husky voice greeted me, but her mood was even lower than before. As we talked, I wanted so much to cheer her up, to spread my mood around. I asked if she'd like to come down to New York for a few days, as my guest, so we could get acquainted. The invite picked her spirits up somewhat.

"Eddie, I would but I'm leaving tomorrow for Phoenix. You won't believe why. I don't even believe it—I want to see my mother, be with her a while. Sounds silly for a twenty-seven-year-old career girl, been on my own since eighteen. But I have to get away from here, from Vin's family and friends, all the places I associate with him. So I'm actually going home to Mama."

"You sure you wouldn't like to stop here for a few days on your way?"

"I would, but she's made plans, we're going to take a little trip together. She's taken time off from work and I've only got three weeks' vacation, actually only two with pay, so I'll be back soon."

"Good, we'll get together then."

"Yes, I'd like that."

The line about only two weeks with pay gave me an idea. "Ginger, give me your mother's address in Phoenix. I want to send you something."

"Send me something?"

"Something from Vin."

"Oh . . ."

She gave me her address in Arizona, then she said, "You know, Eddie, it's been getting worse lately, instead of better. I mean—about Vin."

"It hasn't been all that long, it'll get better soon, it will."

"I hope—doesn't seem like it ever will, not the way I've been feeling. Just—don't care if school keeps, just don't care. I always thought I was a pretty pulled-together gal. Guess I fooled myself."

"I bet the trip and the change will help. I'll help, too, when you get back. I bet I can."

"You sound sweet."

My own high spirits made me say, "I am." She laughed; I loved the quality of her voice. "You take care," I told her, "I'll call you in a couple weeks, when you get home."

The next day I sent off two thousand dollars, twenty one-hundred-dollar bills in an envelope, registered, to Ginger in Arizona. I enclosed a note saying it was from Vin, I'd explain when I saw her. I didn't send a check because I thought she might hesitate cashing it. I got a huge glow on just mailing it.

I knew, of course, I'd at least made off with sixteen thousand five hundred, but I didn't know what the eventual outcome would be with the securities.

The results are now in.

# 48

The following Monday morning, right before noon, I was at the Stock Exchange, up in the visitors' gallery, looking down at the bond room, trying to pick out a likely candidate to approach from the clerks on the floor. Someone who looked hungry.

One fellow, dark-haired, thin, agile, with the slight look of a ferret, grabbed my attention. He appeared to be between twenty-five and thirty. He laughed and made jokes with several other clerks, but there was a certain shiftiness about him when he was going about his business alone. It seemed. No proof, just a hunch.

I stationed myself across the street facing the door they used coming in and out of the main building. The day was mild, sunny, early spring. After twenty minutes or so, he appeared with two other young clerks, all of them dressed in slacks, shirts and ties and the light tan institutional jackets the clerks in the exchange wear as uniforms.

They lit up cigarettes and stood around bird-watching, I think it's called. After a while they strolled to the corner, bought hot dogs and soft drinks from an outside stand, one of those with an umbrella attached to the cart, walked back near the building and sat on a cement ledge eating and ogling. They laughed and joked and occasionally whistled at a pretty girl, even sometimes at one not so pretty as long as she had either good legs, a noticeable ass or large tickets.

There was something about this one fellow, his leanness, his look when he was not occupied talking or laughing that simply gave me the idea he'd ears-up and pay attention at the suggestion of a financial deal, shady or not. He had exactly what I was looking for, a hungry look. Several times he took out a comb and worked over his slick black hair. One very pretty mini-skirted girl walked by; they all whistled. She glanced at them, grinned and walked on. A hurried conference and then my man took off down the sidewalk after her as one of the other fellows called out, "Go, Sal—go, boy!"

Sal caught up with her, engaged her in animated conversation for a minute or so, his hands gesticulating all the while. She gave him her attention but ended up replying to his proposal by shaking her head, no. She walked on as Sal turned, making a shrugging hands-out, palms-up gesture as if to say: Well, I tried, what are you gonna do?

His behavior strengthened my hunch. After they went back to work I crossed the street and asked a guard at the door what time the clerks got off, saying I was coming back to meet a friend who worked there later on. The guard told me around three-thirty or four.

It didn't seem wise to hang around that area for fear of being accidentally spotted by my old buddies, Tank and Mickey. I walked down to the Staten Island Ferry, took it over, had lunch and about two-thirty took the ferry back.

Shortly before four Sal came out of the building, now out of his uniform, wearing a dapper wide-lapeled brown blazer. He was with one of the clerks he'd lunched with. I followed them for several blocks until they said good-bye and the other one went down into the subway. Sal walked another half-block before going into a cut-rate record store. I followed him in, watching him closer as he thumbed through stacks of L.P's in a bin marked "Special: On Sale." When there was no one terribly near, I walked up and began looking through some records next to him.

Whatever my behavior, I knew it should not be tentative. My experience so far had taught me that. I reached to my inside pocket and took out the five-thousand-dollar Treasury note I'd brought as a sample. Putting it down on the records in front of him, I asked, "You know what this is?"

I'd startled him. He quickly looked at me, then back down at the certificate. "Sure," he said. His dark brown eyes regarded me again, he shrugged and said, with well-brought-off casualness, "So what?"

"Supposing a person had a lot of these and wanted to make a deal to convert them to cash and didn't want to go through the formalities of a bank or—"

That's as far as I got. "Let's take a walk." He turned, heading for the door. When we got to the sidewalk, he stopped and looked at me, giving me a quick appraisal. "You want to have a beer?" he asked.

"Sure."

"Come on." As we walked down the street he stopped abruptly and said, "Hey, you know me?"

"Not really."

"Then how come—"

"I know where you work." As he opened his mouth to speak, I added, "Never mind, let's have a beer and talk."

He took me to a plain, no-nonsense workingmen's bar where we sat at a booth. He didn't say a word until after we'd ordered our drinks. Then he asked, "A lot of them, you said?"

"Yes."

"How much is a lot?"

"Let's start off easy." I extended a hand. "My name, for our purposes, is Ted Hogan." He looked at the hand before nodding slightly and saying, "Sal Califano."

"Hi," I said, shoving the hand toward him, forcing a shake, which I didn't quite like.

"Oh, yeah," he said. "Hi." Then: "Someone tell you about me?"

"No."

"Then how come you made the approach?" I liked the language, the "approach" part. I grinned. "What's funny?" he asked.

"Nothing, I just had a hunch."

"A hunch, what kind of a hunch?"

"Just a hunch."

"Oh . . ."

"Was I right?"

"How do you mean?"

"About my hunch, that maybe you'd be interested or be able to put me on to someone?"

He glanced around, darting his eyes the length of the bar, then shrugged, but his voice frogged up when he said, "All depends." Clearing his throat, he showed nervousness for the first time. I liked that, too. Better him than me. His beer and my wine came and I paid. I tipped my glass toward him in a toast. He seemed confused for a moment, then said, "Oh, yeah," and tipped his.

After we sipped our drinks, he leaned in toward me and attempted a smile but it didn't quite come off. His lips were thin and curled down. I thought of my father. "Hey," he said, "did someone tell you about my uncle?" When I didn't reply at once, wondering what they meant, he nudged my hand with his stein and said, "Come on, you can level with me."

"No, what about your uncle?"

"I got an uncle in Jersey who might be interested."

"Good."

"If the terms are right, he might be."

"We'll make them right," I told him.

"Well, that depends," he said, now pulling back in tone, indicating a bit of game playing. I was feeling up to game playing; in fact, I had one all lined up for him. "So, come on," he said, a touch of eagerness in his voice. "What have you got?"

I told him exactly what I had. When I finished, he said, "Hey, you weren't in on that holdup last—"

"Let's not get into the gory details, I'm just telling you what I have, let's leave it at that."

"Oh . . . ?" Another deeper look of appraisal. "Yeah, okay."

"Now, how much would you say my partners and I could get for them?"

"Your partners?"

"Yes."

"How many partners?"

"Three, all of us cops."

"Cops?" he asked, in surprise at first, then a sudden real laugh, the first one from him. "Yeah, cops, Jesus, you guys . . . yeah, go ahead." Now he seemed to be getting a kick out of it.

"That doesn't put you off, then?"

"Cops, hell no, they're just like everyone else. Worse even." He quickly pulled back in his seat, raised a hand and said, "No offense, I didn't—you know what I mean? My uncle deals all the time with cops."

"This uncle, is he in the Mafia?" He hesitated. "Well, no matter," I said, "as long as he can help."

"Yeah, he can help, like I said, if the terms are right."

"How much would you say?"

Now he coughed up a whole line of chatter, knocking the operation, about how even though they were negotiable, the word would be out on them, it wouldn't be easy, the notes weren't at mature value yet (I reminded him they were only two years away) and on and on, ending up with, "You'd be lucky if you got half face value."

"Half?"

"Yes, probably even less."

I'd heard him out, now it was my turn. "All right, I'll tell you what we want then."

"What?"

"We want one hundred thousand, that's the bottom line."

He whistled softly, shook his head. "No, you'll never get that."

"We're sure going to try." I didn't want to get into a lot of messy haggling and backsliding, so I sighed and raised my glass. "Well, listen, if that would be too much for your uncle, we'll just finish our drinks and, what the hell, nothing gained, nothing lost." To display added ease I stuck out my hand again.

He waved it away. "Well, you know, it's not—I mean I have to talk to him."

"Still, we don't have a lot of time to waste. My partners are scouting around, too, so—"

"I'll talk to him, I'll talk to him tonight." He took a notebook out of his pocket and a pen. "What's your number, I'll give you a call."

"No, you give me your number and I'll call you." He started to protest but I laid it out. "Look, we're cops, we don't want trouble. I already know your name, where you work, so what's the big deal? We're not out to pull any fast ones, we just want cash, and we'll take one hundred thousand and *no more*—"

I realized my mistake, the only fluff I'd made so far. I laughed and said, "I mean—no less, not a penny less. If he's interested in that, we'll go ahead."

He wrote out a number on a piece of paper, tore it off and handed it to me. "I've got a roommate, also works at the exchange, but he's very square so if I can't talk—"

"I'll understand and call again."

"Yeah, or leave a number."

"No numbers, names or addresses from me. I'll call again."

"Okay, give me a call tomorrow, around five." He sipped his beer, then shook his head and said, "You know, you don't look like a cop."

That didn't particularly please me. "What do cops look like?"

"I don't know, but I wouldn't take you for a cop."

I glanced around, then opened my jacket and gave him a peek at Mickey's shoulder holster. "What do you think this is?" I asked.

He gave me the palms-up gesture and a shrug. "Okay, so you're a cop."

The television set over the bar came on, a rerun of a Lucy show. Sal looked over, suddenly pleased about the whole thing, smiled and said, "Another drink, I'll buy?"

No, I thought, don't louse it up, you've played your part pretty good, corny as it all seemed, sitting in a ratty bar, bluffing through with a shoulder holster and your bond, trying to pull this deal off. Really getting to be a facile liar. Don't drag it on, don't let's get too chummy. I thanked him, assured him I'd be calling at five the next evening, shook hands and left with a parting word: "Remember, one hundred thousand, no if's, and's, or but's—anything else, we'll call it off, no hard feelings."

"I'll pass it on."

## 49

Anxious all the next day, anxious while dialing Sal's number at five that evening. "Oh, hi," Sal said, "I talked to my uncle last night like I said I would." There was an expansive tone to his voice that indicated he might not just be speaking for my benefit.

"You can talk then, your roommate's gone?"

"Oh, yeah, I took care of that. I'm here all alone." Still the tone persisted. "Okay, so, this is what he said—" Sal went into a long spiel about the difficulties involved in his uncle passing them on, the time, the contacts, the idea that every time the notes changed hands, cash value gets subtracted from the going rate. At the end he tacked on a price. "Top he can get up in cash is eighty thousand. But, man, that's eighty thousand in cold cash, any way you all want it."

"No, that won't do," I told him.

"Well, why don't you check with the others and see?"

I almost said "What others?" but caught myself.

"You all together now?" he asked.

"No, the other two are out in Brooklyn, they've got a contact they're working on out there."

"Oh, where's this other contact?" It was asked for someone else's ears, I was sure. "In Brooklyn?"

"That's right."

"But a good contact, like mine, hard cash, no funny business? A good contact?"

"Yours may be a good contact but it's a cheap one. See, we're all agreed on the price."

"But what if you don't get it, then what?" He was definitely putting on a performance.

"If we don't get it now, we'll sit it out until we do."

Enough, try the bluff. Lingering and hedging only gets you backed into a corner. "Well, okay, Sal," I said, "tell your uncle thanks anyway. Sorry it didn't work out. You probably missed out on some change yourself, didn't you? Thanks again for trying—"

"Hey, wait a minute, hold it just a minute, will you?"

Obviously his hand was over the mouthpiece and he was going over the matter with his uncle or a friend of his uncle's. When he came back on he said, "Okay, here's the top offer—ninety thousand cash!"

I got a kick out of him. He'd either forgotten his "I'm here all alone" or else it didn't matter any more. "I'm sorry, Sal, if I were in it by myself, it would be different but I've got partners and we've agreed on it. It's firm."

Sal showed his stupidity by saying, "Any chance, well, you know, of ditching your partners on this one?" Showed it not only to me but to his uncle, whom I could hear say, "Give me that."

The fumble of a receiver changing hands, then a well-modulated gentle voice, an older considered voice came on. "Hello, you'll have to excuse Sal." He showed he hadn't forgotten what Sal had said when he added, "When Sal said he was alone, he meant his roommate is out." Now the uncle went on in a most logical way, going over all the difficulties Sal had offered earlier and adding a few, ending up, "I understand your problem—you have partners, two of them, I believe?"

"Yes."

"And you've agreed upon your price, but do you realize and do they, I wonder, that my top price would only be a mere three thousand less apiece for the three of you?"

"Yes, I realize and I'm sure they would. They're very bright and they're also very determined and, like I told Sal, there's nothing I can do. But I thank you and"—thought I'd give him a little jab—"I'm sorry you had to come all the way in from Jersey for nothing."

"All right," came the reply in an entirely different voice, cool, sharper, right down to earth: "Your price, one hundred thousand. It's Tuesday, I can have the cash by Friday. How do you want to work it?"

"Good. I'll call Sal Thursday evening, same time. I'll give him the name of a hotel and a room number. Friday Sal will bring the money, nothing higher than hundred-dollar bills. He'll give us the money, we'll give him the securities. It's simple."

There was a pause. "Sal works Friday, I'd rather have one of my—a friend of mine will come by with the money."

"No," I said, "I'm sure Sal told you, we're cops."

"Yes, yes, I know that," he said, brushing it off. "I'd rather have a friend of mine do it, if you don't mind."

I tried a little joke to keep it friendly. "What's the matter, don't you trust Sal?"

He actually laughed, a very pleasant-sounding laugh. "Of course I do, but I'd prefer—"

"No, you see, being police, especially being police, we're worried about too many people being involved, we'd like to keep the cast down. You can understand that?"

"Yes, I can, but how can I be sure you'll give Sal the bonds once you have the money?"

I hadn't thought up an answer for that one. I fully intended to go through with the deal fair and square, so I simply tried to convey that by my tone. "Look, Mr.—ah, I don't even know your name?"

"No, but then I don't know your real name. Fair's fair. On the other hand, you can understand my concern, can't you?"

"All I can say is, we're cops, we've never been involved in trouble before, we don't want trouble now. We have these notes, if we get our price, in hundred-dollar bills or less— that's all we want." He didn't reply. "I don't know what else I can say, it's as simple as that. You get the notes, we get the money and everyone should be happy."

"In other words, you're asking me to take your word?"

"Yes, I am."

"I believe you."

"Good."

"Then you'll call Sal Thursday afternoon at five?"

"Yes."

We said good-bye and I hung up. Suddenly late results came in. Nerves hit, now that that tricky conversation was over. I actually had to walk around the room, arms held out from my sides, snapping my hands from the wrists, to calm myself down.

"Hey, Vin—I think I'm fucking around with the mob!"

The mob. I guessed I was.

# 50

A minor confession: I never get the plots of intricate heists, always miss the clues in detective stories, even find good spy novels hard going. I have to keep turning back every five pages to see—is this guy a Russian pretending to be a German but really working for the British in East Germany, or is he a . . . ?

So in my own case, I was slugging away trying to figure out who would be double-crossing whom? And how would they go about it? The uncle put it in my mind when he asked, "How can I be sure you'll give Sal the bonds once you have the money?"

That remark started an entire landslide inside my head, making me wish I actually had two partners. Then, of course, I thought of Vin. How great that would have been. He'd have been up to it and then some.

One thing for sure, I knew I had to change hotels. I wanted to be registered as Ted Hogan, here I was already down under my own name. I thought of slipping the desk clerk a few bills and asking him to change the registration. I felt safe where I was, but a request like that would trigger suspicions. The more complicated I made it, the more dangerous it might become. So I decided on Thursday to move.

Walking around the Village, I came to another hotel nearby, the Columbine, right off University Place on Ninth Street. About eight stories high, it was attractive with wrought-iron railings and several wrought-iron balconies, New Orleans style, on a pleasant tree-lined block with two small Italian restaurants and one French one. The Columbine was more a residential hotel than for transients. The lobby and desk area was small and homey, with plants, a love-seat, several easy chairs and a large magazine rack.

When I went in, an oval-faced woman in her fifties was humming to herself while going over papers at the front desk. I asked if there might be a double room available for a week—double only because it would be more spacious to deal in, not so stingy.

She smiled and asked if I had luggage, I told her it was at friends', I'd be picking it up when I found a room, and added I'd be glad to pay cash in advance. This satisfied her and she turned to look at a board with keys on it. "Front or rear, that is, facing the street or would you prefer more quiet?"

"Quiet, I suppose."

She turned back with a key in her hand. "Would you like to see it?"

"Yes, please."

Ordinarily I'd never have bothered, but this was a room in which special things were going to take place and I wanted the vibrations to be good. She took me to the fifth floor, along the back hall and into 508.

It was a pleasant spacious room with twin beds, a green and yellow flowered carpet, television set, easy chairs, a small desk and two large long windows, coming down almost to floorlength and facing out on a back garden and, beyond it, the opposite gardens of town houses on the next street. She showed me the bathroom and I told her I'd take it for a week. Downstairs I paid the rent and left to get my things. No big deal, I only had a suitcase and a duffel bag.

The room was fine. I had thought of getting one that would be big-time impressive, at the Waldorf, say, or the Plaza, but large hotels put me off a bit. You seem to be walled up in them more than small hotels.

For the last two days I'd toyed with all sorts of plans to insure I wouldn't be double-crossed. In more than one movie or television show I'd seen plots in which the money turns out to be counterfeit. I worried about that. Or else the money is stacked and masked to look like it adds up to a hundred thousand, but there's really only thirty-two thousand. I worried about *that*. I wasn't going to have time to sit there and count a hundred thousand dollars, bill by bill. Or would I? If I had accomplices it would be easy.

I thought of hiring a couple of guys to pretend to be the

other two cops. Much better, three against one. But then whoever I hired would be in on the operation and could I trust *them?* After Sal left, I'd be sitting there with two strangers and a hundred thousand dollars in cool cash. Temptation. I could picture me trussed up in the bathtub with a sock stuffed in my mouth while my two "buddies" skipped lightly away.

I'd even thought of renting three hotel rooms, all in a row, and perhaps getting Monica and her friend to sit in the rooms on either side of me. I could say the other two cops were there, didn't want to be seen, but would gladly surface if there was any funny business. I could give a signal and have Monica and Alice return a series of raps on the wall. I entertained this last idea the most seriously. At one point I almost went over to talk to them. But again, it would be complicating matters. And if there was trouble, what the hell would Monica and Alice really do? Alice could barely get from one room to the other without  oxygen. It would also be putting them in danger, if danger there was going to be.

In the end, I decided to continue on my own. Superstition also reared its sly head. I'd made out on my own so far. Perhaps if I cluttered it up, I'd set a jinx to work.

But I was depressed to be alone on this. Wanted it to be fun, not a big sweating hassle. So, listen, for a hundred thousand dollars—*does it also have to be hilarious?*

Still, I was more nervous about the switch of goods for money than I had been pulling off the holdup.

Thursday afternoon, after I'd moved into the Columbine, I got a dandy case of the jitters waiting for the time to pass. My nerves were fraying and no matter the little pep talks I gave myself as I finally left the room to take a walk around the Village, they kept on fraying.

I could not stop playing the nasty game of "What if?" What if *five guys* suddenly show up at the door? What are you going to do? *Not* let them in? What if they ask "Where are your partners?" What do I say? "Under the bed, but no fair peeking!"

On and on I went, not helping myself at all.

I'd hoped to walk an hour away, looked at my watch and only twenty-five minutes had dragged by. By the time I got back to the hotel Thursday afternoon around four-thirty, after a complete tour of the West Village, looking at antiques, bookshops, art galleries and boutiques—and not really *seeing* anything—I carried a six-pack of beer for Sal and a bottle of Scotch for my jagged nerves.

At five on the dot I got ice from the buzzing machine at the end of the hall, made myself a light Scotch and water, very light, and just as I picked up the phone, did myself the distinct disfavor of realizing that, if all went well, within twenty-four hours I could be sitting safe and snug with enough money not only to take care of Bebe indefinitely but to carry me comfortably until I decided what I was going to do with my discombobulated life.

How many people had that chance? If only it worked out! If only . . . that's right, build it up, put the pressure on yourself, knot up your eighty-seven feet of intestines.

# 51

A little come-down when the uncle answered the phone. I'd have preferred to deal with Sal. Felt I could handle him all right. Didn't much like the idea that the uncle was in Manhattan with me, would have preferred him in New Jersey.

"We're all set here, we've got the stuff, ready to go," I told him after the opening hello's.

"Fine, I've got the cash. Would you like to make it tonight instead of tomorrow?"

I jumped at the suggestion, I'd had enough suspense, get it over with. Immediately I got back into the acting game. "Wait a minute . . ." I put my hand over the mouthpiece and counted to about ten slowly. "Sure, that's all right with us," I told him.

"Good. Ah, Sal might not be able to make it, but—"

I cut right in. "We don't want to deal with anyone else.

Like I said, we want to keep the cast down. If it's not going to be Sal, we'll wait until he *can* make it."

"What difference does it make?" he asked, coating his words with ease and a tinge of not comprehending, as if it were all so simple. Deliver, pickup, what's the big deal?

"You don't know my partners. They go by the books, what's been arranged. That way there's no trouble for you, no trouble for us. It's relaxed. I'm sure for one hundred and eighty-five thousand dollars in securities, Sal will be able to make it. It would seem worth it."

"It would seem worth a hundred thousand in cash—no matter who delivers it," came the reply.

"No. If it's going to be like that, maybe we better call it off."

A pause while I told my heart to stop beating so loud it could be heard over the phone. "All right, I'll get hold of Sal." This, on a sigh.

"But that's what we arranged." I didn't much like him doing me a favor.

"All right. Where are you?"

I gave him the hotel address and the room number and then asked, "And the bills, are they in the right denomination?"

"Yes, mostly hundreds, some fifties and twenties—mostly hundreds, though."

"That's okay."

"Dammed right it is," he said.

"What time will Sal be here?"

"What time do you say?" Before I could answer he asked, "What about seven-thirty—eight?"

"Good, between seven-thirty and eight."

"Thank you, Mr. Hogan," he said, with a slight edge of the supercilious. "It was good doing business with you. Any time you have anything, just get in touch with Sal."

"Thank you, I will."

Not in a pig's ass. This was it for me. The test results were in. I had not been manufactured to withstand these stresses and strains. I was retiring. Indian, fireman, Chinaman, chief—thief, no! Enough of the thief, this job was my doctorate.

Another miserable two-or-three hour wait, still it was better than an entire day. At six-thirty I walked over to one of the Italian restaurants across the street and ordered dinner, more to kill time than anything else. I picked at the food, I wasn't relaxed enough to enjoy it, it was more to have an activity, to pass the time.

Sitting at a small table by the large front window, I looked out at the occasional Village-ites strolling by. It was a quiet street, not much activity.

While I poked at the tortoni, I noticed a beat-up gray panel truck cruise by the far side of the street, slow down in front of the hotel, stop, then move on. Three men sat cramped together in the front seat. They must have gone around the block because within a few minutes they came around again and slowed up to park on the same side of the street as the restaurant, across the street and about seventy-five yards to the west of the hotel. From my seat I could see the front part of the truck. The three men just sat there, shooting the breeze and smoking.

I didn't think anything particular, only noticed them because I'd been watching the street for lack of anything else to do. When I left the restaurant to go back to the hotel I glanced over at the truck. They were paying no attention to me but I almost froze in my tracks when I saw that the license plate was from New Jersey.

That gave me a start. Trying not to be obvious, I glanced at the men: all three looked to be in their thirties, two dark-haired, one blond.

Entering the hotel, I did my best not to look around to see if they were watching and—not to slip into panic. It was a coincidence that a panel truck with Jersey plates and three men had parked near the hotel, it had nothing to do with me. Or Sal's uncle.

I prayed to Christ it didn't.

Still, when I got to the fifth floor I walked down the main hall to a short curtained window that faced the street. Craning my neck, I could see that they still sat there but none of them appeared to be paying attention to the hotel. I felt better. Something better. Looking at my watch, I found it was already seven-fifteen. Hoped Sal would be on time. Let's *really* get it over with.

At seven-thirty I thought I'd walk down the main hall, turn

left and have a look out the front window to check on the panel truck. It would be a relief to know it had moved on. I opened the door and almost cried out. So did Sal. He was standing right close to the doorway, holding a good-sized gray suitcase with two canvas straps around it.

"Oh, Christ," he said, stepping back, "you scared me, I was just going to knock." His face was flushed.

"Yeah," I exhaled, "you scared me, too. I was on my way to get some ice."

I knew he was lying; he'd been standing at the door listening. Even now I could see him trying not to let me notice his furtive glances past me into the room to see if anyone else was there.

"You're right on the dot," I said.

"Yeah."

"You want a drink or a beer?" I asked.

"A beer, if you got one."

"Sure. I'll just get some ice for myself."

Realizing I didn't have anything to put the ice in, I stepped back into the room and grabbed a glass. To act at ease and allow him to inspect the room at his leisure, I said, "Come on in, I'll be right back."

The ice machine was at the opposite end of the hall from the adjacent short corridor leading to the front window. I filled the glass, strongly tempted to walk around even now and look to see if the truck was still there. I decided against it, taking the affirmative and telling myself it *wasn't* there. Besides, if it was, I'd only be more tense and there was nothing to be done about it anyhow. I couldn't very well tear down to the street and shout, "Would you move the goddam truck, you're making me nervous!"

I went back to the room. Sal sat on the edge of one of the beds, next to the suitcase. I got a beer, opened it and handed it to him. "Thanks," he said. Feigning casualness he added, "I thought your buddies would be here?"

"No."

"They coming?"

"They'd rather not be seen, they're more shy than me," I told him, trying to make light of it, or them, or whatever.

"They're not coming, then?" he asked, pressing it, putting me on my guard.

"Oh, they're here, in the hotel." I added a tinge of impatience to my voice, like I didn't want to be pressured about them. "Like I told you, they don't want to be seen, unless it's necessary. They'll show quick enough, if it is."

Sal looked confused, as if he'd like it cleared up. I decided to help. "They're right here in the hotel," I reiterated, "if that's what you want to know."

"No, I mean—doesn't make any difference to me." He accompanied this with a little shrug.

There was a stretch of silence that was not particularly thrilling either of us, I could tell. "So," I finally said, after taking a sip of my drink, "whatcha got in there?"

"What do you think? A hundred thousand."

"Good. Can I see it?"

"Sure. Where's the other stuff?"

"Right there, in that envelope." Walking to pick it up from the top of the bureau, I grinned to myself: kids, in a cool garage, I'll show you mine, if you show me yours. "Here, look 'em over."

He took the envelope, put it next to him on the bed, but instead of looking right away, he undid the two straps from the suitcase he'd brought and slipped them off. He unsnapped the latches and opened the case, revealing a folded up man's raincoat on top. He gingerly removed it and there they were, stacks of bills, stacks upon stacks of them. A pulse-quickening sight.

"Count it if you want, it's all there, all good money."

I sat down on the far side of the suitcase from him, while he opened up the envelope and began thumbing through the Treasury notes. I gave my attention to the cash, picking up and counting the packets. Each one had a small slip of paper, saying "$5,000—100's" or "$8,000—50's," etc. At random I picked out a stack of 100's marked $5,000. I counted carefully and yes, there were fifty bills, all looking good.

I heard footsteps out in the hall. Realizing I hadn't locked the door, I quickly got up and went to it, slipping the bolt and securing the inside latch-chain.

"What?" Sal asked, looking worried.

"Nothing, just don't want anyone coming in while we're having this little picnic."

"Picnic?" he asked.

"Yes," I said, indicating our respective treasures, "while we've got all our goodies spread out like this."

"Oh . . ."

He was a humorless fucker, I decided I really didn't like him. Decided, too, I was letting my nerves make me punchy, a little coy.

"Who'd come in?" he asked.

"The night maid, anyone, I don't know."

"Oh . . . yeah."

He'd taken a pad and pen out of his pocket and was tabulating the notes. I got a pencil and paper and started adding up the money, according to the numbered slips of paper on the stacks. My hand was trembling but I couldn't help it. For a hundred thousand dollars—go have the shakes! And it did add up to a hundred thousand. I picked out a few more sample packs and counted them. They were true to the slips. each containing what the notation said.

Sal had finished before me, his job of addition being much simpler. By the time I was through he was standing drinking his beer from the can, looking out the rear window at the gardens in back. When I was finished, I stood up. "Looks like it's all here."

"Yeah?" he said, smiling now.

"Yep," I replied.

We stood there looking at each other for a moment. Then Sal glanced around the room and said, "Nice little hotel, you live here?"

"Just temporarily."

"Oh . . ."

He put the beer can down. "Thanks for the beer."

"You want another?"

"No, thanks, I better be going, gotta get this stuff to my uncle."

"Okay."

He went to the bed, picked up the envelope and walked to the door. I followed him. "Good doing business with you," I told him.

"Yeah, same here."

I put out my hand, we shook and I unlocked the door, praying that when I opened it up I wouldn't find those three men from the panel truck standing there with guns. The hallway was empty. I said "So long," Sal said "So long" and walked down the hall toward the elevator. I closed the door but not completely, waiting until I heard the sound of the elevator door opening and closing.

Then I walked down the hall, turned the corner and hurried to the front window. The panel truck had moved back farther away from the hotel, was barely in sight, perhaps a hundred yards to the right. But it was there.

I glanced below me as Sal came down the steps and hit the sidewalk. He walked west, beyond a point opposite the truck, crossed the street, doubled back around and walked up to the passenger side of the truck. Two of the men in the front seat got out, went around to the back of the truck, opened the rear panel doors and got in. Sal took his place in the front seat next to the driver. They just sat there.

Oh, Christ, something very much was up!

That's all I had to see. I raced back to my room, shut the door, locked it and put on the inside latch again. Oh, Jesus, don't let them do it to you! Not now, not after all this.

# 52

I had to get out of there and fast. And it didn't look like I'd be leaving by the front door. I went to the windows and looked out. Five floors down and no fire escape. I wouldn't be leaving by the windows either.

If I could only figure out a diversion to get that panel truck away from there, just until I could get out and away. Far away.

I didn't know whether they'd be coming after me or whether they'd wait until I came out. Looked like they were set to wait. Not wanting to take chances, I picked up the phone and jiggled for the desk.

"Yes?" It was the woman on duty.

"Hello, this is Mr.—" In my fuddle I forgot the name I'd

registered under. "This is 508, please don't let anyone up without announcing them."

"No, of course not, we always announce visitors."

I hung up. Didn't they believe my story about having two partners, I wondered? Christ, if I only had my buddies, the cops, now! Just the thought knocked a wild plan into my scrambled brain. Wild or not I had to try it. I couldn't stay in the Columbine Hotel forfuckingever!

I quickly got out of my civilian clothes and changed into my full-dress uniform, campaign ribbons, cap, the works. (Trembling fingers had a time knotting the tie.) I dumped everything out of my duffel bag, then took the stacks of money from the gray suitcase and stuffed them down inside. I gathered up anything else in the room that might have my name or be able to identify me: other army gear, anything personal, all my papers, also the two guns I had, jamming them down on top of the money. All my civilian clothes, toilet articles, things like that, I left. Those could be replaced.

I sat down by the phone and dialed 9 for outside local calls. I called information and got the number of the nearest police precinct, which turned out to be the Sixth, right down in Greenwich Village. I dialed and took a deep breath. A no-nonsense voice answered: "Hello, Sixth Precinct, Sergeant McCann."

"Hello, listen," I said, breathing hard, "can you help me?"

"Help you? Who is this?"

"I'm in room 710 at the Columbine Hotel on Ninth Street. Have you got that?"

"Room 710, Columbine Hotel—who is this?"

"I just shot my girl friend—I think I'm going to shoot myself!"

I quickly hung up. I'd picked the room number out of the air, hoped they wouldn't call the hotel to merely investigate. No, that would be too tricky, a man with a gun, might endanger lives. Prayed they'd show up in person. I quickly doublechecked the room, to make sure I wouldn't leave anything traceable to me. Then I picked up the duffel bag and went out into the hall. Walked around and looked out of the window. The panel truck was still there, the driver and Sal glued to the front door of the hotel.

Took the elevator to the ground floor, walked down the short hallway leading into the lobby. There were thin curtains veiling the front windows looking out into the street and the truck was parked far to the right of the hotel by now anyhow. I stepped up to the front desk and put my key down. The woman turned, she'd been checking over reservation cards near the switchboard.

"Oh—why, I didn't know you were in the service?"

"Yes, but we wear civilian clothes most of the time."

"Don't you look *nice* in your uniform!"

"Thank you."

She saw the duffel bag. "Not checking out?"

Although I'd paid for a week in advance, I didn't want to get into any accounting or refunds or—even—any more talk, nothing that would hold me up. "No, just going back to the base for the night, I'll be back tomorrow."

"Fine."

I went over and sat down in the love-seat, with its back to the windows. Praying to God my plan would work. I looked at my watch, it had been just five minutes since I'd phoned the precinct. I'd only been sitting there for another minute, armpits dampening, when I heard the first lovely wailing sounds of those New York police sirens, way in the distance at first, but quickly honing in closer and closer.

My heartbeat tripled, at least, as they hit the block we were on. "Good lord," the lady at the desk sighed, making a face at the noise, "*this city!*"

I heard one police car screech to a halt, then another pull up and turn off its siren. I swiveled around and looked out of the window, just as the panel truck pulled away, going on past the hotel and down the block.

Three officers burst in through the front door. Two with guns drawn. The woman stood behind the desk in speechless fright. I stood up and asked with concern, "What happened, something wrong?"

They gave this spruced-up serviceman no more than a glance, then one of the police officers demanded of the woman, "Give me the key to room 710."

She turned and fumbled in the rack, handing him a key and asking, "What happened, what's the matter?"

"Emergency!" was all he said. "Tom, you go up the stairway, just in case. We'll meet you up there."

One officer headed for the stairway and the other two got in the elevator. The woman followed them, still asking what was going on, but the door closed in her face and the elevator ascended.

I picked up my duffel bag and said in a controlled voice, "Hope it's nothing serious, I'll be running along, see you tomorrow."

Walked down the steps as a third police car pulled up, lights twirling, siren winding down. A policeman stood by one of the two police cars that had pulled up earlier, looking up at the hotel windows.

"What happened?" I asked, looking back and up myself but not before I quickly glanced down the block to see if the panel truck had only pulled up ahead and stopped. No sight of it.

"I don't know," the cop said as the other officers got out and trotted up the steps. By this time a crowd of ten or twelve people from nearby buildings was assembling.

A taxi came by and slowed. "What's going on?"

"We don't know yet, some nut called," the cop said.

"Hey—you free?" I called to the cabbie.

"Well—yeah. Not exactly *free*, but ready for a fare," he chuckled.

I hopped in and told him the Plaza Hotel. It would be safe now. As the cab pulled down the street, I kept looking back through the rear window. Just as we got to the stoplight ahead, the panel truck nosed around the corner at the far end of the block behind us and slowed up, right near the corner, way back from the hotel, parking again. They'd been scared off by the first rush of commotion, but they'd only gone around the block.

Timing! Timing was, at last, with me. When the cab turned the corner and headed uptown, I laughed, wondering if they thought my partners had arrived in such flashy style to share in the goodies. Wished I could see Sal's expression. My uniform finally came in handy; not only that, New York's finest came through like pussycats.

Can I tell you about the rest of that night? I had the kind of high that comes from winning an Academy Award for best *everything*, hitting your five-hundredth home run, transcendental meditation *and* the news that I'd been granted Eternal Life!

## 53

Yes, I still have rushes, huge highs, from pulling it off. I still hug my spoils occasionally and look back in loving horror at what I did. But, of course, money does not bring back the dead, cure strokes or make people the way you dreamt them to be.

Most of all, it doesn't—can't—buy you a great friend or a true love.

But it helps shrink disappointments, helps buy the luxury of time to think, to figure out.

Having put it all down, I think I understand why I did it. Life hands you certain curves, God only knows, circumstances force you into certain positions: into prison camp, into doing it with your best friend, *out* of your marriage.

I did what I had to do at the time, had to pitch a few curves back, had to deal with a certain amount of garbage, and if I got a little dirty doing it—send all complaints direct to the Manufacturer, don't bug me.

For the first ten days after the make-out, I was up, up, way up. Helping Monica and Alice get the apartment together and moving Bebe in. Bebe, who's not recovering as quickly as I'd hoped, but coming along *poco a poco* and being good about it. And in my free time I was looking for the right girl to share my manic spirits and good fortune with. Looking too hard. I suppose when you're looking with everything in you, you don't really find.

New York got too frenetic for me. It came to me one day when I was getting on a bus behind one of those distraught elderly women laden down with bundles and packages and paper bags, stockings hanging down her legs like concertinas, overdressed in all sorts of coats and scarfs and a knitted cap, despite the very-warm-end-of-May day it was—getting on the bus with what looked to be the sum total of her worldly possessions. She fumbled a mittened hand in a ratty little change purse, coming up with a fifty-cent piece and offering it to the driver, who snapped, "Only tokens or exact change!"

"What?" she asked.

"Only tokens or exact change, lady!"

She didn't have tokens or exact change. And when the driver told her to either come up with it or get off the bus, she began crying out, "Torture our Lord—let me be. Libras are the whores of the zodiac, all of you. Jackals, you're all jackals!"

Someone in the rear of the bus yelled, "Come on, lady, move it along!"

At that, she turned and directed her yelling at the passengers, shrieking, "Pabst! Blatz! Schlitz! Pabst! Blatz! Schlitz!"

I backed off the bus and took a walk. The city and the people were getting to me. Not only that, it had occurred to me maybe I was pushing my luck, walking around like nothing had happened. Suppose I turned a corner and bumped into one of my ladies from Chez Madeleine? Or maybe Tank and Mickey were cruising around in an unmarked police car? My face was still a little hot for public appearances.

Decided to go away for a spell and pull it all together in peace and quiet. Passing a construction site for a new building, one of those boarded passages thrown up to prevent poured concrete and lumber from clobbering pedestrians, I saw, scrawled on a piece of plywood, "Help Stamp Out Reality!"

I laughed. Yes, get away, let's figure out what's reality and what isn't.

Rented a car and began driving the next day, driving nowhere in particular, but ending up in a few days taking the boat over to Martha's Vineyard, where I'd never been before. The summer people aren't here yet. The island is beautiful. I've rented this small cottage on a bluff overlooking the ocean and I've finished this.

Taking long walks along the beach every day. And thinking. I suppose all my life I've been trying to figure out if we're living in the Good Place or in the Bad Place. I think I really wanted a definitive answer. If it was the G.P., I'd play, if not—well, I just might cash in my chips.

No dice.

Big trouble comes in trying to separate the two. If you say it's hell and play it down the line like that, you miss out on the heavenly aspects, and if you call it heaven—watch out! You're in for some big surprises.

This morning, a morning so miraculously clear and pristine and beautiful that it crept right into my sleep at six-thirty and almost knocked me out of bed, I started making a list of all the heavenly aspects. A list of things I'd miss if I was dead (and my "misser" remained functioning, that is).

I didn't bother to set down obvious major items like the gorgeous sunset of the night before and wide-open people you connect with right off the bat and warm lovers and knock-out orgasms. Obvious stuff like that I left out.

I had decided to make a list of only unimportant little things I dig. Nothing patently fabulous like the circus or the lobster I cooked last night or seeing *Gone with the Wind* or thighs or kelly green and deep blue or a great snug sleep during a rainstorm or the stray cat that's begun taking meals with me out on the deck or the two sea gulls that are trying to incite me to jealousy with their feats of soaring or Bette Midler's recording of "Do You Wanna Dance?" or the third cup of coffee that tasted so sensational five minutes ago.

Anyhow, what happened was—I couldn't get a list together because there were no little things. Everything seemed not only pretty wonderful but important and big. Nothing was small or trivial.

Obviously I am having it pretty good today.

(Three days ago when I was feeling the lonely-blues and experiencing uncalled-for flashes of Lisa and Vin and Bebe, if I'd asked myself what I'd miss if I was dead, I'd have said, not a fucking thing, thanks, you can shove the entire package, wrapping and all.)

So, walking along the beach these days, thinking over all I've been telling about here and trying to add it up in some way that makes sense—all I can come up with is that Eddie is one candy-brained philosopher. There's hurting and there's feeling good; there's living and there's dying; and almost anything you can think up to say about the perverse little ditties dumped on us in between—is true. Is it Hell? You bet your ass it is, even if those two sea gulls turn into angels before my eyes. But how can Hell be so heavenly! I don't know. Maybe the ultimate reality is neither good nor bad. Or both. Or something else we haven't quite figured out. Perhaps what makes the difference between Heaven and Hell is some secret personal approach locked up in each of us. If you don't want to get dizzy thinking about it, just call it life and eat it up, because that's all we have—that we *know about*.

I'm sure they've got some other surprises that we *don't know about*, but they're keeping them surprises, so . . .

Today I'm dedicating myself not only to the pursuit of happiness, but the catching by the tail and dragging down into clover of it.

I phoned Ginger Collins just now. She sounded perkier; her husky voice touches me greatly. She had a good visit with her mother and was all curiosity about the two thousand dollars, which she said came in extremely handy on their vacation. I said I'd explain when I saw her. She's not too happy to be back in Dorset with her memories of Vin. She's seriously thinking of moving away, after she saves a nest egg.

My month is up here at the end of the week and I'm driving down to see her. I didn't say anything on the phone but I've got a legacy for her from Vin. She'll be able to move anywhere she wants.

This is one last thing I can do for him.

A final thought: Whoever I eventually find to lay this all on—I must really love you. That's all there is to it.

## *About the Author*

JAMES KIRKWOOD is the author of three previous novels, *There Must Be a Pony!*, *Good Times /Bad Times*, and *P.S. Your Cat Is Dead!*, which has also been presented on Broadway and in Los Angeles and San Francisco. He is also the co-author of the book for the Pulitzer Prize-winning hit musical *A Chorus Line*. In addition to his writing, James Kirkwood has been a nightclub comic, disc jockey, and Broadway actor, and has appeared in over three hundred television programs.

## Great Movies Available in SIGNET Editions

☐ **THE FRENCH LIEUTENANT'S WOMAN by John Fowles.**
(#AE1095—$3.50)

☐ **THE EYE OF THE NEEDLE by Ken Follett.** (#E9913—$3.50)

☐ **COMA by Robin Cook.** (#E9756—$2.75)

☐ **KRAMER VS. KRAMER by Avery Corman.** (#E8914—$2.50)

☐ **SEMI-TOUGH by Dan Jenkins.** (#J8184—$1.95)

☐ **I NEVER PROMISED YOU A ROSE GARDEN by Joanne Greenberg.** (#J9700—$2.25)

☐ **ONE FLEW OVER THE CUCKOO'S NEST by Ken Kesey.**
(#E8867—$2.25)

☐ **NORTH DALLAS FORTY by Peter Gent.** (#E8906—$2.50)

☐ **THE SWARM by Arthur Herzog.** (#E8079—$2.25)

☐ **THE SERIAL by Cyra McFadden.** (#E9267—$2.50)

☐ **BREAKFAST AT TIFFANY'S by Truman Capote.**
(#W9368—$1.50)

☐ **IN COLD BLOOD by Truman Capote.** (#E9691—$2.95)

☐ **CARRIE by Stephen King.** (#E9544—$2.50)

☐ **THE SHINING by Stephen King.** (#E9216—$2.95)

☐ **TRUE GRIT by Charles Portis.** (#AE1607—$1.75)

☐ **ON GOLDEN POND by Ernest Thompson Introduction by Richard L. Coe.** (#AE1223—$2.50)

---